ADEPT

By Erik Schubach

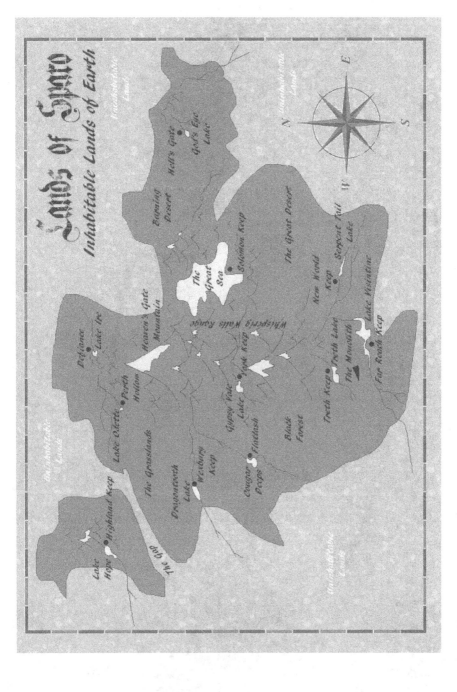

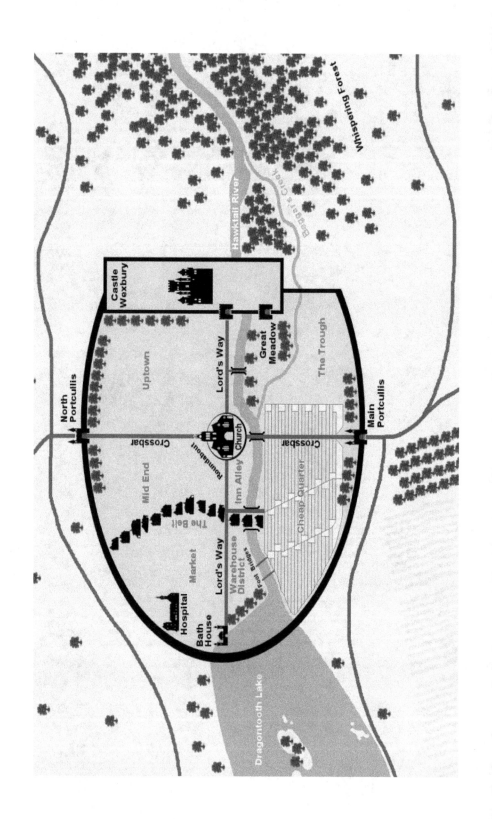

CHAPTER 1 – PORTCULLIS

I yawned as I stepped out of my family's stone cottage with my little brother, Jace, the steel pin hinges groaned in protest. I closed the old wooden door as quietly as I could as to not waken mother. Her health had been deteriorating and we didn't like her exerting herself.

We walked to the pig pen and I grabbed my wooden cart by the handles and started toward the portcullis of the defensive wall around our village. I called back, "After you feed the hogs, bring Matilda to the butcher. She isn't laying anymore, and we could probably get at least two pennies for her or trade for a half sack of grain, she has some good meat on her."

He nodded as he grabbed the bucket to get some of the castoffs from Castle Wexbury we had traded some eggs for. Our feathered ladies were some of the best laying hens in the village and the lords of the castle were partial to them. I smiled. He was only seven but was a godsend around here. With mother down, he was all I had to help me with all the chores while I was out scavenging.

I was not about to marry myself off just to maintain the household, I don't care if I was of age of consent last month or not. No man would have me, ever, and I don't understand why any woman would ever betroth herself to one. I shivered at the thought.

I looked back at the door then added, "Remind me when I get back to grease the door hinges with lard or bacon grease would you?

I don't want that noisy door waking mother, she needs her rest." He nodded in earnest. I smiled at him, he was such a good boy, I was proud to have him as a brother.

I started wheeling my cart to the cobbled road in the twilight of the morning. He called back, "Do you think you'll get enough today Laney?"

I smiled more confidently than I felt and crossed my fingers at him, "Let's hope this batch will get us enough for the medicines." He crossed his small fingers too and smiled and went back to the morning chores.

I walked down the lane, the village was waking up. I started passing people getting to their jobs and had to move for a couple chargers trotting gallantly past as the morning patrol went to replace the night patrol outside the walls.

I looked at them with awe and amazement. To be a noble would be so glamorous. They protect the village and we tithe them so that they can concentrate on that defense. I blinked. One had the crest with a lightning bolt crossed with a sword on her sash. A Techno Knight! I noticed my jaw was hanging open as she passed by and snapped my mouth shut. She noticed my admiration and she winked at me as she trotted past. She looked a year or two older than my nineteen years.

I blushed, she was not only a knight, but a Techno Knight. Her red hair flowed back over her armored shoulders like a cape draping over the studded leather and metal. Her emerald eyes were sharp, and they glowed with the magic potential of a Techno Knight... they seemed to swallow me whole. I looked down in embarrassment when the other knight said loudly, "Looks like you have an admirer Celeste."

She hissed at him, "Don't be such an ass Bowyn." I kept my eyes down but I could feel her eyes on me. I had a little affinity for magic and could tell when it was focused my way. Her eyes were overflowing with it.

She kicked her horse and gave it some rein and shouted, "Hyah!" And galloped off toward the gates. I looked up to watch the other knight urge his horse to catch up. I grinned, being a mere Knight of the Realm, he was subordinate to that Techno Knight. What did he call her? Celeste? He was subordinate to Lady Celeste.

I noted the street lamps in the row I was passing were flickering. I looked at the electric filaments in the globes and they were intact. I stepped over and kicked the ceramic containment vessel which held the magic potential that powered the little copper wound generator. With a scree that was just beyond all but the hearing of the young, the bulbs brightened and remained steady. I grinned.

I absently wondered how the wizards of the old realm of the Before Times powered their tech. I have heard so many ludicrous theories. Like chemical reactions. The old buffoon who proposed it called it batteries or some other nonsense. That would be terribly inefficient, and what would you do with these... batteries... once the chemical reaction was exhausted? Throw them out and build new ones? Non renewable resources were in such short supply and that would be a waste.

But that wasn't as funny as the Techromancer who was laughed out of the conclave for suggesting that his interpretation of the old writings of the Before was that it was with water from rivers. How can water power electricity? The two do not mix. I chuckled at the thought.

No, the wizards of the Before were so much more powerful than us. Just look at all they had accomplished. We unearth more every day. They had to be so far beyond our abilities. It was only the Great Impact that brought down their civilization. I imagined all the wonders I would have seen if I had lived in their time.

As I approached the huge gates at the portcullis, I glanced back to the east, to Castle Wexbury. The great castle with it's soaring towers and waving standards. It was so large it formed two thirds of the east wall of the village itself. Well over a half mile of stone.

There hanging above it in the sky were the Three Sisters. The three pale white moons and the ring of debris around Earth. I tried to imagine what it would be like to see one huge moon in the sky in ancient times, before the Great Impact. A rogue astral body had collided with Mother Luna and tore her in half. I looked at her oblong egg shape and the two smaller sisters, Athena and Freya, which formed afterwards.

They say that Mother Luna will again be round one day as

gravity reshapes her as she spins. She appears to be always looking down on Earth with her red eye. The pale red glow of the vast magma fields on her broken edge will eventually be swallowed. Much like the vast magma fields on the Dark Side of the Earth.

It is rumored there were billions of people in the Before. Over three quarters of the population was wiped out when the debris storm and shock wave had hit the Dark Side. And even more died in the early years. There were rumored to be huge bodies of water they called oceans that covered most of the surface of the planet. I would not have believed it if I had not seen some of the old writings that they have in the castle. The Techromancy Scrolls.

There was a picture in one, of the Earth as a blue ball, covered in water. The language looked so much like English, and I could read most of it, but the old English from the Before was so different than now. Now all villages were built by the few lakes and small rivers that came down off the Whispering Walls Mountain range in the center of the habitable lands.

The young chamber maid, Resme, who cleaned the library had been punished for letting me in to see the forbidden writings. I still feel bad for putting her in disfavor with the lords of the keep. They traded her off to another realm. She had been my only friend here.

I had to take ten lashes at the whipping post for my part. The punishment for trespass into the library was usually twenty, but the magistrate did not wish to be so harsh on a thirteen year old child. I believe he did not strike me with the enthusiasm I have seen in the past, the blows barely left any scars. He explained why the nobles were so strict with public floggings in regard to the library. The scrolls and tomes there are invaluable, and the kingdoms greatest treasure. I did not cry out, I was strong like mother told me to be.

The library had tens of thousands of scrolls and tomes that were falling apart with age. They have had Techromancers working diligently over the centuries to restore them or make modern records and reproductions so that the knowledge would not be lost to the ages.

I was knocked out of my musings when the first rays of sunlight from Father Sol crested the majestic peaks of the Whispering Walls far in the distance. I took a deep breath and looked at the line of people that was starting to form on either side of the gate. We all stayed clear of the knights, and the gate and wall guards.

A man was walking down the line with a checklist asking each person their business outside the gates. The grumpy, heavyset man wearing old, ill fitting, worn leather armor that had suffered most likely decades of disrepair, finally got to me. "Name, station, reason for travel?"

I glanced over to see the Knights just twenty feet away. I smiled a little when I saw Lady Celeste speaking with two other knights of the realm. I looked away and said to the man, "Laney Herder, serf, scavenging." We used our profession to identify ourselves, in case there were more than one person in the village with the same name. My family are livestock herders, so I had to identify myself that way.

He placed his pen down on his tablet and cuffed my ear roughly. "What are you doing scavenging you worthless tramp?! Get back to your animals, the kingdom needs food more than junk!"

I held the side of my face, my cheek stung, but I did not cry out. I worked my jaw trying to get the ringing in my ear to fade. I looked at his feet. "Please sir. I'm scavenging copper, and iron. I'm a sensitive." I pulled my crystal necklace from under my shirt, it hung on a small leather strap, it started glowing faintly amber when my hand came in contact with it.

I heard a large horse approach. A familiar woman's voice snapped out with authority, "Steward! The realm needs metals and machines from the Before as much as food! Maybe more."

He stood at sloppy attention and I kept my eyes down as he ground out, "Yes Lady Celeste. She didn't specify that at first."

Then she spoke again, "You, young miss. Are you of majority? Has your age of consent come?"

I bowed my head a little, looking at my feet. "Yes Lady."

She spoke again with a tinge of amusement in her voice, "Look up, I do not bite." I looked nervously up and she asked, "You have others to tend your animals while you are outside the gates?"

I nodded and my voice wavered when I replied, "Yes Lady. My brother. He's small but is a good worker." She smiled a little and I looked back down.

Then she asked, "You say you are a sensitive, but you said

copper AND iron. Which is it?"

I chanced another look at her up on that grand mount of hers, its coat dark as midnight. "Both, Lady." I tried not to show the pride on my face. It was extremely uncommon to have the magic affinity to more than one metal. That is why I did so well on my last two outings once I was the age of majority and could travel outside the walls without an adult. I also hid the other abilities that I had started developing the past two months.

The Techromancers needed the various metals and machines to maintain and build upon the growing technology base of our village. We were one of the most advanced villages in all the realms. There was so much old technology buried just below the surface, which was so much easier and quicker to use than the mining and smelting of ore from the mines. I was able to save up fifteen iron pennies and two gold coins from my previous outings. Just one more gold coin and I could afford the medicines for mother from the hospital.

She cocked an eyebrow and gave me a genuinely surprised smile. "Truly?" I nodded and then she looked at the man. "Steward, allow this woman to the front of the line, her work is valuable to the realm."

He shot me a glare but bowed slightly to her and responded, "Lady." Then he grabbed the handles of my cart and pushed it roughly to the front of the line, cussing the whole way.

I looked up to the knight and did a curtsy and said quickly, "Thank you Lady."

She shook her head and said, "Celeste. You may call me Celeste, Laney."

I nodded and ran off to my cart. I was blushing profusely. I wondered where all my confidence had gone. I'd never felt so self conscious around anyone. Because Laney you fool, she was a Techno Knight! A Knight of the Realm! I caught myself smiling. I had just spoken to a Techno Knight, Jace was going to be so jealous!

The clock in the church steeple in the center of the village turned over to seven o'clock and the huge church bell started chiming the start of the day. The deep resonating bongs filling the valley. Lady Celeste had her horse sidle up to the receiver beside the huge motors that operated the gate. Then she drew her long sword.

The light of the rising sun reflected off of it. I could feel her magics rise like a pressure on my chest and the little hairs on my arm and the back of my neck stood on end. I could see energy bleeding out of her green eyes, lighting them like twin emerald stars as energy crackled down her arm, arcing from stud to stud on her armor. It traveled into her sword and it started to glow red hot in her hand.

Then she looked over to me and winked again and slammed her sword into the receiving socket. It was like energy just cascaded into the ground, and I felt like I had dropped down three feet. Nobody else seemed to notice any of this. The motors began to turn, the huge iron gates groaned then started to rise and she withdrew her sword and slid it into her scabbard.

The steward was speaking loudly. "The gates close at seven this evening. If you are not in the gates of the keep by the seventh strike of the bells, you must seek your own shelter for the night." As he spoke, the returning knights passed the day patrol. They saluted each other, my eyes were glued to Lady Celeste and she turned back in her saddle as she went out on patrol and I swear she looked directly at me.

I was cuffed on my ear roughly by the steward again. "Are you listening Herder? I told you to start moving three times."

Oh, I had sort of tuned him out. "Sorry sir." I grabbed the handles of my cart and headed out the gates, looking up to the iron gates suspended in the soaring arch above us. I turned east toward the mountains as soon as I was out. I had found a great rock outcropping just a couple miles away that had brought me luck so far.

I made sure to take a circuitous route through the Whispering Forest, mindful of other scavengers that had their eyes on me. They were probably wondering where I was finding so many relics from the Before. When I was certain I was not being followed, I turned back toward Beggar's Creek and Hawktail River that ran through the keep. They emptied into Dragontooth Lake at the west side of the village.

I grinned, this was going to be so much fun!

CHAPTER 2 – SCAVENGING

By mid morning I had reached a rock outcropping that I had been prospecting. I moved a bush aside to see the edge of the embossed aluminum sign that was sticking out of the ground. It was banged up and had a lot of oxidation and some pigment where there was probably paint on it in a bygone era. The raised letters read 'Gus Davis FORD'. I assumed it was the name of the village or the names of the three founders of the settlement.

Aluminum wasn't in high demand since it was the most abundant metal on the planet so I had left the sign as a marker for myself, hidden behind the bush that had grown in front of it long ago.

I pulled my crystal necklace out from inside my tunic, I noted I had another tear in the worn material I'd have to sew up when I returned home, before the weaving started to unravel. "Damn." I held the crystal in the palm of my hand and it glowed faintly amber. I reached inside me to the reservoir of magic I had just discovered as I matured and pushed some of it into the crystal.

I blew across it and it brightened and felt alive on my palm. I could feel energy pulsing through it. I smiled and whispered to it. "Can you find me some copper please?" I started turning slowly in a circle, watching the light closely as it brightened and dimmed. Changing colors as it felt the metals I sought. Blue for steel, yellow for copper. I squinted when it turned a pale pink in one direction. It had never done that before. Was it another metal I was developing an affinity for?

I wondered for a moment how our new magics were different than the powerful wizards that came before us. There are songs and tellings of the Great Impact changing something in the fabric of space around the Earth. Something that woke up long dead magics that our predecessors didn't posses. These reawakened magics were ours.

I kept turning, then went back to where it had glowed yellow the brightest. I slung my tool bag over my shoulder and grabbed my shovel from my cart and started walking. I had to dodge around rocks, bushes and small trees near the rock outcropping. I went maybe twenty paces before the light started to dim. I backtracked until it was at its brightest, then tucked the crystal into my tunic and started digging.

I got almost three feet down when there was the thunk of metal on metal. I grinned and started quickly widening my hole and brushing off an expanse of rusted metal and something else that looked like metal but was not rusted.

It was big, like my first find that took me two trips to scavenge what I could off of it. This one had a metal emblem on the side. It read 'Mustang'. This was a metal horse? Then I remembered the pictures of the metal conveyances from my visit to the library of the scrolls.

I smiled at my discovery. They named the conveyances after swift horses. I wondered how I could get word to the scholars and

Techromancers. This was a minor discovery, but every piece of information gained us more insight into the past. I took out my hammer and chisel and carefully pried the emblem off of the relic and stuffed it into my bag.

I took out my crystal and ran it over the entire length of my find and I was a little confused. There seemed to be copper everywhere in it. Then I smiled. They must have ran electricity through the entire conveyance to run all kinds of marvelous gadgets. The crystal glowed brightest near one end, by the orientation of the emblem I believed it was the front of the conveyance.

I looked closely and there seemed to be a seam. I placed my shovel blade into the seam and started prying. It took twenty minutes but I finally had pried up enough of it that something snapped, whatever was latching the metal down. With the screech of metal tearing I pushed it up and stopped breathing.

I had to blink twice. Good lord! Jackpot! There was a compartment that was stuffed with metals, machines and gadgets that had somehow been preserved fairly well. There were tons of insect nests and something had eaten away some of the casings they had used on the copper wires that seemed to go in all directions, but it was all fairly intact.

Being this close to it, I didn't need my crystal anymore. I could taste all the metal and a huge concentration of copper. I blinked when I saw it. It looked to be an fairly intact electric motor! I've seen these before, the Techromancers called them alternators. They use them in things like the street light chains from this morning.

It was in such great shape, they wouldn't need to use much magic potential to get it operational again. I could probably get an entire gold coin for this alone! I pulled out my flexible steel braided cord with wooden handles at either end, and dipped it into the little bag of crushed carbon. Diamond dust. Then I looped it under the support and started sawing.

Twenty minutes later it broke free and I quickly sat on the top of the conveyance and pulled my brush out of my bag and started cleaning it. It was in better shape than I thought. Whatever coated the hundreds of copper windings inside of it hadn't decayed. The orangeish red coating looked intact.

I looked out of the pit to be sure I couldn't be observed then I pulled my magics to me. I had just started learning I could do this. I let the power flow through my hand and into the alternator. Dirt and debris started falling out of it. I watched as the oxidation on the metals started fading, peeling back the revenges of time and decay. I had to keep this a secret. It was like the Techromancers could do. Only nobles could be Techromancers and they'd throw me in the stockade if they ever learned I was anything more than a sensitive.

When I did all I could, it was obvious it would need more than I was currently capable of to finish the job, but I could get more money for it in this condition. I flicked the flywheel with my finger and it started to spin fairly freely, where it hadn't at all when I pulled it out. I quickly dropped the thing when I got shocked. I had been

surprised, not hurt. Electricity seemed to like me. I had been
holding it with my hand on the terminal and I was definitely
grounded sitting on a metal beast.

I laughed. It worked! It could already generate electricity in the
rough condition it was in. I was surely going to get mom's medicine
with it! I looked around in the compartment and started yanking out
copper wires by the handful, stuffing them into my burlap sack on
top of the alternator. This was like the find of a lifetime.

I found a couple more devices that looked like small electric
motors. How had the wizards made them so small? I pried them out
and placed them in the bag. I could spend a week just here,
salvaging all the wire and steel. I'd have to break the bigger pieces
up, I had plenty of crushed diamond dust for my wire saw, carbon
was extremely plentiful.

I saw something in another compartment farther back from this
one, the roof of the conveyance hadn't been entirely crushed. I
reached in to something glinting inside and yanked a couple times.
With a snapping sound I pulled it free. I looked at it. It appeared to
be glass, with that material that wasn't metal, surrounding it. I
wiped it on my tunic to clean off the grime then gasped.

It was a mirror! The finest of silver smiths must have polished it
and covered it with glass, because it was the clearest oblong shaped
mirror I had ever seen. I looked at my face in it and smiled at the
girl covered in dirt from all my digging. I stuck my tongue out at
her and giggled. I could get some good money from a lord or lady

for such a well crafted mirror.

I ate some goat's cheese and some chicken jerky, and drank from my canteen. Then I noted Father Sol's position in the sky. "Damn!" I pushed the sheet of metal back over the compartment then jumped on it a few times to move it back in place then I grabbed my shovel and started filling the hole again.

An hour later, I was exhausted. But I sprinkled twigs and grass over my excavation then marked it with a stone so I could find it quickly when I next returned. I put my tools and my bounty on my cart and started quickly making my way back down toward the village.

I hadn't gone two hundred yards when I heard horses making their way through the forest to the river. I had thought it to be the knights returning from patrol but froze when eight men dressed in bearskins, riding horses decked out in matching furs, came trotting out into the open. Marauders!

The leader paused when he saw me and he smiled. His teeth had been filed to sharp points and were rotting. He made a motion with his head and the men surrounded me with their horses. They were all pulling clubs and swords. The leader pulled out what looked like the jawbone of an ass that had sharp metal teeth embedded into the leading edge.

He spoke in the guttural language of the Outsiders, it was a mashup of English, Mountain Gypsy, and Welsh. I had learned it from the woodcutter, Corrick, who had befriended mother eight years ago. He had courted her for a year until he didn't return one day. I liked the man, he made me think that that is what it was like to have a father. The night patrol returned the following morning to inform us that marauders had raided the logging camp and all were lost.

The man before me was taunting me, "What have we here? A lost morsel. What should we do with you young one? I bet my men can think of something before we roast you on a spit over the fire." He rode past me, letting his weapon drift lazily past my head, I saw some of my brunette hair drift to the ground, telling me the teeth on his weapon were razor sharp. I stiffened. I don't know why I wasn't panicking. Or maybe I did. I wouldn't give them the satisfaction of seeing me cower before I died, and no man would ever use me. Mother told me to always be strong.

I pushed the jawbone away from me and stood tall and replied in his tongue, surprising him, "Your men would have to kill me before they had their way, I'd bite off their manhood. I hope my flesh poisons you all when you eat me."

He started laughing and the other men joined in. "A scrappy one are you? That sharp tongue will look awfully good on my necklace." He pulled up a string of rotted looking jerky that was around his neck. I realized that they were tongues. I started shaking. So much for not showing fear.

Two men dismounted and started walking toward me from either side. One was pulling his furs away to expose his manhood. No, no, no. A fire ignited inside me and I grabbed my shovel and swung it at the man in one quick movement. I almost vomited as the blade hit him in the crotch, leaving a bloody mess where his manhood had been moments before. I was appalled, but the mounted men were all laughing.

The man I struck screamed in agony and fell to the ground grasping his crotch, his life's blood flowing out from between his fingers. I spun to the second man and held the bloodied shovel toward him. He looked at his comrade on the ground, me, then the shovel. He growled and reached out quickly, taking me by surprise, and he yanked the shovel from my hand and threw it to the ground.

He raised his club and I closed my eyes. At least they weren't going to defile me. I heard the thundering of hooves and a woman's commanding voice yelling out, "Hold!" My eyes snapped open as Lady Celeste and Sir Bowyn burst into the open, their mighty steed's muscles rippling along their flanks as they charged the marauders, swords drawn.

In one swift motion, Lady Celeste hopped up onto her saddle, and continuing the motion, was somehow vaulting into the air, arcing over the mounted men and landed in front of me in a slide. Her blade, crackling with energy, continued it's arc downward, cleaving the man in two and embedding into the ground.

Sir Bowyn was engaging two men. Swinging his non powered steel blade smoothly from side to side. Deflecting blows from both mounted opponents. The other four dismounted and charged the

Lady, circling around us.

I glanced at her, her eyes blazing a blinding green and her arms crackled with power. She was smiling at the men as she did this leg over leg side stepping, around me, her blade stretched out. Like she were designating her reach. I realized she was. She was telling these men that it was a circle of death that they could step into if they dared.

I glanced at her face and she looked down at me for a moment and she winked again. She keeps doing that to me. I was able to contain my fear. I made myself as small as I could to give her as much room as she needed to fight. Damn it, if she didn't have me here in need of protection, she wouldn't have let them surround her. I was worthless and endangering her.

Suddenly she was in motion, she must have read something in the men I didn't see. They were all attacking at once, and time seemed to slow down. She was moving like a dancer. Her blade making sweeping strikes that seemed to be both deflecting weapon strikes and keeping the men at a distance.

There were three clangs and a thud. I looked toward the thud and a man dropped to his knees grasping a bloody stump. His hand and club lay on the ground in front of him. He yowled in pain and anger. Then I heard another thud and he fell face first on the ground, a knife in his back.

I looked to where Sir Bowyn was still fighting his two mounted marauders one hand outstretched, he had thrown the knife. He nodded at Lady Celeste and she nodded back. They were two against eight and it seemed like they had the marauders outmatched. I was channeling my fear and turning it into anger that there was nothing I could do to help.

I was suddenly feeling things all around me. I could taste metals beneath our feet. A horse cried out in pain and one of the mounted riders went down under it. Crushing him. The three men on foot were circling us, looking for an opening. The leader, I'll call him Jawbone... Jawbone was smiling just like the Lady knight was.

He made a spinning motion, swinging his jawbone weapon behind him and sort of did a spinning attack maneuver through her circle of death. She deflected the force of his blow and he reversed his spin and the blade swooshed over my head, sending more hairs drifting to the ground, and she somehow twisted her arm down and her blade stopped the strike that was aimed at the back of her leg. He spun away laughing.

She bent forward and slashed her sword behind her to catch the blade in her other hand and deflected the sword of another man who used Jawbone's distraction to attack. She spun and leapt and kicked the man squarely in the jaw. I heard a crack and he went stumbling back, his face twisted in pain. He started circling with the other men again.

I was breathing hard, I could feel my pulse racing and my head was aching. I could taste the metal in all the weapons around me, I could sense everything in my bag in my cart. There was something of hardened iron or steel just below the surface of the ground to my side.

I heard an anguished cry and a gurgling to the side and watched the second mounted man fall from his horse, blood across his neck. Then Sir Bowyn turned his charger toward us, I heard a whupping sound, then he flew off his horse with an arrow embedded in his chest. He landed on the ground unmoving.

Lady Celeste growled and screamed a cry of anger and rolled over Stumpy's body and came up on a knee with the dagger in her hand. She sent it flying faster than she could have thrown it, backed by a burst of raw energy from her arm and a moment later an archer fell out of the tree with the blade buried in an eye socket.

This caused the last three to charge her. They started pushing her back as she spun and slashed and blocked. She grunted when Jawbone's weapon struck her left shoulder. It cut through her armor, but I could see some of the metal teeth broke off in the leather joints of the armor. Blood was flowing down her arm. They all seemed to have forgotten me as they attacked the Techno Knight with extreme prejudice. She was holding her own and I saw her starting to gather power again.

My eyesight was fuzzing, I was seeing everything in weird colors. I could taste the iron in everyone's blood. My body seemed to be heating up, I saw energy start to arc across my skin. What was happening? I clenched my fists and the object under the soil seemed to move, like it was connected to me somehow.

One man gave her a glancing blow when Jawbone and a big brute pulled her attention to one side with feints. She was hurt! I let out a sound that was part anger, part challenge, part growl and I thrust my arm forward on instinct and the object under the soil burst out and flew at the man who had harmed the Lady. It impaled him and kept going, dragging his body along until it embedded into a tree. It was some sort of metal post with metal placards on one end.

The distraction allowed Lady Celeste to roll to the side and engage Jawbone directly. I looked at the archer and made a grasping motion, I could feel the dagger in his skull like I were holding the hilt. I made a slashing, throwing motion and it flew at the other brute. He saw it coming and deflected it with his blade. The knight used that distraction to change the swing of her blade into a parry, continuing the motion and spinning to embed her blade into the other brute's gut as she kicked the weapon out of Jawbone's grasp.

I just blinked at her skill. She was thinking and reacting to a changing situation at lightning speeds, using any opening. She released her sword, then she was trading blows with Jawbone in such rapid succession I almost couldn't follow them. He out massed her and his blows were more devastating, but he could only land one for every four or five she did. She finally landed a strike to his sternum that had him staggering back a few steps. She snarled and growled out, "Enough!" And thrust her hand forward and raw magic lanced from her, I could actually see her magic reservoir almost empty with my weird augmented vision.

I had expected him to be blasted back into the treeline, but he was still standing. I raised my arms and every scrap of metal around me rose too. I prepared to strike when I realized he wasn't moving. He was just standing there with a look of shock on his face.

That's when I noticed there was a gaping hole burned all the way through his chest as he collapsed onto the ground. I blinked. It was over? All the weapons and tools fell to the ground around me and I fell to my knees, realizing that I was so tired. More so than I had ever felt.

Lady Celeste was suddenly by my side, cradling me as I sat back on my feet. "Are you alright Laney? Are you injured?" I dumbly shook my head and she squeezed my shoulder.

Then she was on her feet and running to Sir Bowyn. She sat him up and I heard a groan. He was still alive! She said, "This is going to hurt. Ready?" He nodded weakly then she snapped the end off the arrow, drove the shaft the rest of the way through him, and yanked the arrow out. Blood spewed in an arc and his eyes rolled back into his head. She pulled upon her almost empty magic reservoir, I could barely make it out as my eyesight and breathing started returning to normal.

Then with the sizzling of power on skin and the stench of burning flesh, she cauterized his wound. She sat on the ground and panted after she lowered him back to a laying position. She watched his breathing normalize while she wrapped her own wounds. Then she shot me a tired but amused smile as she crawled back over by my side and just sat next to me and murmured, "Exciting afternoon."

I blinked at her then chuckled, she joined in. I don't know why we were laughing, after so much violence and death, but it felt good. My laugh slowly turned into sobbing, she just held an arm out and I folded into her. She just shushed me until I could stop the crying jag. I had no clue why my emotions were everywhere like that.

She asked with a hint of a smile in her voice, "Did you really tell them that you hoped they got sick when they ate you?" I laughed and nodded, pushing gently away from her and wiping my eyes on my tunic.

She looked around me at all the weapons and tools then at the man impaled on the tree. "You're not just a sensitive are you?"

I looked at her and fought back a new round of tears, I shook my head and my voice sounded pathetic to me when I pleaded, "Please don't send me to the stockade."

She pulled me back to her and stroked my hair and said, "Nobody's going to put you in the stockade. But we have to keep it just between you and me until I figure out what to do... okay?" I glanced at her and nodded. Feeling hopeful.

She stood and walked to the impaled man, and I followed behind. Trying not to vomit at the sight. She pulled her sword and with great effort, powered it then slashed down, letting the metal post fall to the ground, leaving the man stuck to the tree on a short piece of metal.

She flipped the post over so the placards faced us. I dusted the three sheets off, they were aluminum, the post was steel. One had the vestiges of of red and white, it was octagonal and had letters, S-T-O and I couldn't quite make the other out but it was most likely a P, it made sense. I prompted, "Stop?"

She arched an eyebrow at me and asked, "You can read?" I nodded and blushed. This caused her to smile. "Not many serfs learn to read. The House of Lords is thinking on mandating that every man, woman, and child learn. You are full of surprises Laney. You're quite a woman." Her smile caused a warmth to spread from my core. Her compliment caused my blush to return with a vengeance.

We returned our attention to the plaques. The second one was embossed but had no color left, just the white oxidation of aluminum. I read it, "Dead End."

We both looked at the man, the sign, then each other, she chuckled out, "Pretty much." She shook her head in disbelief. "Death by irony."

I almost slapped her shoulder in disbelief, even if I was thinking the same thing, but was just able to stop my hand from contacting her. Striking a Lady is a death sentence. She caught my sudden fear and she clasped my hand by her shoulder and looked directly into my eyes. "It's alright Laney. Honestly, I'm not one of those snobbish nobles that are sticklers for proper decorum." She looked to the other knight. He was still out. So she said softly, "I'm from common stock. I saved a Lady's child from a runaway horse. Her husband was none other than Prime Techromancer Donovan. He saw my magic potential and they bought me from my uncle."

She smiled and said, "They raised me as their own daughter and the rest is history." Then she relaxed a bit and said in a cheerful tone, "There, now we know each others secret. You can stop being so afraid around me." This coaxed a smile out of me. She tucked a strand of her red mane behind her ear. Did she even realize how beautiful she was? I felt self conscious about how dirty I was.

We turned our attention to the the final plaque. Three quarters of it was just oxidation but there was a faint green tint on the remainder and we could make out 'Lane'. I spoke out loud, "Lane." Then I looked at her in excitement, "This is a road sign." I had just learned another thing. The ancients marked their roads like we did too. She saw my excitement then she looked over at my cart and hefted the signpost and walked over and placed it in it for me.

I blinked at her and she shrugged, "It was your find. I didn't know it was under the earth there." I smiled at that. Then helped her gather all the weapons. And my tools. She got a rope out and lashed Sir Bowyn to his horse, then she gathered all the other horses and used lengths of rope to chain the reigns together.

She slid a gauntlet down and looked at her wrist. I blinked at it. There was a miniature clock on her wrist! She saw my shock and she showed it to me as she said, "The first artifact from the Before that Techromancer Donovan restored. He gifted it to me the day I became a Techno Knight." I smiled and looked between it and her. She added, "It is six o'clock. We need to hurry to get to the gates before seven."

I blinked when she started walking, holding her horse's lead as I grabbed my cart and started pushing as fast as I could go. She could make it to the gates in minutes if she rode. She was going to walk with me the whole way? Why did she look so bashful suddenly? She's the Lady, I'm just a chicken farmer.

Forty five minutes later we were approaching the gate. I paused, and started digging in my sack. She paused beside me and squinted. I pulled out the mirror and thrust it out to her. "I was going to sell this to a Lord or Lady. But I want you to have it. For saving me..." I blushed as I added her name, "Celeste."

She studied it with an inquisitive look, then realized what it was. She smiled at me then looked into it. She whispered, "What amazing silver smiths they had in the Before." I nodded my agreement. She locked eyes with me. "I couldn't accept this, this is priceless." She held it out to me. I shrugged and backed away a half step, not accepting it back.

She smiled at me and cocked her head, then she pulled off a gauntlet, tucked it into her belt, and placed a warm hand on my cheek. "Thank you Laney." I felt a raging fire inside at her touch, I was feeling flush. I realized I was grinning like a lovesick puppy and straightened.

She chuckled then removed her hand and whispered. "You need

to calm your emotions. Your amber eyes are glowing brilliantly. Any mundane wouldn't see it but it is like a beacon to us magic touched. You need to control your emotions or others will know before I can figure out what to do."

I furrowed my brow and she held the mirror up to me and I gasped. My eyes were glowing with an amber light. They had never done that before. Had whatever awakened in me during the battle cause this? I took a couple deep breaths, calmed myself, and the glow faded. I could feel it.

She slid the mirror into her saddlebag then bumped my hip playfully and said, "Again, thank you. But I'm not so sure you needed rescuing. I watched as you didn't back down from eight armed men, you were fearless. Are you aware you killed just as many marauders as Bowyn, a Knight of the Realm?"

I blushed and timidly bumped her hip back and we continued to the gates. The men on the wall saw us, the horses, and a knight lashed to his horse. They started clanging the alarm bell, calling out, "To the gates! Knight down!"

Moments later the courtyard by the gates was swarming with knights and medics. In all the commotion, I slipped away back toward home with my cart, while the attention was on the two knights, where it should be. I caught a final smile from her as she was inundated by questions.

As I approached home I repeated her words into the air with a smile, "Exciting afternoon."

CHAPTER 3 – THE SPOILS OF BATTLE

When I got home, I excitedly shared my day with Jace and
mother when we woke her for dinner, omitting the portions I had
used magic. I was in an especially good mood so I splurged and
made a hearty stew with almost half of our larder. Including salted
beef! I figured I could spend five or ten penny to restock in the
morning if I got as much coin as I thought I would from my salvage.

Jace contributed a nice scone to the meal. The baker's wife had
snuck it to him when he went to trade eggs to them and to sell to the
nobles in the castle. She really liked Jace, she had a daughter a year
younger than him, who they were hoping he might take an interest in
when they reached the age of majority. It was a smart match,
pairing a herder and a baker. And little Elise was adorable with her
golden tresses.

After giving mother a nice sponge bath and changing her
nightshirt, I sent her back to bed. I gave Jace a tiny bulb from my
find that day, which miraculously still had its filament intact. I went
out to do the nightly chores. I buttoned up the chicken coops and
chased the three hogs into their covered enclosure to sleep. I
thought about the day as I pumped a fresh bucket of water from the
well. I was so exhausted, but I was smiling... I had spoken with a
Techno Knight!

I almost skipped back to the straw mat, near the little electric
resistance heater at mother's bed, that I shared with Jace. The heater

was a luxury that Corrick had spent a month's pay to get for us. It allowed us to stay warm without stoking the fire in the fireplace all night and allowed us to conserve firewood for cooking.

I checked the ceramic vessel that held the magic spark that powered the electric device to make sure the seal was not deteriorating. We'd never be able to afford a new power vessel if this one ever allowed the magic potential to seep out.

As I curled under my blanket I remembered that I still had to fix the ratty hole in my tunic. Maybe on the morrow. I looked at my little brother. I felt almost guilty that I couldn't both scavenge and take care of the livestock. He was being forced to grow up too fast. Then I smiled when I saw the bulb I gifted him on a little string necklace hanging from his neck.

I kissed his forehead and made sure he was tucked in, then laid back and drifted off to sleep with a certain smile and wink on my mind, while the last church bells of the night pealed out ten o'clock.

***

The next morning I sponged off a lot of the grime from the previous day, I'd have to go down to the lake to take a swim, or visit the baths to get properly clean for church the next day. I had salvage to sell and hopefully medicines to buy and our larder to restock. I decided that this would be a day in the village to get all the errands taken care of.

I looked at Jace, "After you do the morning chores and see to mother, then spend the rest of the day playing in the market with the

other boys after selling the eggs. You deserve a day off for fun.
You can use a half penny to get sweets if you want." His eyes shot
wide at that.

He nodded enthusiastically, "Yes sister."

I greased the door hinges with lard, then opened the door
carefully, there was no protest. Then Jace and I stepped outside into
the morning twilight and froze. There were two horses tied to the
pig pen. We both looked around cautiously but saw nobody about
except old man Warren down the lane tending his garden. He had
almost a bushel of fresh carrots and green beans in his cart, my
mouth watered.

We stepped up to the horses. There was a stack of folded
bearskins on the rickety bench beside the rain barrel at the base of
the firewood overhang. Two saddles in ill repair rested on the stack
and an envelope with the wax seal of Castle Wexbury on it.

Written on it in grand script with regal looking flourishes was
my name. I looked around again and snatched up the envelope.
Jace crowded me and ran his fingers along the letters. "What does it
say?"

I smiled at him. "Remember mother's lessons? You tell me. I'll
have to restart lessons with you when we get a slowdown this
winter."

He looked at the writing, it was so loopy I wasn't sure he would
get it. Then he asked, "L?" as he pointed to it I nodded in
encouragement. And his small voice continued, "A... N... E... Y..."

Then his eyes went wide, "Laney! That's you!" I nodded and he looked at the second word, after the H he just blurted, "Herder" He looked almost as proud of himself as I was of him as he said, "Laney Herder. Are you going to see what it is? It looks important, that is the seal of the realm!"

Was I in trouble for getting the knights hurt? I was nervous, but not as nervous as breaking an official seal of the castle. But it was addressed to me right? I pulled from my pigskin boot, the little piece of metal I had scavenged, that was hammered thinner than the blade of a knife, which I had fashioned into a blade. It was from my prior find, I had cut the piece out of a large sheet that was so even that I had to wonder about the metal smiths that could hammer the sheets out so smoothly.

I carefully slid it under the red wax as not to break it, It was beautiful and I didn't want to ruin it. With a little pop, the wax came away from the parchment envelope and I slid out a single sheet of parchment and unfolded it carefully. I read it twice and blinked over at the horses.

I felt my breathing becoming more rapid and I could hear my pulse in my ears and I started heating up. I could feel magic escaping from my eyes as the world changed colors, and I closed them and willed myself to calm down. After three deep breaths and counting to ten, I could feel my skin cool and the tastes of all the metals around us recede away.

Jace excitedly asked, "Well Laney, what does it say? Are we to groom the horses for the nobles or board them? We could get two or three pennies a week for that!"

I shook my head and said incredulously, not believing it myself, "No, they are mine."

He blinked, not understanding and I smiled down at him and looked at the letter and read it aloud, "Be it known, that the treasury of Castle Wexbury has awarded to one Laney Herder, maiden of the keep, the bounty of two silver pieces for the heads of two marauders in the battle east of the gates on the fifteenth day after Three Sisters Conjunction, twenty seven and forty two years post Impact. As witnessed by Lady Celeste of the Techno Knight Order and Sir Bowyn, Knight of the Realm."

I tilted the envelope into my hand and two silver coins slid out. We were now just two silvers away from affording the medicines now, and I still had my salvage to sell! I was in shock. I continued, "In pursuant to the rules of combat and the division of spoils, Laney Herder is awarded the prizes of the combatants she has slain."

I read the list, it was an inventory. "Two bearskin saddle blankets. Two saddles in the Mountain Gypsy style. Two tack and bridles. One Percheron stallion, black with white blazing on muzzle, no brands. One Mustang mare, chestnut, no brands." It went on to describe the contents of the saddle bags."

Jace was going through the saddle bags that were more like deerskin sacks tied to the saddles. I grinned at the last part just below the signature of the village treasurer, "Witnessed by Lady

Celeste of the Techno Knight Order, Blade of Temperance of Wexbury, daughter of Prime Techromancer Donovan, Lady of the Court." Then it had her signature that looked far too loopy and feminine for a knight to have. I smiled at it.

At the bottom, it had a wax seal of the ring of the treasury. I folded the letter and slid it back into the envelope and pulled my coin bag from under my waistband and dropped the coins in.

I looked at my brother who was standing below the behemoth stallion, reaching up to stroke the lower part of his neck. I said to him. "We own horses Jace!"

Then he looked at me and said with pride, "Better still, horses my sister won in battle. You're like a knight Laney!" I almost cried on the spot, it was all I could do not to tear up at the pride for me that shone in his eyes.

I looked at him. "Lets get the chores done quickly, I'll help. Then we can brush them out and we can sell the mare. She'll fetch almost two gold coins, that will feed us through winter. We'll keep the big guy." I smiled at him and named him. "Goliath. We'll keep Goliath."

He nodded enthusiastically and looked up at the huge mount, "You hear that Goliath? We're going to be family!" I was imagining how much easier going to market and going outside the gates scavenging would be with a horse, especially a huge draft horse like this.

I looked over to the old hay wagon that had seen better days in the firewood overhang of the roof and smiled.

We finished our chores in record time and checked on mother and gave her the last of the scone we had saved and some of the stew. She washed it down with a glass of water. I noted she was shaking as she moved, her illness was slowly eating away at her. We filled her in, then went out to work on the horses.

After giving them a good brush down and cleaning their unshod hooves, we put the saddles and gear in the hay wagon we dragged out. We tethered the mare to the back of the wagon with a long lead and then hitched Goliath up to the wagon. It had been three or four years since we had a horse to pull it. Mother had taught me how.

After loading the wagon with my salvage and the day's eggs, we sat up in the wagon and I had Jace sit on my lap. He may as well learn sometime. I put the reins in his hand and clasped his hands in mine, released the brake and whipped the reigns lightly, and we lurched forward as Goliath started trudging forward like he had no load at all. Jace was laughing. It was so good to see him laugh.

The village was awake and active now, we got stares from all our neighbors and the people heading to market as we trotted past. We must look a sight, our clothing in tatters and having not one, but two such fine horses as we passed by. I was so very embarrassed. I couldn't help noticing there was no comparison between Goliath and the old swayback mare, Tulip, we had years ago before we sold her to the butcher so we could survive a winter. I loved Tulip, but she was nowhere near as grand as Goliath.

Once we hit market, I sent Jace off with the eggs and a half penny as I promised. I called after him, "I'll see you at home at sunset!" He just waved me off and disappeared into the hustle and bustle of the crowd and all the market carts and tents.

I made my way to the livery stable beside the blacksmith, I set the wagon brake and hopped down and brought the letter and the mare to the big liveryman who was washing down two chargers that had the Wexbury Keep brand on their flanks.

He looked up at me and I said, "Excuse me sir. I was wanting to sell my mare if you are buying." He dropped the thick bristle brush and wiped his hands on the huge work apron he wore and stepped up to me. He looked displeased.

I didn't see it coming, I was seeing stars and my ear was ringing after his big ham fist backhanded me. I kept my footing and refused to cry out like mother taught me. If you cry out and show weakness, then people above your station show more cruelty. He said with a accent of the Northern realms, "Whacha doing ya fool girl! Horse thievery will get ya the gallows!"

I looked at him, fighting off tears from the stinging pain. "But I own her sir, I have the papers that say so. With the official seals." He raised his hand to backhand me again and I just stood tall. He gave a growl and lowered his arm.

I dug the letter from my tunic and handed it to the man. He unfolded it holding it roughly in his hands and wrinkling it. I fought back a exclamation at that, I wanted to keep it in good shape and put it in my hope chest. He looked the letter up and down with a studious look on his face, but I noted his eyes did not track side to side, the man could not read. His eyes dwelled on the easily recognizable wax seal of the treasury.

He nodded and thrust it back at me. I took it and folded it carefully to slide it back into the envelope as he said gruffly, "Aye. Why didn't ya just say so in the first place?" He just ignored me as he stepped up to the mare to run his hands along her examining her and looking at her hooves, and asked, "How did a young thing like ya come to own a horse?" Proving to me that he indeed could not read.

I said meekly, "Spoils of battle." He stopped his examination of the horse and looked back at me in disbelief and I quickly said. "Truly, just like the letter stated."

He looked at the corner of the envelope sticking out of my tunic near my modest cleavage then nodded and said gruffly, "Of course. I just didn't believe it." I gave him his dignity and nodded like I understood.

Then he stood after looking at the last hoof. "Unshod, swaybacked. I'll give you a gold coin for the nag."

My eyes went wide, "Swaybacked? Nag? She's no more than three or four. Strong back and true footing. I could get three times that at the livery in Flatlash."

He squinted at me then he smiled slightly in appreciation then said, "Maybe so, but Flatlash is a two days ride. Then how would you return? Two gold and not a penny more."

I smiled at how quickly he had countered, the mare must be in better shape than I had anticipated. I let my voice go a little sing song as I shrugged and said, "Two gold five penny and a trade for proper saddle and tack."

He looked at me and just squinted for a very long time then asked, "Trade fer what? I stepped to the back of wagon and showed him the bearskins, saddles, and tack. "I'd need something suitable for Goliath there." I pointed at the Stallion.

His mouth was watering as he stared at Goliath. "Would ya be selling him too?" I shook my head and his shoulders slumped. I knew Goliath was worth four or five gold. Draft horses had many uses.

He looked at me then just started throwing the bearskins and saddles over his broad shoulders. A few minutes later, he had me put my mark on a bill of sale and I walked out with a beautiful used saddle, tack and blanket for my Stallion. I grinned at the fact that he may not know how to read but he was just fine reading and writing numbers. His mark on the bill of sale was just some loopy gibberish instead of an X, I'm sure he was used to dealing with people who could not read and wanted them to think he was a learned man.

I hefted the saddle into the wagon with a smile. I had more than enough for the medicines now, even enough to have the doctor out to our place since I didn't wish mother to travel in her current state.

I took off the brake and the man called out, "Young miss."

I called back, "Laney. Herder."

He said, "Laney, come by to deal anytime. Ask for Heath."

I waved at the man and traveled the twenty yards to the blacksmith and dismounted. I learned from my last mistake and had the letter at the ready as I stepped into the smithy. It was ungodly hot with the huge fire pit and bellows stoking the flames higher. Two men without shirts and more muscle and sweat than any four men should have, were pounding out metal on their anvils with skilled strikes of their huge hammers.

One looked over toward me, then quenched the blade he was working on in a bucket. He smiled and started walking over, I sighed in resignation. It was Kyle Smith, the boy mother tried to marry me off to last season. I told mother that I would be betrothed to no man.

He stepped up to me, he had certainly filled out and muscled up in the past year. "Laney! What brings you here?" There was hope in his eyes and I felt terrible for the man, he truly was a good person, I just had no want to court anyone.

Before he got his hopes up. I handed him the letter as I nudged my head to Goliath out the big doors and said quickly, "My horse needs to be shod, is the farrier here today?"

He looked at the letter and whistled. "You fought marauders?"

I blushed and blurted, "Not by choice!"

He chuckled. "Nobody fights marauders by choice." He smiled and said, "You're quite a woman, Laney." I wish he'd stop saying nice things, it made me feel guilty for not returning his affections.

He seemed to sense my unease and said as he walked outside with me trailing behind. "I can handle it. No need for the farrier, he overcharges. I can have it done in an hour for... a penny a shoe?" He squinted at the price knowing how tight money was with mother down.

I nodded and pulled out my coin purse then looked at all the iron strapped wagon wheels leaning against the smithy, then at the wagon. The wheels were in such disrepair, I'd hate to break a spoke while I was out scavenging or bringing things to market. I had coin now and more to come when I sold my salvage. I could look at this as an investment. "How much to refit new wheels?"

He looked at me like I had just sprung a nut. Then looked at the wheels and said, "If you give us your old ones in trade, I could give you the new wheels and the shoes for... a silver?"

I spit into my hand and offered it. "Done."

He spit in his. "Done!" And we shook.

I held my coin purse close to me so he couldn't see the contents and I pulled out one of my bounty silvers and put it in his hand. He blinked at it then smiled at me and said, "Give me some time. Pick it up at noon?" I nodded and took some stuff from the wagon.

He stepped up and looked under the canvas sheet in the wagon and whistled. "I heard you were scavenging now. A woman of many facets."

I shook a finger at him and squinted playfully, "It all better be there when I return."

He chuckled and held his hands up in surrender and headed back into the smithy. I turned toward the hospital and hurried on my way. This was my most important task for the day.

I hated the hospital, it always smelled of herbs, antiseptic, alcohol, and sickness. But it was arguable the most modern building in the village besides the castle. Every room had electric lights and heat, they could even keep the rooms cool in the scorching heat of summer. It also had running water pumped through pipes using electric powered pumps. It truly was a marvel if you forgot the smells and the sick and dying people. They even had machines that could hear the heartbeat and breathing of someone without a stethoscope.

Most of the advancements the Techromancers developed that were not dedicated to the defense of the realm, were dedicated to medical advancement. They say that one day our medical capabilities will rival those of the Before Times.

I walked into the front room, there were a dozen people waiting in chairs. I stepped up to the woman at the front desk and dug out the slip of paper from my pocket that had mother's prescriptions written on it. She looked up at me and smiled as I slid the paper over and said, "Hello ma'am, I'm Laney Herder, daughter of Margret." I nudged my chin at the paper. "I've come to purchase her medicines."

She looked the papers over then gave me a sympathetic look.

She wrote some stuff in a ledger and said with one squinted eye, indicating she knew how painful the cost was, "It would be three gold four penny."

I nodded and quickly pulled three gold and a silver from my coin purse and slid them to her. "Is that enough to have the doctor come look at her?"

She covered my hand and the coins and just looked at me for a long moment until I met her eyes, then she nodded. "He is going out this afternoon on house calls. Where are you located?"

I said hopefully, "We're the chicken herders in Cheap Quarter, near the main portcullis."

She nodded and wrote something in another book then looked at a calendar with writings on it behind her. She said absently as she wrote Margret Herder on the calendar. "He'll be out around seven tonight." She looked up at me, "Is that okay?"

I was nodding fervently. She smiled and stood, "Alright then, I'll be right back with the medicines, or would you rather the doctor bring them in case there has been a change?"

That made sense to me so I nodded again and said, "That would probably be best. Thank you so much ma'am."

She looked happy that I was happy. Maybe the hospital wasn't as bad as I thought. I left the hospital with a weight lifted off my heart knowing maybe mother could get better.

I looked at the clock tower in the church as the bell chimed eleven. The day was just shooting by. I still had to make it to the castle to sell my scrap and I still had plenty of coin in my purse. I turned back toward the market, I was going to treat myself to a mid day meal. I hadn't had one in the market since mother was healthy. I felt a little guilty spending money on myself but I was in an extremely giddy mood.

I glanced back at the west wall, were it extended into the lake, and the swimming hole and bath house. I needed to be clean for church in the morning and I wanted to look presentable when I went to barter at the castle. I made the decision to bathe after I picked up Goliath and my wagon.

In the market I found a Gypsy food vendor, I ordered one of those mouth watering skewers with chunks of meat and vegetables alternating on it, a buttered roll and a large cup of grape juice. I thought about getting wine or mead instead, now that I was of age, but decided against it. It was expensive but worth the half penny. The smell of the food alone had me salivating.

I passed a seamstress on my way back to the smithy then paused to look at the back of the cart. There was a bar with dozens of tunics hanging from it. I looked down at my threadbare shirt and chastised myself as I stepped back and started looking through the offerings.

One and a half pennies later I walked off with one new tunic for me, one for Jace, and a new nightshirt for mother. I stopped my frivolous spending and walked away from the stacks of trousers the seamstress had, before I could waste any more money.

I smiled at the tunic I had chosen for myself. Instead of the usual natural browns and tans of the threads, this one had been dyed a rich hunter green and the seamstress had embellished the sleeve cuffs and collar with yellow leaves that looked almost gold. It was the nicest shirt I had ever owned.

After picking up Goliath and the wagon and stowing my purchases I headed down to the baths. Again drawing people's eyes, most likely wondering why a young woman such as myself had such a stallion. I know it would have been a curiosity for me if I had witnessed it.

I set the brake at the public baths. They weren't busy today. Or perhaps it was because it was midday, I had never visited them during the day.

This was a perk of living in Wexbury. The baths were open to all at no charge, and were famous through all the realms. Wexbury extended into the lake for the sole purpose of this convenience. The founders of the keep determined that cleanliness kept away many of the blights and disease that pestered other realms. So they designed the keep to include a safe area for swimming and bathing within the walls.

I looked around, there was another wagon with two older draft horses at the yoke, and three mares hitched beside it. I took my new tunic with me and entered the arch into the women's side of the bath house. There was a ten foot tall stone wall that divided the men from the women, and the baths had underwater entrances into the swimming hole. They even had a smaller area on the other side of the bath house where they had heated water pools in the winter. I found it odd not to have to stand in line.

I walked over to the elderly matron of the bath, Hannah, and greeted her. The pleasant portly woman was always dressed impeccably for a serf, just as well as any noble. She had the rich speech patterns commonly associated with the nobles as well, indicating a good education. Though she was of lower station, I have always found it odd that the noble women paid her great respect.

She handed me a large white towel and I turned and sat at the benches and undressed self consciously as I looked out to the waters just beyond the benches. There were only nine or ten women in the large fifty foot square waters. Some had oils and soaps they were cleaning with. I was jealous of such luxury.

I undressed and stacked my clothing on the bench, hiding my coin purse in a boot. I wrapped in the towel and started toward the waters when a rich voice called over from the matron. "Laney? Fancy meeting you here."

I froze then turned slowly to see Lady Celeste in full armor with another knight taking towels from Hannah. I walked up to her with my eyes lowered and said shyly, "Celeste."

Hannah spit out quickly, "Mind your tongue girl! Address the lady properly!" I glanced over and then winced, waiting for her raised hand to come down on my cheek. Why was everyone disciplining me lately?

Lady Celeste caught the matron's strike gracefully and far more gently than I would have thought possible. She chuckled out to the woman, "It is alright Hannah, I gave her leave to address me so. We are old comrades in arms, Laney and I."

She shot me yet another one of her winks as I wondered if blushing could be terminal. Hannah was immediately her calm professional self and she simply tilted her head to me in acknowledgment, "I apologize miss, I was not aware." Then she bowed her head slightly to the knights, "Lady Celeste, Lady Verna." To my surprise they both returned the bow if not slightly shallower.

Before I knew what was happening, the Techno Knight had looped her arm in mine and was dragging me to the benches, "You simply must join Verna and I."

I tried to protest but she ignored me and I sat and turned away from them as they removed their armor and disrobed. I turned back when they had towels around themselves. She said, "Laney, this is Lady Verna, Knight of the Realm, and my best friend."

She turned to the woman who appeared to have as much muscle as the blacksmiths but still somehow looked very feminine despite the ragged scar that cut diagonally across her face from the temple down her neck to the opposite shoulder. It made her look dangerous and oddly alluring. Celeste told her, "Ver, this is Laney Herder."

The woman grinned at me and offered a hand and said in a soft alto, "Laney."

I shook her hand, it was like grasping iron and I lowered my eyes in respect. "Lady Verna."

She chuckled, "None of that Laney. If you are a friend of our Celeste here then you can call me Verna. She hasn't shut up about you all day."

She had been speaking of me? I bobbed my head, chanced a look up, and acknowledged the request, "Lady." She rolled her eyes and chuckled and turned toward the water and dropped her towel just before she stepped in. I blinked, even her back muscles had muscles.

Celeste chuckled and I glanced up to see her watching me then said knowingly, like she knew what I was thinking, "Yeah, she's always working out and sparring in her free time. I think it is an obsession with her. She has to compete with the men. Maybe it is to make sure her husband, Sir Kristof doesn't surpass her in the ranks."

We stepped up to the the carved stone steps that led down into the water and Celeste let her towel drop to the ground, and I stopped breathing as she walked slowly down the steps into the water. She... her body... those curves. I believed I had just witnessed an angel. I was feeling so warm and flush. Dear lord, I was aroused!

Verna moved through the water to me and brought her hand up to close my mouth. She had a look of mischief on her face as she said through a chuckle, "Yeah I know, not fair to the rest of us. I feel like a horse next to her." Then she added, "She'll make some..." She paused looking for the words then settled on, "...person, a fine catch."

They both moved to a row of submerged stone benches and I held my towel tight. I was extremely self conscious of my body suddenly. Compared to the two knights, I felt like I had the body of a child. I turned my back to them and let my towel drop. I crossed my arms over my breasts, holding my shoulders and turned to descend the steps.

Celeste's eyes were narrowed and she looked angry for some reason. Had I made her mad in some way? I sat beside them on the bench and Celeste brought her hands up and grabbed my shoulders, turning my back toward them.

I shivered when her fingers gently traced the scars on my back in the water. She growled out, "These are scars from lashing." It was a statement not a question. I saw Lady Verna wince. I just nodded and turned myself out of the knight's grasp and placed my back against the stone bench's backrest.

She just stared at me expectantly. I shrugged. "I don't like to speak about it." She just kept staring at me with that expectant look and I exhaled and caved. "A chamber maid snuck me into the library of the Techromancy Scrolls to show me the wonders it held when I was younger."

Her anger seemed to double, was she displeased I had broken the rules? I shrugged again and said more to myself, "The punishment for trespassing into the library is..."

She finished for me, "Public flogging, twenty lashes. It's

barbaric." She turned me again and looked at my back. I blinked, she was mad about the scars, not about my transgression?

I relaxed a little and put her mind at ease. "The magistrate took pity and gave only ten, he stayed his hand and was gentle."

She growled out, "To punish a child for being curious? That is what children do." Her finger was running along the worst of the scars. "Wait, was that when little Resme was sent away?" Before I nodded she said, "I remember that day. I snuck out to the flogging. Father forbade me to watch. He thought it a travesty that anyone should be punished for seeking knowledge."

Then she got a look of pride on her face. "You say he stayed his hand, but you are incorrect. I watched this little slip of a girl stand tall at the whipping post. She did not cry out as the whip cut unto her back. The magistrate struck more forcefully each time yet she still did not cry out. There were murmurings about the brave child for days after that."

I pushed that day out of my thoughts and said in a tight voice, "Mother told me to be strong, so I tried to do her proud and refused to show weakness."

She grinned at me and sat back on the bench and started washing up. She glanced at her fellow knight, "You should have seen her when confronted by eight marauders, unarmed. Instead of trying to flee or begging for mercy, she just stood there and threw their threats back at them."

Verna rolled her eyes in humor. "So you have told me, seven

times now." They got into a shoving match and I chuckled at their childish behavior. I made an odd realization at that moment. Knights are people too. I blinked at that. I have always seen them as these paragons of right, the larger than life heroes that kept evil at bay. But – I looked at the playful women – they can laugh too.

I relaxed and grabbed one of the bristle brushes tethered to the benches and started scrubbing a week's worth of dirt and grime off of my skin.

They got me talking about the surprise of finding the spoils and prizes of battle at my doorstep in the morning. About being able to purchase mother's medicines. How I was going to the castle after the bath to sell my finds from the previous day.

Celeste brightened, "I'll accompany you if you don't mind. Until Bowyn recovers, I'm stuck at the castle for the next week or two, and I get ever so bored."

I blushed and looked down and nodded. She said as she turned her back to me, "Good! Now that that is settled, scrub my back for me would you? I'll do yours."

I was surprised by the wound on her left shoulder, it was only a series of angry red scars where the marauder's weapon struck. How could it heal so much in but a day?

I shook my head then looked away from her shoulder and I blinked at the flawless skin she presented me. It was marred only by short scars in three places that, as I ran my fingers across them, I realized could only be sword entry wounds. I held my breath as I moved my hands down her back, feeling the smooth skin that I would associate with a noble.

She said in a wavering voice, "Trying to make me swoon is not conducive to getting my back clean Laney." I was breathing hard and felt flush as she glanced back with a demure look. She froze and whispered, "Your eyes. Calm yourself. Breathe." I nodded and closed my eyes and pushed away the heat building inside me. I felt the power fade but the heat was still there. I opened my eyes and she smiled and nodded. I grabbed a brush and she turned and I started scrubbing. Verna seemed to be watching the whole exchange with great curiosity.

After the sinfully erotic experience of having a Knight of the Realm wash my back and run her hands along it, we stepped out of the baths and wrapped in our towels. I kept my back to them as I quickly dressed. I know I will surely burn in hell, but I peeked as Celeste got dressed. Her long legs and shapely butt were... I bit my lower lip and looked away.

I had an epiphany at that moment. Was that truly why I never wished to be wed like all the other girls? Why the thought of laying with a man repulsed me? Was I broken in some way? I couldn't deny the fact that I was extremely sexually attracted to a Lady of the Court. To a female Knight. Hell is too good a place for me. It was not unheard of for a man to lay with a man, or a woman with a woman, though it was exceedingly rare. I took another peek jut to see her looking my way. Caught. I blushed and stood.

I swear she was grinning but I refused to look directly at her after being caught looking. The women took out a hairbrush and brushed out each others hair. Then Verna turned to me and patted the bench beside her. "Come now, your turn."

I absently touched my dark, tangled hair, remembering when I was small, mother had a small hairbrush back then. It has since broken and we never bought another. I timidly sat, and the women, the Ladies of the Court, the Knights of the Realm, brushed out my hair.

I quickly wiped a tear from my cheek. I had no idea why I was crying. I pushed back the odd feelings and just reveled in the attention. My hair was almost dry when they finished with me. Then with quick, deft hands, Verna braided my hair and Celeste tied it off with a ribbon of violet and emerald, the colors of the keep.

The muscled woman said, "She cleans up nice huh Celeste?" I looked down then chanced a look at the other woman grinning and nodding in agreement.

We stepped over to Hannah and looked into the huge polished silver mirror that they kept near the entrance. The silversmiths visited weekly to keep its surface almost glassy smooth. I stood in front of the two tall women in armor, I looked almost like a child compared to them, even though they could only be two or three years my senior.

I absently reached up and touched the braid going down my back. Cleaned up and wearing my new green tunic, I looked above

my station, like a castle servant, not a serf. I smiled then looked
away, it did not pay to be vain, only hard work can put food on the
table.

We bid farewell to the bath matron and I saw the two chargers
lashed to the post near my wagon. Verna mounted her steed in one
fluid motion, then she held her hand down and Celeste grasped
forearms with her as she said, "I'm off to the wall for the rest of the
day. Church tomorrow?"

Celeste nodded. "Aye."

Then Verna reached toward me. I blinked then grasped her
forearm as she said, "Goodbye Laney. I'm sure we will meet again."

I replied, "Goodbye Lady Verna. It was very nice to meet you."
She smiled, nudged her horse and galloped off.

I turned to see Celeste looking at Goliath's shod hooves as she
stroked his flank. She smiled up at me and said, "You aren't the
only one to clean up nicely. This stallion looks to be the pick of the
lot. Very handsome."

I grinned with pride for the horse I have owned less than a day.
"Yes Goliath is. I've never owned a horse of my own before. It is
almost surreal."

She squinted in confusion. "But you have a wagon, how was it
pulled before?"

I shrugged. "Mother had an old nag. We had to sell her for food
a few winters back."

Again she looked unhappy. She kept getting that look around

me and I wondered if I were displeasing her somehow.

She studied me a minute then exhaled and prompted, "To the castle?" I nodded, trying not to show my excitement. I'd been to the castle hundreds of times, trading and selling eggs, but the servant's entrance was nothing compared to the wonders in the salvage intake courtyard. There were so many wonders to see before the Techromancers hauled them off to be repaired, reclaimed, or recycled.

My first time there, someone had brought in a windmill with a motor that generated electricity when the wind blew. In a couple short months two or three windmills had appeared on the highest tower ramparts. The Techromancers were quick to reproduce working designs. It was free electrical energy with no magic cost, courtesy of the winds of the realm.

I had once asked mother why we even bothered with electricity and generators when so many people with magic potential lived in the castle. She explained that energy was energy, whether magic or electric. But we could generate electrical energy whereas we could not generate magic energies. So when a magic user is at their limit, they need to rest, sometimes for days to regain their strength. But as long as a generator is turning by any means, then electric power is produced. The wizards of the Before knew this, that is why so many devices unearthed from that era were powered by electricity.

We had Techromancer apprentices in the castle who's daily duty was to link crystals with their own magic potential and seal the sparks in ceramic pots. These vessel's magic potential turned the generators and alternators that powered our village. I absently touched my tunic, feeling the crystal shard on its string beneath the cloth. If a vessel lost it's potential it would be returned to the castle for the apprentices to re-energize with their own magics again.

Lady Celeste trotted next to the wagon as we approached the castle. I said, "I need to see if I can speak with a scholar. I think I have learned things of value of the Before. Would one speak with me? Or should I just leave a note at salvage intake?"

The look she gave me was full of mischief. "Oh, I think I have an idea of someone you can speak with. I'll go fetch them while you do your business."

I smiled and tried to hide my excitement. I, Laney Herder would speak with a scholar or, I didn't dare to hope, an actual Techromancer... besides Celeste of course. Techno Knights are minor Techromancers who answer the call to defend the weak instead of devote themselves to study.

I couldn't imagine the intelligence of the scholars, having full access to the scrolls and tomes of the library. Mother was the most intelligent person I knew. I often wondered how she became so well versed in about every subject, but she would never speak of it. She always seemed to have tomes around to read but I know not where they came from. She promised to tell me when I reached majority, but she had gotten too sick by then.

We reached the line to the inner portcullis at the intake arch, but

Celeste moved past it saying, "With me Laney." People averted their eyes in respect as she trotted past and I felt more than a little self conscious as I had Goliath follow her.

The steward at the gate bowed as she passed him and his helpers with their clipboards. She simply said, "She is with me steward," before they even asked. His head still low I saw his eyes flick up to me in confusion but they let me pass. My head was turning every which way taking in the racks of wonders from the before as we passed them. There was a fairly intact, rusted back end from a conveyance that caught my attention.

I looked up just in time to stop Goliath before we slammed into Celeste who had stopped and was dismounting at the Purser's huge, iron bound, oak table. I put on the brake and scrambled down behind her. With her left hand, she discreetly made a wiggling motion with her fingers behind her. I took that as a silent prompt that I should be behind her on the left. I had never been in the company of a noble before and I silently thanked her in my head for not letting me make a fool of myself.

She spoke with her commanding tone, "Purser William, please attend my friend, Laney Herder, while I go retrieve someone to speak with her."

He was quick to respond in military precision, "Yes Lady Celeste."

She grinned back at me, "I'll return shortly." I nodded and she strode off like a woman on a mission.

The silver haired man had the look of a soldier but had the smile and laugh lines of a cheerful fellow around his mouth and the corners of his blue eyes that twinkled with vitality. He was in his fifties but held himself like a man in his thirties. I had met him on my last visit to the intake courtyard. They were so impressed with my first load that he wanted to handle my second load personally.

He looked to where Celeste had disappeared into the castle then at me with a grin. "Interesting company you keep for a young herder."

I didn't know what to say but I don't think he expected a reply because he was already jumping spryly into the back of my wagon saying, "Lets see what salvage you have for me today little one."

I climbed up beside him and pulled back the canvas, then opened my burlap sack. His eyes glittered again as he looked into the sack and whistled to himself. "How do you find such treasures? He looked at the signpost and ran a hand over the steel post. I could taste and feel the magics from his hand. His eyebrows went up. "Steel." he said.

He grabbed the signpost and threw it to the ground. The loud clang of it on the cobblestones made Goliath nervous. William jumped down and I followed him with the sack and went to his table. I rummaged in it and pulled out the small motors and placed them in front of him. I saw his magics reach out to them, one shaft turned the other didn't. I wondered why the man was not a Techromancer, but figured it had to do something with the low levels of magic I was sensing from him. Celeste, being a Techno Knight, was low level, but she felt as though she had ten times his power.

I looked at him expectantly and he tapped his fingers on the table, making a steady thrumming sound on the wood as he thought. "Two silver? One each?"

I smiled, I liked this dance, there was something invigorating about dickering. "Three. Two for the free turning one, one for the seized one."

He enjoyed the game too, I could tell as he countered, "Two, five penny."

I held my hand up to spit in it but saw the gleam in his eye and stopped. I squinted at him, "Two silver, five penny, and two penny vouchers in the market."

He chuckled at me and spit in his hand, "Done."

I spit in mine and shook. "Done." He moved them to the side and from his coin belt he counted out the money and placed the coins in front of the motors and then pulled two violet penny voucher slips from his clipboard and slid them under the coins.

Penny vouchers weren't as good as real pennies. You could only use them in the market and the vendors gave no change for them. So you had to be smart shopping in the market with them to get as close to a penny as you could. Vendors had to save up one hundred of them to cash them in at the treasury. It was a sort of credit for the keep.

I grinned then looked in my bag, I took out the Mustang emblem and pocketed it. He squinted trying to catch what I had decided on keeping until I showed a scholar. Then I pulled out all of the copper wires that were covering the true prize. After dickering and letting him get away with paying only a full silver, I smiled hugely at him.

He tilted his head, he knew it had to be good if I saved it for last. I pulled the burlap down to reveal the alternator. He reached for it and I slid it back from him. I pulled a little bulb from my tool bag and used some wire from the stack and connected it. I placed the butt of the bulb on an iron strap on the table then flicked the pulley and the light flickered a little.

I'm not too proud of the predatory toothy grin I gave him as I said, "Three gold." The man was salivating. He wiped his jowls, his eyes glued to my treasure, and I pocketed my bulb and and put the wire back on the stack and slid the alternator across the table to him. He couldn't get his hands on it fast enough.

I felt him send his magics across the device and he froze and pushed it away from him like it would burn him. He was on his feet and his voice held an accusatory tone, "There's residual magics on it! Did you..." I was suddenly frightened, I didn't know he'd be able to tell. I was heating up and my breathing was getting faster.

I saw a reflection of my eyes in his, burning brilliant amber. Shit! He was bellowing, "Guards! Rogue!" Power was starting to build in his hands. Oh god, I was going to the stockade just because I tried to get more coin for the salvage. What would mother and

Jace do?

A deep resonating bass voice behind me said, "Belay that! She's with me William." William quickly lowered his eyes and bowed his head as I turned to see Celeste walking up with a large bald man in his fifties dressed in the robes of a noble. A scholar?

My heart jumped into my throat and I swear I was a moment from passing out when the purser said, "Of course Prime Techromancer Donovan."

CHAPTER 4 – TECHROMANCER DONOVAN

⁓**M**⁓ y vision was starting to swim in the augmented colors of the world. I was aware of every metal around me, I could taste iron in all of the people's blood. Power was starting to arc down my arms. I started to feel lightheaded and realized I needed to breathe. I exhaled and tried to take in a breath without it sounding like a gasp. Show no weakness Laney! Belatedly I bowed low and kept my eyes on the ground.

The big man stepped up to me and placed his hand on my back. His deep bass was soothing as he said quietly, "Breath trough it child. It is alright. Breathe, calm yourself, it will pass. Control it, don't let it control you."

I started taking long deep breaths and tried to calm my center. Besides Duke Fredrick himself, the Prime Techromancer was the most powerful and important figure in all of Wexbury. He was telling me to calm myself. Him standing there was counterproductive to that end. The Techromancers were my heroes.

The colors of the world slowly bled back to normal and I slowed my pulse. I could feel the heat leaving me. I knew my eyes had returned to normal. I stayed in my bow. He pulled me up gently. "There, that's better now. Look at me child." I looked up at him hesitantly. He looked over at William, "This is a child, not a rogue." The man nodded and kept his eyes low.

Then he addressed me again, "When was your igniting?"

I didn't understand and Celeste answered for me, "Yesterday father. Her gift bloomed in defense of a Knight of the Realm. It was spectacular, I'd never witnessed an igniting before." Igniting? She knew something happened and didn't tell me? Oh good lord, this was Techromancer Donovan!

He looked at me expectantly but then his eyes narrowed. "You did not know? Surely you were aware of your gift."

Oh... I said meekly, "I am a sensitive. For two metals sir. Iron and copper."

He snorted then put an arm around my shoulder and looked up at William. "Pay her price and have her wagon moved to the main livery please."

William hastily counted out three gold coins from his coin belt, then picked up the rest of my coins and vouchers and handed them to me. I said to him, "I'm so sorry for any trouble I have caused sir."

William looked at me for a moment, studying me then exhaled and said, "I'm a little excitable. I'll have your wagon moved for you." I nodded and Celeste pulled me from her father and put an arm protectively around me as we followed the Techromancer into the castle, past the onlookers that were gawking at us trying to figure out what was happening. I was in the same boat.

As soon as a heavy oak door was closed behind us the big man asked, "What have you done child? Anyone who was magic touched would have seen that display." I didn't know if he truly wanted and answer or if it were rhetorical.

Celeste chastised the man, "Stop it, you are frightening her father." I blinked, she obviously had no fear of the most powerful magic user in the realm. We moved in silence to the base of the Techromancy tower, just below the great library. We entered a grand office that was in disarray, with scrolls, tomes, parchments and devices stacked everywhere.

He dumped parchments from two chairs in front of a great oak desk and made an ushering motion. Celeste pulled me down into a chair as she sat beside me. Techromancer Donovan sat on the edge of the desktop and looked between the two of us. I could see his mind running at lightning speed in his eyes.

He looked at me but spoke to Celeste, "Daughter, why can commoners not wield more than the magic of a sensitive?" I understood he was educating me by having her explain it for me.

I didn't know much, just that anyone in the village that developed an affinity for more magic, wound up on public display in the stockade, then vanished after a few weeks. I assumed to the dungeons.

She exhaled and looked between me and her adoptive father, and sighed out, "Rogues." It was a single word that was frightening to all that herd it. She expounded upon it, "When commoners started developing the gifts that once only the nobles possessed. The lords of the realms deigned they were not to utilize those gifts. They were under some misconception that a serf was not worthy to be included in the conclaves of magic users in the keeps."

Her eyes narrowed. "Those who broke the edict would be subject to public floggings and imprisonment or execution. This of course did not sit well with those magic inclined who had the audacity not to have noble blood in them to 'deserve' the gift."

I was noticing more and more that even though she was a noble and held the bearing of one, she disapproved of how nobles behaved. She got the same look whenever I was being disciplined by someone. My eyes went slightly wider as I realized it was because she had once been a commoner like me, like she had confided.

She didn't have that noble blood she spoke of. She was a woman of two worlds and she didn't believe they should be separate. I could see her reading my eyes and I caught an almost imperceptible nod from her, knowing I had come to that realization.

Her voice had no emotion. "This caused an uprising and secret societies five hundred years hence. Magic users would flee the keeps to avoid punishment. Large groups organized and were labeled rogues. They may have started as frightened people but they quickly became more dangerous than the marauders and would wipe out entire outlying villages with their magics to raid for supplies."

She closed her eyes, "This put the lords in a no win situation. They had to maintain the archaic rules restricting who could wield magics in order to stop others from rising to power with ill intent inside the walls of a keep, but it also perpetuated magicked people fleeing the keeps. They lords of the keeps were damned if they did, damned if they didn't."

She opened her eyes and looked at me. "It all came to a head fifty years back when the leader of the rogues, Rydell, decided that raiding was not enough. He decided to assault the walled keeps to take them as their own and end the rule of the lords. They first struck Far Reach, killing every man, woman, and child. The Techno Knights, Knights of the Realm, and Techromancers of Far Reach put up a valiant fight but were massively outnumbered and the magical assault was relentless."

I knew of this story from the bards, it was the Great Mage Wars that ended six years before I was born. She gritted her teeth and spoke the next through them, "They mounted the bodies of the fallen Techno Knights and Techromancers on pikes at the main gates as a warning to all. This began the great Mage Wars. All of the realms united under Prince George of Highland Keep to stop the rogues. Their numbers only grew as they swept up from the South, laying waste to all villages and keeps."

She was noticeably aggravated now, "They didn't care who they killed in their wake. Tens of thousands of innocents died with the defenders. The wars raged for over thirty years until one man, from Wexbury. Sir Tannis, Hero of the Realm, lead an assault deep into enemy territory, directly into the heart of Far Reach. The most powerful Prime Techromancer to ever hail from Wexbury. He handed his station down to father to don the mantle of Techno Knight."

She had pride on her face now and her voice was strong. I loved hearing this tale every time the traveling bards traveled through the realm. "He was one of the three Adepts known to live past igniting in that time. He could control all metals and channel electricity, combining magic and raw power. After both sides were decimated, with the keep in ruins, only Sir Tannis and Rydell were left alive. They stood for two days and nights, locked in a battle of raw power. Then it is said Sir Tannis called upon the earth itself to vanquish the Arch Rogue Rydell."

She looked sad as she said the next, "It was too much for Tannis. The knights that arrived to witness the end of the battle rushed him back to Wexbury, but the Hero of the Realm died on the journey home. The rest of the rogues ran and scattered themselves throughout the realms."

Then that fire of disapproval of the nobles was evident in her eyes again as she added to the story, something I did not know. "The travesty to Sir Tannis' family that followed was inexcusable in my own view. His daughter, who had deigned to marry below her station, to marry a lowly commoner, no longer had the ties to Tannis' nobility. As a wife takes her station first from her parents and second from her husband. She was stripped of her nobility and disappeared into Wexbury, never to be seen again."

Then she shrugged it off and looked directly into my eyes, "After that, the punishments were modified for serfs who ignited, they were only placed in the stockade as an example to others, then traded to other lands to be put into a capacity as to never use their magics. These 'disappearances' served as better deterrent than execution. Fear of the unknown."

She looked at her father, "Through recent rumblings and investigations by our spies, it has been determined that there is a man who is organizing the rogues again, and we fear the approach of another Mage War."

I went pale. Another Mage War? The horrors the bards share of the inhumanities people suffered in the last war gave children nightmares after hearing. It couldn't possibly happen again could it? But then my mind caught up with me and I tried to stop the terror welling up inside of me. I refused to let it show. My voice came out in barely a whisper as I stood, avoiding their eyes. "I'm to be brought to the stockades then." It was a statement not an question.

Celeste pulled me back down into the chair and tried to meet my eyes, I only averted them down. The Prime Techromancer sighed and spoke, "If we are to follow the letter of the laws, then yes child."

I didn't look up and he added, "But there are ways around it. It would be a shame for us to lose a Terchromancer who is sensitive to two metals. Yet I believe there is even more to you. You have something about you child, your magics taste familiar, like there is something you are not sharing. I can't quite place my finger on it."

He chuckled out, "Hell, you may not even know you are not sharing if you didn't even know your potential until yesterday. And you have caught the eye of my Celeste. If she is seeing something in you then I would be a fool not to." I stopped breathing at that. Celeste was seeing something she hasn't shared with me.

Celeste perked up and asked, "What ways father?"

He dipped his head to catch my attention. I looked nervously at the man, holding back the energies I could feel threatening to escape me again. He smiled like he were sharing something exciting as he spoke to me, "We could marry you off to an eligible lord in the castle. I hear Count Heinrick's son Edwin is of majority."

I was on my feet instantly, finally losing my calm as energy spilled out of me and every metal object in the room sprang to life and started rotating around me, just above my head. I snapped, "I will be betrothed to no man! No man shall ever have me in their bed!"

Both Cleste and the big man stood, but his eyes were not on her as he absently said, "Most commoner women would jump at the chance to marry into nobility, young Laney. Like a dream come true." He seemed mesmerized by the chaos of swirling metal forming a chaotic halo above me. The lights hanging twenty feet overhead started arching power into the whirling dervish, I hadn't realized they were electric lights.

A warm hand on my arm and a gentle voice beside me pulled my attention and I looked at Celeste through augmented vision, colors swirling. There were so many tastes around me. Everything was getting confusing until I made out what she was saying, "Laney. It is okay. Nobody is going to marry you off. You need to calm down. Laney, look at me."

I turned to lock eyes with her, amber energies trailing from my eyes at the motion. Her emerald eyes were blazing with green power, it was so beautiful. She smiled and said, "Laney, breathe. Think about breathing. Concentrate on one thing." I nodded, choosing her eyes, and took deep calming breaths.

She smiled again and I smiled back, I couldn't help it. Then I covered my head with my arms as she did when metal rained down on us when I felt my vision return to normal. It was darker in the room, half the overhead lights were out now.

Donovan was in motion, squatting and sifting through the mess of metal items around us as he distractedly asked like nothing had happened, "Sell you off to a noble family? It is how I was blessed with the most amazing daughter I could have wished for." He kept picking stuff up and then dropping the items back on the floor to move to the next.

All commoners were property of the realm. I didn't want to be sold, I knew it was the right of the Keep or my mother to do so, but I couldn't leave mother and Jace. I fought the power from rising again, Celeste tilted her head still staring into my eyes. She smiled and said, "She is not cattle father."

His examination of the debris stopped as he suddenly looked up at her with concern and love in his eyes. She glanced away from me for an instant as she held a hand toward him. "I do not feel that way father. I love you. But I admit to feeling that way in the beginning."

He stood as her eyes met mine again, she was like a calming force on me. I did not wish to distress her. Then she smiled and tilted her head toward her father but keeping her eyes on mine. "There is another way father. She could become my squire. As Knight ascendant she would hold the rank of nobility and her family would rise to the station." I blinked, a squire?

The man looked at his daughter for a long three heartbeats then nodded and reasoned it out, "That would have the desired effect. We would not lose a potential Terchromancer and she would be beholden to none but you. But she is a child daughter, she is no warrior. Duke Fredrick would never allow it."

I was about to say something, I'm not sure what but Celeste beat me to it. She chuckled, "But she has already proven herself in battle. She took down as many marauders as a Knight of the Realm did in that same battle. She yet stands and Sir Bowyn is recovering from wounds suffered. She has shared in the spoils of that battle. I think that more than qualifies her. And she is no child, she has reached the age of majority just as I had two years hence." She wiggled her eyebrows at me and I blushed.

He nodded and then looked at me and I broke eye contact with her. He asked, "Would that be more acceptable in the stead of the stockade and being spirited out of the realm? It would be a shame to lose someone with your potential." He looked around the floor as he said the last part.

I looked back and forth between the two. My mind was reeling. Trying to process this. They wanted me to become a squire, a Knight ascendant? Me? Laney Herder? I would be beholden to an angel? Wait, squires live in the quarters of the Knight and their families live in the castle with the servants unless they had a manor. They would want for nothing. Even if I was losing my own freedoms to dictate my own life, it would be worth it for mother and Jace to be cared for.

I opened my mouth to accept but what came out instead surprised me, "My potential?"

He chuckled seeing my own shock at my question. "Yes. What I just witnessed from a newly ignited Techromancer was not normal. He grabbed something off the floor and held it behind his back. "What is the object I am holding made of? Copper or iron?"

I looked at him and Celeste looked intrigued too, she said, "Just concentrate, try to touch it with your mind." I nodded and tried to feel it.

I was getting frustrated because I didn't know how. That frustration caused the heat to rise inside me again as my eyesight started changing. I tried to channel it like I did with my crystal. I smiled as I could taste it. I squinted in confusion. It does not taste like copper, nor steel. It is not the blue of iron, nor the yellow of copper. It is a pale pink."

I remembered that color from when I was scavenging the prior morning there was an infinitesimal amount of it in the conveyance but there was a lot of it in his hand. I grasped it in my mind, trying to understand it and it leapt up out of his hand and hovered above him as two other items on the floor joined it.

He was grinning like a madman and said, "Those items all contain platinum." He bent and grasped a small item into his fist and cocked his eyebrow at me. My eyes flared and I was seeing orange from his hand and I shrugged, "That is even different, I am seeing orange." As I said it another object jumped up and I looked at it. It was a gold coin. I smiled and blurted, "Gold!" He opened his a hand and there was a gold coin that hopped into the air and started orbiting the other one.

He was still grinning. "How many metals can you see around us?"

I looked around it was a rainbow of colors. The items that had all started orbiting themselves fell to the ground as I lost focus on them. I murmured, "There are so many." Then I glanced up and staggered, to be held up by Celeste's firm hand. I was inundated by so many colors and tastes from above it made me dizzy. I grabbed my head and closed my eyes, there was too much screaming at me. I gasped, "There's too much up there." What was stored above his office? That would be the back of the library by the vaults.

Celeste was saying, "Just breathe through it, block it out and pick just one thing and concentrate on it." I looked up and met her eyes. I calmed quickly.

The Prime Techromancer looked too chipper as he hopped up to sit on his desk again. "Now young Laney. Can you feel the electricity flowing through the remaining lights?"

I looked at him and smirked. "You make fun of me now sir. Nobody can feel..." I paled, I could feel the steady stream of power being fed through the bulbs, it felt similar to the feel of my magic, only... different.

He laughed at my expression as Celeste furrowed her brow at him. He said to me with a jovial tone, "Congratulations Laney, you just became far too valuable for the Duke to ever spirit away. You are now one of the five known Adepts in all the realms of the habitable lands." Then he added, as my mind reeled, "What are the odds of one Keep spawning two in the same century?"

Celeste was supporting me. She looked to be in shock too. "An Adept? Truly father?"

He chuckled at her this time, "Have you known a Techromancer to be sensitive to more than two or three metals, and electric power?"

She was shaking her head as she looked at me and a smile slowly grew on her face. My own mirrored hers as I couldn't help but smile at hers. The she asked cutely, "So Laney. What do you say? Be my squire?"

I was nodding stupidly trying to process everything. She hugged me. "Grand! We will get with the Duke and should make it official in the next day or two." I nodded again numbly, trying to fight down the rush of heat and excitement of being in her arms.

I jumped when the Prime Techromancer clapped his hands together and prompted. "Great! Now that we have averted a travesty. Celeste said that you had information you wished to share with a scholar?"

I blinked. Oh. I nodded and he said, "Grand!" and I tried to remember why I needed to speak with a scholar, my mind wasn't working until Celeste released me. I smiled and began.

CHAPTER 5 – THE GREAT LIBRARY

Getting over my prior fright at the thought of sharing what I had learned with someone of Donovan's stature. I smiled and said quickly, "Lady Celeste and I discovered an artifact yesterday that shows they used road signs in the Before Times. It..." I paused, in all the pandemonium I had forgotten about the road sign. I frowned.

Celeste prompted, "What is it Laney?"

I shrugged and said quietly, almost embarrassed, "I never got paid for the post. I ummm... before I..."

She smiled broadly. "I'll be sure to make sure you get a fair price, it was your find."

I took a quick breath then looked to the Techromancer, he had his attention fully on me. "It was a steel post with three aluminum signs on it. One was octagonal that said 'stop', a rectangular one had no pigments remaining but it was embossed with 'dead end', then..." I smiled hoping I was clever. "...a long rectangular one was mostly unreadable but on a green background in white letters it read 'lane'. Marking a road."

He was nodding with an unreadable expression. "Yes, we have seen many such markers." My shoulders fell, well of course they have, why would I think I discovered something new? He smiled softly at me. "Don't despair about it. It helps solidify scientific theories. The more empirical evidence we can gather about any hypothesis, serves to prove that hypothesis out as fact. It is how science works. You just gave yet another example, farther solidifying our observations."

Then he tilted his head, "Your enthusiasm over discovery is commendable and you had come up with the same hypothesis as others, but now I have proved out your hypothesis for you. We have helped each other in a scientific manner."

My hand was outlining the metal emblem in my pocket. I felt silly now. He made me feel better about my uneducated enthusiasm, but I figured they already knew the other thing I wished to share. He was watching my hand keenly, reading me. "There was more?"

I looked at him, trying to figure out if her were teasing or mocking, but he seemed genuinely interested and not condescending. I nodded slowly as I pulled the emblem out of my pocket and rubbed it with my fingers. "You probably already know this too. I thought I was clever when I found this on an old conveyance I unearthed."

I handed it to him and said, "It says mustang and has a carving of a horse. I had assumed that the wizards of the Before had named their conveyances after horses. It made sense to me since they would have replaced the horses with the machines."

I paused at the look on the man's face. His eyes were glittering and he seemed to be full of nervous energy suddenly. His voice was full of excitement and mischief, "I think you may be right young Laney! Would you like to prove your hypothesis out with me?"

My jaw dropped, I was stunned. Not only did he seem like he

was surprised by my assumption, he wanted to help me prove it out... like a scholar? Celeste was smiling at me at my reaction. I nodded and he hopped to his feet. "Grand! Follow me girls." He flicked the emblem into the air toward me with his thumb and I caught it.

I just stood there watching them walk toward the door. Celeste looked back and grinned and stepped back to me and looped her arm in mine and dragged me along. Her voice was cheerful, "Come along my squire, we have science to do."

I blushed and we followed the excited man. I felt warm inside. We caught up with Donovan as we walked briskly up a sweeping curved stone staircase to the next level and I froze and pulled out of Celeste's grip when the big man stopped at the huge arched oak doors at the entrance to the great library of the Techromancy Scrolls.

I stepped back and the Prime Techromancer looked down at me in concern. "What is it child?"

I felt all the blood drain from my face. Celeste stood in front of me and locked eyes with me but spoke to her father. "When she was young, she snuck into the library. The magistrate had her flogged at the whipping post. She still bears the scars."

He shook his head and looked as though he had just eaten something sour. Then knelt in front of me, at my eye level and held a hand out to me. "Nobody will punish you. You are my guest. Besides, are you not now a Knight ascendant?" I paused then took the man's offered hand, mine looked like a doll's in his huge hand.

He smiled at me then stood. He raised a hand and I tasted magic... blue... iron magic. The great doors swung open on their huge iron strap hinges. Then he led me in, my mouth hanging open as I took in the rows upon rows of huge bookcases that reached high into the vaulted ceiling space. Sweeping staircases, and rolling ladders. There were rows of long tables in the middle, made of a rich dark wood I had never seen before, and chairs with cushions in the violet and emerald colors of Wexbury. I had though to never see this glorious sight again.

He paused a few steps in and let me turn slowly in a circle, looking up, trying to take it all in. I glanced away to see the Prime Techromancer and his daughter were looking at me with a fascination of their own. I crossed my arms over my chest, hugging my shoulders self consciously, and looked down.

Donovan said in a faraway voice, "I often forget that reaction to the Library. I miss my own wonder of it. Maybe I should take the time to remind myself how blessed I am to be in the presence of all this knowledge. One shouldn't get so used to something or they take it for granted."

I glanced back up and he smiled then turned back to the shelves, I couldn't stop a smile at Celeste's own smile, and I dropped my arms.

He tapped a finger to his lips like he were trying to recall something. Then he did a combination exhale and sigh of surrender and yelled, "Emily?!" His voice echoing in the huge space.

The two scholars that were busily copying pages of crumbling tomes to fresh parchment, and a younger man who had been using magic to restore what he could on a particularly rotted and damaged tome, all stood up when they saw us and scurried for the door like rats running from a cat. All bowing their heads in respect in Donovan's direction.

He huffed a moment then murmured, "Where has that woman gotten to now?"

Someone cleared their throat and we all swung around to look at the positively tiny woman standing right behind the large Techromancer. She was impeccably dressed in a tunic and long skirt that rivaled the garb of a noble. She had calfskin shoes on, that looked so soft I wanted to touch them, but there was something on the sole of the shoes. At first I thought it to be a thin black board but the way she bounced on her toes like she had too much energy, showed they flexed just like canvas.

She had long blonde hair, that even braided, hung down to the back of her knees. And she wore something on her face. Two round glass lenses that looked like the ones in my spyglass in my tool pouch. They were held in place by intricately carved, graceful strands of silver that held them to her nose and looped behind her ears.

Whatever they were, they made her look, I don't know, studious, and oddly alluring. They made her cobalt blue eyes pop on her young face. I'd guess she was fifteen or sixteen if it weren't for the wisdom of someone in their mid to late twenties reflected in her eyes. It may have been that she was so small, it gave the illusion of youth. Not many adult women were shorter than me, but she was a good half hand shorter than myself.

Then she spoke in a clear musical tone, "Why are you being so loud in my library you blustering lout? And why did you chase off the scholars before they could refile their tomes? I should have you refile them."

He sputtered, "I didn't... they... you..."

She shook her head and rolled her eyes then looked over at me an her smile bloomed, then she waved him off as she took me and my attire in, "You've brought me a helper?" I was stunned. This tiny woman was talking to the Prime Techromancer like he were a child.

He tried to take control of the conversation before Celeste burst into the laughter I could see her fighting off valiantly. He said in a controlled tone, "Emily. Please, I have a guest."

The woman looked up at him with an amused look on her face and prompted toward me with her eyes. He stood tall, perhaps to intimidate the woman who was barely over half his height, and said imperiously. "Emily, Matron of the Library, please meet Laney Herder. Or should I say, Squire Laney, Knight Ascendant, from the house of Celeste."

I didn't know what to do so I curtsied low and kept my eyes down. I probably looked like a fool. She comically crouched and cocked her head up to look into my eyes. "Whatcha doin' down here Squire?" Then she put a finger on my chin and applied upward pressure as she stood, bringing my head up so we looked into each others eyes. "There, that's better." Then she let go of my chin and thrust out a hand. "None of that Matron stuff Donovan is throwing around. Call me Emily." Then after a dramatic pause, she added in a dangerous tone, "Or else..."

The serious look she shot me had me gulping until she suddenly burst out into a giggle and clapped her hands close to her chest at my expression. I smiled nervously then shook her hand. "Just Laney please... Emily."

Then the Prime Techromancer cleared his throat. "Emily, I was just wondering where the tomes about the conveyances of the Before were again."

She looked at him then pointedly over at a row of little drawers in a huge oak cabinet, then she looked back at him and cocked an eyebrow. She sighed in frustration and said, "I don't even know why I indexed every item in the library if nobody is going to use it."

He tilted his head and gave her a warm smile, "It is because we all know, you know where every single item is. Nobody has a better memory than you."

She glowed at the compliment and said in a way that didn't sound snobbish. "That is true you sweet talker." Then she squinted at him and poked him in the side and said, "You're all skin and bones. When was the last time you got your nose out of the scrolls and ate properly?"

She reached over to a bowl of fruit and cheeses that were on the nearest long table, and I realized all of the tables had similar bowls on them. She jammed it in his gut. "Eat!"

He looked sheepish and then took a fruit that was small and orange, like a peach, only it looked to have a tough rind on it. He said, "Yes Emily."

I was grinning at how she handled the second most powerful man in the realm. But glurked when she thrust the bowl toward me. "You too, you look positively starved Laney." I blinked first at her, then the bowl that had so many fruits and cheeses. The smells alone had me salivating. I looked up at Celeste and she gave me an enthusiastic thrust of her chin to the bowl.

I clenched my hands. "I couldn't. I'd feel guilty I didn't share with my brother and mother."

She cocked an eyebrow expectantly and she blurted, "Take some for them too. You can't endeavor in intellectual pursuits in my library if you are hungry, it distracts you from assimilating knowledge properly." I looked around at the three then timidly took a red apple, I had only ever had green ones. She tapped her toe then I took a peach and one of those strange orange fruits and slipped them into my pockets. The odd one indeed felt like it had a rind like a watermelon. She still held the bowl out, so I took a cube of cheese and put it in my mouth.

As I moaned, I thought seriously about marrying the cheese and having its children as it melted in my mouth. She grinned happily and placed the bowl back on the table. Another apple unexpectedly shot out from under her arm. She had thrown it cross-ways, and Celeste caught it deftly with one hand.

The Knight grinned cheerily at the little woman and took a big bite, while Emily smiled like a pleased chipmunk and she chirped out, "Your reflexes never cease to amaze me Celeste."

Then Donovan cleared his throat again and Emily waved him off, "Aisle G8 fourth unit, third shelf from the top. There are ten original tomes, one restored, and two hand copied duplicates. They are low on the priority list so the others will not be restored for some time still."

Donovan leaned way down and kissed the woman's cheek. "As always, you are amazing. Thank you."

She grinned at him then winked at me, "The old man is a flirt."

He actually blushed then tried to regain his wits. "Enough of this, we are performing science here." They shared a smile and we were apparently off as Celeste was dragging me along with them.

I called back as I was pulled along, "It was nice meeting you Emily."

She just smiled and bobbled her head cutely. She was possible the most adorable woman I had ever met. You just had an urge to hug her and keep her safe. She was apparently scary smart too.

I looked up at Celeste, "Does she really know where every item in the library is?"

She nodded seriously. "That woman has a perfect memory. Not only does she know where everything is, but she can recite every tome and scroll she has ever read, or repeat any conversation she has ever had in her entire life, word for word. She befriends everyone and she's simply lovable. She has every man in the castle, like father, literally eating out of her hand as you saw." I smiled at that, I understood the effect.

Donovan was ignoring what we were talking about. His hands were absently peeling the thick rind off that fruit as we walked in one long strip. The smells that hit me were pungent, like nothing I had ever smelled. It was a sweet acidic smell. He was mumbling, "E9, F1..." I looked at the rows of shelves and realized they had brass letters hanging on the end of each. They were numbered and were going up as we walked.

He pulled a section of the fruit away from the rest and popped it into his mouth, and deftly dropped the peel in one of the little brass trash cans at the end of each aisle. He saw me watching him and he paused and tore another section of fruit off. "Tangerine?"

I looked at him then the fruit. Then up at Celeste, "I've never had one, is it good?" I trusted her opinion. Hell, I trusted her, period.

She nodded and said, "It's like a small orange." I screwed up my brow in confusion, then she said softly, "It is an exotic citrus that grows near Far Reach, near the southern most part of the habitable lands." I knew citrus, they used lemons from Far Reach in the bakery to make special tarts for the nobles. They were supposed to be very sour.

I timidly reached out and accepted it, then smelled it. I pulled back and my eyes almost watered at the pleasant, acidic, and pungent smell. Then I took a bite, it was like it was made half of water like a grape, and moisture and tart sweet flavor exploded in my mouth. My eyes went wide and I popped the rest into my mouth and smiled as I chewed and swallowed. "That was amazing." I looked at the bowls of fruit at the tables, wishing I had tried one instead of an apple.

The father and daughter seemed pleased with my reaction and he said absently, "Again, I forget..." Then we were in motion again heading into the G section. I knew what he was looking for now, and dragged along the Techno Knight who had attached herself to my arm.

I pointed at a row. "G8."

Donovan paused and cocked an eyebrow, "You read?"

I nodded, "Some. My mother gave me and Jace lessons."

He nodded in appreciation, then he counted down the units of bookcases, quickly eating the rest of the... ummm... tangerine. He licked his fingers as he stood at a twenty foot ladder and then pulled some soft calfskin gloves from a stack on a little platform suspended under the ladder. He handed Celeste and me a set then put his on. I looked to my Lady. She whispered, "You never touch the old tomes or scrolls with your hands, oils and..." She grinned. "...juices can accelerate the deterioration of the old parchments"

I quickly put mine on. Good lord, I would have just started grabbing them and looking at them. I felt like a barbarian. Donovan went up a ladder then after some rummaging on the proper shelf came down with a little tome in his hand, not much larger than the hand that grasped it. He held like it were priceless, like it were made of solid copper.

He hustled us to one of the long tables at the end of the row, explaining as he had us sit to either side of him. "When I was but a young Techromancer apprentice. I remember my master giving me this tome to file away with the other conveyance tomes. This was before we had our dear Emily to keep things straight for us. I remember getting frustrated at not finding the proper stack in all the chaos. I will always remember the cover because I felt guilty for days after I slid it under the nearest stack in my frustration when he wasn't watching me."

He grinned. "Your postulation that the wizards of the Before Times named their conveyances after horses made me remember the name of that ill fated tome, as it is forever burned into my brain."

He prompted, "Your emblem?" I took it out of my pocket, rubbed my finger across its surface, it felt muted under the glove, then placed it on the table. He smiled and pushed the little battered and crumbling tome to me as he said, "Shall we test your hypothesis with additional empirical evidence young Squire?"

I looked at the dilapidated cover but there was a picture of a mechanical conveyance. It was red and the realism of it had me amazed at the abilities of the artist who had painted it. Their skill was phenomenal. Oh, to have lived in such a time as that. I looked at the faded letters on the bottom of the cover. Then my eyes went wide and I grabbed my emblem and held it in one hand and looked at the tome in my other.

I read out loud, "Charger!" Both horses proved out my guess! The next word was... "Owner's? I know 'owner' but I don't understand the symbol before the s. I only know of the four prime punctuation marks. The period to end a sentence, question mark is self explanatory, the exclamation point for emphasis, and the crono mark for tense."

He nodded, "That mark, the apostrophe, changes an S from plural to make something possessive, indicating ownership." I nodded, I had seen them in a couple of mother's tomes but I never asked because I understood the meaning of the sentences. I was learning! In the Library of the Techromancy Scrolls even! I was hyperventilating at the thought and was getting overly warm.

A hand rested on my shoulder and a sweet voice said, "Laney. Control it, don't let it control you."

I glanced at her and calmed myself down and I could feel energy in my eyes dissipating. "Sorry, this is just so exciting." Then I looked at the last word, sounding it out in my head then furrowed my eyebrows, "Manual? But the machines were powered."

The toothy grin Donovan gave me made me feel silly. He said,

"It is another word that had multiple meanings in Old English. It also means, instructions, or orders."

They looked at me as I put it all together. "So this tome explains how to operate one of the conveyances?" He nodded and I looked away when I saw pride in his eyes.

Then Celeste said, "Well done Laney. Now this new piece of information can be shared with the other scholars. Every tiny piece of information draws a better picture of the world from the Before."

Donovan took his gloves off and put them on the table, Celeste did the same. I went to put the tome back but Celeste laid a hand on mine, stopping me. Donovan said, "Just leave it for Emily. She blusters about people not putting things back, but she truly enjoys doing it herself. She doesn't think I know, but she checks after each person leaves that they placed an item back where they got it from. She doesn't trust anyone not to mess up her system."

I blinked at the fact that someone so high up in the noble ranks cared what those below them thought. I nodded and took off my gloves and went to pocket my emblem but hesitated then offered it to Donovan. "As a thank you for allowing me to see the library, and for entertaining my silly theory."

He looked sad as he cupped my hand in both of his. Did I upset him? Then he nodded once and took it. "Thank you child." He grasped it, rubbing his thumb on it as he started leading us toward the main doors. "As a Squire beholden to a Knight of the Realm, you have free access to the library any time Laney. As long as you follow the rules, and not upset our Emily." He grinned at the last part.

I would have smiled back if I had not been stunned that he had just given me a gift greater than I could ever have imagined. I looked around at all the worlds of possibilities, and limitless knowledge around me, and fought back a tear, just nodding.

We looked back to see Emily skittering over to the table where we had been, like the chipmunk I imagined earlier. She picked up the tome in a gloved hand and looked at us as we reached the door. She shook a scolding finger across the library at Donovan but she had a smile on her face telling me that the Prime Techromancer was right about the woman.

As we made our way back to his office he said, "I will have a writ sent to the lord of the keep, requesting the squireship today. Tomorrow is the Holy Day so he will approve it on First Day. When he reads of what we have discovered of your gift, he would be a fool not to."

He grinned then continued, "As soon as you are beholden to Celeste, you can move your family into Castle Quarters. The head Maid, Earnestine, matron of the castle, will see to it. She runs the castle staff efficiently for the nobility, her word is as binding as any Lady."

Then he paused at his office door and his tone got serious. "Then I wish to participate in your training in all things not under the purview of my daughter. Your magics have such potential."

Celeste was dragging me down the hall away from him. I heard him murmuring as he stepped into his office, "Two Adepts in our realm in the same century..." I looked up at a grinning Celeste then back at her father's office. We hadn't even said goodbye.

She brought me through a maze of corridors. Servants, knights, and even some nobles bowing or lowering their eyes as Lady Celeste passed. I looked back and most were staring back at us with looks of curiosity painting their faces.

We finished our apples along the way, I pocketed my core for a treat for Goliath later. We burst out of a door into the evening air with her chuckling at my bemusement. I was lost in the castle with all the twists and turns, for all I knew we were stepping out into the middle of Hawktail River. We were in the courtyard by the castle livery. I saw the wagon, cleaned up and scrubbed down, and smiled at Goliath, his black coat shiny in the last rays of Father Sol. He looked to be brushed out again and his mane not so wild, like it had been trimmed. There were violet and emerald ribbons tied in his mane at even intervals.

A stable hand ran off when I stepped up to my horse and I ran my hand along Goliath's flank. He even smelled cleaner. I glance at Celeste and she shrugged at my amazement and said, "The castle livery does this for all visitors, it is lauded throughout the habitable lands."

I turned back and patted the Percheron's neck, "You're such a handsome boy." Then tuned to my Lady and glanced at Father Sol again. "I have to get back home, the doctor will be there at seven and I told Jace I would be home at sunset."

She nodded and moved in and it looked like she was about to hug me and I stiffened. She looked undecided and clapped her hands down on my shoulders gently. Then asked, "Will you be at church in the morning?"

I got lost in her gently glowing eyes and nodded dumbly. She smiled a toothy smile. "Grand, Verna and I will be attending. Goodnight, Laney. Stay safe."

I blushed and nodded and she helped me up onto the wagon, not that I needed any help. I admit I loved the way she seemed to take care of me though. As I urged Goliath to start forward I called to her, "Goodnight Lady Celeste. Stay safe. Thank you."

She waved and watched me until I turned off of the Lord's Way and onto the Crossbar toward Cheap Quarter. I know because I kept glancing back. Her smile was burned into my mind and I realized I was smiling too as I started whistling the Herder's Refrain.

CHAPTER 6 – MOTHER

When I pulled up at the cottage, Father Sol had just dipped below the horizon and the world faded into twilight with the pale light from the Three Sisters casting a silver glow on everything. I glanced at them. Freya had just started her traverse in front of Athena as they did their weekly dance in the sky, orbiting each other as they trailed after Mother Luna in a timeless chase. Freya would be hidden from view in a couple nights.

I started unhitching Goliath when the door swung open and little Jace came running out to hug my waist then all his attention was on Goliath. His eyes wide in amazement. I led my horse under the firewood overhang where we stored the wagon after we sold Daisy. Jace threw some hay down then he helped me put up the rail to keep Goliath penned in. I pulled the apple core out of my pocket and gave it to the big guy then turned to Jace. "Remind me to fill the trough for Goliath in the morning squirt."

He nodded and started excitedly telling me of his day and the sweets he purchased. Rock candies. Then he noticed my tunic. "Hey that's new!"

I smiled and reached into the wagon and threw him his new tunic that was wrapped in brown paper and tied with twine, he caught it and almost dropped it. He was blessed with the same terrible coordination as me. "You got one too. You've been such a great help to me little brother." He tore the package open and tore

off his threadbare tunic and put on the new one. Dyed a dark
maroon.

I dusted his shoulder, "Very handsome."

He smiled then he appeared to think of something and his face
got more serious that a little boy's ought. "Did you get enough for
mother's medicines?"

I placed my hand on his cheek and nodded. "And enough for the
doctor. He'll be out in just a half hour. So be a good lad and help
tidy?" He nodded and I reached into my pocket and produced the
tangerine for him.

He took it and looked at it with cute confusion. I hoped I didn't
look like that in front of Celeste. He said, "What is it? It feels like
leather but looks like fruit."

I took it from him and dug my thumbs into it, sprays of that
stinging pungent juice squirted out. I tore the peel off of it and
tossed the rind into the hog pen then pulled a segment off for Jace
and handed it to him. He sniffed it and pulled it away blinking. I
said, "Go on now."

He took a bite then his eyes lit up, "It is sweet and tart at the
same time. It's like candy."

I handed it to him and said, "It is called a tangerine. They just
gave it to me in Castle Wexbury today, and a peach for mom."

He looked pleased at that but didn't say anything as he was busy
trying to stuff all of the segments of the entire tangerine into his
mouth at the same time. I chuckled and grabbed my tool pouch and

mom's new nightshirt, then gently cuffed Jace's shoulder and we went inside.

While Jace tidied, I gave mother a sponge bath and had her change into her new nightshirt, it was white as the driven snow. I gave her the last of the stew then showed her the peach. She lit up at it but she was at the end of her strength, "Maybe tomorrow my Laney."

I helped her into bed and told her the doctor would be around. That agitated her and she looked nervous. I just wish we knew what had sapped her strength so much, it just got worse and worse over the months. The last doctor grumbled about only treating the symptoms and prescribed the medicines. But after a while, the medicines could not keep up until she was confined to bed.

It hit me like a hammer to the chest when the day came months ago, that she passed on going to church on Holy Day. Since then Jace has been a godsend. I don't think I could have kept things running around here and provide for him and mother without his help. He may be tiny but even at seven, he is physically almost as strong as me.

I ran to the well and worked the hand pump and got a fresh bucket of water. The street lamps started flickering to life. Then I ran the chamber pot to the road and dumped it in the iron grates they had in the long stone ditches along each road. I had always thought them ingenious. In the morning before the village awakens, they open floodgates at the Hawktail River where it enters the city, for fifteen minutes, the water fills the channels and washes away the waste into the keep's sewer tunnels that served the castle. Modern conveniences.

I saw a black carriage pulled by two horses and a lantern on a hook coming down the lane. I darted back inside to put the chamber pot in the corner and straightened Jace and my tunics as I said, "He's coming."

A minute later there was a tapping at the door. I opened it straightaway and there was a tall lanky man who looked as though he belonged in a corn field somewhere, scaring off the crows. He looked exhausted and I wondered if that made his long, drawn face look older. I was guessing the man to be in his thirties. He was impeccably dressed but his clothing was wrinkled and the sleeves of his long shirt were rolled up, indicating a rough day. He carried one of those the big black bags one always associated with doctors.

I bowed my head to the man and asked even though it were obvious, "Sir. Are you the doctor?"

He patted my shoulder like we were old acquaintances. "Yes child. It has been a long day and this is my last stop. We can dispense with any formalities. I'm here to check in on..." He looked at a slip of paper hanging out of his bag. "A Margret Herder. Are you she?"

I ushered him in and Jace shut the door. "Margret is my mother." I led him over and mother was asleep. I remembered her teaching me to always be a good host. I quickly asked, "Where are my manners. Would you like a cup of water sir, fresh from the well just now, we have some chicken jerky if you like."

He was setting his bag down beside the little stool we had by the bed and pulling a stethoscope out from under his shirt as he looked at me with a compassionate smile. "No child but thank you. What is your name. I'm Doctor Maxwell, but everyone just calls me Doc.

I nodded and said, "I'm Laney and this rascal is my little brother Jace."

He nodded to both of us then turned toward mother. He paused and looked down at the electric heater at his feet that was blowing toward mother and smiled. "This is positively antique and it still works?"

I know he didn't expect a reply because he was already gently shaking mother's shoulders. "Margret? I'm Doctor Maxwell." Mother woke and looked nervously at the doctor. He squinted. "You look familiar, have I treated you before?" She shook her head. He shrugged and went about asking a lot of questions as he examined her. He referred to the notes frequently. He seemed upset about the notes.

Then he took some of her blood with a needle and put it on some paper. It changed color and he harrumphed and muttered something about imbeciles. Then he sighed and spoke to all of us though he looked at mother. "You seem to be having problems absorbing a hormone our bodies naturally produce called insulin. Plus the iron in your blood isn't carrying enough oxygen to your cells. There are many syndromes that cause this. Coupled with your other symptoms I believe you suffer from Wasting Syndrome."

I cut back tears, we had always thought she had Wasting Syndrome. It would get worse until she didn't have the energy to even wake up. Then she would simply pass away.

He sounded mad as he continued, "My prior colleague was a lazy man. He only treated your symptoms instead of coming to a proper diagnosis. Just because a patient isn't a Lord or Lady, doesn't excuse this sort of incompetence."

But then he brightened. "Lucky for you, I finished my journeyman rotations in Castle Wexbury's infirmary to become a master healer, where they have come up with a new treatment that has been showing great success when coupled with the traditional treatments."

He dug around in his bag and came out with one familiar medicine, but then pulled out two others. He showed the brown glass bottle and said, "Take this as you always have." Then he showed us a blue glass bottle of pills. "This will absorb the toxins produced by your body due to the Syndrome. Take one in the morning when you wake, one at noon and one when you go to sleep."

Then he showed us the red glass bottle. I had once asked why all the medicines had different color combinations of bottles and lids. It was because most of the people in the village could not read, so they color coded everything. He said, "This... this is new, it is an oral insulin supplement. It boosts your insulin levels so that your body can adsorb enough to stabilize your blood sugars."

He seemed happy with that and said. "Now, there is no cure for Wasting Syndrome. But these will stabilize you and prevent it from progressing. You should gain back most of your old vitality within a week or so. But you will be on these medicines the rest of your life. People we treated with these, increased their quality of life and live a relatively normal life span."

I was blinking through tears. Mother would not die? He saw the hope in all of our eyes then he cautioned, "Only if you respond to the treatment. One out of every thirty people do not respond. But I think those are pretty acceptable odds."

He finished up and gave me a script for her new medications and I blanched, they were almost twice the cost of the others. I'd have to step up my scavenging. But then I thought, if I really became Celeste's squire then it would be taken care of by the realm when we moved into our servant's quarters in the castle.

I thanked him all the way to the door then followed him out to the buggy and said, "Doc, wait a moment please." I ran to the coops and gathered as many eggs as I could that were laid during the day and I put them in one of our straw baskets and ran back out to the waiting man.

I thrust the basket at him. "Here Doc, please accept this gift. We don't have much, but you gave us so much hope tonight."

He blinked at me and looked down at the eggs then slowly took the basket, studying me. Then he cocked his head. "Are these the blue eggs they serve in the castle proper?"

I nodded and he beamed a smile that looked so nice on his face, it washed away the fatigue weighing down his features. "Yes sir. We trade them to the House of Lords there. And the Nobles along Lord's Way."

He smiled at that and inclined his head in thanks. "They are the most sought after eggs in Wexbury, so rich tasting, and the odd blue shells they say only come from a rare type of chicken."

He paused and looked back toward the house and murmured, "Margret." Then he shook his head and looked at me. "Your mother looks so familiar but I just can't place her. Maybe from when she traded eggs at the castle."

I shrugged, to my knowledge, mother has never been to the castle proper. She avoids it. The only public places she would ever go are the church and the market. She spent more time trading to the farmers and proper herders outside the keep walls in Wexbury Minor. The small town on the horizon that was protected by the knights of the realm.

They were the workers that kept the keep supplied with most of the meats, grains and vegetables. Us minor herders and gardeners like old man Warren, inside the walls, were few and far between. Not many had the space in the village. We had a double lot.

He had a genuinely thankful look on his face as he hugged the basket to himself and said simply, "Thank you, Laney." He shut the carriage door then his driver gave the horses some rein and they trotted down the lane.

I spun in place, there was hope for mother. I sprinted inside and made her take her medicines and wash them down with a cup of water. Then we all retired. I thought I wouldn't ever get to sleep with all of the events of this most hectic day of my life winding down. But I was fooling myself because I never finished the thought.

Chapter 7 – Holy Day

We awoke to the smell of eggs cooking. Mother was at the hearth, color in her cheeks. She was still moving slowly and looked exhausted, but she smiled at us. "I feel better than I have in months. If we use the wagon to get to Church, I'd like to go to service today to thank God for Doctor Maxwell. I couldn't walk the distance. But maybe in time." Jace was connected to her waist in a hug, and I was just staring at her.

She smiled at me and said, "Now eat. I haven't cooked for you children in ages." We ate and I cried tear of hope, keeping a brave front.

While we did the morning chores, mother dressed in her finest dress, in the colors of the realm.

I put on my peasant dress. The only one I owned, but I needed it for church. I had worn trousers for all my life, the work we do is hard and is no place for a dress or skirt. I blinked, was that why everyone looked so curious about me when we walked past? Besides the Lady Knights, all the women in the castle wore dresses and skirts. They probably all thought me a barbaric savage.

Jace put on his new tunic and his trousers, then I sent him out to hitch up Goliath. Mother smiled and put her hand out and I offered my arm. I could feel her putting most of her weight on me for support. She was still but a shadow of herself. But she was on her feet. "Let us see this grand horse you got as spoils of war daughter.

Jace goes on and on about him."

She stopped outside the door and was blinking at my Goliath. All she said was, "Oh my." I placed a bucket upside down behind the wagon and we helped mother step up. Then we were trotting down the lane headed for the Crossbar. The lane that bisected the city between the Main Portcullis at the south, to the secondary portcullis at the north wall, which was only opened in times of war for the knights or to evacuate the village.

In the exact center of the village in the middle of the turnabout was the largest building in the village besides the castle itself. With it's sweeping arches and tall spires and more stained glass than any four other churches. The Wexbury Cathedral, the villagers just refer to it simply as the Church.

We stopped in front of the Great Staircase that took up the entire front of the cathedral, facing the Castle, and an alter boy helped mother down. Jace hopped out and I traveled around the roundabout and headed down the Crossbar toward Cheap Quarter again until I found the first lane I could leave the wagon. I set the brake and hopped out and hustled back to my family.

Mother was a little shaky but we got her to the front pews below the balcony that arced around the entire cathedral to look down upon the dais. That is where the nobles looked down upon us serfs and commoners in the lower pews.

I always liked church. I don't know if I really believe in God. I mean sure, I hope he is there, but I am a woman of facts, of science.

But the cathedral is what I liked. It was so grand, so beautiful, it inspired you to believe. I liked the feeling of people getting together for the common good. And if there is a God, I needed to thank him for my mother this day. I haven't seen her this vital in months.

Worship in modern times was much different than the scholars had found of the Before. Back then there were many beliefs, but you would pick one and shun the others. Now I'd like to think we have surpassed the Wizards of old in at least how we worship. We all use the same church and a person is left to worship as they choose. Whether it is belief in God, or any other deity, or if you worship technology and knowledge, love, or even luck. Some who believe in none of these simply come for the camaraderie of community.

In the Church, all are equal and there is supposed to be no division between nobles and commoners, all may speak freely. Though I have never seen this in practice as the nobles occupy the balconies and we the lower pews. I have heard of retribution for things a serf may say in the Church at a later date, by a Lord or Lady who felt slighted. So maybe we aren't quite as enlightened as I'd like to think.

The end of the service on Holy Day also gives the Castle a forum to inform the people of new policies, village improvements, or other subjects of importance, since over two thirds of the seven thousand residents attend service. The rest hear it from the criers in the market on First Day. If it pertains to defense of the city, then criers will wander every lane in the village on the eve of Holy Night.

The Pastor walked past us and paused mid step when he saw mother sitting beside us. He smiled at her, and made his way up to the dais. My eyes were on him when someone sat next to me and bumped my hip over to make room. I glanced over and froze. Lady Celeste had an overly cute grin on her face but was staring at the pastor as Verna sat next to her, looking toward me with a smile. "Move your butt over pipsqueak." They were in full dress armor with their violet and emerald dress capes. People all around us were murmuring.

I started to panic, what were they doing down here with the commoners? I looked up at the balcony on the left, where all the Knights of the Realm sat, then at them. I whispered, "What are you two doing down here? People are looking."

Celeste still did not look at me but she said quietly, in an over amused tone, "Control yourself Laney, deep breaths or everyone is going to know." Oh, I hadn't noticed the color changes in my vision. I calmed then just looked at the two as the world dulled out again. Mother cleared her throat.

I glanced at her and gave an apologetic smile. "I'm sorry, where are my manners? Mother, Jace, this is Lady Celeste of the Techno Knight Order, Blade of Temperance of Wexbury, daughter of Prime Techromancer Donovan, Lady of the Court, and Lady Verna, Knight of the Realm, Lady of the Court."

I looked at the knights. "This is my mother, Margret Herder and my brother Jace."

Mother gave a bow that looked too smooth, too polished, like she had a lot of practice as she responded, "Ladies." She took each of their hands by their fingertips tilting her head down. This made Celeste look at their hands then mother with a studious and thoughtful look.

Jace hopped up and was starting to babble, "Knights, here, Laney they..." He stopped as both mother and I lightly cuffed his ears and he looked at us then the Knights and he gave a clumsy bow. "Ladies."

They chuckled at him and clasped his arm like they would a comrade at arms. My Lady said, "Margret, Jace. Please call us Celeste and Verna. After all, we're all about to get a lot closer."

I paled, with all that had been happening and with the doctor visiting last night I hadn't had the chance to tell them what I was to do to prevent myself being put in the stockade for using magic. Celeste looked at their confused looks then my most likely pale face. "Oh, you haven't informed them yet."

I said, "I haven't had a chance yet, what with the doctor visiting."

I tried to change the topic, "You two need to get back up there, people are staring."

Celeste grinned and settled into the pew. "No. I said I'd see you at service. Here I am."

Verna chuckled, "Don't argue with her Laney, she has a stubborn streak a mile wide even when she is wrong."

I grinned at the muscular Knight, "I'm beginning to see that."

Celeste interposed herself between us, "Hey, none of this ganging up, we..." She stopped talking when the alter boys stopped the soft humming they had been doing as everyone was being seated.

She flapped her fingers in a light backhand on my shoulder, winked at mother and Jace, and pointed toward the pastor. Grrr... I'll get the knight for all of this embarrassment. Lady or not.

Pastor Emery had shown up in Wexbury around the same time as Corrick had started courting mother, so eight years ago. The man was in his late forties at the time and was a refreshing change from old Pastor Vick.

Pastor Vick was maybe a million years old, fine, maybe late seventies, and droll and boring. His sermons could put you to sleep at a hundred paces. People couldn't wait for Reflection Hour after the sermon where you were free to pray or think about life. Hour was a misnomer as it was the final thirty minutes before noon, when Church let out.

But Pastor Emery was so much fun and full of energy and asked so many great questions for people to ponder. We got the best end of the deal and I seriously believe he knows the name of every parishioner in the village.

Just before the village announcements and Reflection Hour, he took the time to introduce the two new families and one new noble into the village and looked directly at mother when he added, "And it is so good to see some familiar faces that have been absent for so long."

I started looking around as the village announcements were made and I saw Prime Techromancer Donovan up in the balcony in the private section with Duke Fredrick and the Duchess Lucia. I frowned at the empty chair beside Donovan, everyone had loved his wife, Countess Shavey. It was a tragedy when the Wasting Syndrome took her from the realm nine years ago.

He caught my eye and gave a smile and nod. I gave a smile and tiny wave from my side. Then it was time for silence, Reflection Hour. Most lowered their heads to pray. I did, for once, and thought. Lord, if you are there, I'd like to thank you for Doc Maxwell, he gave my mother back to us. Then I added quickly as I looked at the woman beside me, who looked so... right... to me. And thank you for Lady Celeste who has befriended a simple commoner. Oh, umm... amen? I wondered what amen actually meant. Maybe if they were serious that I could have access the library, I could look it up some time. I glanced to my side then down. I bet Celeste knows.

Then I sat and just contemplated all the good things in my life until the giant bells in the tower chimed noon. Everyone raised their heads if they were bowed and people started pouring out of the Church. It was a day of feasting and rest. All but the people who had animals to tend, guard posts to man, or were hospital workers, did not work on Holy Day, and the market was closed.

Mother was unsteady on her feet and I supported her again. She looked pretty drained, she shouldn't have tried going out in public so soon. As soon as we got into the wide aisle between pews, Celeste was on mother's other side offering her arm, Mother took it with grace, using just her fingertips. Celeste seemed to be studying her intently.

We got outside, mother was leaning on both of us by then. I glanced at the two knights and Jace. "I'll go get the wagon. Be right back?" Jace took my place supporting mother's arm.

Celeste took mother's hand off of her arm and Verna slipped in smoothly to offer her's as Celeste said, "I'll accompany you." People all around were giving our odd group a great deal of attention. I was so embarrassed having these Knights assisting us.

As we jogged down the Crossbar. Celeste asked in a voice that seemed haunted, "Wasting Syndrome?" I nodded wordlessly. She whispered more to herself than to me. "Like mother."

Oh good lord, she didn't need me bringing up her own painful memories. I reached out hesitantly, not sure what to do. Could I touch a Lady to console her when so many people were about in the lane? I changed my destination and started to move my hand toward her shoulder when her hand reached out to engulf mine. She gave it a little squeeze and I shared a look of understanding with her. She smiled back at me sadly.

Then I said almost excitedly. "There is a new treatment now. It isn't a cure, but it allows a better quality of life and longer life for those afflicted with it." Her eyebrows rose. I nodded and said, "Mother is taking the new medicines, though it took most of the coin I had left. But this is the first time she has left home in months." Then I furrowed my brow in concern. "I fear she has overdone it in her enthusiasm."

She had a gleam in her eye, like a cross between vindication and hope. She asked, "Doctor Maxwell?" I nodded and she smiled, "He has been a godsend working with the Castle infirmary to develop new treatments. I'm happy to hear the efforts are bearing fruit."

I realized I was still holding hands with a Knight and flushed with heat then gave her hand a squeeze and looked up into her eyes to let her know how sorry I was for her mother. Even I, as a young girl, remembered the kindness of Countess Shavey before she passed. She gave a smile of thanks and we turned onto the lane where the wagon and my Goliath waited.

I made a squeaking sound as I was suddenly hoisted effortlessly by my waist up into the wagon and Celeste hopped up gracefully beside me. She took the reins and I was surprised at just how badly I maneuvered Goliath and the wagon when she made it look so effortless with virtually no movement of her hands as she manipulated the reins, letting Goliath do the work.

I looked at her then the lane as we turned back up the Crossbar. "Why are you helping? A Knight of the Realm has more important things to attend to than associating with serfs." She didn't say a word, just simply reached over with one hand and bopped me on top of the head. Then she grinned and maneuvered the wagon through the dispersing crowd to the Great Staircase.

Before we hopped down she said. "Come to the feast with Verna, Kristof, and me? They invited me and it is terribly boring when those two fawn over each other like lovesick puppies."

I said in a low voice, "I must get mother to bed."

She nodded. "After then." It wasn't a question. Could I refuse a Lady? Did I want to refuse her?

I shook my head, "What will people say? Consorting with a..." I paused as she comically held her fist over my head to bop me again if I said commoner.

I exhaled and she took that as assent, "Grand. Livery courtyard at three then?" I couldn't stop from smiling at the woman, she looked so pleased. I nodded. Lady Verna and Jace were there at the bottom of the staircase with mother who didn't look well.

The two knights were in tune and Verna simply smiled at mother, saying, "Margret." And lifted her by the waist up to the wagon to Celeste like she were made of straw. My Lady helped her sit then gave her a smile and hopped down lightly. She looked up to me. "Three then?" I nodded then she clasped Verna's shoulder and they made their way back up the staircase to where Sir Kristof waited.

Celeste looked back before they went back into the church while Jace hopped into the wagon. I know, I watched. Mother knocked me out of of my silly grin when she prompted, "Home please Laney.

I overdid it, but it was invigorating to be out in the world again."

Then she was silent, looking back nervously as I urged Goliath around the roundabout. I glanced at mother as Jace idly tied a piece of string he had found somewhere into various knots. "What is it?"

She looked at me and asked, "What did Lady Celeste mean when she said we were all going to be getting closer earlier?"

Oh lord. I took a deep breath then exhaled, gathering my thoughts. But this was a good thing right? To keep me out of trouble for... what... I am. I looked into her eyes, she seemed nervous. I smiled meekly and lowered my eyes and said, "I, what did they call it? I ignited. And yesterday at the castle's salvage intake courtyard, others saw."

She had a strange combination of surprise, pride, and – horror on her face. I quickly assured her, "I'll not be going to the stockades. Prime Techromancer Donovan and Lady Celeste came up with a plan to keep me free. Well sort of free, I'll be beholden to someone."

She looked relieved, curious, and nervous now. I was starting to wonder what was going on. She nodded sadly and laid an ice cold hand on mine on the reins. She spoke softly, "I know you swore you'd never take a man's hand in marriage, I'm so sorry Laney."

I shook my head and said, "No man will ever have me. I will be a spinster first."

She was confused now, then looked appalled, "They've sold you! Barbaric custom! How long do we have with you before they take you away from us."

Those were the same two solutions Donovan came up with. I shook my head. "No. Lady Celeste has claimed me as a squire. I am to beholden to her. Prime Techromancer Donovan wants to train me in Techromancy as she trains me to defend the realm."

She inhaled and then said in a ghost of a voice. "Squire? But that would mean with such a small family, we will be moved to the Castle, assigned positions there. Why did they do that? We can't go back to the castle."

My face fell, did she truly prefer to have me sold into another family? She was... disappointed in me? I said as we were pulling up to our cottage, "I'm sorry mother. The Prime Techromancer said the Duke would approve. He said I was an – adept?"

She put her hand to her chest, I held her shoulders. "Are you okay mother?"

She smiled at me and placed a cold hand on my cheek, "An adept? My baby girl?" Wait, back to the castle? What was going on.

She exhaled and relaxed. She smiled at me, "Well then, I guess there's nothing to do about it then." She shook her head and her eyes twinkled with pride as she whispered, "An adept."

Jace and I helped her down, using a bucket as a step again. "What's an adept?" he asked as he automatically started unharnessing Goliath without prompting.

Mother told him as I supported her toward the door. "A powerful magic user that is not constrained by the usual limitations."

I heard him say in awe, "Woooow." As he led Goliath away.

I brought mother in and helped her into the house and got her changed into her bedclothes. I made sure she took her medicines and then sat at her side and held her hand as she slowly drifted off from a strenuous morning.

I smiled, it was so good to see her out and about. I hope she continues to improve. I looked at her sleeping and my brow furrowed slightly as I contemplated why she seemed so afraid of the castle. It was good we'd all stay together right? If I was sold off, contact is discouraged.

I, like Celeste, thought this solution was the best solution. Except for the fact that I'd make a terrible knight since I couldn't fight my way out of a burlap sack and I'm not much stronger than Jace. I wondered if a squire could be a squire forever. I smiled, I'd be beholden to my Lady forever then.

I thought of the invitation to the feast. It was held in the large livery courtyard at the castle on Holy Day and was open to all. It was devised by a Lady of the Court before I had even been born, to ensure that everyone in the village got at least one good meal a week. Yet another thing that differentiated Wexbury from the other realms. It also gave a forum for commoners to mingle with any knights or Nobles who chose to attend. It started after service on Holy Day and ended at dusk.

Until mother was confined to bed, Jace and I would attend every week, though mother would never accompany us. She always headed to Wexbury Minor instead to donate eggs to their version of the feast. I thought about that and then felt guilty that I hadn't given it a though until now. I'd have to rectify that and start bringing a basket of eggs down to the little village to the south every Sixth Day or Holy Day.

I paused, would I be able to? I'd be a squire now. I didn't think about what it would mean for our chicken farming. Would we be allowed to keep it? Would we have to hand it over to the Castle to assign a new family of herders?

I was getting anxious and recognized the heat I felt building with my rapid breathing, I calmed before I could feel it in my eyes. I smiled, I was already beginning to gain some control over my new magics.

I made a pact with myself to get some of these answers from Lady Celeste at the feast.

It was an unofficial tradition that if you had anything you could spare to share with others less fortunate, that you bring it to donate to the feast or the castle kitchens. I looked around. Our larder was restocked but had meager pickings. I opened the little cupboard that had our chicken jerky and I grabbed four or five strips off the rails and wrapped them in burlap. This would do.

We always had jerky. The hens that stopped laying we would sell off to the butcher, or trade for them making strips for us out of half the chicken that we could make jerky with. It was good protein for rough months and the winter when egg production was low, and it stored well.

When Jace came in I looked at him and smiled. I didn't think anyone would mind so I asked, "Did you wish to go to feast while mother sleeps?" He nodded and I licked my fingers and ran them through his unruly mop of tangled hair.

I smiled and said, "Grand!" I opened the back shutter and looked at the clock high in the cathedral in the distance, we had about two hours to kill. I cocked an eyebrow at the boy, imagining the man he would become then whispered conspiratorially, "Stories?"

He nodded enthusiastically and I went to sit by the bed near the heater and waited as he pried up the floorboard and picked a tome from mother's cache. He handed it to me and sat next to me. I grinned, it was his favorite. A fable. I opened it and wrapped an arm around him so he could read along and I read the story of the cobbler and the stag. When the Church bell tolled twice, I looked at him as I closed the book and handed it to him to hide away.

I stood and he rejoined me and I handed him my bundle and said, "Shall we be off?" On a whim, I also grabbed the basket of eggs by the door, it was marked with the seal of the realm. No sense making another trip tomorrow, I could bring our tithe to the realm today. Every citizen paid a tithe each month, either as five percent of their earnings, or five percent of their craft. We tithed twenty four eggs, once a week.

It wasn't much but it was what we had. It would give ten people in the castle a good breakfast. I smiled with pride that the Lords and Ladies seemed to favor our eggs.

Then we stepped out into the early afternoon and started walking down the lane toward the Crossbar and turned north. Jace chased an escaped rabbit between some buildings with a giggle. That would be Hank's, his family raised rabbits in their large lot at the end of the lane. We occasionally trade a rabbit for a chicken with them as long as they could keep the pelt. Rabbits make for some good stewing.

We had thought of switching to rabbit farming once because the pelts are so valuable. You could get two or three pennies for them and a half penny for the meat of two rabbits at the butcher. Then we did the math. A chicken, in its life, could produce four or five pennies worth of eggs, then we could get a half penny for two at the butcher. Then trade for the feathers we pick up in the coop to fishermen and seamstresses. Chickens also eat half of what rabbits do, so less investment. We had decided to stick with what we knew.

I looked up at the cathedral clock as we passed, we'd be a half hour earlier than Celeste would arrive, but that would give us a chance to drop off our offering to the kitchen and our tithe to the steward.

I never tired of the sight of Castle Wexbury. I looked on in amazement as we approached the looming castle that stretched on for well over a half mile. The towers and spires were awe inspiring and I suppressed a smile at the wind turbines on the ramparts. It was something out of mother's tomes. The granite blocks that comprised the inner walls were like the ones of the great wall around the village, hewn smooth by expert masons. The colors of the reflected sun made the walls seem rich, regal, and full of warmth.

We approached the crowded Portcullis to the livery courtyard and I glanced south across the Hawktail River as it flowed through the keep, and to the Great Meadow down to Beggar's Creek, making the meadow a little island. The Great Meadow was the only area of the city that wasn't packed with buildings. It was a flowing, manicured lawn, like a park hidden in the keep. There were exotic flowers and some trees that just punctuated the beauty of the area. Not may of us commoners walked the park or picnicked, it was usually full of nobles and castle servants, so we sort of felt out of place though all were welcome.

I smiled at the guards at the gate. One smiled back. Then Jace was tugging on my sleeve. "Did you see their swords? One day I want to be a warrior like them!"

I grinned at his enthusiasm then nudged my chin toward the servant's entrance to the north. "Could you please get the jerky to Cook? I'll find the steward, with our tithe. Come find me in the courtyard when you're done or find some of your friends to eat with. In any case, we'll leave at six." Cook was the lady of the kitchen, she was second only to the head Maid, Earnestine, matron of the castle. Her name was Corwin but she made everyone call her Cook.

Jace didn't even look back and just darted through the crowd

with the little bundle of jerky. I headed toward the main castle
courtyard away from the celebration. I found the steward of the
watch at the large table beside the arch. I bowed my head slightly,
"Sir, I've our tithe. For Margret Herder of Cheap Quarter."

I could tell he was grumpy, having to work on Holy Day. Only
the most junior of the stewards pulled this duty while the others
feasted. He wordlessly looked into the thick bound castle ledger and
turned a few pages. Then he looked up at me then the basket and
held his hand out. I passed it to him and he looked inside. The man
was actually counting the eggs!

He grunted, and wrote something in the ledger. I was fascinated
as always with the featherless quills they used. They called them
pens and they didn't require dipping in an ink well to write. They
were like the pencils mother used in our lessons but they used ink
instead of graphite.

Then he roughly cuffed the boy who was sleeping on a stool
beside the table. "Wake up! Make yourself useful, take these to
Cook!" He thrust the basket at the boy who blinked away the sleep
and picked up his page cap that had fallen when he was struck. The
boy grinned at me as he took the basket and ran off. I grinned back,
he was a cheerful sort.

Then the steward looked under the desk and found another
empty basket and thrust it at me. I took it bowed my head slightly.
"Sir." Then turned and made my way back to the feast in the livery
courtyard. He definitely was not a chatty fellow.

I looked around at all the people, they gathered in cliques, though this was supposed to be a chance for mingling. All were welcome at the feast and like the church, this was supposed to be a place where serfs could sit with nobles as equals. Near the main courtyard were the few nobles that came, keeping to themselves at three of the long plank tables. Then the servants as a buffer.

Then there were the knights. Their tables were always crowded, they were sort of the exception to the rule. They loved getting a chance to speak with the people they were sworn to protect. But most commoners were intimidated by them so not many ever chanced sitting with them to break bread. And closest to the livery stables, where the smell of horse and manure were the worst, were the thirty long plank tables where the serfs congregated.

I smiled at the gathering then stepped in the long line by the buffet tables. I grabbed one of the ceramic plates on a table and tin silverware and stretched and bobbed, trying to see the wonders the castle had laid out for us this Holy Day.

CHAPTER 8 – DUKE FREDRICK

I dished up my plate, feeling a little guilty how high I had it piled. There were just so many choices. But I had my eyes set on the large slice of roast beef laying on top of the bed of mashed potatoes and carrots that I had slathered with beef gravy. I haven't seen a piece of beef that large in years, my mouth was watering.

I moved off toward the stables and then saw Jace waving at me I made my way over and squinted at his plate. I said, "No you don't little brother. You get some vegetables and beef or wild turkey on that plate before you eat those sweet rolls."

His shoulders sagged and his eyes dropped. He hopped out of the long bench seat and took his plate, looking at his feet. "Yes Laney." I chuckled to myself. I used to do the same thing.

I set my plate down and started to slide into the seat when a voice I was getting quite fond of asked, "I thought you were sitting with us." I turned and looked up bashfully and brushed some loose hair out of my face. I couldn't help but smile at my Lady.

I looked back at the tables filled with boisterous knights then around at the commoners tables. People were just staring at Celeste, no doubt wondering why a Knight of the Realm was speaking with a herder. I lowered my voice. "I'll not embarrass the knights by sitting there."

She gave me a toothy grin that was half dare, then she sat her plate beside mine and said, "Fine, We'll just sit here then. Let me just call Vena and Kristof over."

She started to sit and I grabbed her arm to stop her, squeaking out, "No, you're a Lady!" Embarrassed for her since she didn't have the sense to be embarrassed for herself. A gasp and murmuring ripped through the nearby tables. I looked at my hand then Lady Celeste and I quickly dropped my hand and bowed deeply looking at my feet. What they hell did I think I was doing? I had laid hands on a Lady.

It was her turn to look around, giving a nervous chuckle and an apologetic smile to all of the people now staring at us. She grabbed my arm and hauled me up. "Stop that Laney, grab your plate and come with me." She picked up her plate again and looked at me expectantly.

I glanced back at the buffet tables where Jace was in line, staring over at us with wide eyes. I lowered my eyes, "I can't, Jace is here."

She followed my eyes then smiled at my brother, "Grand! He can join us to. Now grab your plate and lets go before you make a bigger scene." I blushed again and took a deep breath then grabbed my plate. She looked at Jace and pointed to the tables packed with knights and his jaw about hit the ground.

Then with her free hand, Lady Celeste offered me her elbow. I blinked and placed a hand in the crook of her arm and she stood tall and elegant and walked me to the table where Verna, with a wicked grin on her face, was sitting. I noted she was shortening her stride to accommodate me. I didn't want to embarrass my Lady farther so I walked with my chin up, ignoring all the stares and the sudden silence from where the nobles were gathered.

She helped me into the bench beside Lady Verna, then sat on my other side. Again I felt like a child between these two tall, strong women. Verna had nothing but a mischievous smile for me as she said simply, "Laney." Then looked past me as I bowed slightly, as she said to Celeste, "You're about as subtle as a bull moose you know that?"

Celeste brightened. "I've been told that once or twice." Then added with a smirk, "By you."

Verna added, "You've embarrassed the poor woman."

Celeste's smile dampened a bit and she looked at me. She caught my eyes, "Sorry Laney."

I shrugged and tried to play it off. "No worries. I need to verify my heart is actually beating from time to time."

The knights around me hefted their mugs and bellowed, "Here here!" I had to smile at the boisterous lot as one across from me sloppily poured some juice into the mug in front of me. And then I noted that with that, the nobles seemed to have lost interest and went back to their own conversations.

I was about to speak when I noted Jace was approaching the table, his eyes still bugged out. Celeste followed my gaze then bumped shoulders with a handsome knight with flowing black hair and a chiseled jaw. "Tennison, make room for our guest."

The large man, like Verna was quite muscular. He playfully

pushed the man next to him and who bumped the next man off the end of the bench. Everyone laughed and the ejected knight pulled a barrel over and sat at the end of the table and just kept eating like some sort of machine.

Jace stood there, still in his hero worship shock, and Celeste chuckled at him took his plate and set it next to her and suddenly he was flying. Sir Tennison had just reached back and hoisted Jace by the back of his britches with one hand like he weighed nothing and sat him at the bench between him and Celeste.

My Lady gave him a crinkled nose smile, "Hi Jace. We meet again."

He looked around and just nodded. He'd find his voice soon then they won't be able to shut him up.

Celeste called out around her, "Knights! Laney Herder, maiden of the realm, and her strapping brother Jace!" They all pounded their mugs and made sounds of greeting. I buried my face against Celetes's armored shoulder.

Verna slapped my back and chuckled. "She'll get her's one day Laney, just you wait and see." I smiled back at her from my shelter. Then the large man beside her with short stubbly red hair and a full red beard said, "Let us feast, there will be time for talk later."

Celeste grinned down at me as I pulled away from her, she agreed, "Kristof is right." Then she grabbed her fork and knife and attacked her plate. I did the same. I ate the vegetables first, working around the roast beef. I have a thing for carrots, I've always loved the taste, they were especially good with that beef gravy over them. I tunneled under the beef, getting all the mashed potatoes.

I glanced around and Jace was devouring everything. I don't think we have eaten so much as we had the past few days. We couldn't seem to get enough. I finished the wild rice then I pulled apart a biscuit and used it to sop up some of the gravy on the plate. There were bacon bits in the biscuit!

Then I just looked at that slice of roast beef. I had already eaten so much but my mouth was still watering as I picked up my knife and planned my attack. I glanced up and found five or six knights just staring at me, not eating.

Celeste had a crease between her eyes and Kristof leaned in so I could see him around Lady Verna. "You've been working around that slab of meat the whole meal, like you were afraid to touch it."

I shrugged and just offered with a smile, "We don't get much meat, except chicken. This was just a treat for myself. I've never seen such a slice." Celeste looked mad again. I was starting to get nervous as some knights looked at their meals then sat their silverware down and pushed their half empty plates away.

What? Now I know I had committed some sort of social faux pas. I wish I had paid more attention to the manners and etiquette lessons mother gave me. I tried to ignore everyone and I sliced off a piece of the meat. I made sure to catch some gravy with it then took a bite. I closed my eyes and savored it on my tongue for a moment before I started chewing.

I opened my eyes and noted they were all still watching me. I wasn't sure what to do, so I said with my mouth still full, "This is good." A cheer went up and everyone turned back to their plates except the few that pushed theirs away. As I ate I leaned into Celeste and said, "Are all knights this easily amused?"

She just smiled softly at me and said gently, "Finish your roast."

Verna leaned over and explained, "We knights fight to protect those under our care, to make sure they never want for anything. You just remind us that sometimes the sword is not enough."

I thought I was starting to understand and I started chewing slower. I had shamed them. That wasn't my intent. I smiled a smile I wasn't feeling at her, Celeste placed a hand on my shoulder, and I just kept my head down and finished eating.

I glanced over when Jace asked my Lady, "Is that a real sword? You didn't have it in the church. Is it heavy?"

She winked at him, stood, and stepped away from the table and drew her sword in one fluid motion and laid it across her arm, offering the hilt to him. "See for yourself."

His eyes shot wide. "Really?" Then he sought out my eyes and I couldn't stop smiling as I gave him a little nod.

He took the leather bound hilt in both of his small hands, not quite getting them all the way around. Then he hefted it. The blade was almost as long as him. He overbalanced and the tip drooped toward the ground. Celeste's foot shot out and the tip clinked on her armor before it could hit the ground. Jace smiled at everyone watching him as he grunted and raised it into the air. It must have weighed half as much as him.

He looked at me. "It is heavy."

Sir Tennison stood with a chuckle, he was bigger than I thought, maybe six foot four or so. "Celeste's toy? Here's a real sword." He reached back into his cape and started drawing out a double handed sword from his back scabbard. The blade seemed to go on forever. It must have been five feet long.

Celeste was grinning at the man and retrieved her sword from Jace who was mesmerized by the double handed sword. He placed it in Jace's hands then everyone laughed when he released it and Jace fell to the ground, the blade falling flat and clattering on the cobblestones. Sir Tennison apparently wasn't as picky about his sword hitting the ground as Celeste was.

The big man hoisted Jace up, clapped his back, and said, "Do me proud and work hard, get strong, and one day you may be a knight with your own sword when you are grown."

Jace nodded enthusiastically, "Yes sir. I promise." The man pushed him back then looked around, holding his had out to keep people clear as he walked a circle around his sword then with a scooping kicking motion of his toe, He flipped the sword into his hand and he made a complex slashing display, switching from hand to hand

He transitioned to a double handed grip, and made two slashing upward strikes then swung at the ground with all his might. The blade tip stopped less than an inch from the ground, showing his great control and strength to stop it. He tapped the ground with a little "ting" then stood and deftly slid the blade into his back scabbard.

Everyone clapped and he bowed at Jace then sat back down. It was then I noted the crest on the sash over his armor, the lightning bolt crossed with a sword. He was a Techno Knight like Celeste!

She was still standing there with her sword. She made some silly wiggling movements with hers and did a funny slash in the air and deftly slid her blade into her scabbard without looking as a counterpoint to her comical display. She stuck her tongue out at Tennison and everyone laughed and clapped. The big man got a kick out of it.

She sat back down with me, her eyes twinkling. I had to look down as heat spread across my cheeks. Then she tilted her head to look past me as she made an "Eww" face. "See what I mean? I needed you to save me from that lot." She nudged her chin.

I glanced over and covered my mouth with my hand in surprise. Lady Verna and Sir Kristof were kissing. Celeste mimed sitting back in a chair as she folded her arms behind her head and prompted, "So tell me more about Laney."

For the next hour we just sat and chatted. I had almost forgot where we were and the other knights around us. I only had eyes for her and I ate up anything she shared about herself. Jace would sometimes chime in to add embarrassing corrections to some of my stories.

When she asked about my first scavenging run from the keep after I had discovered I was a sensitive for copper. I spoke of the wonder and excitement of it all. My first find and how excited I was in the salvage intake courtyard with all the wonders around it. Then my shock at how much coin I received and how it would help to purchase the medicines for mother. When I finished, I looked around and found that some of the knights had stopped what they were doing and had sat in rapt attention as I spoke. Verna was holding a sleeping Jace on her lap.

I looked back toward the church, forgetting I was in the courtyard and couldn't see the clock from behind the inner wall of the castle, so I looked at the sun. Celeste pulled down her gauntlet and showed me it was half past five on that wondrous tiny clock. I smiled at Jace and said, "I think all this food and excitement did the poor little man in a little early."

Sir Tennison chuckled behind me, "I feel the same myself."

Suddenly all the knights stood at strict attention. Lady Verna sat tall, chin up with Jace still in her lap. My blood ran cold when Celeste said in a firm tone, "Duke Fredrick sir." I turned to see the Duke, the most powerful man in the realm of Wexbury. He was a man of modest height, late fifties, dressed in exquisite violet and emerald robes. His dark hair, shot through with distinguished grey was trimmed neatly and his short gotee and mustache looked just like the paintings.

Duchess Lucia was on his arm and the paintings did not do the woman justice. The delicate woman's gown was beyond words and her face did not show her fifty plus years. Her honey blonde hair was in curls and it pooled around her shoulders and down her back. She had a regal air to her.

I dropped to my knees, hands in front of me on the cobblestones, my eyes down. I peeked up, nether took any notice of me, thank goodness. The Duke made a waving off motion with his hand and the knights sat except for Celeste.

Fredrick motioned with his head toward the lower arch that lead out to the Great Meadow. "Walk with me Celeste. Tell me of the papers I signed for that new..." He paused, I could tell he was taking in where he was as he chose his words carefully, "..squire."

The Duke and Duchess started walking as Celeste said, "Sir." Then she looked down at me and just started walking away saying, "Laney, you are with me."

I looked up from where I was and at her retreating back then at Verna. She had an urgent look on her face and kept nudging her head toward Celeste. I leapt up and hurried off. Verna was whispering after me, "On her left."

As I approached, Celeste didn't look back but she was giving that discreet wiggling finger motion to her left. I got in step behind her feeling acutely aware of the fact I was following her and the rulers of the realm.

We reached the lower arch and there were four guards stationed there that fell into step behind us. The Duchess pulled Fredrick to a stop. "You go on ahead, I find business of the realm tedious dear. I'll retire to our chambers."

The Duke gave her a quick peck on the lips and nodded as he said, "Alright dear, I won't be long." She left us and two of the guards peeled off like her shadow and followed at a discreet distance.

We walked in silence into the Great Meadow to a little secluded area I hadn't been to before. It was some sort of sunken rose garden with trellises and a small gazebo. When we started walking down the little slope into the garden he made a cutting motion with a flick of his wrist and the guards stopped and turned their backs to watch the approach.

When we were out of earshot and approaching the gazebo, the Duke turned with an amused smile. He glanced at me then Celeste. "So this is the young adept then?" She nodded once and he tilted his head and looked at me up and down like one would a horse they were looking to buy.

He spoke to me as he furrowed his brow. "I thought you'd be... I don't know. Bigger?" He made a scrunching motion with both of his hands as he squinted, indicating I was small.

I lowered my eyes. What do you say to that? I replied, "I'm... sorry?" Then added quickly, "My Lord."

He chuckled then looked at Celeste and grinned, then made a sweeping motion to the little gazebo. We went in and each sat on a bench on either side of the little space. I looked around and just stood by Celeste's left side. I bit back a gleep, as she yanked me down to sit with her. Then she said in answer to him, "She packs a mighty punch."

He sat silently a moment then he concentrated and held his hand out toward me. I could feel power building. I had never heard the Duke was a magic user! I didn't like magics focused on me and I made myself as small as possible as I felt the heat gathering inside me. I looked to Celeste as my eyesight changed, her eyes had a soft green glow lighting them from within.

I turned and saw silver light trickling out of the Duke's eyes and flowing from his hand. I didn't like how it felt and mentally slapped at it to keep it off of me. I saw amber light dripping from my eyes like the overflow at a well, and the Duke flinched back, his power fading.

He inclined his head at Celeste, not me and said, "Ouch. Though not as much power as even you yourself Lady Celeste. I remember Sir Tannis' power was almost a physical thing it was so overwhelming."

She defended me. "She ignited just days ago my Lord. Anyway, as a wise man once said, it isn't the amount of power that wins the day, it is how that power is used that makes it formidable."

He chuckled, "Quoting my father again are we?"

Celeste chuckled more openly than I thought one should around the ruler of the realm. Then he looked at me and shook his head,

"Another adept, in Wexbury, who would have thunk it? And a serf no less. Can you show me?"

Celeste seemed a little aggravated and said, "Fred, she's a human being not a trained circus dog." I blinked, she called Duke Fredrick Fred?

He exhaled and dropped his head and looked at her as he admitted, "You're right, where are my manners? You're mother would have cuffed me soundly for that." They shared a sad look between them again. Then he looked at me again and said, "Please accept my sincerest apologies." Then he added, "Squire."

He looked over at Celeste while I processed the fact a Duke had apologized to me. I was starting to hyperventilate. He said almost like an excited child, "I signed the papers just this morning. You'll have to have the criers announce on the morrow and since she is a commoner, get her to Bernadine in records to have her lands assigned. And quarters and jobs for her family in the castle, if she has any. This is a whole bottle of worms you've opened up here Celeste. Why squire? Why not just marry her off to some handsome..."

Celeste's sword started rising on its own toward me, and she held up a finger to stop the Duke and turned to me and said softly, "Remember Laney, control it, don't let it control you."

I nodded and whispered, "Pick just one thing and concentrate on it." She nodded back with a smile and I stared into her emerald eyes. They made me feel safe and I felt the heat leaving as my eyesight return to normal.

His head was cocked, "I've never seen an amber power signature before."

Then Celeste answered his question, "We'll not be marrying her off of selling her into a family like was done to me. This was the best way."

He looked thoughtful then nodded slowly. "I guess, but that will make her training difficult with the Techromancers if she's training as a knight."

She shook her head, "She is my squire and her training is up to me. Father already said he would take her under his wing for all things magic."

He cocked an eyebrow then smiled a little. Then his face got serious. "We can't let it out that we have an adept among us before she can properly wield her power to defend herself. Many realms will do most anything to have an adept since there are so few."

He looked at me like I understood everything they were talking about and implying. I got the general gist, I was to be a secret of the realm for now. "So for now you are, Squire Laney, Knight Ascendant, from the house of Celeste. Do you understand? Tell no one until the criers announce it on the morrow."

I nodded dumbly and he smiled reassuringly then asked, "You do realize that binds you to her, you are beholden to her and her house. Your actions reflect on Lady Celeste."

I swallowed. I knew I would do my best for my Lady. I bowed

my head slightly and said, "Yes sir."

He stood suddenly and slapped his knee. "Grand!" Then he looked back the way we came and said absently, "Now I must get one of those sweet rolls while Lucia isn't around to protest." He walked off and called back, "And welcome Squire Laney."

I watched him leave, the guards following. There was something about his gate, it was too precise, too powerful. I think the Duke was a much more dangerous man than he covered up with his aloof act.

I turned and Celeste was watching me and turned to see the Duke disappear up the hill and she smiled a little. I think she knew what I was seeing. She picked one of the yellow roses goring up the trellis of the gazebo. She handed it to me and I just about melted into a puddle. She had no clue what effect she had on me.

She said quietly as she tucked strand of her red hair behind her ear, "Sorry about that. That was almost an ambush. Curiosity was killing him. The only adept any of us ever met around here was Sir Tannis, but that was before my time."

I smiled then blurted out, "Lands?"

She started giggling and pulled herself together, she raised a hand toward me, hesitated, then cupped my cheek with an amused smile. I closed my eyes to bask in the contact as she said, "That's what you took away from all of this?"

I opened my eyes and she still had my cheek, heating it. I shrugged, "It was so confusing, only nobles hold land in the realm."

She nodded and prompted like she wanted me to think it trough, "And you are Knight Ascendant. That makes you..."

My eyes went wide and she pulled her hand back slightly as I asked, "A noble?" She was nodding and I was shaking my head, "I'm a commoner, a serf, a nobody."

She slapped my cheek lightly with the hand she still had next to my face and she said with anger tinging her voice, "You are not a nobody! I don't ever want to hear you say that again, is that clear?!" She calmed and placed her hand on my cheek again, "And yes, you and your family are nobles now. You will get a proper title when you become a full Knight. Lands will be assigned to you, it is rare for 'commoners' as you say, to be taken as squires, but it is not unheard of."

I nodded, wondering what sort of unreal dream or nightmare I was in. Then she smiled and I was lost. Alright, definitely not a nightmare, too dreamy. I realized I must have looked like a lovesick puppy and straightened up and she pulled her hand away.

She stood and grabbed both of my hands and pulled me to my feet with excitement in her eyes. "Come along, let's get Jace home. Then I will expect you at the Castle proper at ten, that should give the criers time to announce your appointment throughout the keep and Wexbury Minor." She didn't let go of one of my hands and just dragged me giggling behind her.

CHAPTER 9 – LADY MARGRET?

I was so thrilled that Celeste insisted on walking me and Jace home. He ran into the house babbling at mother about the feast and the sword he held. We grinned his way then she stepped close and brushed some hair off my cheek. It felt a million degrees with her standing close, I swear I could feel the heat of her body.

I smiled up at her. "I'm beholden to you now."

She smiled and whispered, "Only as long as you wish it." Then she kissed the top of my head and walked away, looking back with a smile, "On the morrow Laney."

I bunched my fists under my lips, averted my eyes and murmured, "On the morrow," back to her with a wistful smile. She was now my Lady in truth. I would do my best not to disappoint her. I stopped at the door to watch her almost skipping down the lane, she looked back as she turned onto the Crossbar. I couldn't wipe the smile off my face when I went inside to tell mother all that had occurred.

We talked into the night until the last bells of the church pealed, echoing through the keep. It was hours later I was able to finally get to sleep as my mind was going a thousand miles an hour.

***

I woke up to Jace shaking my shoulder in the dim twilight of the morning. The light filtering through the window. Mother was making breakfast again. She looked even better than the prior day, she seemed to have a little spring in her step though she was still weak from muscle atrophy of months of bed rest. I knew it would likely be months before she were back to her usual energetic self if the medicines could hold her symptoms at bay like Doc Maxwell said.

He was saying, "Laney, wake up! The criers are coming!" He was so excited. Mother was just grinning at his enthusiasm. Sure enough... I could hear the hand bells coming down the lanes. I pushed some of my own hair out of my mouth with my tongue then pushed it back off my face with my hands. It was a mass of tangles. I pulled on my boots and gathered my hair back and tied it into a ponytail with a strand of string from an unraveling burlap sack by the door.

Mother pulled the pan off the heat and wiped her hands on a rag then joined us. We stepped outside onto the stoop. I could see the Three Sisters dipping below the horizon. And marveled at the whitish glow of the debris trail behind them with a backdrop of only the brightest stars in the heavens that hadn't been extinguished by the impending arrival of Father Sol. My brow furrowed slightly. When was the last time I laid out by the hog pen to watch the glory of the night sky?

The page walking down the street toward the lane crossing ringing his bell was followed by people stepping out of their cottages bundled up against the chill morning air. I could hear other bells throughout Cheap Quarter. I knew the same thing was playing out throughout the village and soon in all the lesser villages of the realm.

The man was older for a crier. They were usually boys just barely of majority as they worked their way up the ranks in the Keep. This man was in his late twenties easily. He wore the stylish uniform of the Keep in the colors of the realm. He had the heavy coat of Violet and matching page boy cap barely containing his wild red hair.

He stopped at the lane crossing and I felt mother grab my hand to hold it as the man said in a rich tenor voice that carried well. "All bear witness!"

He stopped ringing the bell then looked at the parchment he carried, then around to all the people within earshot, before he looked back down and started reading the proclamation. "Be it known that on this eighteenth day after Three Sisters Conjunction, twenty seven and forty two years post Impact, as witnessed by Lord of the Keep, Duke Fredrick of Wexbury, and Lady of Wexbury, Duchess Lucia of Wexbury."

He looked up and said the next without looking at the parchment, "That the son of Baron Reston of Wexbury, Bexinton, has been awarded the title of Squire and Knight Ascendant under the house of Sir Kristof, Knight of the realm. And as such is accorded all the rights an privileges associated with his post." That was exciting, we only saw two or three Squires a year be appointed, now we would have two in one day! And he was a baron. Which made sense since most knights came from noble stock.

He paused and looked around and asked formally, "Witnessed?"

We all mumbled, "Witnessed." In response, and people started to turn to go back in their dwellings

Then he glanced at the parchment and cleared his throat and added, "Also..." Stopping the people.

He seemed to like the power of that word as I could tell he restrained a little smile when everyone turned back to him. The man was having fun with this. I would assume it was a tedious job, but he seemed to rise to it.

He looked up and said, "The daughter of Margret Herder of the keep, Laney..." He paused and looked around as everyone started murmuring and looking to where I stood with mother and Jace. The man smiled at me and inclined his head slightly. He knew he was speaking of me! He spoke in a more powerful and clearer voice now, enunciating clearly. "Has been awarded the title of Squire, and Techno Knight Ascendant..." He paused again to let that sink in, the murmuring got louder.

My lord, Techno Knight? They just declared me a Techromancer. But I realized it only made sense. Others have witnessed my use of magic and this way they were still able to hide that I was also an adept. Then he continued, holding the parchment before him but looking over it slyly to gauge reactions as he finished. "...under the house of Lady Celeste, Techno Knight of the realm. And as such is accorded all the rights an privileges associated with her post."

He lowered the parchment with a smile to all and asked like it was a given, "Witnessed?"

A much louder, "Witnessed!" Came from our neighbors. I was so embarrassed I wanted to pop back inside but mother held me tightly in place.

She said quietly to me without moving her lips as she smiled at the man. "Be gracious and strong. It is your new station." I nodded and stood tall and proud for her. The man smiled over to us and I inclined my head slightly which he returned, only lower. Then he almost jauntily started strolling farther down the lane, ringing his bell.

I acknowledged the stares from our neighbors with another tilt of my head then we turned and entered our home. Jace was bubbling with excitement. "Techno Knight Ascendant! My sister!" Mother smiled and ruffled his hair as I stood by the door, still trying to comprehend that this was really happening.

I just sort of mumbled, "He was a happy sort."

This caused mother to chuckle as she dished out our food onto plates. "He most likely fought to get our area to announce. He is probably the most senior crier of the keep. It is so rare for a commoner to rise to the station of noble and he took great pleasure in watching our, and our neighbor's, reactions."

We ate in relative silence and then I stood. "Jace, help mother clean up the dishes, I'll attend to the flock and morning chores. We have to attend my Lady at ten to finalize my appointment." I smiled at speaking that out loud... my Lady. It sounded good saying that about Celeste.

I went about the chores and stutter stepped. Was this to be my final time doing them? I hadn't thought of what would happen to our flock and home once we were moved to the castle. I sat on one of the rain barrels as Father Sol rose above the horizon to warm the world. This was all I knew since I was old enough to walk. I was a herder, like my mother and father before me. I finished the chores in a daze.

I was sweaty and dirty and was going to the castle in... before I could look up the church bell pealed nine. Shit! I ran inside and almost fell over when I looked at mother. The locked trunk that was in the corner, covered in an old quilt, was open and mother was in an antique dress that would have been fit for a lady of the court if it hadn't been so moth ridden. Her hair was pulled back loosely with an emerald ribbon. She had Jace cleaned up and in his new tunic.

I blinked at mother, if it weren't for the condition of the dress, her gaunt features and sick pallor, she would have been stunning, regal even. I asked in my confusion, looking at the trunk that had been locked my entire life. "Mom?"

She smiled at me and then motioned me over to the bed. "Come, we need to get you presentable." I sat and she sent Jace out to hitch Goliath to the wagon. Then my mother bathed me with a bucket and a towel like she did when I was small. After I dressed in my peasant dress, she used the handle of a fork like a pick, to weed out the tangles in my hair, then let it just drape down my back without braiding or putting it in a ponytail.

Then she went to the trunk and pulled out some slippers like I had not seen before. They had that black flexible stuff on the soles like Emily, matron of the library, had on her calfskin shoes. She smiled, "These were to be yours on your wedding day. I fear that will never come to pass, so for you, for your appointment to noble status."

I put the slippers on and they felt soft as silk and were padded like a goose down pillow. They were made of calf skin and had the musk of disuse and storage. The tan hide was dry and cracking at the seams, they needed a good oiling, but they were simply gorgeous. I asked her, "How?"

Her eyes were sad and she said softly, "I fear all your questions will be answered soon enough sweet Laney. Just know how very proud I am of you." She smiled and stood, "We mustn't keep your Lady waiting. All you do now reflects on her, so punctuality is now more important than ever. As Squire, you are beholden to her as your master until you become a knight."

Then she added with a cute smile that made her look younger, a smile I have never seen on her before, "And we..." She moved her hand from herself and toward the door where Jace had gone. "...are of your house. You are baroness now, but cannot use the title until you are appointed knight."

How did she know so much about what was going on? And what treasures did she hide in that chest?

She smiled at the door as we stood, "And little Jace is now a Lord as I am a Lady. To change to baron and baroness when you can freely use your title." She held my arm and I could still feel her using me for support as we headed outside. She was overdoing it again.

We helped her into the wagon and then I had a thought and ran back inside to grab one of the baskets of eggs I had gathered that morning. When I took the reins with Jace on my lap so he could practice, mother gave me a questioning look. I said, "A gift for my Lady."

She smiled and got a thoughtful look on her face. She seemed to soften and more stated than asked, "You're quite taken with her."

I blushed and urged my beautiful stallion on toward the Crossbar. It felt sort of ominous, like I were leaving my old life behind. I paused and looked back at our little cottage. Mother's hand rested on my arm. I gave her a sad smile and continued on.

We reached the castle and I wasn't sure where I was to go. I pulled us into the livery courtyard. A stable boy ran out and helped mother down and I blushed when the boy offered a hand down to me. I shrugged at him, that was just silly. Then I hopped down myself with Jace landing energetically beside me. I was surprised at the springiness of the slippers, that flexible sole took most of the force of my landing. I grabbed the basket then the boy hopped into the wagon and grabbed the reins.

I looked at him then said, "Excuse me. I'm Laney Herder, I'm to meet Lady Celeste at ten. I'm not sure where I'm supposed to go. Then I added hastily. I'm her new squire."

He nodded excitedly and bowed, "Everyone knows who you are Lady. The chicken farmer who would be knight. It is all over the keep." He said it in a way that was not disparaging, instead his voice was tinged with pride and excitement. Then he pointed out of the courtyard toward the main entry. "Lady Celeste had been waiting there for you since nine. She's pacing and making everyone nervous."

I looked over then at him as he was about to urge Goliath on. "Excuse me, where are you taking our wagon?"

He looked at me like I were daft. "The Lady instructed us to put your horse in the stables and have the wagon looked after." Oh. I nodded and he smiled, giving us a bow and they were off.

We walked to the main entrance with me supporting mother. As we reached the great doors the two doormen standing at attention by the two guards armed with swords and long pikes stood at attention. The doormen grabbed the huge iron rings and heaved. We stepped into the foyer and the doors shut behind us.

I smiled at two familiar figures. Lady Celeste and Prime Techromancer Donovan were talking and turned to us when we stepped in. We bowed our heads, mother slapping Jacc's shoulder and nudging her eyes down until he caught on and bowed. We looked up and I only had eyes for my Knight, and her smile was making my heart ache. We both paused when Donovan's voice, barely a whisper, broke the silence, sounding as though he had seen a ghost, "Lady Margret?"

CHAPTER 10 – SQUIRE LANEY

We all looked between Donovan and my mother. Mom just smiled a fond smile and stepped to the Prime Techromancer, curtsied like she had done it all her life then laid a hand on his cheek, kissing the other. "Hello Donnie."

He looked half shocked as he smiled and stepped back to look at her. "We all thought you dead or beyond the walls." Then he straightened and gave a slight bow. "Welcome home Lady." Celeste looked as confused as I was and she looked at my mother, her attire, and then gave her slight, hesitant bow.

Donovan started looking between her and me then he tipped his head back and barked out an amused laugh. "I should have guessed." Then he just smiled fondly at her, amusement twinkling in his eyes, "And now we know why we've been blessed with the second adept in our keep in the same lifetime."

Celeste started to look annoyed. "Would you two care to clue the rest of us in as to what is going on here?"

Mother gave her a warm smile and 'Donnie' said, "This my dear daughter, is as the commoners called her so very long ago, the Lady of the Keep."

He said it like a title and Celeste's eyes went wide as she looked at mother while she prompted her father, "This is THE Lady Margret?" She bowed lower this time to mother, who just laid a hand on her arm and coaxed her head back up with her own eyes.

I couldn't handle it anymore, I blurted out in frustration, "Who is the Lady of the Keep? What is going on here?"

Mother was blushing and Donovan looked at me. "You truly don't know?" He turned to mother, "You never told her?" Mother shook her head once and he looked back at me and grinned, "Surely you've heard the stories of the Lady who championed the castle feast on Holy Day, and opening the Great Meadow to the common folk? The Lady who's ideas of the possibility of opening a schoolhouse to educate the public freely and free medical care are still being hotly debated twenty five years later?"

I paled... everyone knew of the Shining Lady, or less commonly known as... that's right, the Lady of the Keep! She was generous to a fault and loved the villagers. She had been stripped of her title by the petty Duchess Lucia over twenty years ago when the Lady dared marry a commoner.

I paused again, not just a commoner... I swallowed... a herder. When she left the castle, she was never heard from again. I looked at the woman who raised me. The woman who was so knowledgeable about so many thing. The woman who taught me to work hard and appreciate life. Who taught me to live and love. To read, to stand tall, and never show weakness.

She had been a noble? She was the Shining Lady? My head was spinning. I asked in barely a whisper. "Mother?"

She smiled at me sadly and shook her head, hugging my arm. "That was another life Laney. I had a happier life as Margret

Herder. Wife of Nicholas. Mother to the two most wonderful children who have done me so proud." She looked down at Jace who still wasn't sure what everyone was talking about. She cupped his cheek and gave him a warm smile.

Mother closed her eyes and held on tighter to me, she looked dizzy for a moment. She said to our hosts, "I apologize. Can we sit? My strength has not returned to me."

Celeste whispered into Donovan's ear, but I caught it just barely, "Wasting Syndrome."

Donovan was suddenly by her side, pain in his eyes, supporting her as he would a porcelain doll. "Of course. We can send the girls off to do all the tedious things that are required. Why don't you and this strapping young man..."

"Jace," mother offered.

He nodded, "Jace, come sit in my office? The girls can rejoin us when you are needed." He looked at us, it was an instruction, not a question.

He led mother away and said, "Come young Jace. Tell me, have you ever seen a spyglass?"

I think my brother surprised him as he followed eagerly by saying, "Yes. Laney has one in her scavenging toolkit." I grinned at his enthusiasm. Mother had given me the tool pouch before I went out on my first scavenging run. It was my father's, Nicholas. It was the only thing of his I had. I wish I had known the man. He had farmed chickens and still found time to go scavenging once a month to support mother. He was not a sensitive, he relied on his tool kit and a keen gut to find the treasures of old.

Then I was alone with the woman I admired. I was feeling awkward and I looked down, realizing I had a basket of eggs hanging in the crook of my arm. I clumsily thrust it out to her. "A gift for my Lady. As a thank you for your kindness."

She graciously accepted, beamed at me, and looked inside. She pulled out an egg and shook her head. "I don't know how your family produces such large eggs. I'll be the envy of the barracks. The other nobles fight over these, none have the same taste."

Then she looked in the direction her father had just led my family and then to me. "You are just full of surprises, Squire Laney." The 'Squire' made me blush. Then she was all business, "We have a lot to get done today, are you prepared?"

I shrugged and she chuckled and offered her arm to me again. She treated me like a lady. I timidly placed my fingers on her arm and we started up a grand staircase to the third level where there were dozens of offices down one of the many halls we passed. She stopped a maid who was hustling past. "Miss?"

The maid bowed and asked, "Yes my Lady?"

Celeste handed her the basket. "Please get these to Cook. Ask her if she could please use them for something special for my squad? Courtesy of Lady Laney." Lady Laney? Oh good lord. I swallowed but my mouth was dry. I was noble... bottom of the heap, but a noble.

I blurted, "And one for yourself, for your trouble Miss..." I left a question in the air.

The maid dipped her head to me with a smile as she saw the eggs inside. "Yvette, my Lady."

I smiled and repeated, "Yvette." Then added, "Laney please."

She shook her head and said, "I don't know if I can do that Lady. But thank you." Then she was off, hurrying down the hall.

Celeste looked full of herself as she grinned and started dragging me down the hall almost comically, as she said into the ether, "And she's generous too."

Our first stop was in records. My Lady verified my station was registered and the clerk, Reinhardt, had me make my mark next to the Duke's signature. I think I surprised him by signing my name. He'd been looking down his nose at my attire the whole time. It made me feel like a charlatan.

Celeste seemed perturbed by the man's attitude. We moved over to the Assayer's desk in the back corner. The lady there seemed frazzled, and she had those same type glass lenses on her nose that Emily had in the library. The woman was around sixty, going on one hundred and her silver white hair was pulled back in a tight ponytail, the frizzy ends shooting out wildly like a hissing cat. She was lanky and taller than me but not as tall as my Lady.

The area behind her seemed in a disarray. Stacks of maps and rolled up scrolls on every surface. A wall full of tubes behind the desk were stuffed with rolls of parchments and maps. She squinted up at Celeste and smiled like someone would to a grandchild. "You seem taller ever time I see you Celeste."

The woman felt comfortable being familiar with her. She sort of reminded me of Emily in that way. So competent that nobody would correct her. I grinned. Celeste just chuckled, "No Bernadine, you're just getting shorter in your old age."

The woman pursed her lips and waved that off, "Pish. I'm just reaching my prime." Then she seemed surprised to see me standing there too, like she hadn't noticed me before. She squinted at me. "You, I don't know." Then she straightened, "What can I do for you ladies?"

Celeste said, "Assayer Bernadine, this is Squire Laney, Techno Knight Ascendant."

The lady brightened and offered her hand. "Oh yes, the herder girl. So exciting." I shook and couldn't help feeling amused at the woman. Then she said, "So you're here to get her lands assigned, not visit?" She harrumphed.

Celeste chuckled at her, "No, just business I fear. Your gossip always leaves me exhausted."

The woman winked at her, "You've always been a lightweight ever since you were small Celeste."

The woman turned and went back to the ungodly mess and looked around for a second then said, "Ah." And grabbed a map that was under a huge stack of papers. In one deft movement she whipped the map out from under the rest, leaving the stack undisturbed. That was kind of impressive.

As the woman smoothed the map onto the large desk the best she could over the mess on it. My knight leaned down toward me like she were confiding in me. "If you ever need information about anything that is happening in the keep, Bernie is the woman to talk to. Though she'll almost literally talk your ear off."

The older woman didn't even look up, she just grabbed a melted glass glob from the desk and threw it at Celeste while she studied the map. It clanked on the armor below the knight's tunic and fell back to the desk. Celeste asked, "Ow?"

The silver haired woman looked up and just said, "Drama queen." Then she looked to me and asked, "Which lands?"

I looked at her and shrugged. "They didn't tell me."

A strong hand laid on my shoulder. "No Laney, she's asking you to choose. Your title gives you fifty acres. Any of the shaded areas of the Realm of Wexbury there are lands already assigned."

I blinked. I got to choose my own lands? That was such a foreign concept, I would be a land owner? I looked at the map, two thirds of it were expertly shaded by thin lines drawn parallel to each other, thinly spaced. I looked back at the redhead with those mesmerizing emerald eyes. "What did you choose?"

She chuckled. "I didn't choose. As father's daughter, I am heir to his lands. Though he did gift me a small portion of them, The Scales and The Grove on my majority."

I blinked again, I seemed to be blinking in shock a lot theses days. I blurted, "You own The Scales and The Grove?"

The Scales were a series of little islands in the middle of Dragontooth Lake. They weren't very large, the biggest being five acres with a little caretaker cottage and two small cabins. There were two small islands to the south near the shore that were also part of the Scales. Two years back, the Scales were declared a Treasure of the Realm by the owner and opened up for the use of any and all citizens, and the cabins made available for use by any fisherman who needs to overnight in them or take shelter from a storm. Two years? That was when Celeste reached majority. When they became hers. I smiled at her generosity to the people of the realm.

The Grove was the portion of the island that was formed by the Hawktail and Beggar's Creek outside of the walls of the keep. The portion inside was the Great Meadow. The Grove was a heavily forested area that had a patch of crab apple trees in the center of it. It had also been declared a Treasure of the Realm a couple years ago and opened to all citizens of the realm.

There were no bridges to it. The only way to access the island was by boat. This was by design as the castle bisected the island so it was more for defense than anything else that bridges were not built.

I had borrowed a small row boat last fall from a fisherman I had traded some feathers to tie flies with. And I gathered twenty pounds of crab apples to sell to the baker for pies and tarts. I got two pennies and an apple pie for my troubles. The island was beautiful in the shadow of the castle walls.

I smiled at her, she had turned her gift from her father into a gift for the people of the realm. I wanted to be as altruistic as her. I bit my lip and studied the map. Most of the taken lands paralleled the rivers since water was life. Also most of the north Grasslands were taken where large herds of deer and wild cattle roamed. I was seeing a pattern... water was life and food was life. Most people seemed to stay clear of the castle except to the south where the Realm owned Orchards, Farmland, and Ranches were between Wexbury Keep and Wexbury Minor.

Then I smiled as I looked at that buffer the other nobles were giving the keep, it was about five miles. And there, two miles away on the Hawktail, in the middle of the unshaded zone, was a familiar turn of the river where I knew there was a outcropping above.

I looked at both of the women then stabbed my finger at the location squinting an eye in question. They were quiet then Bernadine asked, "Are you sure you want lands that close to the keep?" Like it were distasteful or something. I'm sure I'd get an education later.

Celeste's eyes narrowed and looked at me. "That is where you faced the marauders." I nodded and then paused a second, knowing I was about to give out a secret, a secret I didn't need to keep anymore, being a Squire meant my family would want for nothing.

I licked my dry lips. Then looked between the two women. "I... found it. When I was scavenging." I exhaled and just spilled,

"There is a settlement from the Before Times just below the surface there. That is where the wondrous salvage I have been bringing in to sell has come from. I think the village was named after the founders. Gus Davis Ford."

They blinked at me and Celeste suddenly chuckled and spoke to the air, "And even more surprises."

I stabbed the map again. "Can I. Can I make it a Treasure of the Realm and have it excavated?"

The smiling look I got from the elder woman as she bit the tip of her tongue told me nothing. She held up a finger and turned to the organized chaos behind her. Celeste chuckled, and said, "It is your land, you can do anything you wish with it."

Bernadine was back with some parchments, another map, and a ledger. She smoothed out the map, it showed the area of my find in much larger detail. With smooth strokes using a calligraphy quill with a brass tip and inkwell instead of one of those self contained pens, she wrote Baroness Laney of Wexbury on the map, and with a ruler she deftly marked out a fifty acre parcel. The uneven north edge through the middle of the Hawktail.

She added something in the ledger then started putting parchments in front of me pointing at a signature line. "Land title." I signed and then she and Celeste signed the witness lines. Then came, "Assignment of Treasure of the Realm." We all signed. "Writ of intent for archaeological dig and spoils share for lands assigned to Treasure of the Realm under your stewardship."

Then she smiled and offered a hand, I shook. She placed her
other hand over mine as we shook. "Congratulations, Laney you are
now a land owner who signed her lands away to the public." She
looked at Celeste with a grin before she released my hand. "I'm
happy to see she lives up to all the hype circulating the keep." She
shook her head in amusement and murmured, "A settlement from
the Before."

Then she looked at me. "You have one year from today to
assign a steward or trustee to oversee your holdings. Eighteen
months to start the archaeological dig." I nodded dumbly. I'd figure
out how all that worked later. She finished with, "I'll have copies of
all of the records sent out with the monthly couriers to the other
realms." She smiled, "It truly was a pleasure."

I nodded. "Likewise."

Celeste winked at me, I melted, and she offered her elbow which
I gladly accepted. She keeps winking like that and it turns my legs
to jelly every time. She said, "Bye Bernie. Thanks for your help."

She wiggled her fingers like she was dismissing us. I said,
"Goodbye," as I was dragged off. I got my legs back under myself
as she brought me down to the ground floor and to a back room past
the great hall. I was giggling at her haste. "What next?"

She responded smugly, "Now the painful stuff." I looked
around, we seemed to be in a seamstress parlor.

The rest of the morning was filled with fittings, trips to the
armory to find I was better suited to knives and a very small sword

the length of my forearm. It was all I could heft. The Man at Arms said it was really just a short sword used as a parrying blade in two bladed combat, usually used in the off hand while the fighter wields a long sword in the other. Okay, that was embarrassing. Celeste commissioned a custom sword for me and passed my measurements to the armor smithy.

Then we slowed down as we headed to Donnovan's office for lunch. She told me. "There will be days of little things here and there that have to be done to get you set up for your station. The only major things left are to get your family into some quarters and to the seamstress for proper fittings of appropriate clothes, to move your belongings in, and to assign duties to your family."

That got me thinking about home again. "What happens now. I mean to my home? And our flock? I mean..." I wasn't sure what I was asking and was probably coming off like a fool.

She saw my frown and chimed in, "This is a rare occurrence, but believe me, there is a procedure for every contingency in the realm. We will have some porters help your family move in the morning. The property will revert back to the control of the keep and a son of a herder who is of majority will be assigned the cottage. Your mother will be recompensed for the stock."

I was sort of saddened by that. It was my home. It was all I knew. I know we never owned it but it is where we lived and mother and father made a successful chicken farm on the double lot. But if we could not live there.... I looked up at her and asked, "Can we make a suggestion as to who would get it?"

She nodded and mused, "Of course, someone you know the abilities of would be better than some random pick or lottery among the herders."

At least if it is someone I know, the sting wouldn't be as bad. "Then I recommend Hank, son of Joseph and Ursula Herder. I have known them all my life and they are successful rabbit farmers. Hank is their youngest son and has reached majority. He would do well with the chickens."

She nodded, "I'll make the recommendation then."

We reached Donovan's office and I heard laughing. We stepped in and mother was almost in tears as Donovan chuckled. Jace was looking between the two with a grin as mother choked out between spurts of laughter, "No? Tell me she didn't. Laney did something similar on her twelfth birthday. Only she didn't wind up in the..."

She paused when she saw us walk in and looked at the Prime Techromancer. They burst out laughing again. I was smiling at their antics. I hadn't seen mother laugh like that in such a long time. "What, you two?"

Donovan waved us off as he composed himself. "We're just talking about raising headstrong girls in these modern times." Celeste and I shared terrified looks.

Then the big man smothered a smile and asked. "How did you two fare, daughter?"

She replied in a matter of fact tone, "All of the pressing matters have been addressed. All that is left for this day, is to get Laney's family some quarters in the castle or an Uptown manor if any are available, and have them assigned duties. The porters will assist in the move." Then she added with a mischievous smirk at me, "And the armory needs to figure out how to fit a hilt onto a letter opener."

I opened my mouth wide in a disbelieving smile. "And here I thought you to be a lady... my Lady."

She chuckled and acted innocent, "What? I have knives longer than the blade you chose Laney."

I blushed profusely and feebly attempted to defend myself, "I'm not a fighter. I'll make a terrible knight."

She had fire and... pride? In her voice as she said, "Tell that to those two marauders. You bring a shovel and a signpost to battle and you walk away unscathed while two Knights of the Realm suffer injuries."

She pushed that aside and smiled at her father, "She has released her new lands as a Treasure of the Realm." His eyebrows arched in question. She looked sideways at me as she told him, "Yet another secret she has harbored. The remains of a settlement from the Before Times." He looked impressed and it was mother's turn to look surprised. I just shrugged at her.

At that, Celeste's father straightened and said as he made an ushering motion with his hand to the door, "Shall we break bread before we attend to Lady Margret and Lord Jace here? I'm sure the day has been most tiring for the Lady. It would be best to get them settled in somewhere..." He paused looking at mother's dress. "...and get some attire more befitting a Lady."

Before we could say a word, Donovan offered an arm down to mother. She took it lightly and stood from her chair. I could see the man skillfully supporting her without being obvious like he had practice at it. Then my heart fell realizing he had. His wife Shavey had suffered from the same affliction and succumbed before this new treatment had been developed.

I grinned when Jace comically offered his arm up to Celeste, mimicking her father. She smiled at him, crinkling her nose cutely and took his arm. She gave me an imperious look as she strode off with him. Leaving me chuckling as I ran after them. Taking my place behind the Knight to her left.

We entered the main dining hall and moved back to a smaller dining hall I didn't know existed through an arch behind it. There were only five decent sized tables and it appeared to have a private entrance directly into the main kitchen. There was a couple siting in the far corner, their elegant robes told me they were high-ranking nobles.

Donovan moved us smoothly to the farthest table from them to give them and us some privacy. He held out a chair for mother so she could be seated. Jace quickly did the same for Celeste and me before hopping into a chair beside mother. I grinned, he was learning manners by proxy. I think he had the same hero worship I had of the Prime Techromancer and his daughter.

Then Donovan looked at Jace when a woman dressed all in white came rushing to the table and started laying out linen napkins and formal silverware place settings. You needed more than one spoon fork and knife? "So young Lord Jace. Is there something in particular you'd like for lunch? The matron of the kitchen can prepare anything your heart desires."

Jace scrunched up his brow in thought. "Some beef or pork jerky stew? Or perhaps some biscuits?"

We all looked at him with fond smiles. The big man said, "I think Cook can do a little better than that." Then he turned to the woman that was now just standing by Donovan's side. He looked up to her and said, "Dear, could you just have Cook prepare something to welcome this new family into the fold? And Emily is always going on that I'm losing too much weight, I'm sure Cook is in cahoots with her and will know what the Queen of the Scrolls means."

I could hear the fondness in his voice when he spoke of Emily, it was the same tone Emily had for him. I also was not blind to him looking at his daughter every time he said Emily's name. I think the man was ashamed of his affection for the woman since she was barely older than his daughter. The sad look Celeste shared with me told me she was aware too but was sad her father felt he could not act on it.

The woman tittered a little and echoed softly, "Queen of the Scrolls."

Donovan's eyes went wide and he sputtered out in a panic, "That's not to find its way to her."

The woman bowed out and started toward the door to the kitchen. "Of course not, my Lord, of course not."

He looked at Celeste. "She didn't sound sincere." Then he glanced at mother. "Did she?"

Mother reached over for the pitcher of water at the center of the table and poured a glass as she said mischievously, "I wouldn't count on it. I remember how quickly gossip travels in the castle. No doubt word has already reached her."

He placed his head in his hands and shook it slowly. Then he straightened with a smile. "What is done is done."

Then Celeste jumped out of her seat standing at attention when a woman's voice from behind us said, "Margret? We heard rumors you were dead." My eyes bulged when I turned to see the Duke with the Duchess on his arm entering the dining room. I was on my feet and bowing deeply. Donovan just stood and inclined his head. Mother was in a deep curtsy too. She slapped Jace's shoulder and he hopped up and bowed.

Then Duchess Lucia detached herself from Fredrick's arm when he made a dismissing motion with his hand and we all stood. She took a step toward mother, looking her up and down and she smirked. "Or that you went to work in the brothel in the Trough. Judging by your dress that is a quarter century out of date, that one was closer to the mark. But no, I hear now that a herder was the rank you rose to." The Trough was the seedy area of the village, where the taverns, beggars, and brothel were. It was the lower east portion of the village across from Cheap Quarter and below Beggar's Creek.

The Duke cleared his throat. "Lucy, please be civil."

Then Donovan spoke, "And you would be familiar with the brothel how?" With a smirk he added, "My Lady?"

My eyes snapped open, that was as close to a personal attack on one of the rulers of the realm as you could get. He could get the stockade for that. Mother just stood impassively and the Duchess raged. I felt the hairs on the back of my neck stand on end and silver sparkling energy was pouring out of Lucia's eyes as power gathered in her hand. "You dare?" Not only the Duke but the Duchess had magic? Why did nobody know of this in the village?

Donovan's eyes narrowed dangerously and he cocked his head. The Duchess paled and then looked at her husband as her power dissipated. "Are you going to let him talk to me like that?"

The Duke looked tired. He had patience in his tone and softness you have for someone you love behaving badly. "To be fair love, you did fire the first volley, unprovoked."

She seethed then glared at mother as she hissed at him, "You always did take her side." Then she stalked off calling back over her shoulder, "I'm not hungry anymore."

We watched her retreat as the Duke chuckled. "I knew it wasn't a good idea bringing her here, but I just had to confirm the rumor that our dear Squire Laney here had returned our Shining Lady to us."

He stepped up to mother and took her hand and kissed the back of it. She grinned and kissed his cheek. "Hello, Fred."

He smiled at her then looked away with a touch of shame in his eyes. "I'm sorry that Lucy had used that archaic law to strip you of your titles for marrying a commoner without your father's title to protect you. It was a terrible manipulation, but my hands were tied."

Mother nodded and went to sit, he held her chair for her. The rest of us sat and he sat after Celeste and I did. Then she said with an encouraging smile, "It is the past, and all has worked out."

He nodded then assured her, "Well rest assured that such a travesty of justice will never occur again, as we petitioned Highland Reach and had that law stricken from the books."

She nodded and something clicked into my head when he mentioned her father dying. I remembered the story of what had happened after the Mage Wars. Grandfather was Sir Tannis? The Hero of the Realm? I started breathing hard and then calmed when a warm hand forged of steel slipped into mine. I looked over and Celeste gave me a smile of encouragement.

I swallowed and smiled back. It looks like I wasn't the only one in the family full of secrets and surprises.

The servant came out and quickly bowed and set up another place setting for the Duke. Thay quickly brought him some wine. Then I just sat in stunned silence as 'Fred', 'Donnie', and my mother caught up.

A few minutes later, three people came out of the kitchen with serving trays, followed by Cook! I liked Cook a lot, she was always fair to my brother and me when we came bearing eggs for sale or trade. The woman covered her mouth over a little squeal and ran to the table as mother stood. "Margret, so it is true! You've returned to us!" The ladies hugged each other before mother sat down once again.

Mother said through her smile, "Hello Corwin."

Then Donovan blustered out, "Does everybody in the keep already know of this?"

Cook slapped the top of his head playfully. "Now Donovan. If Bernadine knows of it, then all of the Realm does by now."

He nodded with a sly smile. "You're right of course, Cook."

Then we were served a four-course lunch. I still don't know where I was putting all of this food!

The Duke talked mother into resuming her position as the head of Special Projects for the Keep. The office was dissolved when she left. And he set Jace up as a runner for the Knights after having fun testing his knowledge of different locations in the village. He said it really wasn't a job for a Lord, but he was young and needed to learn the workings of the keep from the inside until he hit his majority.

Then he smiled and said, "Margret, instead of the small nobles quarters in the castle, your old manor in Uptown, just outside the Castle gates had been sealed, and Bernadine has made sure it remained vacant on the odd miracle you ever returned to us. Don't ask how she accomplished it, but it is best not to ask questions about her methods, even I'm smart enough not to." He grinned.

Mother tilted her head in acceptance and said, "Thank you. It is good to be home Fred."

He excused himself and Celeste looked at her father, who was already deep in conversation with mother. "Can you see them to the seamstress father? For proper wardrobes? I need to get Laney situated in the room off my quarters."

He nodded and we stood. I kissed mother on the cheek and was pulled toward the kitchen. As soon as we got into the noisy kitchen she smiled. "I just wanted to get you to myself for a bit. It has been such a hectic day I haven't had a moment alone with you."

I blushed as she dragged me up to Cook. She looked at me then smiled and asked, "Have you ever had ice cream, Laney?"

I furrowed my brow. "I get good cream in the market."

She grinned and wiggled her eyebrows at Cook then held up two fingers. Cook just pursed her lips in a tight knowing smile. They evil women were conspiring against me. The elder woman popped away and the came back a minute later with two small china bowls with what looked like a glob of butter in them and two spoons. We took them and she started pushing us out the outer door into the courtyard. "Now shoo, I have a few hundred knights and servants in the main dining hall to feed."

We stepped outside and my hand was getting cold and I looked down at the bowl. I put my finger on the butter and it was quite frigid, I knew that the ice mongers supplied the castle, the butcher, and some of the vendors in the market. They cut the ice from the Whispering Walls Range and the glacier on Heaven's Gate Mountain. It was quite a luxury. It was even rumored that some of the estates in Uptown had ice boxes in their larders.

She smiled and scooped a small bit of it onto her spoon, held it toward me in a prompt then ate it. The smile she had, as she put it in her mouth, was almost seductive. I melted then took a big spoon full and she caught my hand. "You want to take small bites. Too much at once and you can get an ice headache."

I nodded then took a small scoop and brought it to my nose. It smelled sweet, of vanilla. I stuck my tongue out and took a taste. It was like the icing on a sweet roll. I smiled and took a bite. It was freezing and tasted like nothing I had ever eaten. I closed my eyes and savored it as it melted off my spoon in my mouth. I opened my eyes and took the spoon out and said, "Oh my lord. That's amazing!"

She gave me a knowing nod as we both dug in as she started us walking south. Before I knew it, we were stepping out of the archway into the Great Meadow as we ate the sinfully delicious dessert. She had a million questions for me, but I refused to answer unless she answered my own questions in turn.

After a while, we found ourselves stepping onto the bridge across the Hawktail, toward Lord's Way. Celeste stopped a page who was running past, and handed our bowls to him with our thanks. Then she offered her arm to me. We walked slowly and I pulled her to a stop midway over the bridge and released her arm to watch a fisherman float below us in a little rowboat.

I turned to her timidly and asked a question that had been plaguing me, "Why are you so nice to me Celeste?"

She tucked my hand back into the crook of her arm and just watched the man in the boat below us cast his line. She shrugged and said simply, "Because I like you."

That answer seemed so loaded to me for some reason, but before I could ask her to elaborate, something cold and wet hit my cheek. We both looked up as the heavens opened and rain started falling all around us. RAIN!

We were all smiles, staring up at the sky and laughing. People were coming out of buildings in Uptown to look at the sky in wonder. It isn't that rain is unheard of but this far out to the Fringe, near the uninhabitable lands, we only saw rain two or three times a year. Not like they got in the central area or in the mountains. I've even only seen snow twice in my life here.

If it weren't for Dragontooth Lake, the streams, and rivers that we use for irrigation of the crops, and the plentiful ground water, Wexbury would not exist.

There is virtually no place in the habitable lands that you can't dig a shallow well to get water, except the deserts. And it is why the grasslands don't dry out. The scholars say that there was no way that those oceans I saw on that picture were all vaporized during the Great Impact. They believe that the continental shelf is resting on a subsurface ocean, which has been proved out by deep drilling.

But rain... rain was free water with no effort. It was a treat as amazing as the ice cream had been. There were rain gutter systems, water barrels, and troughs all throughout the keep to capture this gift.

I watched as Celeste untied her hair and let it fan out down her back as she ran her fingers through it like a river of flame. It was mesmerizing. I followed suit, and we just stood on the bridge with our arms spread wide, eyes to the sky and reveled in the rain as we slowly spun.

I glanced over. She was so beautiful, and almost innocent looking in the rain.

CHAPTER 11 – SQUIRES

After the storm, which lasted two hours, where we were even treated to a couple lightning bolts with rolling thunder, we met with mother and Jace at a beautiful manor. It was huge, we could have fit our entire cottage in one of the three bedrooms in it. It was, as Duke Fredrick stated, directly outside the main castle gates in Uptown. It was the prime location, you walked off the lush grounds and into the main arch. I wondered how Bernadine had kept it vacant for more than twenty years.

Then we said our good nights and we met with Lady Verna and Sir Kristof at the livery. They were speaking with possibly the thinnest boy I had ever seen. Gangly would be an overstatement. He had extremely short, light blonde hair and I swear his freckles were so numerous they formed one huge freckle on his face. The only thing that broke them up was a severe case of acne. He had a pack on his back with tubes or wires or something strapped to his arms going down to some gloves. He was dressed in a noble's tunic that draped on his thin frame and he had it tied off at the waist with a belt that had at least a dozen pouches. Over the top of it all he had the sash of a Squire with the crest of Wexbury, and house crest of Kristof and Verna.

Don't get me wrong, I thought the guy was cute in an awkward way and he had a smile of excitement that seemed to be full on, full time.

The knights greeted us and clasped my arm like they would a peer. The Verna said, "Lady Celeste, Squire Laney, we'd like to introduce Kristof's new squire, Bexington."

The young man offered his left arm to Celeste as she offered her right. His gear squeaked as he switched arms and then bowed slightly, almost headbutting her as he said, "Lady." Then he offered his hand to me and I shook as he repeated, "Lady." We couldn't help but smile at the poor boy. I no longer felt the most awkward person in the group.

I bowed slightly. "My Lord."

Celeste looked about to say something, but Verna beat her to the punch as she backhanded my shoulder lightly. "None of this Lord and Lady stuff you two. It gets tedious. All knights are nobles, and we'd get nothing done if we played the titles game. That's not to say we don't follow social protocol in non-casual situations, it is paramount then, but among our group, do not. Also, if any knight gives you leave to ignore it, or prefers to enforce it, then do as they ask."

Then she got a grin on her face at the next part. "And Laney, you do not bow to Bex anyway. He is a baron and you a baroness, the same station, yet you actually outrank him as Techno Knight Ascendant as he is just Knight Ascendant."

Celeste grinned at her friend. "Well said." Verna playfully inclined her head to my Lady.

I stood tall and then said to the young man, "Laney is just fine.

Should I call you Bexington?"

He had a toothy grin for the group. "Bex, please. It is less cumbersome and more dashing."

I couldn't help but smile, he reminded me of Jace so much, with his enthusiasm. I assured him, "Quite." Which just got a smile from Verna and Kristof.

Then Celeste offered, "Celeste." He nodded and stopped himself from bowing again. Then she said to the group, "We need to get into some dry clothes and I need to get Laney here situated in my quarters. We also need to get Laney's family moved tomorrow. Will we see you on the training grounds tomorrow afternoon?"

Verna shook her head and offered, "Take Bex with you tomorrow, he's got able hands and a strong back. It will be easier if we train the two concurrently, then we don't have to go over the same orientation material up front. Until they have to split Laney off for Techromancer training with that magic shit you do. And I'm sure she'll need education too."

Celeste grinned at the 'magic shit' then beamed a proud smile at her. "Laney can read. And I'm sure she knows her maths as well?"

I nodded and blushed. "Mother insisted that Jace and I were learned."

Kristof boomed out, "Grand!" You could tell that he, like my mother, was a proponent of everyone in the village getting a basic education.

Celeste inclined her head at the three and said, "On the morrow then." Then to Bex she added, "We will be in the livery courtyard at daybreak." He nodded.

Then she offered her arm to me again. I timidly took it, in front of her peers, and she strode off with me in tow.

I don't know what I was expecting, I'd never seen a noble's quarters before. And I still wasn't sure I had. This was a knight's quarters, they were the entire south end of the castle closest the livery stable. I knew from stories in Cheap Quarter that the knights who chose to bunk there instead of living in a manor, were set up three to a room, unless they were married, then they had their own quarters. Squires would bunk in the small anterooms attached to the chambers.

They were situated close to the livery in case of emergencies, that way they could mobilize as quickly as possible. Twice a year they had war drills, which were a wonder to see. Over a hundred knights came thundering out of the castle to the huge bellows powered war horns of the keep. Their charger's hooves pounding the cobblestones and shaking the ground as they passed through the north and south portcullis. The Techno Knights leading the charge.

Unlike any other realm except the Capitol up in Highland Keep, we were possessed of four Techno Knights in our ranks. Only the capitol itself had more, with eight among their one thousand Knights of the Realm.

It was things like this that that made Wexbury so special. We were the third smallest keep in the eleven realms but had the fourth largest defensive force. One hundred and fifty Knights of the Realm and seventy in reserve. I learned today, through our talks, that Celeste was in charge of the mobile battalion. Whereas Techno Knight Tiberius was in charge of the home defense battalion. Then we had two other techno knights that could take over if the leaders fell. May that tragedy never occur.

Other keeps usually had but one Techno Knight as Techromancers were vital to the upkeep and modernization to any Keep and could not be spared for defense. Except Solomon Keep, across the Whispering Walls, who had two Techno Knights, and the second largest fighting force in all the realms.

Solomon was the jewel of the Lower Ten; The ten realms in the largest expanse of the inhabitable Lands of Sparo, or Lands of Hope, that were across The Gap from Highland realm. Soloman was located at the south of the Great Sea. A lake so immense, it was over two hundred miles long and over a hundred wide. It was the largest known body of water on the surface of the planet and was surrounded on all sides by mountains. What a sight that would be to see, water all the way to the horizon, fed off the mammoth glaciers on Heaven's Gate.

We passed a young page stationed in the long hall, which I knew was repeated on all levels of this wing of the castle. Then we walked past seven arched doors before entering the one at the end, Celeste's quarters.

I looked around, the living chamber was twice the size of our

cottage and was adorned with beautiful wood furniture and chests.
Tapestries hung on the walls to give warmth and life, in all the rich
colors of nature, to the otherwise cold and lifeless stone walls.
Thick rugs and runners adorned the marble floors that shone with a
high polish.

A great fireplace commanded the inner wall with paintings of
the forest, and of a young Techromancer Donovan, a beautiful Lady,
a boy of maybe five, and a cute red headed girl around six or seven
who had a mischievous smile on her face that matched Celeste's.

I turned toward the outer wall to the east, and there were the
three smaller alcoves. I could see draperies pulled aside on one and
could see a grand bed on four posts through it and blushed.
Celeste's sleeping chamber. There were two small arches at the far
end of the quarters with iron bound oak doors. There were three
narrow, operable stained glass windows, letting in the natural light
on the far wall.

I glanced back at the other two alcoves that had heavy drapes
hiding the small rooms beyond. "How many others share the rooms
here?"

She smiled at me and looked a little embarrassed, and said as if
she were reading my mind, "As commander of the mobile battalion,
I have private chambers."

I blinked at her and looked around again, my eyes landing on the
two great brass chandeliers above, realizing the dozens of glass
domes in them were electric lights and not gas or candle powered. I

stuttered, "All this space?" I would be alone with my Lady?

She chuckled. "This is actually one of the smallest. I chose it because it is one of only two on the outer wall that have an unobstructed view of the Grove and Whispering Forest below. That is why the windows are so narrow, too narrow for an enemy to enter even if they are somehow able to attack from the Grove and scale sixty feet of sheer polished granite. There are steel shutters without, that can be closed to prevent projectile attacks."

She grabbed both of my hands and walked backward with a grin. "Would you like to see your antechamber my squire?"

I grinned in excitement, and that excitement bled through in my voice as I said, "Very much so."

She pulled me through the second heavy oak door at the end of the great room. There was a space as large as my cottage with three small alcoves large enough for someone to sleep on a straw mattress.

I knew this is where the squires for the three knights that would usually be assigned to the chambers would live. Two alcoves had fine cushions in them with dozens of colorful pillows. The other had been fitted with a great chest with many drawers and a cushioned chair in front of it with a mirror of finely polished silver above the chest with a silver tray that had a variety of brushes and combs on it.

Obviously none of this was what was normally in any of the sleeping spots.

But the thing that held my attention was the grand bed that looked a smaller version of what Celeste had in her space. Four great posts and a canopy of white fabric that was lit up in an array of soft colors cast by the single thin, operable stained glass window on the south wall. There was a fine white bedspread on it and more pillows than a single person could ever hope to use.

There was a thick forest green rug covering the stone floor in the place with only the fringes of the marble visible at the edges. There were various antique chests and what looked like a small writing table with a matching chair and a reading lamp. I had never seen such finery.

She was searching my eyes then she reached over and turned a knob on the wall and the small chandelier chained high in the anteroom sprang to life, lighting the room. It had electric lighting as well. She shrugged and asked, "Do you like? It was the best I could have done since Sixth Day. Father knew the Duke would approve your squire appointment.

I looked at her in disbelief then back at the room. Logically I had known my life had changed before, but for some reason this brought it all home for me. This was mine. This was my life now, Cheap Quarter left behind. I was beholden to a Lady of the Court. An angel that had taken my family into this new world.

I nodded with tears in my eyes and she looked distressed and pulled me to her as I sobbed uncontrollably. I still don't know why. I buried my face in her tunic as I cried, and my Lady patiently held me. Stroking my hair and murmuring things like, "Shhh... I know Laney. It's okay." And "I felt the same so long ago."

Finally, I pushed away and looked down. "I'm sorry. I don't know what came over me."

She smiled and shrugged. "It is a lot to process. But this is your space now."

I looked at the bed and pushed my hand down into the mattress. It was soft with some sort of springy support. It wasn't packed with straw. And felt to be only padded by goose down the top couple inches. I grinned at her and she nodded and I launched myself onto it. The bedspread was of the finest cotton stuffed with goose down and I bounced on the bed when I landed.

She chuckled at me as I beamed at her. Then I thought about how dirty I was from the day's activities and still slightly damp from our excursion in the rain earlier and scurried off the finery. I smoothed it down with my hands. She was just watching me with an unreadable expression on her face.

Then she turned away when I heard a light knocking at the door. "Be right back." She gave me a grin and stepped out of the anteroom and crossed the great room to the door and said, "Enter." A young woman came in and mumbled something to her and handed her some parcels wrapped in paper. She bowed and left the room in a hurry.

Celeste rejoined me and handed me the parcels. "The seamstress has finished one outfit for you and one for your training. The others will follow in the next few days." She nudged her chin to the parcels. I sat them on the bed and hurriedly opened them. There was a grand dress in the colors of the realm, with some accessories I didn't know what to do with. And a pair of shoes that were of the finest calfskin with that odd coating on the soles. It looked like the type of outfit a lady wore from day to day.

I squinted at the dress then at her, then said, "There isn't much utility to a dress."

She actually laughed out loud at that. "No, but I bet it will look pretty on you. I think that is father's doing."

Then I looked at the other packages. Some trousers made of thick canvas-like material with multiple pockets and flaps. A tunic as fine as any I have seen. Then I paused and lifted a sash. I blinked at it then ran my fingers timidly along the emblems embroidered on it. The crest of the realm with a sword and lightning bolt crossed before it, with the addition of a small silver star, the crest of a Techno Knight Ascendant! And the coat of arms of the House of Celeste, marking me as hers.

I pulled it over my head and smiled and dashed over to the mirror. I was no longer Laney Herder. In her place stood a Squire of the Realm. I turned to where Celeste had been just standing silently, watching me. I smiled at her and ran my fingers along her coat of arms on the sash. "I'm of your house."

She nodded then said softly, "Take a minute to clean up and get into your new clothing. Perhaps... maybe we can just call down to the kitchen for a meal in our quarters here. It would be nice to just sit and decompress from all of the excitement of the day."

I nodded and she stepped out of the room and called back as she wandered out, "There is a washroom with running water in the door next to yours. You go first. I need to inform the page in the hall of your station."

Running water? I dashed out and into the other room, there was a basin there and two chains above it. I pulled tentatively on one of the chains and water started flowing from a cut in the granite in a smooth sheet into the basin. I felt the cool water. When I released the chain, the water continued to flow for a minute before stopping. I pulled the other chain and the flow started again and I was floored when I put my hand in the stream and it was warm!

I giggled to myself at the wonder of water inside of the building. I had only seen something like this at the hospital. Only it was just cold water there. It was a whole different world here. I looked at the polished silver mirror over the basin. Then behind me where there was a seat that had a box suspended high on the wall with another chain. I pulled the chain and I heard water under the seat flowing. I pulled up the seats, there were two. And looked into another basin filling with water.

I pondered this a minute then wondered why they needed two basins. One that allowed the water to flow away and one that held the water until you pulled the chain. Was it just opulence to have two rather than just plug the other one?

I grabbed one of the many washcloths and towels from a stack and was about to kneel and start washing in the basin, but all the sounds of flowing water reminded me that it had been hours since I relieved myself and I begun to shimmy. So I walked out into the great room in search of a chamber pot. There wasn't one, so I looked in my chamber, there wasn't one, but there was a basin with a pitcher of water in it. I knew that was for washing myself in my own room.

I danced over to Celeste's alcove and peered in from the great room and there was no chamber pot I could see and I didn't want to intrude into her space without permission. I headed back to my room to wait for her to return. I took two steps when she walked back in.

I did a little shimmy dance and scrunched up my face at her. "I can't seem to find a chamber pot."

Her eyes glittered in extreme amusement, and I said, "I'm glad my bladder amuses you." Then I looked at the floor quickly for being so flippant.

She reached out and took my hand. "Follow me." She led me back into the washroom and pointed at the seat and pulled up the top seat. The second one had a hole in it.

She said, "It is an auto-pot. Sit there and umm do your thing. When you are done pull the chain and it all gets washed down into the city sewers. If you umm, you know. Then there is a stack of soft papers that you can clean yourself off with and they just get washed down to the sewers too." It was far too cute how uncomfortable she was talking about bodily functions.

But then I paled. Shit! I was about to wash my face in that basin! It was an indoor outhouse. I wondered why they kept water in the basin, I'd ask later when I wasn't blushing in embarrassment. I whispered, "You must think me a barbarian."

She shook her head and said plainly, "No, I just forget how I reacted to all of this all those years ago. It is a different world, and I'm still not sure I am suited for it."

I took her hand and was immediately afraid of being so bold and told her, "You are a Lady no matter your past. Tell me about how you came to be of this world?"

She squeezed my hand once and smiled. "I will trade you that story for the story of how a young herder came about finding a village of the Before Times."

I nodded back then smiled and pushed her gently by the waist out the door and spit into my hand, "Done. But not until I pee!" She grinned at me then looked at my hand then spit into hers and shook, sealing our pact and then I shut the door quickly in her face and heard her giggle at my antics. The lady's giggle was so contrary to a knight, but something genuinely hers and a pleasure to hear.

Okay, I stared at the auto-pot as I dropped my trousers and mumbled the battle cry of the Hero of the Realm... my grandfather, "To the line! We shall not toil!" I sat.

Not going to share that different experience with you but to say, it was different. I did like that I didn't have to carry the chamber pot outside to drain it. I think I liked auto-pots.

I cleaned up in the other basin with the warm water that was heavenly. I even cleaned out my tangled mess of hair the best I could. Then I toweled off and dried my hair the best I could. I saw a little basket with used towels and dropped mine into it. I'd clean those and find where to hang them out later after we ate.

I redressed then snuck out and into my room, I saw her taking her armor off in her bed chamber and hanging each piece on hooks on the wall. I shut my door and looked at the new clothing that was mine. I hadn't paid a single iron penny for them. That sort of made me pause. Then the people of the realm paid for it.

A little rational voice in my head said, "Well of course they did, that is why they tithe, you are a squire of the realm now Laney and you defend those same people." I nodded once to myself and just needed to have the last word over myself and said, "Okay, but I don't have to like it." Take that rational me!

I looked at the dress for a long time then sighed and folded it and placed it into one of the drawers. Then I went to put on the new trousers and paused and looked at the underpants in the miscellaneous accessories. I squinted at them, daring myself. Mother had a pair she always wore.

I put them on then the socks and pulled up my new trousers. They seemed to conform to me. Well, they were made for me so I guess they would. I put on the belt that had so many useful pouches, then the new tunic that felt really nice against my skin.

Then I put on the heavy boots, I was surprised how well they fit and that they seemed to be padded and insulated. Finally, I pulled the sash on. I was proud to wear it.

I put the rest of the clothing into the drawers then put my dirties in a basket by the door. I started out, when the mirror caught my eye, and the brushes below it on the tray. I looked at the door then back at the brushes and I hurried over and brushed my hair.

I closed my eyes and enjoyed the pampering. When I could brush the entire length without any snarling I looked into the mirror and saw someone unfamiliar. I blushed and then noted some ribbons and hair clips on the tray. I clipped my bangs out of my eyes and then took a deep breath and stepped out.

I wasn't prepared. My Lady was in a set of dark green silk pajamas that did nothing to hide her feminine assets. A matching top and pants. She has a loose gold silk robe over them. I stopped breathing. I had never seen her out of her armor besides that one time in the baths. And even though she was naked then, this seemed more... more something... I don't know, I wasn't thinking much.

She smiled at me and seemed to sigh. "You look amazing Laney. I forgot we don't have any night clothes for you yet. You can use some of mine until we get some. Though it will look like a tent on you." She grinned with that.

That snapped me out of my inappropriate attraction as I smiled at her in shock. "Hey! I'm not that small!" Then I looked down.

"You look spectacular."

She looked at the door and then at me. "What would you like to eat? This is your day, we need to have our own quiet celebration and relax. Tomorrow will be just as hectic."

I shrugged. "Just some soup or stew." Then I felt like a pig and asked, "And bread?"

She regarded me for a moment then she did that winking thing again that made my eyes go weak. "Soup and sandwiches it is."

She went to the door and opened it and cleared her throat and the page was suddenly there. She murmured something to him and he dashed off. She had me sit on a long lounge in front of a low table by the fireplace. She set up a small fire burning in it and there was a knock at the door when she was done. She said, "Enter." The page and a girl dressed in the white of the kitchen staff walked in and placed two platters down on the table and the left.

Then I had some of the richest tomato soup and roast beef sandwiches with my Lady. We shared our stories as we ate. It was well past late chime when I yawned. She grinned and put the platters in the hall before she disappeared into her space. She came back out with a silky nightdress and handed it to me.

She placed her forehead against mine then said as she locked eyes with me. "Get a good night's sleep. I'll see you in the morning." All I could do was nod, feeling her hot breath on my face. Then she was gone. I watched her until she pulled her drapes shut.

I went into my room and changed into the nightdress, it pooled at my feet but it was silky on my skin, and it smelled like Celeste. I laid in the overly soft bed for a long time, but couldn't sleep. It all felt wrong.

I wound up back in the great room, by the embers of the fire, lying on the lounge. I just stared blankly at the red glow of the coals. I wasn't really thinking, I just watched the embers with that sense that something was wrong. I understood finally. I was alone.

The lounge shifted and I looked over at the shadowy form of Celeste. She whispered, "What is it, Laney? Are you okay?"

I shrugged. "I don't know. It is stupid but, I have never slept alone. My whole life I shared a mattress with mother then Jace when he was born. I felt... alone... in that room."

She just nodded sadly at me then she laid down behind me. She wrapped an arm around my waist and whispered, "Get some sleep, Laney."

I sat almost paralyzed, feeling the heat of her body. I listened to her breathing even out as she drifted off. I smiled, I didn't feel alone anymore. I drifted off to sleep with a content smile on my face.

CHAPTER 12 – IT WAS MY HOME

I woke up screaming. The massive monolith behind me was cracking and my body was burning. There was so much energy flowing into me then directed to the oncoming enemy. Someone had my shoulders, shaking me gently. "Laney! Laney wake up!" I could still feel the searing pain as I focused and realized I was in Celeste's chambers on the lounge. But it all seemed so real, and there was a shadowed beast with the eyes overflowing with red energies which had been approaching like a specter.

I swallowed and focused on Celeste as the dream faded away. I sat up. "Sorry. It was a nightmare. Monoliths, red-eyed monsters, and pain."

She nodded then said, "You are safe now. It was just a dream."

I nodded and sat up and looked at her sheepishly. She slid off the lounge and smiled. "It's time to get up anyway. Another hectic day of running around in circles lays ahead of us. I promise it will all settle down soon and we can get into a training routine between squiring and magic training."

I smiled at the magic training part. I asked, "Does that happen... umm... in the library?"

She got a sly smile on her face. "Sometimes, but mostly it will be gauging your abilities and limits at first. But the library of the scrolls is open to you anytime you wish to visit. You need to realize you are both noble and a magic user now Laney. It is your right to seek knowledge when you wish to."

I grinned and tried to hide it behind my hand. I could see all the wonders of the library whenever I wished! I watched as she headed to her alcove. "Get ready and we'll head out." Then she added, "You will be required to wear your squire clothing anytime we are on duty. Anytime you are in public it needs to be either your uniform or a dress. Social protocol.

I nodded. I had the one set of clothes that the seamstress sent yesterday, more were supposed to come. I went to get dressed. I dressed quickly and then froze when I looked at the nightdress I had laid on my bed. Wait, Celeste had laid with me on the lounge all night so I didn't feel alone?

I checked my hair and brushed it and pulled it back and tied it in a ponytail with an emerald ribbon. I made sure I looked my best, I didn't want to make my Lady look bad.

The padded boots I slipped on last were a wonder. It was as if I were walking in calfskin with no soles. That flexible material would bend with me no matter which direction I twisted or stepped. Typically a cobbler would take three of four layers of toughened rawhide, glue and stitch them together, then sew those to the bottoms of your shoes.

When I stepped out, Celeste was walking back to the main door. She smiled and said, "I sent the page out to the livery to have them saddle our horses." She went back and sat on a chair by her bed and I watched in fascination as she first checked each armor piece, polished any burnished spots with a cloth and beeswax. Then went about gearing up over her light clothes.

Then once she was satisfied she slipped on a tunic and sash. The last thing she did was to lash on her scabbard and test drawing her sword.

Then she prompted me, "Well?"

I didn't know what to say. "Beautiful? Deadly?"

She looked to the ceiling and grinned. "I think I can live with that." Then she offered her elbow. "Shall we see about getting your belongings?"

I placed my fingers on her elbow and curtsied to be cute. She chuckled and we headed out. I don't know why she always insisted on leading me around on her arm, but I wasn't complaining one bit. She made me feel special. Like I was somebody.

We got out to the livery and Bex was already there and we said our good mornings. He had a grand chestnut colored charger by the lead. Celeste excused herself and I stepped up to Bex and his horse. I put a hand out toward the horse's flank. "May I?"

He nodded enthusiastically. "My father insisted on buying Shadow here. He was the largest charger in the herd and father told me it was important for me to make an impression on the other knights since I'm not very strong, or coordinated, or... Well anyway, Shadow is the largest horse in all the realm."

I patted the horses flank, he was at least a hand taller than Celeste's. He snuffled and brought his muzzle down to me. I stroked the soft fur between his eyes. "You're a handsome fellow Shadow." Then I looked at Bex. "He's beautiful."

He looked genuinely proud of his horse. Then he said to me as Celeste walked up behind him. "You're pretty tiny, Laney, and probably need an added advantage too. You are a baroness, so maybe one day you'll have a steed as grand as mine."

I smiled at him as Celeste stopped beside Shadow with her Charger and Goliath. Goliath stood two hands over Shadow. I grinned as Bex's eyes went wide at the size of my Percheron. I looked at the new war saddle on him. Good lord, it looked magnificent against his black hide. I said with a wink to Celeste, who was grinning like an idiot at what Bex had just said, "Maybe one day. Until then, I have Goliath."

I looked up at the saddle then down to my short legs and saw a problem. I looked at the gangly squire who was just staring at my horse, and asked him, "Bex, could you give me a boost, I've never ridden him with a saddle."

He turned away and smiled at me then stepped over to Celeste's Charger and bent and cupped his hands. I tried to cut back my giggle as Celeste said, "Thank you squire, but I'm capable of mounting Canter myself." In one swift motion, she was up in the saddle and her feet in the stirrups. Just using her legs she had Canter side step away from us as she adjusted her gauntlets before even grabbing the reins.

I stood by Goliath and us women just watched as the gears

turned in the young man's head then he shook himself out of it. He quickly squatted and I stepped into his cupped hands and he hoisted me up. It felt like I went up forever before I could swing a leg over and get seated.

Then he finally found his words. "I thought you were a serf until yesterday." It came out like a question, but I just shrugged. He asked, genuinely curious, "Where did you get such a monster?"

I checked my feet in the stirrups and took the reins and urged my boy forward. "Spoils of war."

He squinted up at me as I moved beside Celeste then smiled at the perceived joke. "Pull the other one."

Celeste laughed out loud as she called back to him as we started toward the courtyard archway. "She has more kills than seven of the knights of the realm."

The poor boy paled and Celeste urged her horse into a gallop. "Hyah!"

I loosened the reins so I could urge Goliath, but he was already in motion. He was all muscle, power, and grace as I almost got whiplash when he galloped up to Celeste's side. I was pleasantly surprised that with my horse's extra height, it put us at eye level with each other. The ground looked a hundred feet below me.

She shared a chuckle with me as we looked back to see Bex hurriedly mounting his steed and hustling to catch up as we stopped at the gates, looking out onto Lord's Way.

He finally wound up on my left as I was on Celeste's left. Then

he said with a crooked grin and said to me with humor in his voice,
"You could have at least stopped me before I put both feet in my
mouth. Us new squires have to stick together. The other three are
almost ready to get their Knighthood."

That made me remember a question I wanted to ask my Lady.
"How long does one serve as a squire?"

She said, "Five years before a squire obtains knighthood.
Quicker if they prove themselves capable of defending the realm
sooner."

I know she was just two years past majority. "But you are
commander of the mobile battalion and are just two years past
majority."

She chuckled, but Bex answered for her. "You can be become
squire at fifteen. Then you would be a knight at twenty. But not
Lady Celeste. Surely you have heard the tales of her Squireship?" I
shook my head and he smiled and she blushed as he explained, "The
youngest Techno Knight Ascendant in the realm. On her fifteenth
birthday, she was named Squire. At seventeen her knight was in the
group who held the gates at York Keep when they called for the aid
of Wexbury. They were being overrun by a large group of
marauders that were organized under the commander known as the
Reaper."

I paled. That was four years ago, the time of the Great Raid of
York. The Reaper lead the Horde, a group of a hundred and fifty
marauders. York lost forty knights and Wexbury and Flatlash

answered the calls for aid. Flatlash lost ten knights, and Wexbury lost four in the battle at the gates of York Keep, but we liberated the keep.

He said with pride, "The Horde was about to break the line, and Celeste's knight, Sir Edwin, had already fallen valiantly to the prior enemy probing attack."

He glanced at Celeste, then me, and lowered his voice. "It is said that a squire stepped out onto the battlefield to face the Horde and challenged the Reaper to single armed combat. This woman stood toe to toe with the man, crossing swords. They say you could see her sword shining for miles as she ignited. On her next slash, she cut through the enemy's broadsword with her magicked blade and ended the man."

I squinted at both of them and called bullshit. "All know the tale of the death of the Reaper. Sir Edwin had challenged him and they battled for hours and with a mighty blow they killed each other. Edwin's last act of valor was freeing York." They didn't say anything and I prompted, "Right?"

Bex shrugged. "Then explain Lady Celeste gaining the mantle of Techno Knight at seventeen and being awarded the command of the mobile battalion when she reached majority."

I squinted at them then asked my Lady, "Is it true?"

She didn't make eye contact and only said, "Until the day I die, I will swear upon the bravery of Sir Edwin." That was all she said, and it wasn't really an answer, now was it?

We were about to leave the castle grounds when Jace came running out to us wearing the uniform of a page and the sash of a Messenger of the Court. He had already started his duties. He attempted a bow as he panted, looked up at Celeste, and handed a parchment up to her. He gasped out, "Lady... Celeste... Assayer Bernadine asked me to deliver this before you left today."

Celeste grinned down at him. "Thank you, Jace. You look very handsome in your uniform." He blushed then bowed again and ran back toward the castle. He was full of energy.

My Lady looked at the parchment and then smiled. "You may wish to handle this Laney." She handed it to me and I scanned over it and smiled like a mad woman, rolled it up, and slid it into one of the four saddle bags on my new war saddle.

Then we urged our horses forward I said, "Thanks for joining us today Bex. We don't own much, but the more hands, the more quickly we can do this."

Celeste nodded her thanks too but added, "We'll mostly be supervising the porters except for any personal items you may hold dear."

I was almost blushing at the looks we were getting from people as we passed by. Instead of those odd looks of curiosity, when I was dressed in my regular clothes. Now it was that look of awe and respect which I always had whenever a knight rode past.

Bex was eating it up. I'm sure the awkward Lord enjoyed the respect. I tried to shrink down in the saddle away from the looks.

Celeste reprimanded me under her breath, "Sit tall Laney. You represent the realm now." I nodded and took a deep breath and sat tall in the saddle, I would not embarrass her. She didn't look at me but nodded once and with a little smile said, "Better,"

We turned onto my lane and for some reason that struck me as a sad notion. This was possibly the last time I would be doing that. This place I had known my entire life was no longer my home. I felt a physical pain in my chest as my heart ached at the realization. Shouldn't I feel elated to be moving up in station?

I made sure to say good morning to all my neighbors by name as we passed. Most were happy to see me, a couple had looks of disgust on their faces that I had never seen before. We got to my cottage and it appeared so very small to me for the first time in my life. There were two large wagons in front of it in the lane, with four porters standing by. I almost snorted, what we had would fit in one with room to spare.

We were one of the few families that had double lots like this. In all of Cheap Quarter, there were only twenty-five like ours. They were assigned to vegetable gardeners or small animal herders like us. The only lots bigger were the three along the keep's wall, spreading out from the gates. Those were for grapes, strawberries, blackberries, and potatoes. The three richest people in Cheap Quarter.

Combined with the few vegetable gardens in Mid-End, and the spices almost everyone grew in their window boxes, the herders and gardeners of Cheap Quarter and the fishermen of the inner river were the only sources of fresh food if the keep were ever under siege and we were cut off from outside supplies.

There were supplies enough and stores of food in the Warehouse District by the Market, and in the castle, to ration to all the people of the keep for twelve months. With us, we could stretch that to eighteen months.

I looked at the place. The cottage itself was like the others, fifteen feet square, constructed of stone and timbers with tiny glass windows inset on three sides. The roof overhang that doubled as a firewood overhang and stable for one horse. A normal lot was twenty feet square while ours was forty by forty-five. What little land remained on our lot had chicken coops and the small makeshift pig pen we had cobbled together for the hogs until we sold them.

I took a moment to take it all in as Celeste and Bex dismounted. I blinked and looked down and Celeste was looking up at me with a tinge of concern in her questioning face. I shrugged and said, my voice cracking a bit as my eyes watered, "It's my home." Some sort of understanding, like that of a kindred spirit, crossed her face and she just nodded once then put her hands up toward me.

I smiled at her, she treated me like I was so fragile, but I wasn't going to argue with a woman who looked that cute and dangerous all at the same time. I swung my leg over and hopped down and she lowered me to the ground by my waist like I didn't weigh anything.

She looked around then made an ushering motion with her hands toward the door and I led them in, porters trailing behind us. She said, "Any gear or supplies needed to tend the chickens and those big hogs out there needs to be left behind for the new herder. The porters will do an inventory after we get packed up so that your mother can be compensated fairly for the livestock and supplies."

I nodded absently as I looked around at the place. She said, "Go ahead and collect any personal mementos that you or your mother may need right away. The rest will be shipped to your family manor."

I sat on the bed and pulled the quilt up to my face and inhaled. It smelled of mother and home. I draped it over my arm and looked around. We didn't really own too much. I looked at her and then pointed at mother's previously always locked chest. "That's mother's most precious things. I think they are from her prior life as a Lady." That still sounded surreal to me.

She nodded then pointed to a porter then the chest. "That needs to be delivered to Lady Margret first thing." The boy nodded and grabbed it and headed out.

I grabbed my tool pouch and slung it over my shoulder. This got a raised eyebrow of curiosity from my Lady. I unslung it and opened the flap for her and Bex to look in. "It is my scavenging tools. It was my father's kit."

Bex whistled and held up the spyglass and a brass device I was never quite sure what it was. Celeste arched an eyebrow. "Sextant?"

I shrugged. "I'm not quite sure. Some of the tools, I don't know what they are for."

Bex looked excited about some of my gear. I hung it back over my shoulder and looked around. Was there anything else I needed? There was my saddle outside, but I had a war saddle now. The porters started packing up the heater and my eyes fell to the floorboards.

I stepped toward them then hesitated. Would we be in trouble for this? Celeste furrowed her brow. "What is it?"

I shrugged and admitted it to her. Somebody was going to find it so I may as well come clean. "Our treasure."

Bex perked up at that and my Lady repeated, "Your treasure." I nodded and stepped over and got on my knees.

I paused as I reached down. "Nobody knows we have these." Then I pulled up the loose floorboard and pulled the chest out. I sat it in front of Celeste and placed my hand on top of hers when she went to open it. I pleaded with my eyes. "If we are to be punished for having these, mother won't survive the whipping post. I will take the lashes for the family."

The furrows in her brow deepened and she looked a little concerned as she glanced at the porters then Bex then me. Bex cleared his throat. "Give us the room please." The porters cleared out. I was a little saddened to see that they already had most of our stuff already packed up and moved out. We had so little to mark our lives.

When they shut the door, Celeste gently grabbed my hand, which was still covering hers and moved it to the side. She hesitated. "What is it, Laney?"

I whispered, "Our greatest family treasure."

She steeled herself and opened the chest to reveal our collection of tomes. When I was younger we had but four. But somehow mother obtained more and more over the years to read to us and to give us lessons and have Jace and I read to her. I don't know where she kept getting them or where they came from. But our tiny library grew from those original four.

I I reached out and ran my fingers lovingly along the cracking and faded spines and whispered reverently, "Knowledge."

Bex was all smiles and Celeste may as well have been carved from stone as she pulled out a couple and looked at the titles. Then she finally smiled and pulled out a child's tome with its half missing cover and brittle pages. One of the one's mother used to teach us letters. Each page had a letter in the alphabet, then a colorful caricature of an animal who's name started with the letter.

I grinned at it. "Mother used that to teach me the letters. P is my favorite." She flipped through carefully, looking at the amazing animals from the Before Times. It is said that thousands, if not millions of species were wiped from the Earth. Like the A for Aardvark, and the L for Lion. Then she stopped on P and gave me a genuine smile.

I said in a reflective tone, "P is for platypus."

She looked at the picture. "What kind of animal is it? It has the bill of a duck and the tail of a beaver."

I shrugged. "One of the many creatures lost to the Impact. It looks to be a noble animal that had evolved to overcome any adversity with its varied evolution. I imagine it was quite adaptable... and formidable like a wolverine." She nodded in agreement with my assessment as she looked at the picture.

She thumbed through the other pages, stopping at T for tiger. A great striped feline, like the cougars and lynx which still exist. Cousins to the little barn cat strays that infest Cheap Quarter and the Trough. They are tolerated because they keep the rat and mouse population down to almost nothing. Some people even treat them as pets.

Bex stopped her on the last page. "A striped horse?" Then he read, "Zebra." We were all silent when she shut the tome, then Bex murmured. "All the wonders lost to us... oh, to have lived in that time." We nodded.

Celeste put it back in the chest and shut it then produced a stick of red wax and a ring from a tunic pocket. I saw emerald energy shimmering as it dripped from her eyes and the end of the wax heated. She pushed the stick across the seam of the lid and then pushed the ring into the soft wax, leaving behind her house crest.

She placed the wax and ring back into her tunic pocket then called out as her beautiful energies faded, "Porter." A young man came in quickly and inclined his head in a bow. She made sure he saw the seal on the chest. "This is to go directly to Squire Laney's quarters. It is her family treasure so treat it as such." He nodded, took the chest, and went back out.

I looked nervously at her. "How will I be punished?"

She shook her head. "It is not a crime to have a tome or scroll. They are salvage like anything from the Before. And it is certainly no crime to seek knowledge. True, the scholars would want the tomes in the library of the Techromancy Scrolls, but it is no law. They pay in gold coin for any writings of the great wizards of the Before."

Then she grinned at me. "As you said, it is your family's treasure. And what a treasure it is." I thought about that, mother wouldn't be in trouble for hiding them away? Then I wondered. Now that I supposedly had access to the great library. Would we need them anymore?

I looked around and said, "That's really it." They both looked around the small space then followed me outside. I murmured, "I'll need to sell my new saddle."

I stuffed the quilt into a saddle bag and Celeste chuckled when I failed to mount, and offered her cupped hands. She teased, "We'll need to get you a little booster stool or a smaller horse more your size."

I looked down at her, trying hard not to smile as I said, "Oh hush you, Goliath is mine." I don't know why I had such pride in a horse I had owned less than a week. I think it was because he was truly mine. Borne out through the most terrifying day of my life.

She was nothing but teasing grins as she mounted her charger like he was part of her. Bex wasn't quite as smooth. He looked at us and smiled. "I thought I'd be doing heavy lifting all morning." Then his smile faltered and looked back at the cottage with an almost upset look on his face. I think he was just then realizing the disparity between the life of the serfs and the nobles.

I remembered the parchment in my saddlebags and then turned Goliath and headed up a cross lane toward the Belt, Celeste and Bex at either side. Two lanes up I stopped at a rabbit farm on a double lot. A handsomely rugged, muscled man looked up from tending the hutches. He quickly stuffed a rabbit in a cage and wiped his hands on his tunic as he hustled over.

His eyes went wide when he saw me then he looked at the others and bowed. "My Ladies, My Lord." His eyes drifted up to mine. "What can I do for you today?"

I rolled my eyes and slid off Goliath and landed with an extra hop. I retrieved the parchment then I slugged the man in the shoulder. "It's still Laney, Devon, you big oaf. Just... different clothes."

He said, "Oh, Laney? Is that you way down there?" He chuckled at his short joke as he put a hand on my head when I swung at his gut, missing at the distance his long arm held me at. I slapped his hand away playfully. Devon was the eldest son of Joseph and Ursula Herder. He would inherit the rabbit farm from them, which is why I didn't recommend him. But his younger brother Hank, who was my age, would never be his own herder unless he won a lottery when a herder of the keep died without heirs.

I asked, "So where's Hank? We have important business with him today." I strode past him toward the cottage, making sure to stomp his foot as I went past. Celeste chuckled at the grunt Devon made as he started hopping around. She and Bex dismounted but stayed with the horses.

Devon pushed me from behind and bellowed, "Hank, get your lazy ass out here. Knights to see you."

Hank opened the door quickly and his mother stepped out with him, they both had looks of concern and curiosity until Hank saw it was me. I guess his father was not home. Hank shook his head in amazement. "Laney. Wow, I heard but it was so hard to believe." Then he quickly corrected, "Lady Laney." I blushed. He saw Celeste and Bex and quickly bowed.

I said, "This is for being the troublemaker of Cheap Quarter." I slapped the parchment to his chest. He stared at it, looking nervous. Then at his family. Then he handed it back. "What does it say?" There was some waver to his voice.

I smiled at him, he always teased me for being "brainy" since I had learned to read. So I always gave him a hard time for the teasing. I held the parchment up as Devon and his mother stood beside him.

I started to read, trying not to smile as I did so, "Be it known that on this nineteenth day after Three Sisters Conjunction, twenty-seven and forty-two years post Impact, as witnessed by Assayer of the Keep, Bernadine of Wexbury, and Clerk of Records, Reinhardt of Wexbury; that Wexbury Keep has awarded to one Hank Herder of the keep, son of Jopseph and Ursula Herder of Cheap Quarter, Farm Lot number sixteen and the livestock therein as its master, upon recommendation of Lady Laney of Wexbury."

I slapped the parchment back on his chest and he took it. He and his family just stared at it, stunned. I got to the horses as I heard Ursula start to cry. Celeste boosted me into the saddle as I tried not to cry myself. This meant everything to them, and Hank would now be able to take a wife now that he had a place to call his own.

My colleagues mounted up and I took a deep breath, getting myself under control and I turned back in my saddle. "Take care of the farm, she's a good home." Then I added, my voice wavering slightly, "Congratulations."

I couldn't do this anymore. With that act, my home was gone. It was Hank's now, to raise his own family. Everything I knew was gone, I was a new person with a new life that I was so ill prepared for. I kicked Goliath's sides and gave him all the rein he wanted. He reared up slightly and then his hooves were pounding the cobblestones with mighty thrums as I galloped off. Celeste and Bex pacing me.

Celeste reached over and slowed Goliath when we turned and started crossing the great bridge at the Belt up toward Lord's Way near the Market. I turned to her, trying to wipe away the tears with my tunic. She tilted her head and Bex was silent. I shrugged and laughed out a final tear. "It was my home."

She just nodded and we proceeded to the castle in silence, her making sure to be in my view at all times, giving silent consolation to me. I don't know if she realized just how much that helped or that she was even doing it.

CHAPTER 13 – TRAINING

The next two months went by in a rush. I was a woman of two worlds. The physical pain of working out and training to become a Knight of the Realm on one side, and the exhausting mental exercises and probing of my magic capabilities on the other. On the plus side, I had free range of the great library. It was like heaven, all that knowledge, and nobody, not even Emily had been through everything that was hidden within it.

Mother was getting better by the day with only one relapse and Jace had already become known as the fastest runner for the Knights. He had an uncanny knack of finding shortcuts through the alleys and lanes to deliver and pick up whatever the knights required.

One thing that Prime Techromancer determined with certainty was that I was among the weakest of all the Techroromancers, my power was on par and slightly less than what Celeste possessed. But the variety of my abilities crossed the whole spectrum. Electricity seemed to feed me and not harm me, so if I could get a boost from any electrical source, I could convert that into magic potential so long as it wasn't too much.

I told him what my mother had shared with me that power was power, whether it was electricity or magic. That we could generate electricity but not magic. He had a sly grin for me when I shared that, telling me it was most likely him that told her that.

I was also telekinetic when it came to objects made of any type of metal. Which we already knew from the whirlwinds of items that would swirl around me when I lost control of my emotions.

Bex and I were sort of the joke among the Squires. Most of what knights do is physical, and between Bex and I, our muscles might have added up to half of a Squire. He was using his intellect to make up the difference with all sorts of odd inventions. He couldn't wield magic so he said he would just have to become a self-made Techromancer.

I was fascinated by his gadgets though his clumsiness and absentmindedness were a recipe for spectacular failures.

I had been gaining more agility and strength through the rigorous physical training Celeste was putting me through and I was sort of liking how much stronger I felt.

Sir Bowyn was released back to duty and he was just as smug but capable as I remembered. He did not go easy on me in training since Celeste was his partner and any mistakes I made could put her in danger.

I was knocked out of my musings by Celeste's growl as she came slashing and hacking at me with a blunted practice sword. I raised my small blunted sword to deflect each strike and rolled away. Bowyn was at my back and I barely got my sword up behind me to deflect a blow that would have done some damage, blunt sword or not.

I couldn't defend against two! I tried retreating and blocked a couple strikes. The other squires were chuckling at me. Celeste started hacking down at me with both hands over and over as she drove me to my knees then rested her blade on my shoulder lightly.

I looked up at her panting and sweating. She had only a smile for me as she nodded once and said, "Good. You are getting better." Bowyn offered an arm and pulled me to my feet like I was a child's toy.

I gasped out between breaths, "Why am I only learning to defend? Why aren't you teaching me to fight?"

She looked upset at the question and she stepped up to me and snapped out in a quiet tone that only Bowyn and I could hear, "Because you didn't choose this Laney. I chose it for you. I didn't know any other way to save you, and I don't want you to become a killing machine because of my decision. Concentrate on your magics and gaining knowledge in your studies. That is where your heart is. I see your eyes light up every time you are in the library."

Then she spoke in a normal voice as she slapped my bottom with the flat of her blade, causing me to squeak. "Besides, defense is the most important thing in any fight. If the enemy cannot strike you, they cannot injure you. That is as powerful a weapon as anything, and can win the day."

I was frustrated, I wanted to be as great a knight as her. To make her proud. I knew I was the butt of the jokes in the barracks. I countered, "So I'm to hide from a fight while the knights protect me? What use is that?"

She bounced her blade in her palm, looking frustrated like Donovan did when I wasn't grasping a lesson. The she grinned and handed me her practice weapon and drew her longsword. "Bowyn, Verna, Kristof, Tennison, Colby, Tremaine. Assist, please. First blood skips a patrol and eats in the Market on me."

They all grinned and swords were drawn. Deadly blades. Then Verna squinted at her blade. "You using magic shit or not?"

I backed away as they all started forming a circle around her. Celeste said with a grin, "I'll not use my magics so your precious Gertrude is safe." I grinned, Verna called her massive broadsword Gertrude for reasons that eluded me.

Celeste walked in a circle with her blade extended, lightly clanging her blade on theirs, marking out her reach as she spoke, "Laney is not allowed to spar with her magics so neither will I. She believes that defense is a waste of time and not a weapon for a Knight of the Realm. I thought a demonstration was required."

I muttered, "I didn't say that." She crinkled her nose at me. She was teasing.

Then she explained to me, "I will not attack and will only defend." I swallowed looking at all the deadly blades pointed at my Lady. She could really get hurt here without the practice swords. The other squires stepped up beside me by the wall.

Bex asked nervously, "Is this wise?" I shared a concerned look with him.

Mason said, "A silver says she doesn't last a minute. My master,

Tennison will make mincemeat of her without her magic."

Without looking I spat in my hand and offered it, he spit into his and shook. The other two, Kent and Brenda offered the same. Shit. Three silver? That would hurt my coin purse. Then I looked at my lady with her cocky grin as she batted Gertrude side to side with the tip of her sword. I said, "Done and done." We shook and I looked to Bex. "Sixty seconds." He pulled his protective gauntlet back to reveal the monstrosity of a wrist clock he had constructed. It also doubled as a timer.

Then Celeste called out as more knights were moving over to watch the match. "Laney, start us if you would." Then she reminded the others, "First blood." They all nodded and I saw all of their muscles tense. I held up a glove and dropped it to the ground. All of them had one eye on the glove one on my Lady.

It was like a bomb went off as the glove hit the ground. Three of the Knights struck at her instantly. She had somehow got two of them crossed up and blocked them with her blade. The third went wide when she deflected it with a long dagger that was almost as long as my sword. The tip of Colby's blade hit Tennison's leg, where he stood to the side preparing to strike when the other three disengaged.

Celeste pirouetted away laughing, dodging another slashing sword "You're out Tennison." The huge knight looked down at his leg to see a small patch of blood.

He lowered his blade then looked at Colby in shock. "Son of a bitch Colby! You cut me!"

Colby grimaced at that as he tried to press the attack while Tennison put his sword across his broad shoulders and draped his hands over it as he walked over to my side. He growled at me, "She did that on purpose to get me out of there before I could take a swing." I looked up at the man with a touch of concern and shrugged.

He chuckled at me and bumped my hip, causing me to stumble. I backhanded his gut and realized that it must be what backhanding a stone must feel like. He was nothing but smiles.

What followed was amazing. The Knights hacked, slashed, thrusted, and swept with their blades. Celeste was spinning and blocking everything, including strikes at her back. She seemed to be always in motion so she was aware of everyone's locations and stances. She caught Kristof's slashing arm between blades, but I could see her pull back quickly during the block so she didn't damage him.

She said, "Kristof is out!" He looked at the back of his arm and saw a spot of blood.

He lowered his weapon and stepped back. "Damn it!"

Verna chuckled. "No love here hon. Don't worry, I'll take you out to eat in the Market on Celeste in a..."

My Lady almost sang out, "Verna is out!"

We all laughed loudly when the muscular woman said, "God damn it, Colby! You're supposed to be on our..."

"You're out Colby!" My Lady interrupted.

Everyone laughed as Verna grinned. "Good."

Then Bex called out, "One minute." I held out my hand blindly as I watched the fight. A few seconds later I had three silver in my hand and grumbling from three Squires.

Now with only two opponents, Celeste started just stepping around in a circle, with both hands outstretched, her smile was wicked. She kept her blade on Tremaine's and deflected a strike from Bowyn with her parrying blade.

When he was off balance she pulled her sword from Tremaine's. He thrust suddenly but she was ready and she swirled her blade around his almost faster than I could follow. She moved her hand to the side in a sweeping motion and Tremaine's sword flew from his hand to embed in a wooden sparring log. "You're out Tremaine." I was about to ask when I remembered that in first blood, disarmed is the same as wounded.

Now it was Celeste and Bowyn. I knew this is what Bowyn was waiting for. My Lady has told me on many occasions that she is the third best swordsman in the realm. Tennison is number one and Bowyn is number two. That is why she used Colby to eliminate Tennison before the big man waded in with that sword of his, which was bigger than me.

I asked once, why Tennison wasn't in charge of the mobile battalion then, since he was a Techno Knight too. She had winked at me and said, "While he is better with a blade, he does not have fine control of his magics. I am better with my magic. So my skills combined will defeat his on the field every time."

Bowyn could move freely now without allies getting in the way and the two partners clashed. It was a thing of beauty like a deadly dance as their swords met time and again. She had sheathed her parrying blade and was switching from hand to hand with her sword as he made probing attacks. She blocked and parried every blow though there were some close calls. It went on for over five minutes.

Then in a series of swift strikes ending in a backhanded spin, all the action stopped as he held his blade delicately at the back of her neck. He said smugly, "You're out."

There was cheering and she turned around with a big smile and clasped his hand. "Well done."

I blinked. "He beat her."

Tennison slapped my shoulder, leaving his mammoth hand there. "Of course he did. She wasn't allowed to attack. This was a demonstration in defense. Once it got down to one on one, she couldn't use the others against him. Think about what she just showed you. It could save your life one day."

The two Knights were all smiles as they joined us. Celeste looked at me with a smirk. "How much did we win?"

I grinned hugely at her. I held up the three silver. She cocked an eyebrow in appreciation. She took a silver from my hand and flicked it to Bowyn. "There's your meal in the Market." She clasped hands with all the participants. "Well done everyone."

Then she looked at all the squires. "Defense is life. It doesn't matter how strong or fast an enemy is, if they can't hit you, all they are doing is tiring themselves out. It takes a third of the energy to block a strike than to swing your sword. If you can wear down an opponent before attacking, you have the upper hand."

We started to disperse when Mason opened his pie hole again when he saw me looking at Celeste with pride. "She may be tough, but that doesn't translate to the ducks." That was what the other Squires had taken to calling Bex and me, since we were such odd ducks to be squires. Most of the knights disciplined them, explaining that a brother at arms is to be respected, they may have your back one day.

Celeste stood straight. "Hold!"

Mason paled, he knew better than to talk down to me when she was in earshot. "Squire Laney, which squire holds rank?"

I blushed, this was going to end badly in the future, the others would double the harassment. I said softly, "I do as Techno Knight Ascendant."

She said, "Are you going to allow him to speak to you in a disrespectful manner?" What the hell Celeste? Just let me go hide.

She looked at Mason then the other two. "Do you believe you could best Bex, and Laney, a techno knight? Speak plainly, nobody will admonish you."

Mason nodded. "Everyone knows she is the weakest magic user

in the ranks. She doesn't know how to wield that toothpick of hers properly. And Bex is a disgrace to the Knights of the Realm with those toys of his.

Tennison started looming over Mason's back with anger and sadness in his eyes. He looked to be about to discipline his squire, but Celeste caught his eyes and shook her head.

Celeste looked at the three then at me and Bex. "So, if Lord Bexington were allowed to use his toys, and Lady Laney were allowed to use her... weak magic, the three of you could take them?"

They all murmured agreement. Celeste was trying to get us killed, I realized that now. She looked to all the masters of the squires, "Shall we put it to the test then?"

The others looked concerned about Bex and I, but agreed. The predatory looks on the other squire's faces made my blood run cold. Celeste said, "Grand! Practice weapons only, no honed blades. First blood."

All the gathered knights said, "First blood." I was ready to pass out.

Bex looked to be jelly legged as he looked at Sir Kristof, who just gave him a confident nod. He said to the young man, "Physical strength is nothing against a sharp mind." Bex shrugged into his backpack, put on a padded glove, and connected a copper lead to a practice sword with blunted edges. I saw sparks fly. This was his answer to a magicked blade and was almost as dangerous to him as to others.

He always had well-meaning ideas, they just didn't work out like he envisioned in the practical application.

He placed the blade down for a second, it sparked on the ground then he pulled on something new. A gauntlet that had copper wires running all around it and he strapped something on his arm. It looked to be a quartz crystal and some sort of lever. He pulled the lever five or ten times and I could hear a dynamo spinning up as power arced through the crystal. What the hell was that thing? He grabbed his sword again and stood. Looking as if he were ready to pass out, like me.

Celeste handed me my practice blade and said out loud, "Here's your toothpick." Then she put her forehead against mine and said so only I could hear, as I drowned in her emerald eyes, "Remember, a battle is not won here..." She grabbed the blunt blade. "It is won here." She tapped my forehead with a finger. Then added, "Even the smallest thing can turn the fiercest battle when it is not expected."

We moved out into the courtyard where the other fight had occurred. Bex and I stood back to back. We must have looked a sight, a short woman with a tiny sword with a tall and gangly man with more wires and harnesses than sense. The other three circled around us like wolves. Showboating by spinning their weapons and slashing side to side, loosening up.

This was not going to end well. Verna looked as concerned as me, but oddly Celeste and Kristof looked happy. My lady held up a glove, then stopped and turned back with a thoughtful look on her face. "Wagers? I have a gold on Laney as last man standing." She had four takers. There was a betting frenzy that followed. Anything from the first blood to Bex pissing his pants.

I was starting to hyperventilate and I could feel my pulse beating in my head. Tennison suddenly stood up straighter when he looked at me, his eyes glowing blue, as my vision changed. I could see amber sparks dripping from my eyes when I moved. I could see and feel all the metals in the courtyard, they all glowed in different colors of the spectrum. I could taste the iron and other trace metals in everyone's bodies.

Power was sparking and skipping across my skin. I was about to quell it all like I had been taught the past few weeks, but then realized this was one time I was supposed to let it flow. Celeste turned and she got a sparkle in her eyes when she saw me. She winked, which just made me want to swoon. Then she dropped the glove.

Mason charged, bellowing a challenge at the top of his lungs as he hacked down at me again and again. The force he was using would seriously hurt me even with a blunted blade. I was knocked to my knees but was able to deflect blow after blow.

I rolled away but still kept myself in a position to protect Bex's back. That's when I saw Kent's blade strike Bex's. It was an explosion of sparks as the electricity stored in the vessel in Bex's backpack arched from his blade into Kent's.

Kent's back went rigid as his eyes flew open. He spasmed and Bex pulled his blade back and Kent's tumbled from his hands as the bigger squire fell to a knee. Holy crap!

I kept blocking and parrying Mason's relentless assault as Tennison said firmly, "Kent is out!" I was outmatched, I could simply yield and end it, but I would not yield and make Celeste look bad.

I rolled under an overpowered slash from Kent and came up behind him, shoving him away to give myself a second to breath, to think.

Brenda had a tunic wrapped around her sword hand as she exchanged blows with Bex, sparks flying as their blades collided. She had him outmatched in skill, speed, and strength as well. She crossed swords and went to shove him back when he laid his other hand on her arm. Nothing visibly happened, but she stiffened and started convulsing wildly as Bex lowered her to the ground, gently cradling her head so it didn't hit the cobblestones.

Verna's exclamation, "Brenda is out!" Was followed by a clank as I realized Mason had outmaneuvered me and he was between Bex and me, and he slapped Bex soundly across the face with the flat of his blade. Far too hard for sparring. Bex went down on top of Brenda, out cold.

Celeste called out, "Bex is out."

Then I was being pushed back by a renewed assault by the big squire. I wish I knew why he had such a hate on for me. I glanced at Bex as the Knights were looking him over, avoiding touching any of his gadgets.

I mused over the fact that he had actually powered his blade so he could fight like a Techno Knight. Could I do the same? I concentrated and let my energy flow from within and down my arm. My blade started glowing amber and it sparked with energy. My blade sunk deeply into his with each hacking strike he made, as I went to a knee under the vicious onslaught yet again. I wasn't going to last much longer. I was never taught how to attack. The top four inches of his blade sheared off and landed ten feet away.

Celeste had said to use my head, to out think him. I couldn't do much, he wasn't giving me a chance to even breathe. What could I do? He was right I wasn't that powerful, and physically he was dominating me.

Wait... the littlest thing... I spun out of the way of a backhanded slash that he tried to get under my guard and my hand shot out. A moment later the tip of his blade flew up from the ground and impacted with the side of his head, leaving a small bloody cut across his earlobe. Tennison said, "Mason is out, Laney wins."

I dropped my guard and exhaled in relief, then froze as three blades shot over my shoulders, all crossing, catching the late strike that Mason was swinging down at my forehead. I swallowed, looking at the blunted blade, just an inch from my nose.

I turned on wobbly legs to see that Tennison, Celeste, and Bowyn had all intercepted the strike. Tennison looked to grow even bigger than his normal impressive stature as he flicked his double handed sword, which knocked Mason's blade forcefully from his hand, onto the ground. He stepped up to him, glaring as he sheathed his sword on his back.

He cuffed the side of Mason's head so hard the man fell to the ground. "What in the hell were you thinking? That could have killed her! This was just a sparring match! I've been far too patient with you and your attitudes toward your comrades at arms. I want you gone within the hour. You are to be stripped of your title of Knight Ascendant. Go back to your parents in their manor, there is no place for you among the Knights of the Realm."

Sir Tennison turned his back to the man and waited until he heard him retreating to the castle. Celeste was frantically checking me for injury as the big knight stepped in front of us. "Please accept my apologies, Laney. I did not teach him to be like that. He had such promise when I took him as Squire three years ago. I don't know what happened."

I dropped my blade and pulled away from my Lady and ran up to Bex in concern. He was conscious now and smiling. Brenda was up and looking between the castle and me. Bex asked her, "Are you okay Brenda? I didn't want to hurt you with my shocking gauntlet." She actually smiled warmly at him before schooling her face.

I stood and Verna said to the quiet crowd, "Laney is the winner." People clapped, then Celeste's eyes got a mischievous glint in them while she said, "You can let the power go now, Laney."

I closed my eyes took three deep breaths and I could feel the energy bleed out of me. Verna was speaking with someone behind me, "She took every one of his strikes, deflected every blow." I was blushing. Someone noted I was severely outmatched, why hadn't I just yielded? Verna's quick response was, "Laney does not yield, I don't think she knows how." I saw a couple Knights asking Bex about his powered blade idea. Other knights were slapping my back in congratulations.

Then I tried to pretend I didn't almost pee my pants. I asked my Lady in a voice I was able to keep most of the waver out of as I fought the adrenaline, repeating her words, "How much did we win?"

She grinned as she started looking at the other knights, holding her hand out. "Twelve gold." Then her smile doubled as people started paying her. She asked me, "Penny vouchers?"

I smiled back and nodded fervently. "Grand idea!"

She found out I had arranged for using most of my squire's stipend, one gold each week, to convert into penny vouchers. At the end of each month, one penny voucher would be distributed to each family in Cheap Quarter, and the Trough. That way I knew they could have a nice meal besides the Holy Day feasts, or get something they needed for their homes once a month.

I kept only one coin a month, I had no need of anything as the castle provided for my every need.

Celeste and seven other knights followed suit, and my mother had the village Treasury set up an official program for it. To my embarrassment, Bernadine has informed me that people of the village are starting to call me the Penny Lady.

After training, we headed off across the village to the baths. I had become so accustomed to bathing every Sixth Day, so I was clean for Holy Day. The other days I spoiled myself with sponge baths using the heated water in the washroom in our quarters, I felt almost guilty about it.

Celeste and Verna chuckled at me when it took two tries for me to mount Goliath. I crinkled my nose at them and stuck out my tongue. At least I was improving, and my beautiful boy was very patient with me. We turned toward the arch when Squire Brenda came trotting up next to us. She stared at me a moment, then asked me instead of my Lady. "Mind if I tag along?"

I smiled and shook my head. Then we all burst out laughing when she asked with a blush as we started to ride, "Do you think Bex is a virgin?" I did a double take. Oh, good lord, she liked him! That just made me smile, what a smart match that would be. His brains, her brawn. Though I'm pretty sure he'd end up calling her ma'am. Then I sobered as I looked at my Lady. That was more than I would ever have.

Like she could read my mind, Celeste sidled up to me and just rode at my side all the way to the baths. She always knew when something was bothering me and she always treated me like I mattered.

CHAPTER 14 – MISSION

When we returned to the castle, I was pretty sure that Brenda was well on the way to making reparations for the way she and the others treated Bex and me. I believe that both her and Kent were just following Mason's lead.

We all chuckled when we got back. She snapped out to Bex who was busy strapping something that looked like an electric motor onto my old hay wagon, "Make yourself useful and get my horse into the livery."

He hopped up and nodded as she dismounted and he took the reins. She called back to him as she stalked toward the castle, "Dine with me at my quarters at seven." It sounded like a demand, not a request.

Bex squeaked out an "O-Okay." We all chuckled again. I knew it! She was sweet on him!

Verna, I think just to be funny, because she was much smarter than that, asked, "Why didn't she just have the stable hands handle her mare instead of ordering the poor boy around?"

Celeste eyeballed her accusingly until Verna laughed. "Fine. Young love is so cute." We all grinned as we handed our mounts off to the stable boys.

I looked up to see Jace rocketing toward us, his little legs churning. He bowed and handed a note to Celeste. She winked at him and ruffled his hair. He blushed and headed back to the castle.

She arched an eyebrow as we all walked while she read.

She looked at our musclebound friend. "Looks like we won't break bread with you tonight Verna. The Duke has summoned me and Laney." She flipped the note front to back indicating that was all the information on it.

Verna shrugged then gave us each a hug. "I'll see you two in church tomorrow then?" Celeste nodded and I followed behind her to the left. I always made sure to follow protocol and not embarrass her on official business.

She said to me without looking, with a little smile on her face as we navigated the labyrinth of halls to the grand staircase. "You really did good today Laney. That was the woman I saw on that first day. You didn't back down, didn't run, and didn't yield. Do you ever get scared?"

I snorted then eeepd in surprise and covered my mouth. "I was scared shitless. I thought he was trying to kill me."

She nodded with a proud grin. "Yet you kept your head and found a solution to win the contest."

I shrugged and she offered an elbow. But we were going to the Duke. I hesitated, but she kept her arm provided. I placed my fingers on her arm and basked in the warmth spreading through me. We reached Duke Fredrick's office, which was next to Prime Techromancer Donovan's, only the Duke's office was three times the size.

She looked at the two guards stationed outside the great oak doors and nodded to them then raised her hand to slam the great ring of iron hanging on the doors, three times. Immediately the Duke's voice echoed out, "Enter."

We stepped in, she placed a hand over mine in the crook of her arm so I couldn't withdraw it. I looked around in shock as we both bowed to the room. It was the veritable who's who in the village nobility.

There was a map spread out on the great table in the middle of the space that was in front of Duke Fredrick's grand desk. It was the largest and most detailed map of the Lands of Sparo I had ever seen. There were wooden markers all around the southern region of the habitable lands.

Next to the Duke was Duchess Lucia. The Magistrate, Man at Arms, Prime Techromancer Donovan, Sir Tiberius, who was the commander of the home defense battalion, and two people in the purples and crimson of the realm of Far Reach were gathered around the table. Also a few scholars I had seen around but did not know personally. One was taking notes.

Fredrick gave us a nod and we looked up. "Celeste. Let me introduce Techromancer Kendell, and Magistrate Lars of Far Reach Keep." Then he turned to them. "This is Countess Celeste of the Techno Knight Order, Blade of Temperance of Wexbury, daughter of Prime Techromancer Donovan, Lady of the Court." Wow, he was using all of her titles, I took it he wanted to impress the men. By their raised eyebrows I believe he was successful.

Then he added, "And on her arm is Baroness Laney of Wexbury, Techno Knight Ascendant, Lady of the Court." I squinted, he was using the Baroness title which I wasn't supposed to be able to use until I was appointed Knight. He really was trying to impress people since there is nothing impressive about a squire.

The men gave us a courteous head bow which we returned. I just followed my Lady's lead. Fredrick motioned us toward the map. We stood at his left side and he started speaking to Celeste. "I'm sure you have heard about the increasing number of rogue raids in the southern realms the past few months?" He was pointing at some of the markers. Some were black and some were red. Mostly smaller villages on the fringes of Far Reach, Treth, and New World.

She nodded looking at the map with a furrowed brow. "Yes, they are increasing in frequency and there are rumors of new rogue warlords trying to organize the rogues again."

The Duke nodded solemnly. "It appears the rumors are true. This new leader, Raneth, is emboldened after a successful attack on New World Keep and the assassination of Count Eric, the Prime Techromancer of New World, before the home forces could lend assistance to drive the growing band of rogues off." I gasped at the news of a Prime Techromancer's assassination.

Celeste paused and looked up at this too. Fredrick nodded at the men. "Word just arrived of this today with Kendell and Lars." He paused then went on. "It seems that Raneth is trying to merge with a second group of rogues, making their leader, Poe, his lieutenant. If he is successful, they would have a magic fighting force half the size of the one Rydell commanded to start the Great Mage Wars."

Then Techromancer Kendell spoke, "None of the realms could stand alone against a group of magic users that large. So we are beseeching all the realms to come together for talks on a renewed joint defense pact. So that we can exterminate the enemy before they grow to the extent that Prince George has to step in.

I understood that. Highland Keep, across The Gap, was the capitol, and Prince George gave all the realms autonomy except when it became apparent that war was inevitable. It had taken five years after the end of the Great Mage Wars before Highland released autonomous control back to each realm. I was sort of in awe of the Prince since he never had to release control in the first place. But the leaders of each realm felt a certain amount of discord with the capitol calling the shots.

So they wanted to solve this problem before the need for the overwhelming force of Highland Keep was necessary, to bring peace to all the realms again. I didn't know much about political things, but at least I knew that much.

Duke Fredrick took over and said, "So I will need an expeditionary force to escort myself and the Duchess to Far Reach for the conclave. Assume the area between Treth and Far Reach is hostile territory."

Everyone was silent as Celeste looked at the map again. "We'll need to keep it small, so we are mobile and nimble. If we cut through the Black Forest and come down through the mountains, past Treth, that would keep us out of the open on the Treth Plains."

Then she nodded to herself and looked directly at Fredrick. "I'd say, seven Knights of the Realm, four archers, two Techno Knights to handle any magic attacks. With that, we should be able to punch through either of the groups and get you into a keep if we come under attack." Then she cautioned, "But if they have already come to an accord, we couldn't stand against them with that small a force. We would be compelled to hold them off as long as we could while you retreat back to Treth Keep or Flatlash."

Lars spoke up, "Why not send your entire mobile battalion?" I didn't like the sounds of that and apparently neither did anyone else.

Celeste held a cautioning hand to the Duke before he could protest. She explained, "That would leave the realm virtually unprotected with only the Home Defense Battalion at the keep." She shook her head and squinted a little at Lars, reappraising him, then finished, "No, we do this with a small, agile force unless your Duke Hannibal cared to hold the talks in Wexbury."

Fredrick gave her a discreet smile then said in a plain tone, "Lady Celeste is my most trusted military adviser, so we will go with her recommendations." Then he looked at Kendell. "How many realms have agreed to the talks?"

The skinny white-haired Techromancer replied thoughtfully, "When we left ten days ago, York, Defiance, New World, Treth, and now Flatlash."

Lucia spoke up, "With us in attendance that gives us a majority. Hopefully even more have accepted by now."

The Duke stood up straighter and looked directly at Celeste and me, and said in a commanding tone, "Then make the preparations, we shall leave on First Day."

We bowed and said, "My Lord," We exited the room quickly.

I opened my mouth, but she held a cautionary hand up and tugged her ear and looked around. I nodded, the walls had ears here, and she grabbed my hand and dragged me to our quarters.

We sat down on the lounge, where Celeste still insisted on sleeping with me to protect me from my nightmares, which were coming more and more frequently, and much more vividly. It was still that giant Monolith and all the power relaying through me. Pain and terror. But now there was a new dimension to the horror. A Mountain Gypsy caravan with rounded wagons. Lightning engulfing me, searing at my soul. A broken and bloodied Celeste laying in front of me, her eyes wide, whispering, "Run Laney!" And a bald man with studded leather armor burning the flesh off of me with red magics, fire magics.

She looked at me and was formulating something to say when I said, "I didn't like weasel boy. What kind of suggestion was that?"

She chuckled out loud and shook her head at me. "Weasel boy? I like that, it fits. It wasn't likely I'd leave our lands unpatrolled and leave our villages open to marauders. Only a bad tactician would make an error like that and he should have known better."

She smiled at me. "Have you ever wanted to travel?" I smiled at her and nodded excitedly, and her return smile warmed my soul. I thought about the ten-day journey, maybe eleven or twelve since we were heading into the mountains, this would be the adventure of a lifetime for me. We wouldn't be back in Wexbury for close to a month depending on how long it took to negotiate a joint defense pact.

She took my boots off for me and said, "Get cleaned up and ready for bed. I'll be back soon. I need to get the ball rolling on a couple things. The rest can wait for after Church tomorrow." I nodded and she left our quarters like a woman on a mission. I laughed at myself because she actually was a woman on a mission.

CHAPTER 15 – THE ADVENTURE BEGINS

By the time First Day came around, everything was organized for the peace mission. The representatives from Far Reach continued north to speak with Perth Hollow up at Lake Odette.

As we checked our saddles while Bex double checked the supply wagon, and the enclosed coach the Duke and Duchess would ride in, Celeste turned to me and checked my new armor that had been delivered by messenger late the prior night. It was mostly leather armor with a light breastplate and bracers made of what tasted like titanium to me. It had the crest of Wexbury in the center, and the crest of the house of Celeste to the left of it. She drew my sword and snorted at it. I slapped her shoulder. "Not funny woman."

She winked at me. "Yes, it is." Then Celeste said, "I forgot to ask yesterday, I saw that Hank kid talking to you at the feast. What did he want?"

Kid? He was my age. She seemed overly curious. Was she jealous? I teased, "He wanted my hand in marriage before I left today."

Her eyes narrowed and I saw a shadow pass over them and said in a dangerous voice, "He didn't."

I shoved her shoulder playfully and chuckled out, "No, he didn't. You already know I'll be betrothed to no man." I stopped myself from adding that besides, I loved someone I could never have. I smirked at her and she smirked back and rolled her eyes at me as she sheathed my sword in my scabbard. I wondered if I looked as ridiculous in the armor as I felt. Like a little kid pretending to be a knight.

She prompted me to speak with the look in her eyes. I caved. "He was just asking what we fed the chickens. They aren't laying as large of eggs nor the same quality as when we raised them. I shared what we fed them and he verified he hasn't changed a thing."

She just nodded and said absently as she checked our bedrolls. "Because your mother isn't there."

I paused and looked at her. "My mother?"

She looked up at my question. "Oh, you really don't know? Haven't you heard the stories of the Shining Lady?"

I shrugged. "Just a few."

She squinted at me. "You know your mother is a nature elemental right? You've seen the lavender power in her eyes?"

An elemental? Mother? How many more secrets did she hide from me? I shook my head slowly. She nodded sadly. "She's probably just so used to hiding it from you when she raised you." Then she smiled. "It was said that the small gardens in the castle were more bountiful when Lady Margret was around, and the milking cows Cook keeps in the livery gave a sweeter cream."

Then she shook her head. "Nobody ever put it together that the incredible eggs brought in by the herder children may have benefited from the Shining Lady. All thought her dead."

I smiled. "Mother is an elemental?" I froze, dear Lord, that meant not only had mother hidden from her children she was a Lady, but also that she was a Techromancer! I saw the satisfied smirk Celeste gave when she saw me adding two and two.

She said as she scrunched her nose, "And we have a winner."

I rolled my eyes at her and pushed past her, yanking her cinch strap out of its buckle as I moved past her horse. "Your saddle is loose, evil woman." I grinned at the explosive laughter behind me.

I grabbed my tool bag off the bench against the stone wall, and slung it over my shoulder then adjusted it so it didn't interfere with drawing my sword. She called over from where she was adjusting her saddle again, "Why do you insist on carrying that stuff? You could check out a proper took kit from the castle stores."

I looked at her and said with firmness, "Because, like Goliath, it is mine." I know it was stupid, the keep provided me with anything I needed, but I had pride in ownership of my horse and my father's tools. They were something extraordinary from my prior life in the keep. She softened at that and simply nodded.

Then we both turned and looked at the expeditionary force. In addition to the knights and archers, we were three Squires, two porters, and one coachman strong. The only two missing were... the castle trumpets sounded the arrival of the Duke and Duchess in the courtyard.

I took a deep breath of the crisp, chill, morning air. The first frosts would arrive in the next few days with winter on their heels.

I looked at the spectators who were there to see us off, both inside and outside the courtyard archway. Plenty of nobles and commoners lined Lord's Way, and Mother, Jace, Donovan, Emily, and Cook; as well as Tiberius and a few knights of the home defense battalion.

While the coachman assisted the nobles into the coach, I walked over and gave Mother a hug. "If all goes well we should be back in a month, before the heavy freezes." She nodded and kissed my cheek. Then I looked at her accusingly. "An elemental?"

She squinted an eye in mock pain and said in a question, "Yes?"

I chuckled at her shaking my head. "Secrets upon secrets..."

She said with a sly smile, "Says the pot to the kettle." I had to grin at that.

Then I said, "Love you, see you soon."

She released the hug and I bent to hug Jace. He almost squished my neck and then he stood tall. "My sister the Squire."

I grinned at him. "Take care of Mother for me. You're the man of the house." He nodded far too seriously for a young boy and I said, "Love you."

He smiled hugely then asked, "Bring me something from your adventure?"

I nodded and went to return to Celeste's side when I passed Donovan said softly, "Remember, battles are won with this..." He touched his head. "... and this..." He touched his chest over his heart. "Not with a blade."

I smiled at the man. "It is only a boring escort duty. We'll be back before you know it." He grinned then I stepped up to Celeste.

I had to smile when I heard Emily saying to the Prime Techromancer, "Now come on and get back inside. It is chilly out here and you're not dressed properly you fool."

Celeste winked at her father when he said in a resigned tone, "Yes Emily."

Then everyone gathered chuckled when she started shooing him inside while grumbling, "Queen of the Scrolls indeed."

We knights and squires all mounted, well the knights and all but one squire mounted. I know I heard some snickering coming from two female knights who so enjoyed teasing me when I got up onto Goliath on my second try.

We slid into formation. Four knights and three squires in front of the supply wagon followed by the archers, then the coach flanked by two knights with one trailing. This would be our standard formation. The archers protected at our center with virtually a three hundred and sixty degree line of fire. The squires were to float from front to back of the caravan on occasion, to look everything over and to keep anyone observing us guessing as to the fighting strength of any given point at any random time.

I smiled at Bex. This is the first time I had seen the armor he had commissioned for himself. He looked like a clockwork man to me with all his gadgets, wires, and gizmo's fastened to hard points on the leather and steel. There were pinned brackets where he could attach various wonders he kept in his backpack and saddle bags. He looked even more awkward than usual, but I supposed I did as well... the little girl playing a knight.

I had to grin at Squire Brenda though. She looked just as beautiful and regal as Verna and Celeste in her armor and she rode next to Bex. Who, by the dreamy look on his face whenever he looked at her, is no virgin anymore. I'm sure she pretty much owned the poor young man now, and I was happy for him, as odd as their pairing looked on the surface. I'm thinking it had something to do with him besting her in the training battle.

Celeste had her business face on as she stared back at the coach awaiting the signal. Fredrick put a hand out a window and made a slight shooing motion with his hand, Celeste turned forward in her saddle and raised her arm to the sky, we all slid to attention in our saddles. I was late, we hadn't gone over any of this in training yet.

Then her hand swung down and she pointed forward and the huge bellows powered war horns of the keep sounded their deep rumble in one single long burst and we were in motion. It felt almost like a parade to me. As if it was some big show.

When we exited the castle grounds and out onto Lord's Way into the cheering of the spectators on the side of the lane, I realized that was exactly what it was. It was a show meant to inspire the people of the village. To demonstrate the strength and majesty of the ones that defended those people's lives and showed them that while that even though we were not the biggest realm, why Wexbury was among the greatest realms to live in.

I was looking around at first until I caught that all of the knights just watched the cobblestone road in front of them with single-mindedness purposefulness. And there I was, gawking like a fool. I forced my eyes forward and concentrated on not looking silly on my huge steed. I caught a slight tick of a smile on Celeste's face in my peripheral vision. Oh, good lord, I was amusing her.

I whispered, "Shut up." She aborted a snort and I could see the strain on her face as she tried to stay composed. Now it was my turn to hold back a smile.

We took the long way around the roundabout at the cathedral and down the Crossbar. People were lined up the whole way. Had they sent criers out to inform them of the Duke's departure? I remember watching processions like this on many occasions and looking up at the Knights of the Realm and dreaming. This was so surreal. I was now up on one of those mounts in armor, at my Lady's side.

I rose my chin slightly, I would not embarrass her here. The guards at the portcullis and the ramparts above saluted us as we left the keep. We continued the slow trot as we passed by the orchards, farmland, and grazing herds between the keep and Wexbury Minor. Nobody spoke. I had so many questions that I would have to ask later.

The few people of Wexbury Minor, who were not out tending the crops and livestock, clapped as we trotted through the little town. It wasn't until we were over a mile south of the village that everyone

seemed to relax and we picked up the pace. I looked over at Celeste
with my brow furrowed.

She smiled and explained, "We owe it to those we protect to
show a strong force that makes them feel safe. It gives them
confidence, to see a well-oiled machine." This made sense and I
thought it admirable that they thought of things like that. Then she
said much louder, "Good thing they don't know Verna." This got a
chuckle from the knights and some of the archers.

Verna was quick to respond jovially, "So sayeth Faceplant."
She said it like a title as Celeste and the other knights laughed.

I again looked at her in question. She just shook her head,
refusing to explain. Verna came forward to my other side and she
sat forward in her saddle to look around me at her friend. "Oh come
now Celeste, don't tell me you didn't share the adventure our first
patrol with our knights as squires."

Celeste was blushing and intent on the road again. Verna sat
back in her saddle, satisfied, then looked at me and said in a
conspiratorial tone loud enough for it to carry to the back of the
group, "Our venerable leader and her young stallion Canter there
were on our very first patrol mission from the gates. We were
heading east into the Whispering Forest."

She grinned and looked behind her, making sure she had
everyone's attention. "Young Squire Celeste here excelled in
everything she put her mind to. There was nothing she could not
do... well except for to choose a suitable mount it seems."

She mocked reverence. "You should have seen her sitting tall and proud in the saddle as we followed our Knights, barreling down the trail and coming out at Beggar's Creek, where our Knights decided to do a sweep of The Grove before we continued east."

She looked ready to burst as she continued, "Without slowing, Sir Edwin and Lady Anita rode into the stream, where the waters came above the chests of their chargers. We followed suit... well I followed suit. It seems ol' Canter there had a fear of water back then and came to a sliding halt in the mud on the shore."

The pleased look on her face just made you smile as she finished. "The look on Celeste's face, as she went flying out of her saddle, over her mount and face planted in the stream, was priceless! Sir Edwin and I were laughing too hard to notice she didn't surface. Her armor weighted her down. A chuckling Lady Anita waded her charger back into the stream and reached down to pull Celeste to her feet by the scruff of her neck. She looked like a wet puppy."

Everyone was chuckling now and my grin was splitting my face. It was good to know that my seemingly unflappable Lady was human too.

Celeste just put an imperious look on her face and patted her steed's neck as she rode. "You do just fine in the water now, don't you boy?" The she shot a grin at me that I returned. I liked it when the Knights had fun like this. We sometimes forget that they are people too, we see them as an ideal, a symbol, but they are just like us under the armor. I looked down at my ridiculously small breastplate and mused that I would be like them one day too.

Since Verna was smugly riding beside me and seemed loquacious, I looked over at her and asked, "What really happened in the Great Raid of York?"

Her eyes showed a touch of sorrow and she said, "Until the day I die, I will swear upon the bravery of Sir Edwin." Not answering my question. She gave a sad smile to me then drifted back to Sir Kristof and Bex again.

It was so frustrating! Why would nobody tell me the truth of what occurred that day in York? Was Celeste really the hero of York and they were hiding it for some reason? Or was it truly Sir Edwin that stopped the Reaper that day like everyone in Wexbury was told?

I huffed in exasperation which only put a smile on Celeste's lips. Graaah! But then I grinned, imagining the sight of my Lady going through her igniting on the field of battle, it must have been a sight to see.

It was exciting really, this was my first adventure. I had been to Flatlash once when I was very young. It was a two-day ride in our old wagon with Tulip pulling. I'm not sure why we visited, I was too young to remember much except the excitement of traveling to another realm. We never went in the keep. Instead we did something at Flatlash Minor, outside the gates, before returning home.

But now, I would be traveling through the lands of five realms.

We would be in Far Reach, where the temperatures never fluctuate more than ten degrees and they get over thirty rainfalls a year.

I drifted back along our ranks when Brenda did. We took some time looking at the supply wagon and coach wheels for damage, pausing with the archers in between. Then trailing the caravan for a few minutes, scanning the horizon in all directions.

Sir Bowyn told us that this would be the norm for the next thousand miles. If we stayed on the flats of the Fringe of the habitable lands, we could get approximately one hundred miles in each twelve-hour day. Figuring ten miles per hour with two breaks for the horses to rest, and a midday meal for us less durable humans.

By diverting through the Black Forest below Flatlash and into the mountains, we would add two, possibly three days to the journey in the rougher terrain. We'd be in the realm of the Mountain Gypsies though, so the mountain pathways should be clear.

As we rode, I wondered how sore I was going to be by the end of the first day. I had never been on a horse for so long. The knights and archers kept everyone entertained with their stories of their own travels, encounters with rogues, marauders, and Gypsies. Some of them clearly embellished and some quite humorous.

Sir Marrin, a tall rakish knight who was always three days unshaven and flirted with any woman who walked past him, got us laughing as he shared the time he was relieving himself into a stream. He was patrolling on the Fringe, close to where the Hawktail river flowed into the uninhabitable lands.

He heard a noise beyond a bush and he leaned forward to look around it. On the other side was a marauder, in the same state as he was. They looked at each other then down at their business and Marrin held up a finger, and they nodded to each other. They both finished then rapidly fastened their trousers and drew their weapons. Then Sir Marrin nodded at the man and said, "Alright then, let's be about it," They fought. He said they did joke about it as the knight rode the then injured marauder back to the keep in chains.

As the novelty of being on the road and seeing something new, started to wear off as we moved steadily south toward Cougar Deeps and Flatlash Keep I grinned at myself. I was bored. Come on Laney it's an adventure! I looked east to the mountains, that is somewhere I longed to see.

So maybe it was just that the flats of West Wexbury, where the Whispering Forest dwindled into the lower grasslands, weren't very interesting to see. I chuckled at myself. I passed the time listening to the stories and realized now why the Knights did it, they were bored too. I looked at Celeste's sash with the crossed sword and lightning bolt.

I asked a question that has always been on my mind to nobody in particular. "So why Techno for magic users? As in Techno Knights, and Techromancers? Weren't they wizards and mages in the Before Times? I've always wondered."

Celeste grinned off into space, not really looking at me as she explained. "When the old magics reawakened, people found they could manipulate the elements. It was found that with all the seeming variety of magics that could affect the earth, fire, air, water, and nature... there was one commonality."

She looked at her hand. "No matter what kind of magic you wield, your magic can be converted to electricity and you can manipulate technology to some extent. Whether it is operating a manual pump or, or turning an electric motor, or even peeling back the ravages of time on relics from the Before by reversing oxidation and decay."

Then she turned in her saddle to me. "So since technology is the common denominator, that is where the Techno comes from."

I smiled at her then squinted in thought. "But what about Mountain Gypsy magic? I hear it is something... else... and they are not considered rogues."

She looked to think of that for a moment to determine the best way to explain, but we were surprised by Duke Fredrick's voice. He was looking out of the coach. I grinned, he must be bored too. "What they wield is something different, we think it may be the magics the Wizards of the Before possessed. It cannot be converted to energy and they seem to weave it in spells, charms, and potions that can be imbued into items and persist. It even gives some, the sight, the ability to see the future."

His brow furrowed a little. "They had their magics long before the first Techromancers and have always kept to themselves. They are peaceful and have never turned against any realm like the rogues have done. They never disputed the claims all of the realms made on their mountains. Even though they were clearly there first, long before the people of Highland Keep crossed The Gap in their explorations, and started settling the great expanse of the new world. But the mountains are recognized as their domain and they have autonomy and free range to travel them in all the realms, that is an undisputed fact."

He smirked a little. "That and I'm sure nobody really wants to anger them enough to find out just what their magics can really do. I know Wexbury doesn't." Everyone chuckled with that. I was learning more just then than my random stumbling in the Library of the Scrolls. Though Emily was far too much fun to speak with, as she herself was quite random.

We had finally settled in for the night with the small settlement of Sleepy Creek on the horizon. The Duke and Duchess retired into a tent and the rest of us sort of made a ring around the large campfire and electric space heater. The porters cooked a hearty beef stew and biscuits. Verna told us Squires to enjoy it because, "Tomorrow night will be the last night we will have an open campfire. We will use the electric space heater after that so there are no open flames to pinpoint our location to marauders or rogues."

Bex asked why we didn't just overnight in the town. It was a good question, I was curious too. Kristof said, "Too many places to hide, and too many chances of an ambush outside of the keeps. Odds are nothing untoward will happen the entire mission, but with the Duke and Duchess at risk, it is always safer to err on the side of caution and have a defensible position.

After the meal was over and checking on the horses, we spread out our bedrolls. An archer named Peter, and Celeste took first watch. Us squires were not needed for the watch since we were not experienced enough. But they would always have at least one knight on watch in three-hour shifts and an additional man to watch our six. This way everyone got at least six hours of sleep.

I shivered in the cold and pulled the cloak, which was fitted for me, out and wrapped myself in it, pulling up the hood. Then I walked Celeste's over to her on the small rise above the camp where she watched the night. I knew not to speak to give her position away.

I smiled and handed it to her and she smiled back and draped it over her shoulders with practiced ease. I shivered and was about to retreat when she held an arm out, her cloak open. I sat with her and she wrapped her cloak around me, holding me and keeping me warm while her eagle eyes scanned the night.

Next thing I knew she was nudging me awake. I looked up at her, safe in the nest of her cloak, she was smiling. I looked over to see Verna, who winked at me. We left her to her watch and made our way down to the small blessed cone that was heated by the tall space heater. Before I could slide under my blanket on the pad on the ground, Celeste again held her blanket open invitingly.

I didn't need more of an invitation and I slipped in and she held me tight to her to share her body heat. And she protected me, like every night since I moved from my home into her chambers. I've never asked why, because I feared she would stop if I did, and I had become accustomed to lying with her, with my Lady.

She whispered, "You don't need to sit with me on watch Laney."

I turned and the light of Earth's ring and the three sisters glittered in her eyes. "I know, but I want to. I... enjoy your company." She gave me an indecipherable smile and hugged me and kissed the top of my head proprietorially and whispered, "Get some sleep, big day tomorrow, Flatlash Keep."

CHAPTER 16 – FLATLASH

The next day felt like a replay of the previous day, with the exception of a few of us gathered around Bex. The previous night he had taken a couple of reed thin extendable tubes that attached to a ring over his canteen cap. They were splayed out and held a taut sheet of green silk between them with a lot of surface area like a sail. When we asked what silly contraption he was working on he told us, "Wait until morning and I'll show you."

We watched as he shook the silk sheet to get the last few drops of morning dew to funnel down into his now almost full canteen. He grinned as he retracted the tubes and rolled the silk up on it. It fit in the palm of his hand.

He grinned at the archers and knights that had looked at him in confusion. He said, "The silk catches the morning condensation, there is moisture in the air everywhere, even the desert. So I am able to fill my canteen with fresh water without using our supplies, nor drawing it from a river or stream and boiling it."

One archer, Linus I think his name was, said, "Well that's just silly boy. There is water within a four-hour ride anywhere in Wexbury, especially in the mountains where you can't fart without tripping into a stream."

Bex replied with pride, "Yes here, but in the Great Desert, and Burning Desert, this would be a great boon to extend water supplies. Imagine draping a couple hundred square yards or so along the perimeter of a camp. You could extend your water supply greatly for only the infinitesimal weight of a bolt of silk in your gear. Or reduce the amount of water you would need oxen to haul on an extended mission in the desert."

He was grinning and I grinned too. It was useless here, but actually pretty brilliant in an instance like he described. A chuckling Kristof walked up to his tinkering squire and slapped his back jovially. "But my stalwart squire, have you not noticed..." He looked around at everyone then back to Bex with a fond smile. "This isn't the desert."

Everyone got a good chuckle and he was a good sport about it. The poor boy's head was always in the clouds. Celeste spoke up after joining in the laughter, "What Kristof says is true. However, I believe you should share your experiment with Hell's Gate and New World Keep scholars. I think it has great potential for them. Keep coming up with ideas, never stop thinking, you never know what could be found useful, knowledge is never something to be wasted."

The other knights and the Duke, who was getting back into the coach, all chimed in with a "Here here." Then we started moving out.

Things on the cobblestone highway were uneventful except after our mid-day meal, Tennison and Celeste pulled ahead to speak for a moment. When they returned, Celeste made some eye motions to the other knights, then moved beside the coach and whispered into the Duke's ear when he hung his head out. He nodded.

We picked up the pace to get to Flatlash before mid afternoon. They had us squires, drifting to the back at irregular intervals about twice as often. I rode beside Bowyn as I rotated back along the line. "What is it?"

He just kept looking forward and said, "Do not look around." That, of course, caused a need to look around. You don't just tell someone not to do or think something, then that is stuck in their head. I saw a wry smile on his face as I tried not to look all around me.

Then he said, "We've picked up a ghost. It may be nothing but a merchantman heading to Flatlash, but they are keeping their distance, using the terrain to obscure themselves. Though when we picked up the pace they did not. However, Celeste picked up another shadow to the west."

He shook his head. "She's always had a knack for getting an itchy feeling when she is being watched."

I asked, "Who could it be?"

He shrugged. "Could be nothing but a coincidence, could be marauders keeping tabs on us." He paused. "Could be rogues. They could have found out that Far Reach is worried and is asking for talks of a renewed defense pact against them. Too many possibilities."

Then he grinned. "In any case, we believe that some sort of game is afoot. Just keep up with your position changes until we are in Flatlash Keep. If their delegation hasn't left yet, we can double our numbers, and that alone would deter all but a war party. We wouldn't be as agile, but we would trade off that agility for better security."

I nodded in understanding then peeled off to continue my movement around our group. The Duke nodded once to me as I passed the coach. I tried to track the various knights eyes as they flicked in different directions without turning their heads. Celeste, Verna, and Bowyn were all concentrating on the west by the Fringe.

I saw nothing of course but knew these Knights of the Realm did. My mind wandered as I thought of what mother had taught me about the Fringe, and why it is the inhabitable lands were called the Lands of Sparo... the Lands of Hope.

Every year, water seeps farther and farther out into the rocky landscape of the uninhabitable areas, and wind and rain erosion slowly builds up the land; grasses slowly spreading outward. The inhabitable lands on the Fringe are continually growing by about a hundred yards a year all around the perimeter of the realms.

That is thousands of square miles of inhabitable lands added each year. This gives hope to the idea that one day, life will return to the entire planet and will be like the Earth that Was one day. When the great expanse of the new world was discovered by Highland Keep almost fifteen hundred years ago, The Gap was over one hundred and twenty miles across and The Grasslands between the Hawktail River and the mountains were almost non-existent.

Now The Gap is just over forty miles across and shrinking. Just in my lifetime, almost a mile of new grasslands have appeared as the two lands come closer to merging.

With the idea of the Great Bridging that Prince George has, I may see the two lands connected before I die instead of it occurring naturally in about eight hundred years. He wants to excavate soil from the mountains on either side of the gap and run an irrigation canal, to build a grassland bridge over a mile wide between the lands. It would be an engineering marvel and would take almost forty years to complete.

Most of the keeps see it like Bex's ideas. Pie in the sky and pointless since The Gap can be crossed easily on horseback in less than a day now. But he sees it as a boon as it would increase the grazing lands for both lands and allow wildlife to migrate between the lands. It is one of those types of selfless and noble thoughts that makes me respect the man, no matter what his critics or detractors say.

Celeste moved over to my side. "Your head is in the clouds." I looked down bashfully. She added, "It isn't an admonishment. I just think the look of wonder you sometimes get on your face is a marvelous thing."

I shrugged and gave her a little smile. "I was just thinking about the fringe since that is where our shadow is. How it is steadily growing. It would be a sight to see when the Earth is alive again."

She looked out wistfully before returning her gaze to me. "That would be something wouldn't it?" I nodded then she jutted her chin down the road. "Cougar Deeps, we're almost upon Flatlash Keep. We'll be in their realm when we cross the Great Viaduct over the Cougar River just east of the Deeps.

I smiled as I saw where the grasslands gave way to the forest that surrounded the lake of Cougar Deeps. It is said that the Flatlash scholars have dropped a line over five hundred feet into the deeps, before the weight snapped the string and they still didn't find the bottom of the lake. They postulate that it is an impact crater from debris from Mother Luna. Flatlash Keep is tucked into the southern crook of the gourd-shaped lake.

We entered the thickening forest and came out on an overlook over Cougar Deeps. A myriad of sailboats and fishermen dotted the lake. Father Sol reflected off the mirrored surface of the black lake. I knew it to be a trick of the depths, that the water was not black. Sunlight couldn't penetrate far enough to illuminate its secrets.

Brenda pointed with a smile. "Look!" This was one thing I had a vague memory about Flatlash. The Great Viaduct! When The Ring, the cobblestone highway that connected the Ten Keeps of the Lower Realms, was built hundreds of years ago, great bridges were constructed over all the waterways.

To avoid the marshes west of the Deeps, a grand engineering marvel was constructed. On the smaller, north side of the gourd-shaped lake, before the drop off into the crater, a bridge like no other was built. Spanning the half mile wide neck of the lake and ending in a great clearing before Flatlash Keep.

It was constructed of seven large stone arches on the first level, rising out of the lake. Then on the backs of those arches, fourteen smaller stone arches that support the grand promenade of the cobblestone bridge deck. The Viaduct is so broad that ten horses could ride abroad and still have room to spare. I was too young to have appreciated it as the modern marvel it was before, but now I looked on in awe as we saw people, horses and wagons moving along it like ants from our vantage point.

I looked back the way we came and was met by another spectacular sight from our position on top of the rise. Across the canopy of trees and into the grasslands of the flats, was a huge heard of bison, maybe a mile away that stretched most of the way to the horizon. Small herds of whitetail deer and elk dotted the landscape closer to the trees.

I looked from the Viaduct to the bison, not knowing which was a more majestic sight. I glanced over as Celeste settled in beside me. She cocked her head at me with a wistful smile full of question. I said in a voice full of reverence. "Sights of wonder I never thought to see." Then added as I tried to hide a smirk. "It almost makes the last two days of tedium worth it."

She tilted her head at me then looked at the Viaduct and the big herd of buffalo. "This is only the beginning Laney. The sights you will see after this are almost humbling in comparison. There is a whole world out there just waiting for you."

Then she held an arm in the air and let it fall forward and our company started down the hill toward the great Viaduct. She didn't leave my side until we were on the mammoth causeway. I looked back in my saddle then forward again, knowing that as soon as we had set foot on the Viaduct, we had left Wexbury and entered the realm of Flatlash. Celeste winked and took point again and I melted a little and fell behind to her left.

The looks we were getting from travelers and merchants as we passed over the gorge, high above the waters of Cougar Deeps, were those of curiosity mixed with excitement and a little wonder. I knew the look well, I had worn that same look every time I saw knights. I pondered that a moment and wondered when I had started getting used to being in their company.

True, whenever I thought about it or saw larger groups of knights, I still felt the familiar awe. I just hoped I hadn't started taking them or anything else for granted. I knew where I came from and the heights I had risen to by pure happenstance and luck. I looked to my Lady and smiled knowing that it all began with her, that morning on the lanes of Cheap Quarter. The day I ignited.

We proceeded off the causeway to a large clearing that was possibly a quarter mile or so in diameter. There were roads in three directions from where we sat, one to the mountains in the east, one to the southwest, around the keep to Flatlash Minor, then the short three hundred yard approach to the grand portcullis of Flatlash Keep and its forty-foot high rough stone walls.

I knew the Keep to be one of the oldest, and twice the physical size of Wexbury, but it hosted almost three times our population. It was designed in the days of old before anyone thought of sustainability in times of war or siege, so I knew they possessed no internal gardens or livestock herds except what little their castle grounds had.

It sat on the southern shore of Cougar Deeps and the Cougar River. The only water they had internally was from the network of groundwater wells inside the keep. That was about all I knew of them from what mother had shared over the years.

Now Celeste held up a fist to stop our company and she called back, "Verna, Laney, you are with me." The rest of the company surrounded the Coach and waited as we rode up to the grand portcullis in a purposeful manner. I noted a couple windmills fitted with electric turbines on the ramparts of the castle looming in the distance, and smiled. Information sharing was improving the tech level of all the realms, and this one began in Wexbury.

We paused when we were fifty yards from the gates, and a group of men and women on horseback came out to meet us, weapons drawn but held lazily in their grips. I recognized four as Knights and the other four had uniforms I assumed to be Guards of the Gates.

My Lady was all smiles as she sat almost casually with her reins and hands relaxed across her lap as the riders approached.

The knights saluted Celeste and sheathed their weapons. One man with a scruffy salt and pepper beard rode up to my Lady and they grasped arms as the man said, "Salutations Wexbury. What brings you to the keep today?"

She smiled and said, "Salutations Flatlash. We seek respite for the night in our long journey to Far Reach." The words seemed too rehearsed to me, this must be the formal greeting between knights of differing realms. Maybe since each Knight represents either realm they are addressed like that? I'd have to ask Celeste or Verna later.

Then the two chuckled and they tightened their grips and gave slaps on the back as the man ground out in his gravelly voice. "Of course Celeste, how many? And how have you been? I haven't seen you since..." He tailed off then finished in a haunted voice, "York."

She released his arm and they sat back in their saddles. "Yes... York." Then she brightened. "Twenty-one. We are escorting our Duke to the defense pact talks down in Far Reach."

She looked at the man and me and said, "Sir Roderick of Flatlash, this is my squire, Laney of Wexbury." He leaned the other way toward me and I had Goliath step up and I grasped the man's arm.

The man was a jovial sort as he chuckled and surprised me by pulling me in and slapping my back like he did my Lady. He released me and smirked. "Pleased to meet you, Laney. Last I saw this troublemaker, she was a squire herself."

Then he had his steed step back as he glanced back at Celeste as he studied me, his eyes on my sash. "You're making them awfully tiny up there in Wexbury I see." Then he added, "And a Techno

Knight as well." He squinted at our group and shook his head in mock disgust when he saw Tennison. "Three? Three Techno Knights in escort duty? We'd give anything just for a second. Sir Ian is getting up there in age."

Celeste squinted an eye in apology, shrugged, and joked, "It must be something in the water up Wexbury way." Then she looked at me with a smug grin. "And we figure the smaller they are, the harder they are to hit."

The man laughed so hard I thought he'd drop over dead from lack of oxygen. I couldn't stop grinning at the man even though the two Knights were making fun of my height. I offered, "I'm just the right size, thank you very much."

He regained his wits and just motioned with his arm to our group. He smirked at Celeste and me and said, "Duke John left just this morning with an escort to the talks. Get your raggedy band inside the gates, I'm sure we have a pig pen somewhere we can host you at the castle."

I caught the ever so slight nod that my Lady gave to our people and Sir Tennison got everyone in motion. We took our places as they caught up with us, and we followed Sir Roderick through a large portcullis that was twice the size as our South Portcullis. The rest of his group took escort positions around us.

Roderick looked back at Celeste with a furrowed brow. "Is she as powerful as you were back then?"

My Lady played it off with a shrug and said, "Not by a long

shot, but she's twice as dangerous. She uses her head." I'm really going to have to ask why they seemed to cause as much confusion as possible when it came to what our magic users could do. I understand it to a certain extent, never let the enemy know your actual strengths. But Flatlash has always been our longtime ally.

I took the time to look around at the keep. It was positively packed to the gills. Not much open space anywhere. All the buildings were at least two stories, and touching each other by stairs along the lanes. It looked like they were stacking families with private entrances to the upper floors through those stairways.

Their serfs looked like ours, their clothing no richer nor poorer and they all had looks of curiosity and wonder on their faces as we passed. Outside of the buildings, were covered wooden walkways that bordered the lanes. I didn't see even the meager four-foot wide strips of grass that passed for yards in Cheap Quarter. They seemed to utilize every square inch of space here.

There didn't appear to be any organization to the keep as storefronts were intermixed with dwellings. I may be spoiled, coming from Wexbury where the entire structure and organization of the keep had been engineered from the start.

Now don't get me wrong, I was amazed at Flatlash Keep. It seemed to have layers upon layers and each layer built up to the castle that was in the center of the keep. All lanes appeared to be like the spokes of a wheel so you would wind up at the castle when you took any of those spokes, and it was in view from about anywhere in the village.

I thought Castle Wexbury was huge, but Castle Flatlash, while not as long as at home, was multiple stories taller, reaching toward the skies, with parapets and towers. With spires that reminded me of the castles in the tomes mother would read to us. One odd thing was that there was no inner wall surrounding the castle. Instead there were a ring of water, twenty-five yards across surrounding the Castle and there looked to be three drawbridges spanning the water.

On the other side was the only green I had seen in the keep. A meadow about three hundred yards wide, which ringed the castle on the artificial island. There were hundreds of people on the lawns. They all looked to be in the bright colors of nobles instead of the drab, natural colors that commoners wore.

We were challenged at the main drawbridge by a group of knights that didn't have the black and greens of the Flatlash knights, they instead wore crimson. Bowyn must have noted my curiosity and spoke from just behind me, "The Duke's Elite. They are similar to our castle guard who are autonomous of the ranks of the Knights of the Realm. They answer only to the Duke as our castle guard answer to Duke Fredrick."

I nodded in understanding. Our castle guard didn't wear full armor like this though they were armed.

Sir Roderick answered the challenge and pleaded our business. The leader of the Duke's Elite made a hand signal and stepped aside, giving us a bow as we proceeded. I followed Celeste's lead and bowed in response as we passed. I looked back and the Elite gave a soldier's salute to Duke Fredrick as the coach passed.

A runner went ahead of us and by the time we crossed the meadow there were maids, guards, and a woman dressed in black and green finery assembled at some great iron bound oak doors that were twenty feet across each. I could see a courtyard with fountains and a turnaround by a grand staircase through the doors.

The company halted when the coach was in front of the group. A footman ran out as our coachman dismounted. They placed small steps by the door of the coach and the door opened. A slender hand in an emerald glove, extended to take the footman's arm and Duchess Lucia stepped out of the coach as regally as I had ever seen. Then Duke Fredrick stepped out beside her and the footman transferred her hand from his arm to the Duke's, then disappeared as rapidly as he came.

They stepped up to the Lady and then the women smiled and Lucia hugged the woman and said, "Camille, it is so good to see you."

The other woman was all smiles as she made a shooing motion with her hand and the maids attacked the coach like a well-oiled machine to get the Noble's belongings. "Lucy, it has been far too long," then she leaned her cheek over to the Duke. "Fred." He kissed her cheek, then she looked at Sir Roderick. "Please see to our other guests. They are to be treated as honored guests of the realm." Then she turned and took an arm of each of my rulers and marched them through he doors.

Roderick smiled as he watched them go. He turned to Celeste. "We could double bunk you all in the barracks or set up tents here on the Fairy Ring. He indicated the meadow. Celeste slapped his back in a friendly manner. "The Fairy Ring would be just fine, we don't need to inconvenience your knights."

He nodded and motioned his men and they rode through the doorway into the castle on his unspoken order. He finished with, "They'll have porters set up the tents and we'll have a feast set up for you on the lawns. Then we can catch up."

She nodded and leaned into him and looked around and whispered, "We have two shadows, east and west."

His eyes narrowed and he nodded once in understanding. Then he followed his men, clasping the arms of each of our knights and archers as he went. He whispered something to the young runner who nodded then ran like the wind back the way we came.

Celeste looked at Father Sol, hanging low on the horizon, then smiled at me. "Another night under the stars." I smiled at that.

Before I knew it, there were four large canvas tents set up and porters and maids were setting a feast on long plank tables. A lot of Flatlash knights joined us in the feast and I sat back with a permanent smile listening to their knights and ours trading apparently exaggerated tales of battle and adventure. I thought it wonderful that two separate realms could share such camaraderie.

As the night wound down and the Flatlash Knights started

trickling back into the barracks, Sir Roderick walked up to me where I was staring at the lights of the village which resembled a wagon wheel of fireflies. The lights flickered, so they must have been oil or some sort of piped gas instead of electricity. Such waste of resources.

I looked at him, then to their church down the hill for the time, but they had no clock in the bell towers, though they did chime the hour. He smiled and leaned against a bollard beside me and looked over his village. "There is no need for you to sleep out here tonight Laney. There is room in my bed."

I didn't know what to say. I know it was meant as an offer and he wasn't being rude or lewd, just letting me know he appreciated me, and if I wanted...

I blushed at the offer and looked down. "I'm sorry my Lord, but..."

Then a warm hand was on my shoulder and Celeste's chin rested on my other. I could feel the heat of her body behind me and caught a hint of her scent as she told him softly, "But she is with me, Rod."

I was ready to melt though I knew she didn't mean her words the way they sounded. Sir Roderick just bowed gracefully at us with a knowing smile and said, "Then I bid you ladies a good night."

I smiled. "Good night Sir..." He tilted his head and I rolled my eyes with a smile. "...Roderick. Good night Roderick."

The cheeky man gave Celeste a knowing wink as he left. I whispered, "You know what he is thinking don't you?"

She just grinned and moved to my side, her arm around my shoulder as she shrugged. I followed her eyes to the sky, to the nightly meteor showers. Freya and Athena were passing in front of Mother Luna now in their yearly orbit of the larger moon. She noted me shivering and pulled me closer. Then we saw a flash on Luna. A debris strike. Only two or three occurred each night. She whispered, "Make a wish."

I smiled at her, I hadn't wished upon a strike in years. I looked back up then at her beautiful profile in the moonlight and made my silent wish. Then she asked, "What did you wish for?"

I just shook my head. "If I tell you, then it won't come true."

She shared a smile with me then started pulling me toward the tents. "Let's get you inside where it is warm. You need your sleep, the Black Forest awaits."

CHAPTER 17 – BLACK FOREST

I woke up screaming with Celeste rocking me. "Shhhh... It's okay Laney. It's just your dream again." I buried my face in her shoulder. It felt so real. I could handle the pain, I couldn't stand the sight of Celeste's bloody face as she told me to run again.

I looked over to see half the knights in our company sitting up looking at us. Nobody said a word. Verna just stretched and stood yawning. She pulled up Kristof and kicked Tennison's leg. "Let's retrieve the horses from the livery and get the wagon hitched. It is going to be a long trek to the mountains from here."

She looked at Celeste. "Time?"

Celeste looked at her wrist and said, "Five thirty." Then added, "Get everyone fed and we'll depart at eight."

Sir Bowyn stood and stretched and I averted my eyes. The man slept the way he came into this world. He pulled up his trousers then scratched his head and started following the others as he pulled on a tunic.

He paused beside us and asked, "What if her dreams are a premonition?" He watched as Bex exited the tent.

Celeste shrugged and replied, "Then we deal with it when the need arises." She looked away from him and down to me. "You okay now Laney?"

I nodded, she released me, and we started getting ready for the day. I noted the morning wasn't quite as crisp as it had been on the lower plains of Wexbury. I knew that would change soon, fall in the mountains can be unpredictable and it was always cooler there.

We broke bread in the barracks. I noted that for a larger village, they didn't seem to have the variety of foods that Wexbury had. Then I realized it was most likely my earlier observation, that they had no gardens and livestock inside the walls. I wondered what kind of crops and livestock they cultivated outside the walls of the keep. Was the bulk of their foodstuffs produced by Flatlash Minor?

I smiled over a piece of bread and Bex asked, "What is it?"

I shrugged and explained, "It seems I have more questions than answers, and not enough time to ask."

He took a bite of egg and grinned. "I always ask until they tell me to shut up. Knowledge is power."

Celeste chimed in like she had a secret as she chewed, "Laney has always been inquisitive. A rare quality." That made me think of her watching a young girl being flogged at the whipping post all those years ago. My hand absently went to the back of my shoulder where I could feel the outline of a scar. She tilted her head as she looked at my hand then she seemed to sober and look down, absently tearing her bread to small pieces.

I repeated my mother's mantra. "A question unasked is knowledge wasted." I looked at Celeste and caught her eyes. "I already have so many questions I'll need to ask when our escort mission is over. There are so many things I don't know about the keeps."

This coaxed a smile from her. "I'll answer all I can. If not I can find the answers." I smiled back and crinkled my nose at her.

A Flatlash voice sounded behind us, "Oh get a room you two. Are they always like this?" And everyone laughed at my blush as someone answered, "Worse."

We finished the meal and retrieved Fredrick and Lucia. Duchess Camille spoke as they boarded the coach, "Fair weather and godspeed."

We all bowed to the Lady of Flatlash and then mounted up. I actually made it up onto Goliath on my first try though it probably looked like I was hanging on for dear life until I was settled in the saddle. I kicked Verna in the leg when I saw her smirk. This just made some of the other evil Knights chuckle.

I watched as huge electric motors lowered the three drawbridges they had raised the prior night. Sir Roderick and a small contingent delivered us to the gates. Roderick rode up between Celeste and I and clasped her arm and they slapped shoulders. "Fair weather. We will see you on the return?"

My lady nodded then Roderick turned to me and gave a soft smile. I went to clasp arms and he instead caught my hand and kissed the back of it. "If you ever wish to trade up. I'm always here my Lady."

I don't know why I felt so brave around my red headed knight, but I grinned at her then at the man. "What? And have you break the hearts of all the maidens in the keep? Perish the thought my

Lord." This got a guffaw from the man then he winked and moved off. He really was a pleasant sort. I find so many knights that way, and I wouldn't have thought it just three months prior.

He moved closer to Celeste and spoke quietly, "Our scouts put one shadow at the west end of the Deeps, in the great marshes. We could not locate the one to the east."

She nodded a thanks to him, then the motors on the huge portcullis started pulling in the giant chains when the big man motioned to the guards. They strained against the immense weight of the gate, and soon it was lifting high into the archway. Celeste turned to look at our company, raised a hand and let it drop, and we resumed our journey.

I smiled as we made our way around the keep, giving us a spectacular view of the forty foot tall Walls of Heinrick the Bold. They had never been breached since Flatlash was conceived. We reached a crossroad, a 'spoke', in The Ring. The ten foot stone pillar with a brass signposts at the top and a dragon weather vane at its apex. One road sign pointed back the way we came, it read Flatlash, another pointing south read Treth. A third pointed east toward the mountains, reading York. Then the final one pointed down an unpaved, packed earth roadway to the west. The sign for that road read Fringe. Someone had painted a skull and crossbones on that one.

This is where we would lose our shadows I thought. They wouldn't conceive of us traveling the mountain roads. We turned east into the beginnings of the Black Forest with a thick canopy of trees stretching to the horizon. I was excited about this. The old growth deciduous forest was so named because even when Father Sol is high in the sky, the thick canopy blocks out most of the sunlight and it is like a perpetual twilight below.

That alone was intriguing, but with the weather cooling with the seasons, it looked as though the forest was ablaze with colors. Swaths of brilliant reds, yellows and oranges made the trees look like a fantasy painting on canvas. I took a moment to behold the splendor of nature before falling into position.

Duchess Lucia smiled at my childlike delight as the coach passed me. It snapped me out of it and I urged Goliath on. Her smile for me was just that jarring and unnatural. The one-sided feud she seems to have with mother, usually spilled upon me. I don't think the Duchess has said two complete words to me since she learned who my mother was.

I grinned at the smile Celeste had for me when I fell in at her left. She always had a knack for making me feel special. I said, "The forest is so gorgeous. The Whispering Forest isn't as thick and it has so many conifer pines breaking up the groves of leafy trees. The colors here are amazing."

My companion squinted at me and tilted her head then looked around like she was just now seeing things around us. Then she nodded and said wistfully, "I'd almost forgotten to look around me. I'm always lost in the patrol. Thank you for reminding me. It really is beautiful Laney."

It was like a curtain was drawn when we entered the forest. Rays of sunlight streamed in small points, lighting the way enough to navigate by. I could hear dozens of types of bird calls and other animals chittering about, though I didn't see much.

I noted the berms just ten or fifteen feet off the road and pointed. Bowyn gave me a start when he answered from directly behind me instead of Celeste. "The royal road crews. They are sent out every spring to make sure The Ring is clear from fall and winter debris. That is hundreds of years of leaves removed from the roadway. Some of the richest compost in all the lands."

I nodded thanks then smiled and peeled off, it was time for a random traverse. The other squires joined me. I asked, "Have you ever seen such wonders?"

I remembered my station when both of them chimed in, "Yes." It reminded me of their noble status and that I was just a girl from Cheap Quarter. Of course, they have seen these wonders. Nobles can afford to travel the realms. Bex read this in my face and said, "But it is a marvel to see someone's first impressions." Brenda just nodded her agreement.

It was on my third rotation that Celeste called out, "Sir Scot, ride ahead with a hunting party, we'll break for midday meal in an hour, fresh meat would be nice." I was surprised when he called out, "Laney, Peter, with me." I looked up at Celeste and she shrugged and grinned. I was no hunter. First time for everything I guess. I

urged Goliath on as Sir Scot and an archer galloped past, he easily
kept pace with them.

I glanced back to the smug look on my Lady's face and narrowed
my eyes. I think she planned this so I could have another first. I
smiled to myself as we rode. Scot was in instructor mode for me
since Peter was obviously a seasoned soldier. "We serve triple duty
here in areas where there is limited visibility."

He counted off on his fingers as we barreled down the shadowed
roadway. "First, as advanced scouts. A small group is more nimble
and can retreat to warn the others of danger faster than we could turn
our caravan around, no matter how small it is."

Then he smirked. "I think Celeste is allowing me to take you out
because we haven't reached what we are designating as the hostile
territory between Treth and Far Reach. I'm sure she'll never let you
out of her sight once we get there, you are her favorite." He winked
at me and I blushed.

Then he held up a second finger. "Once we ride hard for a half
hour, we hunt for wild game as the group catches up." Then a third
finger. "Then we find a clearing or other defensible position for the
caravan to stop while the porters make a meal of our catch."

Then Peter chimed in, "Be sure to not be too good in the hunt or
you will be cursed to be in the scout position for eternity."

This got Sir Scot laughing boisterously. "You should have
thought of that before you became the best shot in the realm now
shouldn't you have, Pete?"

The other man just shot him a playfully poisonous look. Then he softened and looked at me. "Have you hunted?" I shook my head and he prompted, "Snares? Or can you use a bow?" I shook my head again and he grinned like a fool and said to Scot, "We have a virgin here."

I blushed for other private reasons, then narrowed my gaze and shook a finger at the men. "I'll not fall for a snipe hunt. I may be green, but I'm not simple." This got a chuckle from the men and they held their hands up in surrender. "I'll not be out chasing my tail and making a fool of myself seeking out imaginary creatures."

We slowed after a bit and we circled ourselves then dismounted, lashing our mounts to a limb just over the berms. Pete took his bow and slung the quiver over his shoulder. We walked for a couple minutes, both men scanning the ground then Scot put up a hand then pointed at his eyes then the forest floor to the right. I saw pebbled scat, there wasn't much, so it wasn't anything big like Elk. I figured it was deer.

We followed a trail I couldn't see, but each man made a point of showing me scuffed bark on a tree or a snapped over stem on a plant. I started looking closer for anything that seemed out of the ordinary. I was beginning to get the hang of it, though they saw dozens of things I did not. It may have well been a red string leading them to the small clearing we approached a few seconds later. They crouched and I crouched behind them.

We were crosswind from a three-point buck maybe thirty yards

away. I looked around the clearing as Peter knocked an arrow. I
was about to look back at the buck to watch the kill when I saw
something at the edge of the clearing, and I slapped Pete's arm up as
he released. His arrow made a swish sound as it arced high into the
air.

Both men looked at me as if I had gone crazy. I whispered.
"This buck is hers, I will not steal from the mouth of another." They
followed the finger I was pointing and they saw the caramel pelt and
the tip of other's tail stalking toward the deer.

I had never heard a cougar scream before. But as it pounced on
the back of the buck, digging her front claws into his flank, it
screamed out a battle cry. Birds exploded from the trees into the
sky. Her fangs sunk into the back of his neck and she shook
violently and I could hear the snap from where we sat in the
shadows. The deer stopped struggling. I went pale. A cougar could
do the same to me.

Scot sighed in disappointment at me as he signaled us to start
getting back to the horses. When we were out of earshot, we
stopped at a fallen tree trunk for Scot to shake a pebble out of his
boot. He spoke quietly. "Well, I guess squirrel stew it will be since
we wasted so much time on the buck."

I squinted a challenge, "He wasn't our buck." He actually
grinned at that.

I heard something behind the log that I recognized immediately,
and I smiled as I reached for the boot scabbard Celeste insisted I

have. Scot looked at Peter. "Pete, can you find a squirrel or two? I'll head back to meet the caravan."

I dove over the log with my little dagger in my hand I grabbed my prey, and with one slash silenced its cry, just like I would a chicken. I popped up smiling to see to a sword and an arrow pointing at me. I gulped then held up my prize, "You two are welcome to the squirrel, I'm looking forward to a good turkey lunch."

Their weapons dropped and I'm sure you could hear Scot's bellowing laugh a mile away. I grinned as I held up the big Tom. The Knight teased, "Bested by a tiny waif of a girl Pete. There will be retellings of this at the campfire tonight, I assure you."

I grinned as the archer rolled his eyes and reached for my turkey. I started to pull away and Scot held a hand up to me. "You did the killing, the others do the hauling." Then he added as I let Pete take my prize, "Actually this is much easier since I don't think you would have been much help to me hauling that buck back."

I pouted. "Hey. I'm not that weak." He cocked an eyebrow and I crossed my arms then smiled. "Fine. Maybe I am, but shut up, I bagged lunch for you."

Pete chuckled as he walked past both of us with the Tom slung over his shoulder, "Touche. She's got you there big guy." I was treated to Sir Scot's laugh again as we headed back to the roadway.

We had just got to the horses and found a small clearing by a brook when the company came to a halt on the roadway. We walked out to greet them and Peter threw the turkey up to the porters in the wagon. Lady Beth said, "Grand! Turkey! Good show Pete."

Sir Scot laughed and said loudly for all to hear, "Actually that is Laney's kill. We needed something to eat after Peter missed a shot at a deer." I heard a couple gasps. I guess he doesn't miss much.

He protested in good humor, "Hey, she knocked my arm away."

I raised an eyebrow imperiously at him and repeated, "It was not our buck."

Scot laughed and told a thoroughly amused Celeste, "A cougar was on the scent before us. Laney wouldn't let us... what did she say? Steal from the mouth of another." Then he pointed at my leg. "So then she used that tiny paring knife in her boot to bag the trophy to stop our whining."

Everyone chuckled at that and then started laughing harder when I said, "Hey! It's a dagger, not a paring knife." I grumped until Celeste slid off her mount and bumped my hip. Then you couldn't have wiped the grin off my face.

Less than an hour later we were all eating a hearty turkey soup. I was surprised when Fredrick ushered me in front of him and Lucia in the line to dish up first. I must have looked terrified because Lucia prompted quietly so the others didn't hear her showing me a kindness, "You supplied the meal, you are served first."

Oh. I bowed to her, then turned with my bowl and one of the porters, Darin I think his name was gave me an extra half ladle with a grin. Then we all sat as Sir Scot recounted the tale of Lord Peter's first missed shot, to our company's amusement. I was ready to melt as Celeste had me sit between her legs and use her as a backrest as we ate. She whispered, "You are one surprise after another."

After we had been on the move again, Celeste was fidgeting around in her saddle, with the minimal head movement I could tell she was scanning the forest. I fought off the compulsion to look around like my head was on a swivel. I asked, "What is it?"

She responded in a low tone, "There are eyes on us. Start a rotation and discretely let the other squires know to double the frequency at random intervals. The Knights will pick up on it and understand." I nodded and she added, "They have to be a lot closer than when we were traveling through the flats, visibility is limited in the forest, so keep on guard."

Without a word, I peeled off and motioned to Bex and Brenda with my eyes as I passed and they started a sweep with me. Under my breath, I filled them in, prefacing it with, "Don't react and don't look around. Our shadow is back." They nodded and we tarried at the back of the caravan for a few extra minutes.

I could see the knights and archers react to the change, they seemed to all perk up and were more alert, nobody looked around. If you hadn't been specifically looking for it like I was, the casual observer would have seen no change. I marveled at how much more aware of things the Knights were than I was. Was it instinct or was it something learned with experience I wondered.

Two of us moved back to our Knights, leaving Bex to move

back whenever he felt like it made it a shell game how many defenders were at any given point at any given time. I understood the strategy now. Unless they were directly upon us, none would know that we were simply squires and not knights.

We pushed on into the night until a suitably defensible position was found at a clearing under a rock overhang near a little vale. No open flame was the order of the night. Pete and another archer disappeared into the forest after the horses were tended and we broke bread. After laying out my bedroll next to Celeste's, I made my way silently around and up to the top of the overhang where she sat first watch. It was just above the trees and the night sky looked to swallow the world, blanketing it in a quilt of stars.

She just smiled at me as I walked up. She held open her riding cloak and I nestled in as she wrapped me in it. Then we just sat and watched the night, knowing that somewhere nearby, it was watching back. I actually made it through her watch without dozing off this time.

Celeste nodded at a grinning Lady Beth as the burly blonde relieved us. The Knight reminded me of a smaller Verna... nobody had the muscles of Verna. We made our way down. Pausing once when my Lady cocked her head slightly, listening intently, then we went down to the camp, our breath fogging the chill air.

The cone of heat from the electric space heater was a godsend. We laid on my bedroll and she pulled her blanket over the both of us as she draped her arm over my waist and we fell asleep in our familiar configuration.

I awoke with a start, the world was lit brilliantly and the colors were so rich and vivid. Celeste's hand was over my mouth and she was scanning the party. When she knew I was fully awake, she released me as her keen eyes scanned the area. I noticed brilliant emerald sparks were dripping from her eyes and I had matching amber trailing my head as I followed her gaze.

It was still night, it was my magics allowing me to see as though it were day. I tried to figure out what had awakened me and Celeste in this state. Then I could feel it, taste it. Someone was using magic nearby. They were quick because the position kept shifting. She slowly drew a dagger that was almost as long as my sword, I drew my own dagger.

Tennison was on alert and I saw Duke Fredrick poke his head out the tent, silver power sparkling in his eyes. All the magic users were awakened by the taste of magic in the air. Tennison gave Fredrick a reprimanding look and the Duke disappeared back inside the tent.

Celeste whispered, "We are missing one. Figuring three sentries, we should have eighteen here. A porter is missing." She made a hand motion to Tennison and the other knights who were awakening. Then she whispered, "With me Laney." We slipped into the woods. My heart was threatening to pound out of my chest as we made our way around the camp.

I saw one of the porters ummm... squatting by a tree, doing his business. Then everything happened at once. Celeste's eyes shot up above us then over to a stump near the porter. She held a hand out and I had to squint as the very air around the stump got unbearably bright. I realized it was just my enhanced vision. She was illuminating the area.

There was a man in a dark brown cloak crouched by the stump, he was looking at the porter and energy was gathering in his hand. He had been preparing to strike at the man when he could not defend! How cowardly was this magic user? And I heard the first arrow fly from almost directly above us.

The Rogue redirected the power he was going to use to attack the porter to deflect the arrow and he ran. Weaving through the trees so the archer who was sitting in the tree above us couldn't get off another shot. I went to peruse, but Celeste had a grip on my collar.

She grinned at me and shook her head. "Not in the woods at night Laney. I know the fire in your heart. Just know our man is safe."

The porter had fallen over on his ass during the excitement, uttering a, "The fuck?" I looked away from the partially exposed man. Celeste chuckled then looked up and made a slight motion with her head and I saw the archer bound away from tree to tree in pursuit of the Rogue. I think it was Pete.

Celeste chuckled, "For god's sake Henry, wipe your ass and pull your britches up." I waited until he joined us to turn back around again.

He looked back to where the rogue had been then at us. "What the hell is going on my Lady?" She rolled her eyes and gently shoved the man back toward camp. We followed and I kept looking back, Celeste whispered, "He'll not be back tonight."

We arrived back at camp and it was bustling with activity. Three knights were guarding the tent. Celeste spoke loudly with humor tinging her voice. "Henry went out to take a dump and wound up almost shitting himself when our shadow decided to thin the herd. He was a target of opportunity."

There was restrained chuckling and she got serious. "For the duration of the mission, nobody leaves camp without escort, buddy system, and nobody leaves camp unarmed. The assailant was a rogue. Peter is tracking him now." Everyone sobered and gave nods of understanding.

Tennison called over to me, "For the love of God Laney, turn it down a notch, he's gone." I squinted at him and looked down to the rivulets of amber energy arcing down my arms and dripping onto the ground." The big man smirked at me and I sighed and closed my eyes and took three deep breaths, calming myself. I opened my eyes and the world darkened to twilight. Sunrise was maybe thirty minutes off, with tinges of orange on the horizon. Tennison chuckled and winked.

Bex stepped beside us. "What was he talking about?"

I shrugged and went to start rolling up my bedroll. Celeste said in a voice full of humor, "Magic users tend to bleed power from their eyes and it is visible to other magic users. Laney, for how under powered she is, is pretty spectacular to look at. She has an unusual amber signature, and it seems to flow over her entire body."

He looked at me and squinted. Kristof cuffed him lightly on the back of his head and said with humor, "She's not doing it now, and even if she were, we can't see it. But you start to get a feel for it. The hairs on your arm and neck will stand on end whenever one of the techno-dweebs powers up."

He deftly caught the pebble Tennison chucked at him for the insult and grinned. Celeste rolled her eyes with a smile and backhanded him in the gut and joined me breaking camp.

Peter reappeared just as Father Sol peeked over the horizon. He looked annoyed and just shook his head once at Celeste. The Rogue had escaped. He passed Tennison and grumped out, "Fuckin' magic users." Which just got a chuckle from the big man and they exchanged smiles.

I got a smug look on my face when I mounted Goliath on my fist attempt. Then I promptly rode into a branch and almost fell off while I gloated. Celeste just chuckled at me as she rode past. We waited, eyes scanning the shadowed forest as the wagon and coach were checked and loaded. Then we were on our way along the cobbled highway.

I don't know if it was the close call earlier that had me nervous or not, but I think I felt the uneasiness Celeste did when she was being watched. I scolded myself. Just great, don't get paranoid Laney.

Things were pretty routine and the novelty of the never ending dark forest was starting to wear off by lunch. I mean it was beautiful and spectacular, but there were only so many trees you could marvel at, at one time. I did enjoy the more frequent little stone bridges over small creeks we crossed over as we neared the Whispering Walls.

I've heard so many stories of how plentiful running water was in the mountains and was just starting to witness it in the foothills of the forest. I noted we had been steadily heading uphill for hours when we stopped for the midday meal.

After we broke bread, I sat on a stump and pulled out my father's tool pouch. I got a thread and needle out to repair a small hole I got in my riding cloak when I dove over the log to catch the turkey. Lady Beth was watching me intently.

I finally broke and stopped as I was tying off my stitches. I looked at her and then she blinked. "Oh, sorry Laney. I didn't mean to be rude. You can sew?"

I gave a crooked smile. "Of course I can sew. Everyone can sew."

She shook her head. I was about to ask what kind of person didn't learn to sew. Then paused and asked, "Who mends your clothes for you." I nudged my hands toward a hole in the tunic she wore under her cloak as I bit the thread to sever it. Then I checked out my patch.

She made a chuffing sound and said as if it were common sense. "We just send it off to the seamstress for repair or a new tunic and cut up the old for cleaning rags."

I nodded and patted the stump next to me. Celeste was watching our exchange carefully. Beth sat next to me as I knotted the end of my thread and started repairing her tunic. I asked, "And what if you couldn't? What if you had to pay for that new tunic, but you had no coin and the seamstress was away?"

She grinned. "Then I'd have a chambermaid or a..."

I stopped what I was doing and looked at her, meeting her eyes when she paused, understanding lighting her eyes. I said, "Serfs do not have the luxury of chambermaids and servants. The keep does not furnish their clothing. They have to pay for every scrap of clothing they own, and the coin is far too scarce. So they learn to repair what they have, get the most use out of it. It is as natural to us as reading is to a noble."

She cocked an eyebrow as I bit off the thread and checked my repair on her tunic. "Us?"

I exhaled as she smiled at the patch. Then I said, "I do not forget from where I hailed. I am no noble no matter what my title may say. This is not my world. I do my best not to embarrass you true knights, and do you proud." I looked over at Celeste, who was pretending not to listen. "To do my Lady proud."

Beth looked at me then exhaled. "Do not undersell yourself

Laney. You've given me things to ponder here." Then she looked down at her tunic again and asked, "Teach me to sew sometime?" I nodded once and she offered her arm and we grasped forearms to seal the deal.

The smile Celeste gave me, when we mounted up to continue our journey to the towering mountains which we could now see above the treeline, had me blushing for the next mile. She never said a word, but she had me smiling for some stupid reason as we scanned the forest.

I had been noting various heavily traveled trails off the highway and even a dirt road or two as the forest thinned a little. I stopped at the back of the caravan to look down one of those roads during one of our rotations. My brow furrowed when I tried to think of what villages were down that way.

I wasn't as familiar with all the towns in Flatlash as in Wexbury, so maybe a village I didn't know of was off the spoke of the Ring there. I smiled at myself, I knew all twenty-three village names in Wexbury.

Brenda and Bex held back with me a moment, following my gaze. Brenda cocked an eyebrow in question. I shrugged and said, "I've been noticing these small unmarked roads and trails and was wondering where they led."

She grinned and said, "Mountain Gypsy roads. We are entering their domain." I looked back down the road again and at her. She rolled her eyes and pointed as she said, "See the deep ruts from wagons heavier than any wagon of the realms? And the cloven hoof prints? Oxen, not horses. Pound for pound they are much more powerful than horses and can pull those houses on wheels the Gypsies have."

I smiled at that, I hadn't even paid attention to the tracks. I said, "Oh." Then we hurried to catch back up with the group. I asked, "Do you think we'll meet any Gypsies? I've only seen them when they carnival at the keep in summer."

Bex nodded. "It is hard to avoid them in the mountains. It is their domain and the realms have no sway nor say over them. It was after all, their land before Highland showed up and divvied it up."

I found that exciting. Mother had made sure I could speak Mountain Gypsy when she gave me lessons. Welsh is the only language she did not teach me since she says virtually nobody speaks it anymore. Corrick taught me Outsider, which had some Welsh in it. Maybe I could talk with the Gypsies if we met any on our journey.

It was just getting to be dusk when we broke into a clearing on a rise, and I saw rising out of the Earth, possibly the most spectacular and awe-inspiring view I had ever witnessed. The Whispering Walls towered into the clouds. My breath caught at the majestic sight. Maybe God was real, what else could have created such beauty in a world that was almost destroyed? I had seen the mountains in the distance many times but had never seen them from a vantage point at their base. I felt humbled and small.

Celeste's leg brushed against mine as she sidled over to me. She said in that low tone she got when she appreciated something I had done. "You'll need to breathe at some time Laney." I looked at her and realized my lungs were burning. I had been holding my breath. I grinned and exhaled and gulped in another breath. Then she almost purred, "You're holding up the caravan, let's get moving so others can appreciate the view too."

Shit! I had stopped the entire group. I blushed and tried to make myself even smaller on my mammoth mount and urged him on. Celeste's low chuckle got me grinning for reasons I didn't know. I took one last glance at the snow-capped peaks and then sat taller as I realized that I, Laney Herder, was going to travel through the Whispering Walls. What an exciting adventure this was turning out to be!

Chapter 18 – Fall

We stopped at the foot of the mountains by a rocky outcropping that gave us a good vantage point and a defensible position. Celeste gave a soldier's salute toward the mountains and I followed her gaze. I could see a man on horseback a ridge over from us. How had my Lady even seen him? He wore the colorful garb of a Gypsy and his horse had a bright blanket draped over it. He gave a cocky flourish of a hand and bowed in acknowledgment. Then he leaned lazily on his saddle on an arm to watch us.

I looked at her and she said, "Mountain Gypsy lookout. He's been shadowing us half a horizon away since we crested the rise at the base of the mountains."

I narrowed my eyes in mock warning at her. "You need to teach me how you do that. How you can find anyone who is watching us?"

She winked and teased, "If you teach me how to sew as well." I squinted an eye to see if she were teasing then crinkled my nose and pulled off a leather gauntlet and spit in my hand, offering it to her. "Done."

She did the same and clasped my hand as she grinned. "Done."

As we ate, Scot recounted the tale of how a ferocious mountain lion stole a buck away from Lord Peter and causing him to miss his target. He ended with, "And when pressed as to how it had occurred, Pete insists he missed on purpose because he would never steal from the mouth of another." Everyone chuckled and I blushed.

Bex turned to him and prompted, "I thought he missed because Laney knocked his arm away." Which got boisterous laughter from the group. Kristof clapped him on the back.

I said into the biscuit I was eating, "They tease me and Peter." He looked from Scot then me then to Pete, who had a toothy grin as he ate. Then all the cogs and gears in his head connected and a smile crept upon his lips. I had to grin. For someone who was so brainy, some things just escaped his grasp.

I stood when I had cleaned my tin plate and stretched as I looked out over the mountains, Verna joined me. "Wondrous isn't it?" I nodded. She clasped my shoulder then went to rejoin her husband but paused. I followed her gaze as she called out, "Celeste."

I saw the Gypsy lookout on the other ridge looking our way, and he was holding a spyglass in front of himself in a prompting motion. Celeste stepped beside me then asked, "Laney?" I looked at her and she dipped her eyes to my pouch.

Oh, yes. I pulled out my spyglass and handed it to her then the man looked through his to our north. She followed suit then lowered the glass and bowed her head to the man. He waved it off then went back to his aloof vigilance.

She handed the spyglass to Verna, who searched for a moment then said, "Two."

Celeste leaned over her with a hand on her back and nodded. "They must have joined up. I wonder how the west shadow knew we went this way unless he never lost sight of us when we turned to the mountains."

I looked at the women, and Verna handed me the spyglass she pointed. I scanned a rise to the north and passed something orange and panned back to it. It was a tiny campfire, so small I would have missed it. There were two dark shadows moving around it. The two ghosts? Then I had a thought. "How do we know it is them?"

My Lady explained, "That is a perfect elevated location to see our camp. They will be able to see where we go in the morning and follow easily." I nodded and shivered. The wind was biting. She saw this and was suddenly stuffing my spyglass into my pouch and wrapping me in her riding cloak. "You're freezing Laney. Let's get you back to the heaters."

I nodded but would rather just soak in her heat like this. I noted we were starting to get a bit rank. I'd have to sneak away to give myself a sponge bath the next day.

She took last watch that night so she could keep me warm. I hugged the arm she had around my waist as I slept.

I again awoke to her hand over my mouth. The world was lit up by a crackling amber light, my heart was racing as the nightmare receded and I gained control of myself, bringing my power back under control. Though I still felt the last of the terror ebbing away, I had to smile at Celeste deftly catching the two tin plates and a dagger that were orbiting my head like a halo.

She let me get my wits about me, then I scrunched my head and crinkled my nose as I whispered, "Sorry." She just shook her head and cupped my cheek. I closed my eyes and leaned into the heat.

Then she whispered, "My turn for watch, I'll be back at sunrise." I shook my head and stood with her, bringing a blanket. We relieved an archer who I believe was named Samuel.

She took her position where she could watch the shadow camp, and the approach to ours, and I snuggled in on the ground with my head in her lap. She absently ran a hand through my tangled hair as her eagle eyes scanned the perimeter. I loved it when she did that.

I tried to stay alert and started to doze when the first hints of orange tinted the sky to the east. Celeste looked down at me and gave a silly face that made me have to contain a snicker. She tickled me to my feet. I couldn't get away fast enough, I'm extremely ticklish. She stood and stretched and said, "Let's wake up the camp, but first..." She held out her hand expectantly. I pulled out my spyglass and she took a look at our shadows breaking their own camp.

I asked as we walked back down to the others who were already starting to rise on their own. "So is all this people watching people watching people par for the course?"

She seemed to ponder it a bit. "For the most part, though all realms are allies, we still keep an eye on other knights in our territory. I wouldn't be surprised if some Flatlash are out there now in that people watching game. But it is done out of prudence not out of suspicion. And never would another realm attempt to kill someone from another realm's traveling caravan."

She nudged her head back the way we came. "Those are most likely spies for the rogues that are amassing down Far Reach way. Given that we know at least one of the shadows is a Rogue magic user himself, that makes it all the more likely they work for this Raneth or Poe." I nodded at the logic.

I gave her an apologetic look as we roused the ones who hadn't already awoken. "Sorry for asking so many silly questions."

I stood up straight then turned and bowed as Duke Fredrick spoke from behind me. Stretching as he stepped out of the tent. "There are no silly questions. Nobody will fault you for seeking knowledge." My hand absently went to my shoulder where my scars began and Celeste placed a hand on mine to stop me. Fredrick added, "And you ask the exact right questions if you are to one day be a Knight of Wexbury." He held the tent flap open and the Duchess stepped out, looking as perfect as ever, not a hair out of place. I bowed again.

We packed everything away as the porters prepared simple fare. "Last of the eggs," Darin said aloud. "So eat up." After eating and relieving, ourselves in the woods, we mounted up and continued into the towering mountains.

Sir Randolph, who I don't think had spoken a single word on the entire journey started singing, 'Bonnie Lass of Solomon'. We all chimed in on the merry tune.

It was getting close to midday after climbing peaks, just to drop into lush valleys which would make beautiful backdrops for paintings. Bowyn cantered up to Celeste and I. "I'll scout the next ridge for our midday meal."

Celeste nodded. "Take two and get us some fresh game? I do not look forward to the dried and smoked meats."

He nodded and called out "Samuel and..." He looked around then grinned at me. "...Laney, with me." He winked at Celeste. "The Penny Lady here seems to be the camp's good luck charm, maybe we'll score a buck this time." Everyone in earshot heard that and chuckled. They were never going to let Peter and me live that down.

Celeste crinkled her nose at me in goodbye and I surprised Bowyn by kicking Goliath into motion and giving him all the rein he wanted as we charged off down the road. I heard chuckling behind me as he and Samuel pushed to catch up.

Bowyn pulled up beside me and playfully pushed my shoulder and I shot the men a grin. We rode hard for a half hour, our eyes peeled for anything. I noted a Gypsy on another ridge. I couldn't tell if it was the same man or if they had sentries sprinkled throughout the Whispering Walls.

We dismounted on a ridge with a decent clearing and a ravine below on one side, giving us natural defense. I looked down and swallowed, it must have been five or six hundred feet down. Like a great crack in the Earth.

We set out a rope line between two trees and lashed the leads to it, giving the horses plenty of line to graze. I cupped a hand and poured water from my canteen into it to let Goliath drink his fill. The greedy gut emptied my canteen. I scrubbed his ears and shook my head at him.

Bowyn nodded at me when he saw me take out my spyglass. I scanned behind us and I could sporadically make out between breaks in the trees, our caravan slowly making its way through the forest toward us.

I turned slowly around trying to pick out any other movement or anything out of the ordinary. Besides the Gypsy, who was the same man as before, I saw nothing. I shook my head and Bowyn said, "Grand. Then let's find lunch."

We all went into the forest on foot. I followed the men then saw something and placed a hand on Samuel's shoulder. He looked at me and I picked up a stone and nudged my head toward some underbrush. He slowly pulled an arrow from his quiver and nocked it, drawing back on the string then he nodded and I tossed the stone. Pheasants exploded from the underbrush. A large male went down and Samuel drew fast and took a female out of the air.

Sir Bowyn retrieved them and returned the arrows to Samuel. "Great shot Sam." Then he grinned at me. "You really are a good luck charm." We spent another fifteen minutes and wound up with a large jack rabbit and a squirrel before we started heading back to the horses. I blushed in embarrassment, as all I carried out for Sam was the squirrel. Bowyn carried the good meats.

As we set the game on a rock beside the cliff, I suddenly spun around as my eyesight sharpened and the world bloomed in color. Someone was using magic right there! I yelled, "Rogue!" as I dove in front of Bowyn, drawing my sword and jamming it into the ground as I let my power flow into it, causing a river of power to go to ground as we were hit by a powerful blast of raw energy.

I screamed as I channeled the burning magics through me and my sword into the Earth. It was the only magic defense Celeste had taught me so far. I was able to shield Bowyn, who instantly had his sword and parrying blade drawn. Every cell in my body was on fire.

Samuel caught the edge of the blast but was able to loose an arrow before he stumbled back. I dove at him and grabbed his arm as he went over the cliff. I held on with both hands for dear life as I heard swords clanging behind us as Samuel's weight was slowly pulling me over with him. I just needed to hang on for a moment longer. I could hear grunts from our attacker as Bowyn pressed the attack so that the man didn't have time to gather his energies again.

I was spreading my body out on the ground to create more drag as Samuel shook his head at me and said, "Let go Laney or you'll fall with me."

I shook my head and hissed, "No." I pulled my energy to me and tried to push back against the drag, we slowed a little. I heard a gurgled cry of a man run through with a blade. Then Bowyn yelling, "Laney hold on!" Just as we went over the edge, dragging anything loose that was made of metal with us.

I don't know why, but the analytical side of my mind noted that Samuel didn't make a sound as we fell and were pulled apart. He was brave to the end. I, on the other hand, was not so calm. I really didn't want to die. But nobody does. I didn't want to disappoint Celeste, I had to try something. I "Oof"ed as I bounced off an outcropping. It may have hurt, but I couldn't feel anything with all the adrenaline pumping through my veins and sheer terror in my mind.

I exploded into a sparking amber energy trail and I reached out for something, anything. I could feel the metal in my gear, even the metal from our gear on our horses above. I could actually taste my fear, it had an acrid taste. And I could taste... the iron in the red rock face I tumbled past!

I mentally pulled with all my might at the iron I had already passed. Letting it drag at me, slowing my fall, but not enough. I reached inside and screamed with the effort and yanked at that iron as I passed. Rocks and debris were pulled from the cliff face and I slammed into it with the magical draw. My whole body was vibrating from the contact as I slid down the irregular cliff face. It slowed me down as the drag of the strings of amber I could actually see coming from me stretched and snapped over and over.

I was down to the speed of a dead run when I hit a rock near the bottom, hard. The wind was knocked out of me and I bounced off and lost the hold on my magic, there was a new pain in my chest. I had just thought I had failed when I hit the ground on my back a couple feet later.

I couldn't breathe and my vision was fading out when I saw my own sword hurling down upon me. With the last of my strength, I lifted my hand and pushed with anything I had left in me and the blade diverted course just the tiniest amount and sank into the ground right beside my face. I turned my head to look at it, and the last thing I saw was Samuel's broken body maybe ten feet from me when the world went black.

CHAPTER 19 – GYPSIES

My eyes fluttered open, but I wasn't on the lounge in Celeste's quarters. And I couldn't feel her warmth behind me. I hurt all over and I wrinkled my nose, why did Celeste's chambers smell like a wet horse? Why was I wet? I felt steady motion under my belly and my chest was on fire. I lifted my head into the freezing drizzle to realize I was lashed to the back of a horse, and we were moving slowly through the trees. Everything came rushing back to me.

I looked up at the rider who was wearing a bright purple riding cloak. I knew that man. He was the Gypsy lookout. I shivered in the cold then croaked out in Mountain Gypsy, "What's happening?"

The horse stopped and the man turned around in the saddle to look down at me. He smiled a toothy smile at me. "Ah good, you are awake. You are a tough one to survive a fall like that. I think there is more to you than meets the eye, yes?" Then he added, "You speak the tongue of the people?"

I nodded as he dismounted and I winced at the pain in my chest and said, "Yes, but not well."

He started undoing the ropes lashing me onto the horse, and said in English, "We will use the tongue of the Altii then." I nodded. Altii means Others. That's what they called those of us who came to their lands from Highland Keep so long ago.

He helped me down to sit on a log at the side of the little trail we were on. I winced as I tried to take a deep breath. He said, "Easy there little one. You fell from the heavens and survived, I think you may have broken some things here and there on your way down." He waffled his hand back and forth. His grin was contagious.

I took shallower breaths and realized my sword was in its sheath now, and all my weapons and tool pouch were still on me. Then I really looked at the man. He was actually a beautiful man. Can you say that about a man? He had long black curly hair, a dark complexion, and eyes so dark they looked black. His features were chiseled and he had dimples when he smiled. I'm sure the women were swooning all over the man.

He gave me a drink from his canteen. Good lord, the water felt great going down. I nodded that I was okay, and he grasped my shoulder. "Good. We are close to my clan. We can get you where it is dry and warm. To our vrajitoare healer to get you patched up. Then we can see about getting you two back with your people."

You two? I glanced at his huge draft horse and then my breath caught at the form rolled up in a blanket draped over the back of the horse. I saw Samuel's boots then wretched as I fought back tears. I bit back scream at the pain in my chest as I threw up.

He saw all of this then said in a soft tone, "If it is any consolation. He made a hell of a shot before he fell. He had tagged that vrajitor in the shoulder before that big guy finished the assassin off." It wasn't of any consolation at all. I had let him fall. I wasn't strong enough.

I shivered as the rain increased in intensity. I realized it was a pitch black night with the clouds blotting out the moons. How long had I been out? He saw my shiver and helped me to my feet. "Come, let's get to camp before you die from exposure little one." I nodded and he helped me up into the saddle with as little pain as possible, and then swung up behind me. Shielding me from the frigid rain the best he could.

Then he said in his thick Gypsy accent, "Alexandru, of the Lupei family. But please, my friends call me Dru. Except my sister Sylvia, who just calls me lazy." He grinned at the joke.

I smiled up at the man and said, "Laney. Umm... just Laney. I... was... Laney Herder." He inclined his head and then turned his piercing eyes back to the night and started humming a Gypsy tune. I absently wondered if Bowyn was okay, and if Celeste was as well. If only one of the shadows attacked us, did the other hit the main caravan? Were we a target of opportunity again?

I thought about the attack. The man wielded even more power than Celeste. In practice, she had only used half of her potential for me to practice grounding out. I always felt great pressure with hers but never pain. I looked at my gauntlets, which were burned through, and I had burns and blisters on my hands. He was just that confident in his power that he could take three of us.

If I hadn't felt the magic, he would have blown the three of us over the edge. But thanks to Sam's speed the bastard was injured, and with a swordsman like Sir Bowyn pressing him, no magic user would have time to pull more magic to him than to defend with.

I drifted in and out of consciousness and wasn't sure how far we had traveled. But we emerged from the trees under a huge rock overhang that kept the camp dry in the rain. The area was lit up by various burning torches and a large campfire in the middle of a group of amazing wagons. Though it was night, there were people all about, dancing, laughing and singing to a lute and tambourine.

They all silenced when we entered the torchlight. People were suddenly in motion and an old, silver-haired woman, possibly in her late sixties, in flowing gossamer rainbow colored robes, stepped out of one of the wagons and stepped swiftly up to us. Dru slid off the saddle then helped me down as gently as he could. He supported me as I swayed on my feet.

He bowed to the woman and said in the tongue of the people, "Mother, some of the Altii were attacked by a vrajitor assassin. This little one is hurt."

She stepped up to me and put her hand on my forehead and I felt a kind of magic I had never felt before. Wisps of white power swirled around her gently, it felt so warm and inviting. The silky texture was nothing like the raw, jagged power of Techromancer magic. Though I had a feeling the way it draped upon her in layers, that she was possibly more powerful than Donovan himself.

She didn't really, 'look' at me, but through me. The touch of her magic so gentle, like gossamer sheets of silk enveloping me, cocooning me in radiating peace. Then it was gone and she waved him off with me, saying, "Sylvia, then me. The child has something unresolved, we need to suss it out." That didn't make much sense to me, maybe I didn't understand Gypsy as well as I thought.

He motioned an arm toward one of the wagons, I took one step with him and started to collapse, but he caught me and picked me up in his arms like a doll in one smooth movement. I winced from the pain in my chest.

I took in the wondrous wood framed wagons. Some were stretched pentagonal shapes and some like a barrel on its side. All were around fifteen or sixteen feet long and had little stovepipe chimneys and overhangs over the driver's seats to keep the elements of the mountains off the drivers. Some had little round glass windows and some square.

I swallowed hard, the wagons were like in my nightmare. I shook it off.

To me, they all looked to be cottages, with large wagon wheels. Like the fanciful drawings and tapestries sold in the Market. I had seen a couple before, when they came to Wexbury for carnival. But not as regal looking as these.

I saw a small boy sitting in a tree off to the side of the wagon, hiding in the shadows, his eyes wide with curiosity. A thin woman stepped out of one of the pentagonal wagons that had a peaked roof like my cottage had. Her arms were crossed over her chest and her long, colorful dress reached her ankles. She had a warm looking hooded jacket of dyed rabbit furs over it, with matching rabbit pelt boots.

Her attractive face was creased in concern as we approached. She had black curly hair, and dark eyes, like Dru. They looked related. She looked to be in her mid-twenties. She said in Gypsy, "Quickly you fool, get her out of the cold."

I looked up and Dru grinned hugely at her and he said like a petulant child, "Yes Sylvia." Sylvia... his sister? She held the door open and he went up the fold down steps into the warm wagon. He stooped a little then he put me on a bed on one side of the space that was lit by oil lanterns.

He pulled a blanket over me and turned to the woman crowding him. "Sylvia, this is Laney. She is in need of your assistance."

She was pushing him toward the door. "I can see that you oaf. Now get out so I can see to her." He shot us both a toothy grin and stepped out. I noted a little wood burning stove near the door, it was warming the space nicely, ingenious.

The woman pulled back the hood of her coat, and she indeed looked gorgeous like her brother. She grinned at me and rolled her eyes and said in exasperation. "Men. I swear they are all just little boys inside." I chuckled then gasped, winced in pain, and her brow creased. I could tell she didn't like people in pain.

A little door opened at a wall that seemed to divide the inside of the wagon into two spaces. An older, middle-aged woman poked her head out the door asking, "What is all the ruckus? I'm trying to sleep."

Sylvia said, "Nothing mother. Go back to bed." The woman

looked at her then paused when she saw me then retreated back and shut the door silently.

I asked in English, "Mother? But I thought Alexandru called the other woman in the camp mother. Isn't he your brother."

She seemed surprised I knew what they had said, then chuckled as she poured some water from a pitcher into a basin and pulled up her sleeves to wash her hands. She spoke in accented English, "Yes, he, unfortunately, is my kin. The lazy man." But she was smiling, showing she teased.

Then she explained, "No, our mother is Elaine here. The woman out there, Udele, is the leader of our clan, Mother is her title. She would be like the leader of a keep for you Altii. Each of the fifteen clans has a Mother." A matriarchal society? I did not know that about Mountain Gypsies.

She reached for the blanket and prompted with her eyes for permission. I nodded and she pulled the blanket away. Then the woman went about undressing me. She seemed familiar with armor. Oddly, I didn't feel self-conscious about it. It felt almost like a serene ritual for some reason, as she cupped each piece gently and placed it carefully in stacks on a little table that had three small chairs next to the stove.

I winced when she rolled me onto my side to detach my breastplate. She looked at the huge dent in the armor for a second, then she removed my trousers and tunic. I crossed my arms over my chest and crossed my legs in modesty as she folded them carefully and placed them next to my weapons and armor.

She turned back to me and shook her head and gently took my arms and placed them at my side. Then she took a cloth and dipped it into the basin and proceeded to wipe my skin clean. She hummed a slow tune as she washed me and gave me a reassuring smile. She paused at the red and blackening bruises on my chest and looked back at my breastplate. She said softly, "Your armor saved your life."

She rolled me to one side to clean and examine my back, she paused and stopped breathing when she traced the scars there, then she started breathing again and continued her tune. When she was finished, she stopped humming and held my hands to examine the burns and blisters from the magic attack. She smelled them and almost growled, "A vrajitor attack."

I nodded and said hoarsely, "Rogue."

Her eyes narrowed then she said as she placed my hands back at my side, "We will get back to your hands, the most pressing are the broken ribs, you may have internal bleeding. May I..." She trailed off looking for the words then said in Gypsy, "May I use invasive magic to heal your body?"

I blinked. Magic could be used to heal? Then I remembered how different Mother Udele's magic had felt. Maybe they could reverse injuries like we could roll back time on the decay of metals. I nodded and she smiled and she stroked my hair with one hand then put both hands together and held them over my chest.

I was enveloped again by a tapestry of fine white mists and I felt warm and at peace like I was swimming through translucent veils of mist that were all around me. I reached my hands out and I could actually feel the gossamer fabric of the magics, like the fluttering wings of butterflies.

She stopped and the mists seemed suspended around me as she smiled slyly at me, "You are elemental like us, I have not seen your like, it is an amber presence that encompasses so very much. That explains how you survived that strike to your chest that should have killed you even with your armor. You need to relax your power, let me in."

I looked at her and realized everything was brighter and richer in my vision. I was so fixated on the mist that I hadn't realized my own power had risen up to meet it in a joyful dance.

I closed my eyes and took deep breaths and calmed myself. My magic receded, then suddenly the mist intensified and seemed to suck into her hands and I could feel them press into my very being from where her hands hovered a hair's width from my chest. I grunted as I felt the warmth press against my injuries. Soaking into them, numbing the pains. I smiled at her in wonder. She had strain on her face and her eyes were closed.

She whispered in English, "You have some damage to some organs. One moment." I felt heat bloom in my gut and serenity wash through me. She started panting and I could see sweat forming a sheen on her face. Then she smiled. "There, now the bones." I could hear a crinkling sound inside me and the pain went almost fully away.

She gasped and opened her eyes and panted. Then she looked up at me and said, "I will need to rest to deal with the bruising, but it is just superficial. I wanted to use what I have left in me tonight to give your hands relief."

She prompted with her eyes and I gave her my hands, she turned them palm up and said, "They were done with corrupted..." She searched for the word and said it in Gypsy, "power," Then continued in English, "There may be some scarring."

I shrugged in indifference, I was no stranger to scars and I knew I would never be beautiful. She concentrated again, she looked worn out and had to strain. I watched in wonder while the blisters seemed to reduce as the red and burned skin slowly returned to a healthy pink. There was a little twisted flesh on my palms and left thumb left over, but it was nothing compared to the scarring that would have resulted had the burns healed naturally.

I realized I could feel again. A lot of my sense of touch in my hands had been numbed and deadened by the burns and I realized that when I was feeling her magics flow across my fingers, it was my magics I was feeling it with, not my hands. She slumped and her mists seemed to dissipate like a morning fog burned off in the sunlight.

Then she stepped to a cupboard on the wall that separated the space and opened a door. She rummaged around and found a nightdress and handed it to me as she said, "That was all I could do for you tonight. I can try to help more after I get some sleep."

I slipped on the nightdress and smiled at her. "You have done more than enough already Sylvia, I don't know how I could ever thank you."

She placed a hand on my arm and smiled. "You are very sweet Laney. Now get some sleep. I will have your things sent out for cleaning and repair."

I squinted at her. "Mother Udele said I was to see her after you were done with me."

She pushed me back on the bed and pulled the blanket up over me and said with a wry grin, "She can see you in the morning after you sleep. You need that as much as what I did to heal properly and she knows it." Then she chuckled. "Besides, it'll do the old woman good to have to wait on someone for a change." The playful and devious look on her face made me smile.

I couldn't argue if I wanted too as I felt my eyes getting extremely heavy as she turned down the lamps, I was beyond exhausted. I was barely cognizant of her picking up all my gear and opening the door and calling out, "Eli." Then she said in Gypsy, "Please have our guest's things tended to right away."

I heard, "Good night Laney," as I drifted off to sleep with Celeste on my mind.

CHAPTER 20 – SEEING

I awoke in a sweat, to a child sitting on top of me, shaking my shoulder. "Lady... lady, you were screaming." I opened my eyes to an overly cute little boy who reminded me of a younger Jace. I recognized him as the boy in the tree the prior night.

I felt warm bodies pressed up next to me, and looked down. A small girl perhaps three or four was curled up against my chest, asleep, and of all things two of the tiniest goats I had ever seen. I almost laughed. There were itsy bitsy goats in bed with me. They little boy shooed them off the bed and hopped off with them.

What had Sylvia called him last night? Oh yeah. I looked at the little boy and said in Gypsy, "I'm sorry Eli. Just a bad dream." He grinned and then I almost jumped out of my skin when I looked over to see Dru, Sylvia, and Elaine eating at the small table by the stove just a couple feet away.

Dru was grinning so wide as he ate it was almost comical. Sylvia said, "Good you are awake. Let's get some food into you and we can go see Mother."

I looked around at them then sat up carefully, cradling the little girls head and putting a pillow under it as I slid out of the bed. I smiled at the adults then back at the girl and Sylvia said softly, "Ingr, my heir." That was Gypsy for an angel. Then she looked at the little rascal who was playing with the goats. "Eli you apparently know."

I looked around for my things as Dru vacated a chair. All I could see was my sword laying atop its scabbard. The blade had been nicked and dulled by its fall from the cliff last I saw it. Now it was freshly polished and honed to a fine edge with some sort of white symbols etched into it, and adorning the fresh leather on the hilt.

It was crowded in there, a little smaller than my cottage was. Then I remembered it was a two rooms so there was actually more room in it than our cottage and that again amazed me about these little homes on wheels. He motioned for me to sit as he licked something off his finger.

I started to argue, "Mother Udele wanted to see me, won't she be..."

Sylvia cut me off as she shook her head. "It is a good lesson in patience for her." Elaine chuckled at that, as Sylvia shooed Dru off with a grin for him. "Out with you, take Eli. You've lounged around enough this morning you lazy lout. You need to bring the Altii to her."

The boy opened the door and a gust of chill air hit me and I shivered as the men of the house vacated, taking the tiny goats with them. Dru gave a flamboyant bow to us all then chuckled as he shut the door.

I looked at the women with a small smile on my lips. "I've never seen such tiny goats, and their hair was so long. Are they good eating?"

I must have said something wrong as Sylvia blanched and Elaine
chuckled at her reaction and said, "Goodness no child, they are pets.
We harvest their hair twice a year for fiber for thread and yarn.
They are Mini Silkies and won't get much larger, they sleep inside
away from predators." Then the woman added with a smirk, "Not a
lot of meat there to eat anyway."

Sylvia tried to fight a smile as she slapped the woman's shoulder
playfully. "Mother. Don't let Ingr hear you speaking like that."
Which got me a wink from her mother.

The healer patted the table as she stood and retrieved a bowl of
some divine smelling porridge with maple syrup on it, and a
cornmeal muffin from a hooded warmer by the stove. She then
poured me a mug of apple cider. I looked at the women and said,
"Thank you so very much for everything you have done for me. I
don't know how I can ever repay you." Then I perked up. "I have
coin!"

The elder waved me off. "It is what human beings do for one
another. Would you not do the same if we turned up in need on
your doorstep?" I thought of it and she was right, I wouldn't turn
away someone in need if I could help. I nodded and she smiled and
pointed at the food.

It was quite good and I was apparently starving. I had to stop
myself from scarfing it down, I remembered mother drilling into me
that there was no excuse for bad manners. I paced myself and felt a
little self-conscious as the women watched me eat.

When I had soaked up the last of the syrup with the last bite of corn muffin and washed it down with cider, I gathered the bowl and mug. Elaine took them from me and I protested, "At least let me help clean up. It is the least I can do."

Sylvia smiled and returned to the wall cupboard with the clothing in it saying, "That can wait until Mother speaks with you. Here get dressed, your clothing should be mended and cleaned before midday."

She handed me a dress. And what a dress it was. Soft and light material dyed in rich purples and yellows and greens. It had long billowy sleeves and went down to my feet and the women chuckled as I cinched the waist with the sash. I looked at them and furrowed my brow. Sylvia said, "You are little larger than a girl. That one comes to my knees." I crinkled my nose at her. Was everyone in this world of ous bigger than me?

Then she gave me some rabbit skin boots and a dyed pelt coat with a hood. It was almost overly warm in the heated wagon. I looked at her and she stood so I went toward the door. She cleared her throat and pointed at my sword. I shook my head. "I do not need to be walking around your camp armed. I'm your guest and I shall not offend."

She shook her head and handed it to me. "It would be a bigger insult if you did not. It is part of you. You are a warrior woman of the Altii."

I almost laughed as I lashed the belt around my waist and slid the scabbard around to my left hip and accepted the sword and looked at it and said with a grin, "I'm no warrior woman. I'm a simple chicken farmer who fate decided to play a trick upon. It was either become a squire, or face the stockade for using magic. I am now beholden to the most wonderful woman. A true warrior woman."

Elaine paused at that and cocked her head with a wistful smile on her face. "You speak of her fondly."

I nodded and slid my sword into the scabbard. Then Sylvia took my arm and led me out into the crisp morning air. Sylvia said, "I can attend to your bruises after you meet with Mother. I have regained my strength." I absently pressed my hand on my chest and nodded. They were just bruises, she didn't need to exert herself for something that would heal on its own.

I looked at the immense stone overhang the camp was under then to the forest, it had stopped raining sometime during the night. There had to be twenty wagons and there were dozens of people moving about, just like in a village. Most stopped to look at me with curiosity. I looked at the healer. "There are so many."

She said as we walked, "There are two hundred and five in this band of the Lupei family, with eleven others just like this. We are one of the smaller families, but more possess The Gift in the Lupei family than any other clan." She had pride in her voice.

That was less than three thousand, not even half the size of Wexbury Keep. They were indeed a small clan when it was

estimated to be over seventy thousand Mountain Gypsies that
traveled the ranges of the Inhabitable Lands. But looking around it
seemed to be a huge number of people out and about doing various
chores. A group of children were playing some sort of game with
sticks and a barrel hoop.

We stepped up to one of the rounded wagons as the woman from
the previous night, Mother Udele, stepped out to greet us like she
knew we were coming. She put a hand out to me. "Come child." I
looked at Sylvia who prompted me with her eyes, and I took the old
woman's wrinkled hand. She held the door open while I stepped
inside.

She looked back with a sly smile to the healer. "Keeping me
waiting like this child? You're just lucky you are my favorite or
you'd be on ox duty for a week."

Sylvia shot back with a smirk, "I love you too you old crone. It
does you good to wait." Then to me, "Come back to my wagon
when Mother is done with you and your gear should be there by
then. The metal-smiths say you have some wondrous toys." I
nodded with a grin then swallowed hard when Mother shut the door.

She looked at me and smiled, putting me at ease. "It is okay
child, I do not bite. I hear your name is Laney, yes?" I nodded and
she inclined her head in greeting as she sat at a table that had
possibly the most intricately woven lace cloth covering it, draping
down to just above the ground. A small wooden box was secured to
the wall just at tabletop level. She motioned for me to take a seat.

"I am glad to see you looking better than last night Laney. You may call me Mother or Udele."

I looked around and the walls were all covered with hanging tapestries that the artisans in the keep would drool over. There were chests and cupboards stacked up along on wall. This wagon too had a dividing wall and a wood stove to keep it warm though there was no fire burning and the place was quite toasty.

I nodded remembering my manners and bowed my head as I sat. "It is a pleasure to meet with you, Mother." I couldn't bring myself to use her name, it seemed disrespectful not to use her title. Then I added, "I thank your clan for everything you have done for me."

She waved it off like Sylvia had. "It is what people do for one another." I really liked their philosophy, I wish more people thought that way, then expeditions like ours to forge defense pacts would not be needed.

She looked at me and tilted her head, her blue eyes much sharper than I would have thought to see in someone her age. It was rare for someone in modern times to live into their sixties. Non magic wielders saw an average of sixty-two years. Magic users though, depending on their power, could live to almost a hundred or more in some rare cases. I guessed that was the case here since I had felt such power from the woman the previous night. However, I felt nothing from her but curiosity as she sat across from me.

Then she spoke, "You are elemental, like the touched of the people. May I see?"

I wasn't sure what she was asking. "My magic?"

She nodded and held both hands out. I tentatively laid my hands on hers and she gave a gentle squeeze. I took two breaths then I pulled my power forth. She blinked then smiled widely. I saw white mist cloud her eyes until they were solid white.

She said in English, "I have only seen such an amber signature once. A great Altii many years past. A man of great compassion for his fellow man. Tannis of Wexbury. He gave all, that his people may live. You are of his blood?"

I smiled thinking about Sir Tannis, Hero of the Realm, and what I had recently learned. I said, "My grandfather." Then I prompted, "What do you mean by elemental?"

She smiled and then sighed and took on a teaching tone as she said, "You Altii are so young still. All magiks have their roots in the elements. You see the colors of magik, yes?" I nodded and she said, "They are from the six base elements."

I interrupted, I knew this much. "There are but five. Earth - green, Fire - red , Air - black, Water – blue, and Nature - purple. Depending on the mix in any particular Techromancer, the colors vary across the rainbow." I smiled thinking myself clever.

She chuckled. "In the loosest sense yes. But the element lost to most Altii is the magik of the people. The spirit element. White magics. But even the people don't know all there is to know about magiks, take you, for instance, how do you explain amber energy? The yellow that dominates it is unknown to us."

I tried to wrap my head around what she was saying, there were six elemental magics, not five? And she pronounced magic with a hard k. She saw me working through it. Then she said, "I can taste your strong affinity for earth, but something more that binds it to your very core. And..." then she smiled as her eyes returned to blue. "And what has your power in flux, unresolved. You have not yet blossomed."

Blossomed? Oh, did she mean. "But I ignited a couple months back."

She shook her head. "That awakened what you call your Techromancer magics. I am speaking of the magik of the people, it wars inside of you, needing release. I fear your other energies are interfering. You must allow the two to coexist or you will be stuck in between like this."

Then she opened the box and pulled out what looked like a clear glob of melted glass about the size of a fist and she put it on the table. I could see white wisps of energy dancing within it. She smiled at my surprise and said, "The energies of the spirit are much more versatile and malleable than the energies you wield, it can be imbued into objects as tools for the people, charms, wards..." Her lips twitched into a wicked smile. "...curses."

She smiled at my reaction then said, "You Altii are starting to realize the potential of your energies and are beginning to build crude tools to do the same. Like when you capture a magik spark to power your machines." That caused me to raise my eyebrows, so we were starting to realize what the Mountain Gypsies seem to have mastered long ago.

She looked at the glass on the table and said, "That is a seeing stone. Those blessed or cursed with the Sight like you and I can use it to focus our sight to reveal possible futures."

I whispered in awe, "Possible futures? Not the actual future?"

She shook her head with a gentle smile. "No child. People have free will, and depending on decisions they make at the moment, they can alter the outcome. What we see is what will come to pass if a person's decisions remain the same."

Then she said something mother, Donovan, Fredrick, and my Lady Celeste have all said. "Even the smallest thing can have a huge effect on the outcome of any event. You kick a pebble off a path as you walk and the fastest horse in your realm, who was fated to split a hoof on the pebble, is spared the pain. So instead of going to the livery to have it checked, that horse and its rider are tasked to deliver medicines to stem a plague. Being the fastest horse, he arrives a day before any others could have, saving dozens that would have died had you left the pebble be. That single, seemingly unimportant decision, made all the difference."

That sent shivers down my spine, realizing how delicate fate really was. Then something she said earlier sprang to mind and I asked, "As you and me?"

She nodded and said, "Yes child, you have the sight, but it is locked inside, you need to bloom. Hold the seeing stone and let it guide your vision."

I looked at the stone and asked, "What vision?"

She smiled and said softly, "The one keeping you up at night. I saw this day coming and knew I had to help you see, lives depend on it, but I do not know how."

Lives? I looked at her then the stone and reached for it. It slid away from me. She chuckled. "You must not use your Altii magiks, they interfere with your spirit energies." I looked at her and looked at my hand, covered in arcing amber energy that was dripping all over the table and the floor. I calmed myself and felt them receded back into me and my vision flattened.

I looked at the seeing stone and it was just clear glass now. I reached out timidly and it let me grasp it this time, and I screamed when the lightning struck me. No, it was my dream again. There were just those snapshots in time. Incomplete but clearer than they had ever been. I dropped the stone as Celeste turned her bloody face to me and said, "Run Laney!"

I was back in the gypsy wagon hyperventilating and amber energy thrummed through me and silverware and tin plates and other metal objects were swirling around me like a tempest. Mother didn't even blink, her eyes were on mine.

Then she reached through the whirlwind of metal, somehow avoiding being struck and she took my hand. I could see the white mists coil up my arm and they caressed my face, filling me with calm warmth. Then all the metal clattered to the ground as my energies seemed to go to sleep.

She asked as I looked around in embarrassment and started picking up the metal clutter around the ground and on the table, "Did your vision resolve itself?"

I shook my head and she made a placating gesture and said, "Sit, don't worry about that."

I sat feeling the blush of my embarrassment. Then I thought about what I saw and said, "It was clearer now and I remember all of it now. It was as if it were actually happening this time."

She blinked at that. "Transference? You are full of surprises child." Then she picked up the seeing stone. "Let me see if I cannot see more now that the stone has tasted you."

Without my power, I could still feel the immense energy the woman gathered to her and seemed to feed to the stone. Her eyes went white again and she sat unmoving for ten minutes. Then she blinked and her eyes were back to the sharp blue. She pushed the stone away from her like it might bite her and she was breathing hard.

She shook her head. "You poor child. So much depends on your decisions the coming days."

I was getting apprehensive and asked in a shaky voice, "What did you see?"

She shook her head. "Two possible futures for you, both filled with pain. Depending on your decisions, you will either save the people of the lands or be their downfall. All depending upon how much pain you can endure."

I asked, "What was it, Mother? What did you see?"

She shook her head. "I may have already said too much. I dare not influence your decisions." Then she held up a finger. "But I know I must give you this. I saw it in both visions." She dug in the drawer and came out with a slim silver necklace with a small silver goat charm on it.

I swallowed, trying not to panic over the ramifications that she had eluded to. I was a nobody, with virtually no power. The fate of anyone but myself shouldn't be in my hands. I reached a shaky hand out to it and accepted it with bowed head. I could taste it as soon as I held it. It was made of magnesium.

I tried to remember the lessons about metals Donovan had been teaching me. There were trace amounts of magnesium in the human body. It burned at such high temperatures it put out a blinding light. It could be mixed with other metals to lighten them without losing strength. That was all I remembered.

She stood and walked behind me and pulled my hair back, running her fingers through it. "Such lovely long tresses." I blushed and put the necklace on wondering why it was important.

I said, "Thank you, Mother."

She nodded then said, "Your people will be here three minutes before sunset. Until then, rest, have Sylvia look at your chest, you move stiffly, I fear you are not fully healed."

I absently touched my chest. "It is only a bruise, she has already done too much for me, as have you."

She cocked an eyebrow almost playfully. "Are you refusing our hospitality?"

Oh, dear lord. I bowed in haste. "No, ma'am. I'll go see Sylvia."

She chuckled. "Good girl, you'd make a fine Gypsy."

I looked down at my mess and the door, she squinted an eye. "Shoo."

I couldn't help smiling at the woman as I left, saying, "Goodbye."

I shook my head as I walked across the camp, why is it everyone here is cleaning up after me? I feel like a worthless layabout. I was aware of all the little ones either watching or following me. One ran ahead to tap on Sylvia's window before rejoining his friends.

I grinned and reached out with my power, I saw a wisp of amber grab the steel hoop the children were playing with and had it spin up into the air. They giggled and cheered as I made it dance in the air as I walked, then got it spinning quickly as I released it. It hit the ground and rolled off quickly away from the children as all the momentum of the spin pushed it along the ground.

I laughed with them then turned and almost ran into a smiling Sylvia, who was standing at the base of the fold up stairs. "Oh! Hello there." I blurted out as I gave her room.

She chuckled then said, "Hello yourself Laney. I take it, Mother, sufficiently scared you into a fetal position?"

I nodded. "You know what she said?"

She barked out a laugh in genuine amusement. "No, but she scares everyone she does a seeing with."

I cocked an eyebrow. "But you know she did a seeing with me?"

She smiled and winked and held a finger to her nose then moved it in front of her and twirled it around at the playing kids. "The camp has ears and news travels like water through a sieve. The little ones make the best spies." I chuckled at that and nodded as I watched the children play.

Then I turned to her and looked down in embarrassment. "Mother sent me to have my bruise looked at. I told her it was nothing."

She shook her head and rolled her eyes at me. "It is nothing really Laney. I am happy to do it. Come on in before the little ones twist you around their fingers." I nodded and followed her in.

CHAPTER 21 – REUNITED

𝕬fter she healed my bruises and tried to do more for my hands, which she actually was able to reduce the scarring a bit, we sat and drank tea. She asked as many questions about living in a keep as I asked about life in an always moving caravan.

I found it so much fun switching between English and the tongue of the people. I was getting quite used to it. I noted a shelf at the ceiling with a rail I assumed prevented a row of tomes from falling when the caravan was in motion.

She followed my eyes and her smile bloomed and she nodded at me and she nudged her chin. Really? I could touch them? I looked around for gloves. She saw my hesitation. I had been hanging around the great library too much. She chuckled and said, "Go ahead and look."

There were tomes about healing, about gypsies, about nature, plants, animals. Then a large amount of tales for entertainment. I bit my lower lip, I just wanted to consume them. My hand faltered on three marked Lessons - Year One and Two, Lessons - Year Three and Four, Lessons - Year Five and Six. I looked back at her.

She smiled. "I'm also the educator of our band. It falls to me to teach the young ones. To introduce them to reading, writing, math, and languages."

I squinted my eyes. "All children are taught to read?"

She nodded and said in a bemused tone, "Of course. Knowledge is power. Do you not do the same in the keeps?"

I shook my head slowly as I said almost in shame, "No. Only the nobles are learned. I only am because my mother chose to teach my brother and me."

I sat with her and thumbed carefully through the well worn lesson books with amazement. This is what mother had proposed when she was first a Lady. I made the decision to try to press for the same when we returned to Wexbury.

At midday, we went out to gather the children and I helped prepare a meal at the large campfire that was still burning with some of the other women of the camp. I wondered when they had stoked it, I saw no wood around, yet it burned merrily, chasing away the chill mountain air. Just as I completed the thought, a woman walked past with a man and he absently tossed a piece of wood on the fire.

I saw various other people do the same at random intervals as we fed the children and any adults who cared to partake. Then I realized what I was seeing and I looked around at the camp again. It appeared that people were helping out wherever and whenever they were needed. Everyone was contributing to the camp as a whole. With only a few people having specialized jobs like Sylvia or the metal smiths or leather workers.

I asked the healer quietly, "What is the hierarchy here?"

She blinked like she didn't understand the question. But then her eyes widened slightly as she realized the extent of the question. She gave me a sly smile that told me I was not the first Altii to ask. She put her hand up in the air and said, "There is Mother." Then she held her hand down a notch. "Then there are the people." She grinned like she was amused.

I waited and then slowly grasped what she was saying as I looked around again to confirm my observations. She chuckled and said, "We are all the same and are all responsible for our band, working together. We help where we can and if we develop and affinity for something like weaving or healing that will benefit the clan, then we do that as well. We all raise and look out for each others children and maintain the wagons and prepare food. Whatever is needed whenever it is needed."

She pointed at a couple men, though I didn't see nearly as many in the camp as I saw the prior night. "Most of the men do the hunting or patrols as they are physically more able. Or when needed, defend against any Marauders or rogues foolhardy enough to threaten our wagons."

Then she smiled down at my sword. "Few women have the mettle to be a Femeie de Sabie. Though we can certainly defend in other ways. That is why you get the stares from the people. You must be a great warrior to stand with your men in battle." She said 'Femeie de Sabie' or Woman of the Sword as it was a title, like Mother.

I blushed and shook my head. "I am no Femeie de Sabie, I have only been taught to defend myself, not to attack."

She nodded sagely and repeated something our Knights have

told me, "Defense is life."

I nodded then I added for clarification, "My Lady Celeste is a true Woman of the Sword, I am beholden to her and her house."

She paused and tilted her head to regard me with a gentle smile on her face, "You say that with reverence. She must mean a great deal to you." I nodded. Celeste, like my family, was everything to me. She was the first to see me as something other than a serf.

A little girl popped her head up from behind a stump as we finished cleaning and storing the pots and dishes after the meal. She nodded once at Sylvia then ducked back down behind the stump and ran off giggling with a stream of little girls that moved past.

The healer smiled and faux whispered at me, "My spy tells me your gear is ready. We can get you presentable for your lady later. Would you like a tour of the camp?"

I smiled hugely and nodded eagerly. I had wanted that since I stepped out this morning, now that I wasn't seriously injured anymore. The wagons and people were all so amazing to me, it was like an adventure within an adventure. She looped an arm in mine and started showing me the wonders of a Mountain Gypsy camp. This time I was aware of all the cute little shadows we had.

A little later, I found myself behind a tanner's wagon at a little fold-out table with Sylvia and four other women, sewing up waterskins. Me clumsily, the others like they did it every day. Esmeralda, who we would call a master tanner in the keep, was showing me the fascinating trick to making the bladders watertight.

It was almost like a form of science to me.

Esmeralda's daughter, Cera, took my skin and tested it when I finished. Then she went about expertly decorating it with plant and fruit based dyes as I attempted another. Then she handed it to Sylvia who started moving her hand across the surface of it, imbuing it with her wispy magics.

As I finished the next, feeling a little better about it, the sky was clouding up so there was a twilight cast to the air for a couple hours. I don't know how she knew, but she said, "Sunset approaches, we should get you presentable for your lady."

I stood and thanked the women for teaching me a new skill. Esmeralda grinned slyly and nudged her chin to me. Cera smiled back at her then hung the first skin I had made, over my shoulder. Saying, "For the Femeie de Sabie of the Altii." Though the shape of it was a little irregular, the colorful decoration on it was beautiful and masterfully done. I hugged them both and thanked them again.

As we walked back to her wagon, I noted how busy the camp had gotten with people apparently preparing for some sort of feast. I idly looked at the water skin and noted the faint white runes and sigils on it that tasted slightly of magic, they seemed to glow silver in the flickering light of the fire as we passed it. It could have been a trick of the light.

The magic was similar to what I felt at my leg with my scabbard and sword. I looked at the runes and held the water skin up in question as my eyes trailed amber sparks. She smiled. "I charmed it for you, you will not need to boil your water. It will always be sweet and cool for you." I blinked, they could do that with their spirit magic? For how simple what she said sounded, that was a more complex than anything a Techromancer could hope to accomplish. As Mother pointed out, the only persistent magic we could do was to capture some magic potential in a vessel.

I started noting all of the runes and sigils that covered many of the wagons now that I was aware of it. I smiled at her then she ushered me into the wagon and all of my gear was there and looking brand new. Even the breastplate. It now had a high polish and virtually glowed with silvery white runes and symbols etched into it. I looked closely and realized they weren't really etched in, they were made of that wispy, misty magic of theirs.

Even when I let my power fade inside me, I could still see them with my normal eyes as they were almost there and not there at the same time and it made the armor look almost regal. I found all my leathers, weapons and gear to be the same. Even my clothing, the tears and damage all repaired, and all tasting fairly full of that peaceful magic.

I ran my fingers along the runes on the new leather gauntlets, the others must have been beyond repair. Then I asked, "What do they mean?"

Sylvia started pointing at some and explaining the various protections, charms. Even the luck some were imbued with. My armor would be tougher and the runes on my riding cloak would

make me hard to strike. There were literally hundreds. I looked at
her colorful dress and saw no runes, so why was all of mine
charmed?

I asked, "Why?"

She understood my question and said with a smile, "Every
vrajitoare with the Gift wanted to give something to the little warrior
woman, the Femeie de Sabie of the Altii who fell from the heavens
and lived. By the looks of it, many spent most of the day blessing
your belongings." She smiled. "You are something of a curiosity, it
would have taken most the day for some of these, and tired the
vrajitoare out. The Gift does not come as easy to some."

I felt embarrassed and not worthy, but I smiled and then almost
panicked when I didn't see my tool pouch among my things. There
was a new leather pouch with various pockets there and I looked
inside and sighed in relief. All of my tools were there and in almost
brand new condition. Tied in a little ball was the old pouch in one
pocket.

Then I froze as Sylvia started to take off the rabbit pelt jacket
from me. She had an impassive look on her face as she said, "We
must hurry they will be here soon." I felt very self-conscious as she
undressed me, wiped me down again with a wet cloth, and dressed
me systematically in my gear. Again, it felt like some sort of
official ceremony to me as she seemed to hold each piece in
reverence before placing it on me.

When she was done, she laid a braid of colorful fabric around my neck that hung down beside my sash. Then she made sure the little goat charm necklace was hanging out to be seen. She then grabbed the small tapestry on the back of the dividing door and pulled it to the side to reveal a highly polished mirror. She held out a hand for me to take a look while she started brushing out my hair and putting it into a tight braid, running a colorful scarf into the knots.

Good lord, I looked... I looked almost like a real knight. Almost... pretty. My weapons and what little metal armor exposed were gleaming. The magics I was encased in, set off an almost imperceptible glow that I could taste.

She smiled into the mirror and spun me around and placed her hands on my shoulders to inspect me. "There, a true warrior. A Femeie de Sabie." She looked satisfied and she gave me my riding cloak as I put the leather strap of my new tool pouch over my shoulder.

Then she motioned to the door. "After you Laney."

I whispered, "Thank you, Sylvia." She reached over and squeezed my arm then I put on my freshly oiled and magicked riding cloak and she ushered me out of the wagon. I paused at the last step and blinked. It looked like every Mountain Gypsy of this band of the Lupei family was there. The entire camp buzzed with activity and nervous excitement.

Everything went silent as I stepped onto the ground, all eyes were on Sylvia and I then like a switch was flipped, they went back into motion. The jovial atmosphere was catchy as I found myself smiling. As we approached the central fire, Sylvia moved to my left and took my hand and placed it on her arm as we approached Mother.

We reached her and Sylvia took my hand and put it on Mother Udele's arm. Then she moved away from us. Their timing unnerves me still to this day. As Mother looked out into the forest, two horses emerged. Alexandru and little Eli. Behind them came the caravan from Wexbury. Goliath was tethered to the supply wagon.

My heart skipped a beat at the sight of my Lady Celeste, riding tall in her saddle, leading our group. Her eyes were darting around, taking in everything at once until they brushed past me then locked onto me.

Her lips were pursed, a thin white line on her face as she dismounted as her steed was still in motion. The crowd seemed to split around her as she strode up to me with single-minded purposefulness her eyes were brimming with wetness as she engulfed me in her powerful arms. "Oh god Laney. I had thought I lost you."

She was kissing the top of my head and I was crying freely and I didn't fully understand why. I nodded my head as she refused to release me and said, "I'm okay. My friends here took good care of me."

She released me from the hug but kept a hand on my arm like she was reassuring herself that I was real as she looked around like she just realized where she was. She locked eyes with Udele then bowed deeply, taking a knee as she said formally, "Mother." She was obviously aware of their ways.

Udele reached down and placed a hand under her chin and gently raised her up. "Come now child, stand up. You'll give me a complex."

Then she smiled back when we heard Sylvia with a grin, comically saying under her breath, "We wouldn't want that now would we?"

My Lady said, "Thank you, for Lady Laney's care." Then she swallowed and asked her, "Lord Samuel?"

She exhaled in shared sorrow and said, "We have prepared a pyre for his passing but waited for your arrival, in case you needed any preparations."

Celeste nodded once and then made a signal behind her and all the knights relaxed and Fredrick and Lucia stepped out of the coach. They made a beeline for us with big smiles on their faces. Lucia just stepped right up and hugged Mother saying, "Udele. It has been far too long."

The gypsy leader smiled at her as they stepped apart to look each other over. "Lucy, Fred. It has hasn't it. I was thinking on carnival in Wexbury in a few seasons." Then she smiled and waved her hands around at the feast. "But until then, please, may you and yours join us to celebrate Lord Samuel's passing and our friendship."

The Duke bowed his head slightly to accept her hospitality.

"You are too kind as always, Mother." Then with a twitch of his fingers, our people started mingling and celebrating life with the Lupei family. Then he saddened and said, "We can see poor Samuel to the beyond at midnight."

Then he looked at Celeste and then me and he gave a somber smile as he asked, "You are a durable little one aren't you Laney? Always so full of surprises."

This seemed to be a cue for Udele as she looped her arms in Fredrick's and Lucia's as she dragged them off, saying, "You have no idea. We must talk."

I looked up to Celeste, who was smiling down at me. I can't tell you how relieved and safe I felt with her there. I said shyly, "Hi."

Her smile broadened and her eyes were twinkling and she led me off to the feast, shaking her head. "I am never, ever, letting you out of my sight again. I thought I had lost you and my heart could not take it. Bowyn saw you go over. How did you survive?"

I cuddled into her arm where I could feel her strength radiating to me. I shrugged. "It is a long story. But I honestly would be gone now if it were not for the Lupei family here."

We joined in the bittersweet celebration and enjoyed the music and entertainment put on by our hosts. I was blushing and hid my face in Celeste's sleeve as Bowyn recounted the battle to the people gathered around the makeshift tables. "I myself would not be standing here today if not for the quick reactions of our Laney. She took the brunt magic assault herself, channeling it into the ground. I could smell her flesh burning."

Then he looked around and put a hand forth and clasped it into a fist. "She did not hesitate to dive and grab Lord Samuel's hand as he went over the cliff after he made the shot of a lifetime as he flew through the air."

He looked at me and his tone went soft as I could see things replaying in his eyes. "Laney does not know how to quit. Though his was dragging them both over the edge, she would not release Sam though he pleaded with her to do so. She struggled to hold them both, to save Samuel as I dispatched the rogue. Even in the end she would not release him as they slipped over the edge into oblivion."

Everyone was silent, all eyes were on me. I swallowed hard. Then he showed me mercy and held his mug high. "Lord Samuel!" Everyone repeated and drank, then the music started up again and the spotlight was off me and pointed where it should be, on the brave man that gave all for his people.

Things wound down around midnight and the children were spirited off to bed, then the Lupei joined the people of Wexbury on a ridge, a stones throw away from the camp, as we all said goodbye to Samuel. Celeste took his bow and quiver and handed them to the Duke. Fredrick murmured, "I will be sure his family receives these."

Then we stood under a black sky, the moons, and the stars blotted out by the thick clouds that were amassing, and Celeste lit the pyre. We sat and she just held me as we watched the fire burn brightly for the soul of a protector of the realm.

***

I awoke the next morning to the familiar warmth of Celeste behind me, and her arm wrapped protectively around me in Sylvia's wagon. Oh, how I had missed that. It is funny the things you get used to and find it hard to live without.

I grinned at the other sources of heat burrowed around us in the blankets. It was only fair we share Eli and Ingr's bed with them, instead of displacing them. I looked up and suppressed a giggle as Celeste was absently shooing away one of the tiny goats while she slept. as it tried desperately to lick her nostrils clean.

She finally awoke and pulled back at the sight of a goat in her face then she caught my eyes and my smile and grinned back. The entire camp seemed to be there to see us off after the Gypsies fed us a good morning maple porridge and bread.

Alexandru bowed and kissed my hand with a twinkle in my eye."I hope we meet again little one." Celeste cocked an eyebrow and I waved her off as I blushed. The children, dozens of them, mauled me to get hugs then Sylvia herself hugged me. "Thank you for blessing our camp with your smile Laney of Wexbury."

I held her hand between both of mine. "No, thank you for taking me in and caring for me." She just smiled and stepped back and then Mother Udele said her goodbye to me and added, "Follow your heart Laney and you cannot go wrong, young Femeie de Sabie of the

Altii."

After she had said her goodbyes to the Duke and Duchess, Celeste approached the leader of the Gypsies and she bowed low and said, "Mother, the House of Celeste is forever in your debt for returning Lady Laney to us. Our blade is yours should you ever call, our families bound."

Udele paused and seemed to contemplate that, then asked, "A blood bond?"

Fredrick looked to be about to say something when Celeste said, "Yes."

Then Mother Udele regarded us, smiled, and said, "Then it is done. Our families tied." There was a murmuring in the crowd as she took Celeste's hand in between hers and said, "Stay safe child. Laney will need you in the coming days."

Duke Fredrick pursed his lips as he watched then he disappeared back into the coach. Celeste mounted and I, to my eternal embarrassment, took three tries to mount Goliath to the chuckling of the gathered crowd. Then Celeste signaled for us to move forward and our caravan was once again on the way to Far Reach, through the mountain passes.

I looked back and waved at my new friends and chuckled at the children running after us for as long as their little legs could keep up. I reached out with my magics, I could see a thread of amber reach out to their barrel strap and had it dance a merry dance until it fell spinning on the ground to their giggling amusement.

I paused when I saw Celeste's eyes on me with a wistful smile on her lips. I blushed and urged Goliath to a trot, much to her amusement.

CHAPTER 22 – TRETH

Before long, Verna and Celeste had me flanked at the front of the caravan, demanding to hear how I survived the fall. Verna seemed mad at me, but Celeste explained later that Verna had become quite fond of me and she was shattered by the news of my death. She was just angry because that was an enemy should couldn't fight, and that I had the audacity to be alive when I had caused her such emotional pain.

Later still Verna explained how she had never seen Celeste so angry in her life, so much so that she locked down all her emotions until Dru showed up with news of my survival. Verna tried explaining something that I don't think I quite understood, judging by her frustrated look. "Celeste is yours, you know that Laney?"

It was mid afternoon when the snow started falling. Celeste and I rode ahead a little so I could stand on a ridge to watch the valley below, coated in a veil of white as snow fell for as far as I could see. I had witnessed snow twice in Wexbury when I was young, but it paled to the majesty of the blanket of white I saw below. I had never imagined I would see such wonders back when I lived in Cheap Quarter.

I noticed I wasn't as cold as I thought I should be, usually I'd be shivering about then. I took a gauntlet off and the bitter cold bit into me. I smiled at the runes on the gauntlet as they glowed dimly as I put it back on. The Lupei had insulated my clothing.

As we continued on, Celeste subtly indicated the Mountain Gypsy lookouts that were shadowing us. I thought one I saw up on a trail of packed down snow on a peak, which had to have been made by mountain goats, looked like Dru. I couldn't be sure through the snow, but he had pointed ahead of us and Celeste asked to borrow my spyglass.

She cocked an eyebrow at the new pouch and when I located a side pouch with my now gleaming spyglass it, there were three other lenses that looked about the size of the end of the spyglass. I looked through the eyepiece and slid one on and the magnification doubled. Each of the lenses was more powerful. I handed the spyglass to her with the first lens attached. She grinned at it then said, "Looks like you made a few friends in that group."

I smiled and nodded. "They were extremely hospitable and friendly. I felt embarrassed I couldn't reciprocate in kind." She just nodded then looked to where the Gypsy had pointed. She looked back up and waved to the man, who faded back into the rocks as she handed me the spyglass.

She pointed as she said, "Our shadow is ghosting. Probably meeting up with whoever sent them now that his partner is dead." I looked and didn't see anything until I caught some motion and saw a man on a horse moving rapidly down the valley, only about a mile and a half ahead of us and pulling away.

I asked as I put the tools away, "So they can't track us anymore?"

She shook her head and placed a hand on my arm then motioned her head back to our horses. Then said as we mounted up, "They know exactly where we are going now and where we will be. The only place we can reach from here is Treth. We'll go right past it on our way down to Far Reach."

She added as we rejoined the caravan and relayed the information to the other knights. Tennison nodded. "Smart." I gave him a questioning look and he clarified, "He'll go to whoever sent him and relay all he knows and then he will probably wait for another partner to pick us up at Treth Keep or maybe even the Monolith, and then shadow us from there, looking for any opportunity to slow our progress."

I looked around as everyone in earshot nodded. Verna flanked me letting me know it was time for a rotation. I looked at her and Celeste and whispered while feeling uninformed, "Monolith?"

Verna smiled and said quietly, "A solid structure that stretches out of the earth and into the sky, made of some sort of mortar that does not crack under the immense weight of it. It is believed to have been a place of power or worship for the Wizards of the Before. It seems to serve no other purpose, it is just an immense slab stretching to the heavens, almost a half mile. The base is hundreds of yards across."

Then Celeste added wistfully, "To have built such structures that defy our greatest architects and engineers." She shook her head and said to me, "To have lived in a time of wonder such as that. One day, Sparo will rise to such heights." I smiled at her surety, and could not fault her, when I have witnessed the modern marvels we were already capable of. It couldn't be that far a leap forward to accomplish what those who came before us had.

I nodded my thanks then signaled my chilly looking fellow Squires to do a rotation around the caravan. Celeste always looked anxious whenever I left her side now. I think she really meant that she never wanted to let me out of her sight again. She hadn't said as much, but I think she somehow believes what happened on that ridge with that Rogue was her fault.

By late afternoon, she sent Sir Randolph and Lady Beth ahead with Bex to find shelter for the night. The snow had finally stopped falling as we reached the valley floor and headed toward a gap between two peaks. To what Lord Peter called, the Pass of the Abyss. Because in mid-winter, it was impossible to travel through. All men who attempted over the centuries had given their very lives to the mountain and were never heard from again.

I believe he was just trying to scare us squires by the schooled, impassive looks on the rest of the faces in the caravan. I kept glancing at the imposing peaks, wondering if it were actually true, they did look formidable.

We caught up with Sir Randolph's group where the road passed under an overhang. It wasn't anything as grand as the one back at the Gypsy camp, but it would suffice. There was a small fissure in the cliff that formed a small cave where stones from above had fallen in ages gone by to wedge themselves into the crevice.

It was defensible and looked as if a wolf or wolverine had used it in the past. They could warm it and the Duke and Duchess could overnight in it. After a hearty soup made from dried vegetables and jerky, and some biscuits, Celeste took first watch.

I followed her and she gave me a warm smile and offered an outstretched arm to me, holding her riding cloak open. I shook my head and instead opened mine in the same way and laid it on her shoulder as I snuggled into her. She blinked and said quietly in surprise, "It's warm. Well, warmer. It is like having a couple blankets over us."

I grinned up at her and said softly, keeping my voice low too, "The Lupei family spelled all of my things. Their magic is amazing, they can have them accomplish specific tasks, even long after the magic is cast."

She shook her head with a grin and said, "Only you could convince the Mountain Gypsies to share their magic of the spirit with you. They rarely even let outsiders see it."

I buried my head into her arm as I blushed. "I didn't convince anyone, they just did it for me when they repaired my gear," I said.

She nodded and kissed the top of my head and repeated, "Only you..." Then she whispered almost so I couldn't hear, "I was so scared I had lost you." I nodded and looked out into the night with her knowing I felt the same as I was falling, that I would never see her again, and that it would make her look bad that I was so careless.

We just sat in silence in each others company looking out into the snowy world that was dimly illuminated by the three sisters and the ocean of stars above in the then clear sky.

Sir Scot showed up to relieve us. He gave me a squeeze of the shoulder and a nod as we stood, conveying that he was glad I was back. I smiled and placed my hand on his to let him know I appreciated his concern, then Celeste led me through the snow to the camp. We laid on our bedroll and pulled the blankets up to our chins and stared at the stars together.

She whispered, "I remember, before uncle sold me to father and mother, he would take me out on hunts in the Whispering Forest. We were trappers. We would lay out under the stars and he would tell me the tales of the constellations. I fear I have forgotten much of my life prior to moving to the keep. I find it hard to picture Uncle's face. Contact is discouraged when one is sold into another family. And now it is just like before, with mother gone. Just father and I, always a small family for me."

I nodded and found her hand under the blanket and hugged it to me and whispered back, "You have me now, I am of the house of Celeste, your family grows." Then I smiled hugely at her and whispered, "Celeste Trapper."

She paused and I couldn't feel her breathing, then she turned to her side and pulled me back into her and kissed the top of my head. "Go to sleep Laney, Treth awaits us on the morrow."

I so missed her at my back like this. She made me feel so safe, and that I mattered. I whispered, "Goodnight Celeste." I could feel the smile from her arm as she hugged me a little closer.

We awoke in the morning feeling chilly but well rested. Where my riding cloak was still over me under the covers, I was toasty warm but my face was positively frigid. I sneezed and squeaked, which just got smiles from all in earshot. To some chuckles I said, "Oh be quiet you lot,"

To my surprise, my nightmare hadn't come, that was two nights in a row, after Mother and the seeing. Even though she said I still had something unresolved, that I hadn't ignited yet.

Fredrick had come out to tell Celeste that a storm was coming, that we needed to get over the pass before midday or we would have to divert around the mountain and add a day to our travels.

Nobody questioned the Duke, we packed quickly and tended the horses as the porters made a hearty oatmeal with dried strawberries in it. That was a treat. I had asked Verna, and she said, "If our Lord says a storm is coming, then a storm is coming."

We were on the road again as the first rays of Father Sol snuck over the peaks. It was slower going on the steep road through the pass at mid-morning. It was positively terrifying and awe-inspiring at the same time. The road was cut into the steep peaks, with the only thing between us and a thousand-foot drop, was a low stone wall. I felt as though we were snaking our way between the teeth of some immense dragon.

Black clouds had blotted out the sky by then, and when we were half way back down the pass, the snow started up again, heavier and with driving winds. It cut viability to twenty or thirty yards. Shit. If we had been in the pass when this hit, we might well have been one of the stories told around campfires, of the Duke's Caravan that was lost to the Pass of the Abyss.

I stared at the Duke through the foggy glass window of the coach-door as I did a rotation. How had he known? I thought of the magic he and Lady Lucia hid from the keep, and Mother Udele's more in-depth explanation of how all magic was elemental magic. Was he in tune with the weather? A water or air elemental?

We caught up with Bex, Sir Scot, and Lord Peter, who were the forward scout. In a thick evergreen grove for midday meal, not much of the then moderate snow was getting through the dense canopy of pine needles. Bex, who had nothing but grins. Scot and Peter, who were each holding large snowshoe rabbits, as they threw them to the porters said, "Rabbit stew." It took me a moment to realize why Bex was grinning. The others were carrying the prize which meant... I blurted, "Good on you Bex!"

Lord Peter was shaking his head. "It was the damnedest thing. He laid out a spool of copper on ceramic pins near the burrow and hooked it to a power vessel, then we hid over the rise. The rabbits hit the line and started convulsing. Then our Lord Bexinton here walked over and picked up the limp things and wound up his wire." Everyone made appreciative sounds. The idea of fresh meat was making my mouth water.

I smiled when Bex moved to the front of the line for the meal, he had such a look on his face. Celeste bumped my hip and grinned down at me. I whispered, "What? I'm proud of him. He's starting to fit in."

After a satisfying stew and cornbread, we were on the move again moving lower and lower out of the mountains and leaving the snow behind us.

After a bit I asked, "How much farther till we reach Treth?"

Bowyn chuckled behind me. "Like an impatient child on a wagon trip."

I looked back and made a small fist at him and he mock shuddered. Then he said, "When we passed through the Abyss, we entered Treth."

I exhaled and chuckled. "You are such an ass at times man."

His eyebrows rose in mock surprise. "The rare curse from our Laney."

Celeste chimed in, "You best not tease too much Bowyn, our Laney has teeth." I squinted at her trying to figure out if she were teasing me too. I couldn't tell so I crinkled my nose at her, which she rewarded me with a glittering eyed smile.

Then the frustrating man behind us pointed and asked, "Do you see the end of that lake between the peaks to the southwest?" I nodded and he said, "Treth Lake."

Ahhh, so the keep was there hidden by the peaks down in that valley. I nodded with a grin, we'd be there an hour or so before sunset. I noted the air temperature had risen considerably the farther down the mountains we traveled.

I was excited to see Treth, it would be the first Keep I had never laid eyes on and the third keep I had entered since I had finally been in Flatlash, thanks to this mission. I hear the Iron Walls of Treth were something to behold. Resources are at a premium in the inhabitable lands and waste is almost unheard of. Everything is recycled, re-purposed and reused. But the Iron Walls of Treth were constructed using almost a half million tons of iron produced from the great iron mines of their realm. Such wasteful opulence.

We passed between two low peaks and even from two miles away, the tall reddish orange walls were visible around the startlingly rectangular village. Where Flatlash seemed to be a labyrinth of construction upon construction in a seemingly disorganized maze of roadways and alleys, Treth Keep looked even more organized than Wexbury though it was unremarkable except the imposing wall.

All of the roadways I could see were laid out in a perfect grid pattern with the castle being in the middle. I started to wonder if Wexbury was the only keep with the castle adjoining the outer wall. I made a mental note to myself to ask Celeste later.

We slowed as we came out onto the Ring and the familiar clopping of hooves on cobblestone rang out. We slowed even further and Celeste and her mount were fidgeting and side prancing. Our caravan came to a stop and there was silence. I looked around and all the knights and our archers were all on alert, looking all around us.

Verna rode up between us and asked Celeste, "What do you think?"

My Lady was looking all around us and I noted her eyes were burning green and trailing sparks behind as she looked. I pulled my power to me and looked around too. She tilted her head at the keep then asked, "Laney, what do you see?"

I squinted at the keep where she was looking and saw nothing. I shrugged. "Just the keep."

She nodded and looked back at the caravan. "Well, they have already seen us."

Verna nodded and I made an exasperated sound. The muscular woman gave me a crooked half smile. Then she asked, "What do you see without your magic."

Grrrr. They were going to make me reason it out. I let my power fade then I looked all around us then at the keep again and then said, "I see nothing."

Then she explained, "Exactly. Where are the merchant men and travelers? There is no traffic between Treth Minor to the south and the keep. We are an armed caravan moving through their territory yet an escort has not come out to challenge us."

Then she smiled as I blinked in understanding. Then she continued, "Celeste had you look at the keep with your Techromancer sight and you saw nothing. Meaning nobody inside the keep is using magic. None of their Techromancers or their Techno-Knights? That seems unlikely... unless they are not using magic on purpose, like they are hiding. It feels as if the very valley is holding its breath."

All sorts of nasty scenarios were going through my mind until I pointed. "But you can see the villagers going about their business in the keep."

Celeste nodded then took one last look around as Fredrick came walking up to us and looked up to Celeste. "What do you think?"

She shrugged. "There is only one way to find out." He nodded and she said, "Verna, Peter, with me." I started to move forward and she shook her head. "No, you stay with the caravan Laney. If things go south on us, you and Tennison are magic users and will need to get the caravan to safety." I squinted at her. I knew that wasn't the real reason. She was afraid for me and it got my hackles up for some reason.

I just nodded and she hesitated, she saw the frustration in my eyes. Then I watched as they started down the road to the Keep. I turned away in a huff and Duke Fredrick chuckled at me. "She worries about you Laney. Do not take it so hard."

I said in almost a whine I was embarrassed about as I said, "But I'm her squire."

He nodded and chuckled. "Yes, but you didn't see her when the caravan reached Bowyn and the poor man had grief on his face when he told of your death. Let her have this."

I looked down at the man. He was craning his neck up at me. I closed my eyes and exhaled then gave him a nod in thanks when I opened them again. Then he teased as he walked back to the coach, "And get a horse that fits you, you look positively silly up on that monster."

That brought a grin to my face as I patted Goliath's neck. "Don't listen to them boy. We're a team you and me." Then I turned my attention to the advance party as they made their way to the gates of the magnificent metal wall. I could see from this distance, and taste, that the reddish orange color was rust. I had never felt so much metal before. It almost drew me to it.

From where we were, five hundred yards back, we could hear the horrendous screeching of metal on metal as the giant iron portcullis was raised. A man came out and spoke with our advance party. It was an animated discussion. Then Celeste turned and made a hand signal and we moved forward with most of our fighting force up front and only two behind.

We stopped at the gate and the man in ill-fitting armor in the yellow and purple colors of Treth looked us over. He was nearly as big as Sir Tennison. Then Celeste dismounted and escorted the man back to the coach. I noted her hand was resting on the hilt of her sword as was every other knight in our contingent, so I followed suit and Bex and Brenda caught it and did the same.

Celeste said, "Sir Kent here says that we may not shelter in the keep tonight."

The Duke stepped out of the coach, but I noted he stayed slightly behind Sir Kristof and Lady Verna. Everything was making me a nervous wreck. I peered around and saw more knights inside the keep. They looked a raggedy band, with ill-fitting armor and unkempt hair and beards.

The Duke spoke to the man, "I demand to speak with Duke Vladimir and Lady Sara."

The man bowed and said, "I'm sorry my Lord, but they have traveled south to Far Reach to forge a new defense compact. We were ordered to lock down the keep until their return. Nobody enters, nobody leaves." He kept his head bowed.

Fredrick regarded the man then asked, "When did they begin their journey."

The man said quickly, "Four days ago. They await Wexbury and Flatlash."

Celeste asked like she had not known that Duke John of Flatlash had already left. "Has Flatlash passed by yet?"

The man said, "Nay." Then added, "I'm sorry and wish I could grant you respite."

Celeste locked eyes with the Duke and he nodded almost imperceptibly and she told the Knight, "Thank you and we hope we have not caused you any trouble by opening the gates to speak with us."

He bowed graciously. "Not at all. Safe travels."

We moved off and Celeste led our caravan south in silence. The

Knights shot us squires warning glances when it looked like we might start asking questions. The sun was setting as we passed through Treth Minor. The roads were empty, but we could see people peeking out the shutters on the windows. I had a huge lump in my chest screaming at me that something was off.

We traveled in twilight until the we entered the forest and the light from the Three Sisters couldn't light the way very well through the canopy of deciduous trees that were still green in the warmer southern climate. Then we made an unconventional camp with all of us around the coach with the supply wagon and the archers to the rear.

Then as a light supper was being prepared, the Knights started talking. Bowyn asked us, three Squires, "What did you see?"

Brenda mentioned something I didn't notice. "There was only one guard on the wall above. All the other alcoves were empty."

Then he looked at me and I added my observation, "They need to work on their ranks. They were in disarray and their armor was ill fitting like they had no pride in their station."

Then Bex said, "They sent out a shadow." Another thing I did not notice. I was the worst knight ascendant ever.

Celeste smiled at us all, as the Duke and even Duchess Lucia nodded in approval. Then my Lady said, "Very good. All of that tells us that something is not quite right in Treth. We will not breakfast in the morning and will head out before Father Sol tops the Whispering Walls."

Then Bex added, "And Sir Kent said they had not seen Duke John when we know he had to come by before us."

Kristof clapped his shoulder and said, "That may or may not be. If the Duke stayed to the flat lands to circle into Far Reach he would not have passed Treth Keep. Even though that scenario is unlikely as it would add a half day to the trek.

I understood. Celeste just wanted to see what the man said about Duke John. That added to the implausibility of everything but wasn't necessarily a lie.

We bedded down after the light meal and Celeste set up double lookouts for the night. After she and I had been relieved, we nestled in together on my bedroll and she whispered to me, "Far Reach in two days." I nodded as I dozed off, excited to be nearing the end of our trek.

CHAPTER 23 – FAR REACH

I awoke to Celeste gently shaking my shoulder. "Let's get moving Laney." I inhaled and sighed, then my eyes snapped wide. We would arrive at Far Reach Keep by the end of the next day, and this great adventure would be at an end. If it were not for the tragedy of losing Lord Samuel, I would have said this was the most amazing thing that has ever happened to me. I turned my head to look at Celeste's smiling face and revised that to the second most amazing.

Our caravan was on the move again in the morning twilight. We all ate unseasoned jerky and bland, flat bread on our horses. I asked as I tore off some of the jerky with my teeth, "Why don't we just wait until mid-day meal to eat?"

Celeste explained, "We must always take every opportunity to stay strong and ready for anything. If we are hungry, our bodies are not at their best, nor our minds. And a sharp mind is a sharp weapon." Then she gave a sarcastic grin. "So shut up and eat your jerky squire Laney."

I stuck my tongue out at her then smiled and washed the jerky down with fresh water from my skin. Verna asked from behind us, "Where did you get that ugly waterskin."

I flushed in embarrassment. I thought it was pretty. I defended its honor. "It's not ugly, I made it back with the Lupei band. They cast a charm on it for me, so I never have to purify the water within it and it is always sweet and cool."

She caught up and held her hand out and I gave it to her. She squinted an eye comically. "Odd shape but the designs are beautiful." She took a sip. "Wow." Then she smiled crookedly. "The Gypsies charmed your waterskin?" She shook her head. "Only you Laney. How did you convince them to do that for you? They never share their magics except to heal the injured."

I shrugged and blushed as I stowed the skin. "I just helped out in the camp, contributing what little skill I had, until the caravan showed up. They all just sort of did it and said it was for me because I was... what was it? Femeie de Sabie of the Altii. I told them that I was no Woman of the Sword."

I heard Tennison tease from where he flanked the coach, "Aye that much is true, it is more like Woman of the Toothpick." Everyone in the caravan including my Lady laughed.

I complained through my smile, "It's not a toothpick, it is my sword." Which got everyone roaring with laughter.

Celeste forced herself to stop laughing and schooled her face with great effort and said in a strained voice, trembling on the brink of laughter, "And a fine sword it is Lady Laney."

I sniffed the air regally and said, "You my Lady, are no lady." Then urged Goliath into a trot. She caught up and then we slowed the pace and we grinned at each other. She had these mischievous fun spurts that caused me to smile just as much on the inside as the outside.

I actually caught the movement of our Treth shadow to the east. I was proud of the fact he didn't need to be pointed out to me. I didn't give away that I saw. I said, "To the east." Celeste smiled and nodded. I felt pride in that. I wanted to do good by her. I peeled off to do a random rotation, Bex and Brenda fell in beside me.

Bex said quietly, "Technically, that is a parrying blade, not a sword." Just to have Brenda lean over on her saddle and slap the back of his head. He looked back and forth between the two of us, then said sheepishly, "And a handsome sword it is."

I smirked. "She, not it. Her name is Anadele." The man rolled his eyes and Brenda suppressed a grin and winked at me for teasing her beau. We paused as Father Sol cast his warming rays over the Whispering Walls. I closed my eyes and basked in the warmth a moment. By the time we hit Far Reach, we would be in a temperate zone that never dropped below seventy degrees even in mid-winter.

The forest was not as dense as the Black Forest, and it started to get even more sparse as we traveled. Near noon, we sent Brenda forward with one of the archers, Linus, and Lady Beth. I started to hum an old Herder's tune and the caravan started to come alive. It was a sort of melancholy feeling as we moved along the cobblestone road with the harmony of voices of these knights of Wexbury singing the song in restrained voices.

When we found Lady Beth's party at a defensible rise with nothing but a couple squirrels to tithe the lunch, Celeste and

Fredrick agreed we had distanced ourselves enough from Treth that we could pause for a proper lunch.

One of the porters, Henry said they were going to go all out for the next few meals to use the last of our perishable supplies since we would resupply in Far Reach for our return trip. We had salted beef with a little squirrel meat thrown in and steamed rice with a delicious gravy. The smell alone had me salivating. They made some sort of dumplings with cheese inside of them that were divine. Then they made a desert of cored apples that had been heated in a glaze of butter and cinnamon. For such a simple dessert, it was incredible.

I once again took a moment to compare that meal with any I had before I had become a squire. Besides the Holy Day feasts at the castle, I had never had its like. I stared at the last bites of apple and felt sort of guilty. I paused. Then was startled by Celeste's voice. "What is it, Laney?"

I held up a bite of the apple and shrugged at her apologetically. "Just waxing about my life before now and how this would seem a feast for kings. None in Cheap Quarter eats like this unless it is the Holy Day feasts. I guess I was just feeling a little guilty."

Others stopped eating and looked at their forks. Some pushed their plates away and Celeste got that look on her face that I still couldn't identify. Was it anger, shame? I whispered, "Did I do something wrong again?"

She smiled sadly and whispered back, "No, not at all Laney, on the contrary. You teach us humility."

Then Lucia gave me a cross look, but Duke Fredrick looked pensive and thoughtful as he pulled her away from the plank tables to retire back to the coach.

After tending to the horses, we broke camp. Everyone was so quiet and the atmosphere was somber. I felt terrible to have caused such a mood. I slid back to Bex to see what I could do to lighten things up. We started singing a gay tune the minstrels favored at carnival. The Tavern Maiden's Bonnet.

Before long we had most of the company chiming in and I beamed a smile at my Lady when I saw her just watching me with a wistful smile on her face. I felt much better as we started another random rotation around the caravan.

The sun was low in the sky when we suddenly broke out of the forest into a vast rocky grassland. I had to look back to confirm we had actually been in a forest. I shook my head at how sudden it was. I looked at the ground and it seemed the soil was different. It wasn't the rich dark soil that nurtured the forest. Maybe the trees didn't like this hard packed clay like material we had emerged onto.

Then I pulled Goliath up short and stopped breathing. He cantered to the side and made nervous huffing sounds, his nostrils flaring from my unexpected stop. Celeste held a fist in the air and the caravan stopped as she looked at me in concern. Her eyes flitted from me to the horizon on all sides, "What is it, Laney?"

About two miles southwest, towering high above the horizon,

was a man-made mountain. It was a mammoth rectangular structure that seemed to grow out of the very earth at a forty-five degree angle, defying physics as it stretched for the sky. It was the only thing in this rocky grassland beside the rolling hills. How had the Wizards of the Before accomplished such a feat?

I said in a hoarse voice, the words tasting odd in my dry mouth, "That is the monolith from my dream." I swallowed, it pained my dry throat.

She sidled up to me and said as she reached out and laid a hand on top of mine on my reins. "That is the Monolith that lies on the border between the realms of Treth and Far Reach. It is okay Laney. It was only a dream." I remembered all that Mother Udele had shared with me, that this wasn't a dream, more of a seeing of what was likely to come to pass, but nothing was set in stone. I nodded and the caravan continued on, in search of a defensible position to make camp.

There were a canyon and rocky area that traversed from the west to the east to the Monolith that demarcated the border. We located a large rock outcropping that we could put to our backs, which would make a good lookout with the canyon at its back. After us squires tended to the horses, the entire camp was on edge as the porters made a large meal. I had no doubt that they'd deplete our stores with the last two meals the next day before we arrived at Far Reach Keep.

Tennison and Kristof sat on either side of Celeste and me, and Bowyn, Bex, and Verna sat across from us. The Knights spoke around Bex and me. Tennison said, "Our Treth shadow fell back an hour ago."

Kristof nodded and added, "Our old shadow is back, about a mile ahead."

Then Verna said, "And I believe the Gypsies are out there too. I haven't seen them, but I keep catching something in my peripheral vision, but it is gone when I turn."

Celeste got a twinkle in her eye. "Aye. Aren't we a popular lot?"

Duke Fredrick grunted in assent from the next plank table over. Then he said, "It is well that we will be in Far Reach on the morrow and we can dispense with whatever game is being played out there." He nudged his chin out into the rapidly darkening night.

Celeste sat up with me for a while, as we whispered things about our childhoods to each other. She had a stray barn cat as a pet. I was amazed, we couldn't seem to catch them in Cheap Quarter, let alone tame one. In some of the tomes I had seen, cats seemed to play a big role in the lives of the people pre-Impact. They appeared to be a common pet back then. I smirked. Like a cat could ever be as loving as a dog. But I always thought them as smaller wild cousins to the cougars and bobcats in our area. We tolerate them in Cheap Quarter because they are fine mousers.

I woke to Celeste trying to sneak off to her turn at watch. I grabbed her hand before she could slink off. I saw the moonlight and starlight twinkling in her eyes as I shook my head at her with a little smile and joined her. She whispered, "You don't have to

Laney."

I answered in hushed tones as I stalked past her, "But I want to."
She quickly caught up, opened her riding cloak, and I cuddled into
her side. We walked up to the top of the outcropping and relived the
archer who never spoke a word since the trip began. He keeps to
himself, I think his name was Paul. I felt terrible for not knowing
for sure.

He smiled and nodded as we approached then lowered the little
knife he was carving a tiny boat with, from a scrap of wood. He
tucked them both in his belt then hurried off to the camp below to
catch a few hours of shuteye.

"What's that?" I asked as I pointed to a pinprick of light
wavering on the other side of the canyon. It grew until I could see it
was a large fire.

Celeste looked at it and murmured, "That's where our original
shadow is camped out tonight." Then she started scanning the
horizon and two more fires lit heading down toward Far Reach
about a mile apart. "Signal fires, they are warning of our approach."
But then her head snapped back and we saw fires ignite behind us
too, heading back toward Treth. "Fuck," she hissed.

I looked at her in concern and she said, "We'll need to break
camp before dawn and double time it to the safety of Far Reach
Keep. We may need to leave the Ring and travel side roads in case
whoever is trailing us is setting up an ambush to intercept us before
we reach our destination."

She looked back again. "We can't slow down, as we may have an enemy at our back too."

I swallowed and asked, "The rogues somehow know of our mission? Is it Raneth or Poe?" I tried not to let my voice crack. She shrugged and hugged me in closer and then we just watched the night in silence. I didn't nod off, I was wide awake after I voiced the names of the rogues.

We broke camp early while Celeste filled everyone in. It was jerky, flatbread and water again. And we changed out formation a bit. The Coach rode in a cushion of Knights, the supply wagon trailing with the archers and a single Knight, Randolph. We stayed on the ring until Father Sol blessed us with his warming light. Then we doubled our pace. One knight would ride forward a quarter mile and scout out any possible ambush areas then backtrack to get us off the highway and onto a side road to bypass.

We ate lunch on the move, each of us falling back to the supply wagon one at a time to be handed some dried fruits, nuts, and meats.

In the early afternoon, hours before we would have arrived at our regular pace, we swung southwest as Lake Visintine came into view. We just needed to cross the bridge over the Lynx River and then we would head west again along the shores of the Visintine to Far Reach. I couldn't wait to arrive so I could get cleaned up. Our whole company was getting a little ripe.

The bridge was a worry, we would be vulnerable there, it was the last place a possible ambush could be waiting before the safety of the Keep. We approached with care, sending scouts to both ends of the bridge to reconnoiter the area around it. We tightened ranks around the coach and when the all-clear was signaled we crossed quickly.

Celeste had been fidgety all day, and the closer we got to Far Reach the more she shifted in her saddle. It seemed to be catchy as by the time we crossed the bridge, all the other knights looked uneasy as well. I thought they would have been relieved as the high stone towers of Far Reach were visible over the wonder of the rows upon rows of trees with exotic fruits on them including... tangerines!

I couldn't hold my tongue anymore. "What is it? We have made it to our destination."

Then Celeste shook her head but Bowyn answered for her, "Too easy. Why the shadows, and why the signal fires. We saw no signs of ambush and no signs of the shadows in the morning, they had already bugged out. Like Treth, there are no travelers on the road this close to the keep."

The rest were nodding their assent then he sighed. "But it is no matter once we are within the walls of Far Reach."

We approached Far Reach, there was a huge cobblestone courtyard in front of the main portcullis. It had to be almost a half mile across and a quarter-mile deep. By the layout, it looked to be where they held market, but it was empty. Not a single person could be seen in the entire expanse. I started getting an uneasy feeling as well. As we approached the gates, we could see guards in the towers in the purple and crimson of Far Reach.

Celeste brought us to a halt, halfway across the courtyard. She said, "Stay here Laney. They have not sent an escort to challenge us for some reason." She started forward slowly on her own. She was almost to the gates when they started raising. Goliath was uneasy and I looked from Celeste to the gates to the guards above.

Something was wrong, the guards weren't watching her. I reached into my tool pouch, pulled out my spyglass, and looked through it and gasped. Verna, who had sidled up to me on her mount, heard my gasp and snatched the spyglass from my hand and looked. She muttered, "My god!" The guards were long dead, they were strapped to pikes, holding them up to look like they were manning their posts.

I yelled out to Celeste as she dismounted and kept walking toward the gates. "Celeste, it's a trap!" Then all at once, where there had been nothing at all, I felt enormous amounts of magic energy, as men and women stormed out of the keep on horseback, and on foot. None wore the colors of Far Reach, and almost all of them were gathering magic.

I was aware of amber energy crackling along my body as I watched at least a hundred men bearing down upon my Lady, a man at their middle blazing like the sun with yellowish blue energy. The blood drained from my face as I recognized him. He was one of the men in my nightmares.

CHAPTER 24 – RETREAT

Celeste was awash with her own power, rippling with emerald fire like I had never seen it before. With a mighty slash of her sword, the ground in front of her erupted in an earsplitting explosion of power and debris and a massive wall of emerald fire roared up between her and the approaching rogues.

By the gods, I have never seen such power! Where had that come from? She, like me, was not a very powerful magic user.

The enemy pulled back and the mounted riders paced the length of the flames as Celeste mounted up and galloped toward us yelling, "Retreat!" Some of the men on foot paused in confusion, looking at the horsemen and other footmen who were staring at something or shielding their eyes.

We were already moving as fast as we could back toward the bridge as Celeste was joining us. Bex was yelling to her in confusion, "Why have they stopped pursuit?"

I looked at the daft man and pointed back. "That wall of fire bars their path!"

Verna started laughing and Celeste's serious face broke into a small smile as she said, "An illusion. I don't have that much power, but I can pull off a little illusion like that, which only magic users can see. It felt like most of them were rogues."

I blinked at her then relaxed the hold on my own power and the world around me dulled and I looked back to see our pursuers pacing back and forth watching us go, but there was no flame. Then a couple men ran unharmed through the space the flames had been. That was enough for the magic users to understand the diversion, and they charged through and after us. I almost chuckled. If we lived, I needed to have Celeste teach me how to create illusions like that. It was quick thinking on her part and it allowed her to escape.

The ground exploded to our left and my power snapped back up around me. I could feel the magical assault. They were slinging vast amounts of energy at us. The archers were all riding side saddle facing backward firing off volley after volley from the huge quivers on their saddles. Some pursuers were falling to their shots, but most of the arrows were being batted away mid air by violent magic.

Celeste and Tennison stayed to the back of our group, doing something with their magics together, deflecting some of the incoming magic. Brenda's horse was hit and she tumbled to the ground to be almost instantly hoisted by her belt to the saddle behind Lady Beth as she rode past. I yelled to Celeste over the sounds of galloping horses, clanging of armor, and explosions, "What can I do to help?"

She didn't look back at me. "Keep the Duke and Duchess safe! We can hold them off at the bridge for a while!" I nodded to myself and urged Goliath on and we flanked the coach with the others. Forming a protective ring around it.

Some tin plates from the supply wagon shot out and started to orbit around me. All my weapons began to rise and I put a damper on my emotions and the plates clattered to the cobblestones. I could taste something dark... and could smell ozone building as we crossed the bridge. Lightning struck the road in front of us from a suddenly darkening and roiling sky, sending stones and debris flying like deadly projectiles. Our group pulled up short.

I looked back. Celeste and Tennison had stopped as they exited the bridge and they dismounted and were hurtling raw energy across it. It was a choke point! That was Celeste's plan! But then I saw that man who was glowing with yellowish blue power clench his fist to the sky and yanked in a downward motion. Another bolt of lightning struck between my Lady and Tennison. They went spinning to the ground, pummeled by a spray of rocks and excess energy.

I turned on Goliath and charged back, Verna was yelling at me to come back. The two Techno Knights were stirring on the ground as the enemy charged across the bridge. I dove off of Goliath, drew Anadele, and stood in front of my knights, looking at the oncoming horde. I was beyond terrified. I could taste the dissipating electricity in the air.

Celeste looked stunned, blinking on the ground. She turned her bloody face toward me, then the horde. She was trying to say my name. The man at the center on that white stallion looked like he was tiring, but he snarled and reached for the sky again. Oh, dear lord.

A little voice in my head was telling me that energy was energy. He was about to hit us with the power of the heavens. Could I use that power in some way? I wished I had more training. I looked up to the churning clouds, then bellowed a challenge as I thrust Anadele into the ground, one hand toward the sky as the man's bolt of searing power came down to destroy us.

The cascade of pure electricity that was meant to kill us all was drawn into me. I was engulfed by it, and more pain than I could ever have imagined lit me up inside. Time had slowed to a standstill as I stood inside the torrent of power, burning. My gear was glowing with the runes of the spirit elemental charms the Gypsies had gifted me with. I had to use the power, not be consumed by it, I told myself.

I was grounding the energy like I was taught, then pulled Anadele from the ground through the pain, and thrust her forward. The energy arced through me and my sword, which was glowing white hot. The lightning struck the deck of the bridge, blowing a gaping hole in it, and showering the oncoming enemy with debris and melted stone. A few fell, screaming. I gasped and stared at my hand where my sword was cooling. My gauntlets were destroyed and Anadele's hilt was sizzling my flesh. I couldn't let her go. I could smell burning hair and flesh, I was sure the rest of me didn't fare too well either.

Celeste looked up from the ground in a surrealistic pantomime of my nightmare. "Laney, run!" Then she stood shakily to her feet as Tennison did. "Get the Duke and Duchess to safety! We will hold them off as long as we can here!"

I looked at her then the bridge, which was starting to crumble as the rogues retreated to the far side. Their leader slumped on his horse in exhaustion, he was glaring at me, yellowish blue energy sparking from his eyes. He pointed his sword at me menacingly.

I took a step to follow Celeste's orders and almost fell, my legs were wobbly. I put a hand out and steadied myself on something. Celeste's horse, Canter. I couldn't focus to see where Goliath was. I grabbed the reins of Celeste's charger with my one good hand, and pulled myself into the saddle and urge the steed on. Goliath would do Celeste better in battle.

I rejoined the group and said in a hoarse voice, "We need to get the Duke and Duchess to safety."

The Knights were all dismounting and drawing their swords. Verna said, "You can travel faster in a small group. Laney, you take the Duke and Duchess to safety in the supply wagon. That gives you three magic users. Bex, Brenda, Beth, and Bowyn escort! Take the porters and coachman with you." A tiny irrational portion of my mind that wasn't terrified for Celeste almost laughed at the fact they were all B names.

Kristof tapped Bex's shoulder and took his backpack and electrified sword, then his shocking gauntlet as he pulled the lever to charge it as he geared up. I swallowed, this meant Kristof actually appreciated Bex's ingenuity and was going to use it in the battle against magic users.

Then Verna looked at the rest and growled out, "Let's show this trash the fire of Wexbury!" The others growled back in assent as they ran to the side of my lady, the archers giving cover fire. I blinked, not one even hesitated. They were our Knights, our protectors. I fought back tears and looked at Bowyn. He nodded fiercely once as the Duke and Duchess were lifted into the wagon, then we were heading north as fast as the wagon could travel.

I looked back to see men on horseback crossing the river to engage our Knights, who were outnumbered ten to one. I stopped a sob and let my anger build. I grabbed Anadele and tore her away from my hand. I looked at my crispy flesh, which now had the Gypsy charms from the gauntlet and my sword's hilt burned into my skin. I put her in her scabbard and rode closer to the wagon, I would not let Celeste down. I felt like I was leaving her to her death.

We rode hard. Lady Beth asked over the pounding of hooves and the sound of wheels on cobblestones, "How did you do that Laney? You were engulfed by that lightning yet you still live."

I shrugged and said, "Someone once told me that energy is energy, whether it is magic or electricity. I just used myself as a conduit." I held up my burned hand and flexed my fingers painfully. "There was a price." She stared at my hand then just looked ahead as we charged down the highway.

When the horses pulling the wagon were exhausted, we abandoned it and set the horses free. We took supplies enough for a

couple days, and we all doubled up on the horses. The Duke and
Duchess took Canter, so I rode with Bowyn.

I was silent, then he looked back, and with surety in his voice
said, "She will be back. Celeste is too stubborn to die, and she is
tougher than you might believe." I just nodded and then watched
the horizon. We saw the Monolith a couple miles to the west when
we slowed.

We rode up beside the Duke, and Bowyn said, "We need to give
the horses a rest or they are done." I noted they were all glistening
with sweat and frothing at the bit.

Fredrick said, "Agreed." He looked toward the monolith. "We
can reach it by dark, we can find a defensible position there with the
Monolith at our backs."

We dismounted, watered the horses, and started trekking across
the stony grasslands toward that impossible structure. Lady Beth
and Sir Bowyn started looking at the grass as we walked, resting the
horses. They nodded to each other. Lucia asked, "What is it?"

Bowyn shrugged. "Someone was through here a day or two ago.
See here?" He moved some grass aside and we saw a shod hoof
print.

She asked, "Rogues?"

He shrugged back. "Maybe maybe not, most rogues and
marauders don't have shod horses. But they have apparently sacked
Far Reach so it isn't a given."

The Duke hissed, "Well if we can get back to Flatlash and

Wexbury, they won't be holding it for long!" There was a fire in his eyes and a promise in his voice. It was the fire of Wexbury. We would liberate our allies!

We mounted our horses again and rode slowly toward the Monolith, which continued to grow more imposing, more awe-inspiring as we approached. We reached its base and we all just stared up at that man-made stone surface, eroded over the centuries. How little we know compared to the Before. I felt so... humbled?

Then I tilted my head. I could taste... amber was dripping from my eyes as the entire structure glowed blue to my eyes. I murmured, "They have somehow reinforced the stone with a web of iron, lending it strength. Good lord, their engineers were so far beyond our modern capabilities."

Fredrick startled me when he spoke beside me. "It is not stone. It is a man-made material that incorporates stone. They used it everywhere. It is similar to brick or mortar, but much stronger." I blushed. I knew so little, and when others spoke as if it were common knowledge, it reminded me of the separation of classes in our village. Then he smiled. "Reinforcing it with iron is inspired. I shall have to share that with our Techromancers and scholars if they don't already know."

We gazed out at the horizon and Sir Bowyn announced, "Our shadow is back." I looked and saw him on a rise over a mile out. Father Sol was about to dip below the horizon when the man lit the first signal fire. Shit!

Bowyn looked at me almost apologetically then said loud enough for us all to hear, "Alright, we need to set up camp for tonight before we head north. I mean to bypass Treth, as things did not feel right there, and their signal fires went not only south, but north. We need to ration whatever food we have, Flatlash is a five days ride."

He looked around stopping his eyes on me then Beth. "Those of us who can hunt, we need to supplement our rations." We nodded, then everyone went about setting up camp. Making sure the Duke and Duchess were the most protected. The sun set and Bowyn said to the other knight, "Beth, take Laney and see if you can't rustle up some game. We'll have our rations worked out by the time you run out of twilight. Then we'll eat and rest. Double watch tonight."

It was almost comical, we all spun as one, to a voice in the darkness, "Salutations Wexbury. I may be able to help with supplies." All of us had weapons drawn, even the porters were holding carving knives. The Duke had a long slender blade in his hand, and even Duchess Lucia had pulled a blade, from who knows where, and she stood in a classic fencing stance. My hand ached as I held Anadele toward the threat.

We all lowered our weapons and all of us bowed our heads except Fredrick and Lucia when Duke John of Flatlash limped into view on a crutch made of a tree branch. Even battered and bloodied, the man exuded strength and had an almost royal bearing. His black and green garments were dirty and blood soaked. His mane of wild red hair draped over his shoulders, and his legendary handlebar mustache framed his pained smile.

Fredrick stepped up to him and they clasped arms as the Lord of Wexbury said with enthusiasm, "Salutations Flatlash!"

Chapter 25 – Monolith

~~the Lord of Flatlash joined us around the little campfire we had set up in a little dip by a large stone, obscuring our location as much as we could. The Monolith rose behind us, blackening the sky like a looming specter.

Beth and Bowyn saw to his injured leg, resplinting the break, as he relayed his story. He was approached by the representatives of Far Reach, just before we had been, and traveled with fifteen knights and five archers, to begin talks about a new defense pact. "I am now happy that I convinced Camille to stay behind since matters of state bore her. What those... men... those rogues, did to our Lady Knights after killing the men is unconscionable."

The man was seething in anger. "We arrived at Far Reach to find it overrun. Held by the rogue leader, Raneth. We retreated and ten Knights and our archers stayed on the bridge to cover our retreat."

His eyes looked haunted. "As we crested the hills above the lake, we looked down to watch our men overwhelmed by more magic users than I have seen in one group. They killed the men and... did worse... to the women."

He gritted his teeth. "As we continued our retreat, we were relieved to see an entire regiment coming down from Treth. I was elated we would get our revenge, until they attacked. It was a ruse. They had trapped us between Far Reach and Treth, which is now held by Poe's forces."

He closed his eyes. "The last of my men held them off valiantly so I could escape. It felt like most of them were magic users so I cast an illusion of me riding to the east to escape while I rode west, to the Monolith."

He locked eyes with Fredrick while I digested the fact that he had used magic. He said with a humorless chuckle, "Now I am glad you convince me and the rest of the keeps to hide the fact that the Dukes of the realms are Techromancers."

Then I blanched at his implication as to what the enemy did to the women, and a new pang of pain hit my heart at the thought of Celeste and Verna facing them.

He murmured something that chilled me to the bone, "The combination of magics they were throwing... I think Raneth and Poe are Adepts." Beth and Bex inhaled sharply.

The Duke of Flatlash shook it off, and finished with, "I rode hard into the night, like an idiot. My horse tripped up just over that rise and broke both of our legs. I had to put the poor beast out of its misery. I've almost thirty pounds of smoked horse jerky for your rations. I was going to lay low for a few days before trekking through the lowlands toward Flatlash."

Then he looked around at us. "It looks as though you fared little better." Then he looked at me and shooed Beth and Bowyn away to me. "Good lord people, take care of your squire. My leg is still going to be broken tomorrow. She needs all those burns looked at."

His eyes started dripping silver sparks then he smiled. "Ah, a
Techno Knight ascendant." Then he gave an apologetic look to me.
"With virtually no magic potential." I blushed.

As Bowyn and Beth cleaned a burn on the side of my face I
didn't even realize I had, I was surprised when Duke Fredrick said,
"None of us would be here if it weren't for that squire. When our
Techno Knights fell at the bridge, she stood alone in front of the
horde to protect them. She didn't hesitate, it was like she had no
fear."

I don't know what he was talking about, I had been scared
shitless. Bowyn winked at me as he said, "Our Laney doesn't know
how to run."

Then Fredrick said with what sounded like pride to me, "She
took a lightning strike from Raneth, then destroyed the bridge of Far
Reach to slow the enemy. The rest of our men stayed behind to give
us time to escape."

Duke John looked shocked then looked a little closer at me, then
said over his shoulder, "My condolences on the loss of your men."

Fredrick gave him a dangerous toothy smile as he shook his head
and responded, "Lady Celeste leads them."

John's eyes flew wide and he almost whispered, "Celeste? The
squire from the battle of York Keep?" My Lord nodded smugly and
John whistled. "Then perhaps I should send my condolences to
Raneth." Damn it! I wish someone would tell me the truth about
that battle!

He chuckled and shook his head as he looked at me. "Wexbury indeed produces some formidable squires. Even tiny ones." I blushed, then winced as Beth placed a large bandage on the side of my head.

John tugged on one end of his mustache and nodded toward the signal fires heading north. "Well, they know we are here now. We should move to the shelter I found on the rise there. It is defensible, and they won't be expecting three and a half Techromancers."

I uttered a "Hey!" And the big man laughed heartily in mirth and I couldn't help but grin. Why did everyone pick on my size? I almost screamed when Bowyn poured water over my right hand to clean the burns.

John said, "We have twelve hours or so to fortify or run. Unless Poe was already on the move and at your backs." I thought of the signal fires earlier in the day, I could see the rest of our group thinking the same thing.

After my hand, arm, leg, and face were bandaged, we broke up camp and followed Lord John up the rise to an earthen mound. Near the stinking carcass of a horse, a crevice was worn into the soil by water runoff and there seemed to be a tunnel beyond. We gave the horses long tethers so they could graze and then slipped through the crevice and into an almost perfectly rounded corridor. It looked metallic and tasted of iron, but it wasn't rusted, it had some sort of coating that tasted like zinc to me on it. That was interesting.

Verna cleared her throat. "Would you all care to wait for those of us who can't see in the dark?" I looked around and the lords and lady had blazing sparks trailing from their eyes. Lucia couldn't suppress the chuckle the rest of us valiantly held back as we watched the musclebound knight looking around sightlessly.

A moment later, we all covered our eyes when a brilliant light burst out from Bex's hand. He held a little box with an incandescent bulb in it with a mirror behind it. Thin wires ran from it into one of his belt pouches. He grinned cheekily and said, "I call it a portable electric torch. Or PET."

Brenda slapped the back of his head even though she looked impressed with her beau and grabbed it. "Give me that." He kept at her side as she joined us at the front. Well, he had to as the wires weren't that long, and she wasn't waiting for him.

Duke John nodded appreciatively at the gadget. It started dimming and Bex grabbed a little handle sticking out of the pouch and cranked it a few times. The light flared back up. I would have been intrigued, if that is, we weren't being hunted at the time.

There were the embers of a little fire with a bedroll and some supplies in the center of the space, which was about twenty feet across. At the end of the tunnel, there was a heavy metal door inset in one of those artificial stone walls. I chanced asking, "What is behind the door?"

He shrugged and said, "I cannot get it open, I was able to reverse the rust and oxidation, but it is locked from the inside somehow."

Fredrick said, "Laney."

I stepped up to the door and Duke John stated in a tone not meant to insult, "If I couldn't open it, what can a girl with only a spark of power do?"

I brushed the door to uncover badly faded letters. I read aloud, "Powerplant three." I looked back at Lord John, then raised my hand. Various unsecured weapons from my group and some of the metal items and tools from Lord John's supplies flew to me and started orbiting in a deadly halo. Everyone stood back. Then I reached out with my power. I could feel the locks, they were more complex than a simple sliding bolt, no wonder the Duke had trouble. I forced the mechanism to turn, breaking a half dozen tiny pins in it, then I tugged at the bolt and it slid away with a clank. Then I released my power and the metal objects rained to the ground around me. Everyone retrieved their weapons.

John whispered, "Telekinesis?" Then looked at Frederick accusingly. "How?"

My Lord just grinned and said with a shrug, "We're Wexbury." Then added with a smile, "And Laney holds the least of our magic potential as you have said." I bit the inside of my cheek so I wouldn't smile. Fredrick was misleading him on purpose. But I understood he didn't with anyone to know I was an Adept.

Bowyn stepped up to the door and tried pulling it, it started to budge. Beth grabbed on too and they pulled hard, with a groan of protesting metal the door suddenly pulled open and there was a woosh as air was sucked through the crevice and through the tunnel and through the door.

John said, "It was hermetically sealed. Whatever is inside might be preserved." Bowyn grabbed the PET, and the Knights went first, dragging Bex along by the wires of the pack. Then the Dukes and Duchess went in, followed by the rest of us. The air tasted stale. I could see clearly without the light.

It was like a surreal time capsule. The room was huge, and when I say huge, I mean cavernously huge. I realized the rise we climbed was actually just eons of dirt covering the structure. It looked like it had just been constructed. Everything had only a fine layer of dust on it, which probably settled eons ago before the door was sealed with corrosion.

There was a yellow railing that we all stood by to look down upon what looked like six mammoth electric motors embedded in the floor. Each was ten or twenty times the size of my old cottage. "Oh my lord." Someone whispered I'm not sure who, maybe it was me. I was in awe.

Bex said, "Look at this." We all turned and there were huge diagrams on the walls. They were scrolls as big as tapestries. It had a picture above the diagrams that had a structure that looked eerily similar to the monolith. I read the huge lettering, "Grand cow... coo... no... Coulee Hydroelectric Dam" The monolith was simply a dam for irrigation!? What did hydroelectric mean?

Bex was shaking his head with excitement. "No, here." He stabbed his finger at one of the diagrams that was labeled

'Powerplant #3'. We all looked at it. And then down to those
enormous motors. Then back at the diagram. It was almost
comical, we were like a group of lemmings.

I whispered, "No way." As I pointed at the pictures that were
painted so precisely. They must have had amazing artisans paint
them. It showed tubes filled with water. I didn't understand most of
the labels, but they went down through the dam to one of those
motors, they had labeled 'Turbine'. The water turned the motors?
Then they were not motors they were generators!

I didn't understand the text above the turbine, but Bex whistled
and said, "My god. Eight hundred and five megawatts each? Just
one could power all the keeps in the Lands of Sparo with the
capacity to spare!"

I blinked at that as the Dukes studied the diagrams, nodding in
appreciation. Then I had a sudden thought and again felt so very
tiny. I had laughed with everyone else at the Techromancer that
suggested that the Wizards of the Before Times had used rivers to
create power. I murmured, "He was right."

Fredrick knew what I was saying and said, "Indeed. I think
Wexbury owes the man an apology." I nodded absently, looking at
this diagram it was obvious. It was exactly like the windmills, only
it used water to turn the generator instead. They just isolated the
water from the electricity generated. Common theory was that water
and electricity don't mix. I was already envisioning a dam on the
Hawktail, lighting up our whole realm with free power. I almost

laughed.

Bowyn snapped us all out of it. "We need to see if there is anything here we can use to defend with. We can leave this to the scholars if we survive." We all agreed and we split up after making torches for those who needed them. Beth stood guard at the door as we all explored the cavernous space.

There were plenty of tools to use like clubs, but we had swords. I went into a couple rooms and chuckled. I actually knew what they were. Indoor outhouses like Celeste had in our quarters, complete with sleek looking auto-pots. I looked at the signs on the metal doors. 'Men' and 'Women.' Nothing in there to use as a weapon.

I wound up walking to one of the generators out of pure curiosity. It simply dwarfed me. I reached out with my power. I could feel the shaft bound by something. Then I realized it was the lubrication for the bearings that had decayed. It must have been organic based, like the grease we used. Even if we got it turning, something this size, the weight of it and metal on metal would weld the bearings to the shaft in just a few minutes without lubrication.

I gave one last mental push as hard as I could, and there were a screeching sound and the shaft actually turned half way. I felt enormous amounts of static in the air and it subsided just as quickly as it came when the generator stopped turning.

Lord John was by my side quickly. I blushed in embarrassment and said, "Sorry. I was curious... it still works. Did you feel the power buildup just from that minuscule amount of rotation?"

He shook his head slowly at me. "You could feel it? Electricity, and metal manipulation? I have only ever heard of one other with an amber energy signature." I didn't know what to say, it almost sounded like an accusation.

Lucia actually came to my rescue. "No our Laney is only electric sensitive."

Duke John narrowed his eyes. "But the whirlwind of metal around her, and manipulating the locks on the door. I just command the water elements, but I could probably push the generator shaft with raw energy if I concentrated hard, but she has but a tiny spark of power."

She shrugged and said far too sweetly, "Electromagnetism." Then she looped her arm through his and pulled him off down the cavernous space. I wondered why they didn't share with our ally what I was. It wasn't like I was a threat to anyone with any amount of power.

We searched and found other exits, but they opened to walls of clay and stone. The way we came in was the only way in or out. If we stayed in here, it would be our tomb, like the ten skeletons Bowyn found huddled in a room labeled 'Cafeteria'. He had a couple dozen extremely thin bladed knives from there.

We left the cavern and sat around John's re-stoked fire while Bex and Brenda stood guard just outside. We inventoried our weapons. Nothing that could stand against the hundred or so men that Lord John said that Poe commanded.

Fredrick said, "So it is decided then. We run while we can. We could have Lady Beth and one of the squires leave some false trails to the ravine to the north while we head west. We can meet at the end of the dry riverbed at sunrise."

We all nodded in assent, but Bex yelled, "Riders!"

We all ran out and saw dozens of men riding swiftly toward us from the east carrying torches, they were maybe a mile and a half out. I could see a sea of colors radiating from most of them. I whispered, "Almost all of them are rogues." I could hear the fear in my voice. We looked west and saw a smaller group curling around to meet the others just about when they would arrive. It was too late, we were trapped.

Bowyn and Beth slowly drew their swords started walking down the rise to meet the enemy. There was steel in their eyes, Bex and Brenda began to follow. I shouted, "Wait!" The beginnings of an insane plan forming in my head.

They turned to look at me then the oncoming horde. I mumbled to myself, "Water and electricity don't mix." I turned to the Duke of Flatlash, "Lord John, you said you were water elemental?" He nodded and I looked to Fredrick and Lucia and asked, "Water?" They both nodded.

Then I asked John, "Do you really think you can turn that generator?"

He started to ask, "What does that..."

I interrupted. "Can the three of you bring the groundwater to the surface in the dry riverbed there?" I pointed at the base of the rise then John's head rolled back and he started a bellowing laugh to the heavens. I grinned wickedly at him. He pointed at me and said, "That, we can do." He looked at my Lord and Lady and prompted, "Wexbury?"

They nodded and they all stretched out their hands, I felt an enormous wave of power wash past me and we could see the ground below darkening in the moonlight. When the water was puddling on the surface, they all stopped and Fredrick asked, "Laney?"

I shrugged and repeated, "Water and electricity don't mix."

He nodded and said, "Yes but where are we going to get..." He trailed off and his head snapped to the crevice and a smile bloomed on his face.

John nodded at them. "I'll probably need your help to do this from here. Can your squire do this?"

To my surprise, it was again Lucia that said firmly, "Our girl caught a bolt of lightning, what do you think?" Then she looked at me with an actual grin and said as she rolled her eyes and shook her head, "Men."

I looked around then at the approaching horde. I thought about the cavernous room of Powerplant Three and motioned to everyone with my chin. "You'll want to stand over there at the top of the rise to be safe."

They all hesitated, Sir Bowyn stood beside me and I shook my head, I could tell he hadn't realized what I was about to attempt.

"No. Go Bowyn, it isn't safe next to me."

He gave me an undecipherable look and then said, "It is no wonder Celeste chose you." He leaned down and kissed the top of my head and retreated to the top of the rise to stand guard in front of the rulers of Wexbury and Flatlash. He told the porters and coachman, "You three go hide in that gully downrange. Someone needs to get word back to Flatlash and Werxbury." They hesitated, then nodded and ran off.

I watched as the streams of lights merged then charged toward the dry riverbed as I drew Anadele, perhaps for the last time. I looked back and nodded at Duke John. He thrust his hands down with his eyes closed, I could feel his immense power seeking his target. Duke Fredrick and the Duchess followed suit and I saw their power flow into him, compounding his power. They were almost too bright to look at and even the rest of our group must have seen that much power because they were shielding their eyes.

We heard a screeching of metal on metal even from outside and then I could taste the electricity feel the potential as the generator started spinning faster and faster. I could touch it and held it back using my power to let it build. It was painful but not as painful as the lightning bolt, but I believed it would be enough for what I had planned, especially if I could sustain it.

Fredrick murmured something and the group was suddenly hidden behind a pile of boulders. I blinked in shock, but then realized it was just an illusion like Celeste had used. It wouldn't fool any non-magic users though.

The pain was building inside me and my burns felt as if they were being held over hot coals again. The charms on my riding cloak started to glow. Sweat was beading on my face as the approaching enemy began splashing across the riverbed.

I held Anadele high, I could hear and taste a resonance in her with the thrumming electricity as I yelled, "Who are you, and what do you want!?"

The leader who was blazing with blinding red energy held a fist up and the approaching enemy came to a stop. He dismounted as did about half the rogues. I froze as I saw the bald man in studded leather armor. He was huge, and his eyes blazing red like a demon was exactly what I saw in my nightmare. This was him! I remembered the pain of the fire in my dream.

He seemed amused. "I girl, am the last thing you will ever see before you are sent to your maker. Where are the Duke and Duchess of Wexbury?"

I tried not to let my voice waver as the pain of holding back the electricity was almost unbearable. "I give you this one chance, I do not wish to harm anyone. Walk away now and I won't kill you all."

The rogues started laughing as he smiled ruefully. "This is the best of Wexbury? The cowards send a little child to her death?"

I couldn't hold it any longer. As I let go of my blocks, I whispered, "I warned you." I saw him lift a foot out of the puddle he was in and a look of shock as a tsunami of energy roared out of

the crevice, blowing the hole wider. Man made lighting arced out
and into me as I screamed. I was once again engulfed in raw energy
that felt like it was burning away my very soul.

I thrust Anadele forward and a deafening raging torment of
electricity arced out to hit the wet ground the enemy was standing
in. I couldn't hear a thing through my own screams and the sound of
electricity breaking the sound barrier in tremendous claps of
thunder.

The enemy started thrashing and horses were toppling onto men.
Everyone was convulsing. I knew this was a fraction of the power
of a lightning bolt, but I held it for five eternities as I counted off the
seconds. Then ten. My tears were burning my cheeks, I couldn't
hold it much longer. I channeled every last iota of energy I could
and thrust out Anadele one last time with a final effort. The very air
tasted of electricity.

I glanced up and saw electricity coursing through the Monolith
and with a tremble of the ground and a huge clapping sound, the
Monolith cracked along its whole length. The lower half seemed to
hang in the air a moment then fell in slow motion. The ground
shook and I fell to my knees, losing my concentration as the roar of
the collapse hit us like a shockwave.

I heard a screeching sound then an explosion from below as the
bearings failed in the generator. The skin on my arms was bubbling
and again I couldn't release my sword and could smell my flesh
burning.

I tried to stand but stumbled and fell, my sword was knocked away, when it hit the ground. I stared at my hand, it looked like a burned claw and I attempted to flex it and was rewarded with pain, but it moved. I swayed to my feet and sighed in defeat. Poe was standing there, watching me with a shit eating grin on his face. He had some minor burns but nothing serious.

There was a sea carnage and bodies of men, women, and horses out there. I had killed them. But Poe stood with and about ten others gathered around him with virtually no burns. They must have had the power to channel electricity. I thought Poe might survive since we suspected he was Adept, but ten others? I was already dead on my feet. Now it was time to die for real.

Poe looked around and looked a little hesitant but then he started slowly approaching. "Nice try little girl, but I'm an Adept. Do you know what that is? Someone like you with hardly any of your own magic, could never take me down. You're nothing but a toasty critter now. Not even my men would want to use your body now with those disgusting burns."

I pulled my little dagger from my boot and held it out, I swung it from side to side slowly, taking in the approaching enemy. Six men, four women. He laughed out loud and the others followed, "What are you going to do with that little thing? It is eleven to one child. Time to die."

I smiled and I felt my lip crack and blood shot across my arm. Great, I was falling apart literally. I said with venom, "You may want to get some more men then, to make it fair."

He laughed again as he drew his longsword from his back in a slow movement meant to intimidate, he was almost up to me now as I swayed on my feet. "You're delusional now. Just accept your end child. How do you think you could beat us now?"

I coughed up a little blood and gave him a wicked grin, "Because... we are Wexbury."

He cocked an eyebrow. "We?"

Then Bowyn, Beth, Bex, Brenda, Fredrick and Lucia exploded from behind the illusion, with John hobbling behind. They slammed onto the enemy, swords flashing and magic slinging, leaving Poe to me.

He roared in fury and thrust his sword forward, I could taste the familiar magic from my dream. It was fire, he was burning me alive in my dream. I had to change the dream. Mother Udele had said a seeing was just one possible future. I had to change my future. I grabbed the corner of my riding cloak and whipped it up, holding it in front of me like a shield as a tornado of fire hit me from the tip of his sword.

I could feel the heat rising as the charms on my cloak started glowing brightly. Then he stopped and panted. I released my cloak, it had made the difference! I raised my arms in rage and all the weapons from the bodies of the slain started whirling around me. I sought out all the different metals I could taste around me and called them all to me. I could taste it all, even the metals in the earth around us and in the blood of all the people.

I charged at him and he held up his blade, roaring in rage, and like a wall had been raised, everything slammed into it and fell to the ground. I stood within striking distance of his sword and I would have paled if I thought I had much blood left unboiled.

He stepped toward me and I stumbled back. I felt something cool against my neck and my hand absently went to it. It was the little necklace with the small silver goat charm on it. Mother Udele said it was important in her visions of me. I looked at the man, he was an adept that eclipsed my power by an order of magnitude. How could a little magnesium charm possibly help me?

I thought again of Donovan's lessons about magnesium, and my eyes snapped wide as I yanked the necklace off. I held it out toward him. "Please stop. I don't want to kill you with this."

He stepped forward and started to swing his sword as he asked, "How is that going to..."

I threw the goat at him as I dodged to the left and targeted what little energy I still had inside me at it as I closed my eyes tightly. Even through my eyelids the bright white light of burning magnesium almost blinded me.

I opened my eyes as the light died away and Poe was yelling and covering his eyes. If he weren't such a monster, I would have felt sorry about that little trick as I thrust my dagger into the side of his neck.

He took a step and stumbled, grasping his neck. Then he fell to his knees as blood pumped from his jugular. Then he fell face first to the ground. I fell to my knees. I looked around and only my allies were still standing. They were all looking at me in shock. Duke John said in a hoarse voice, "She killed an Adept." He looked at the group. "With only a little knife."

Bowyn was running to my side as I started to slump. I looked around at the grass fire that Poe's attack had started. It was more billowing smoke than fire as the grasses were green and well hydrated. My eyesight began to dim as I looked around the hazy battlefield. I felt something big and pushed Bowyn violently away from me as lightning struck beside me where he had been, sending me flying.

Five horsemen exploded from the smoke and they pulled back at the sight of the sea of bodies. The leader on his white stallion, was glowing a yellowish blue and my heart sank. If Raneth was here, then that meant Celeste was... I couldn't finish the thought. I backed slowly as the rest of my group started taking stances with their weapons. Raneth rode slowly up to Poe's body and then slid off his horse, pointing his sword at me.

Then slowly pointing his sword at each of our party, the big man hissed to our group, "Who killed my son!?"

His... son? Wait, they were both adepts and it seemed to run in families. Of course. And that would be why two rogue warlords would work together! The others dismounted to form a line beside their leader. Everyone was choosing targets. This was just like training in the courtyard. I saw our people moving slowly apart so their circles of reach with their blades didn't overlap.

Raneth didn't seem concerned about it. He screamed at me, spittle flying from his mouth, "Who!?"

I knew I was dead. I had survived until now by sheer dumb luck. This man didn't even look tired from his battle with the Knights of Wexbury. This man killed my Lady, the woman I could never confess my real feelings for. How could I face someone like this? I reached into my well of energy and it was almost empty, a mere trickle. I could defend against possibly one attack.

I smiled and said through the taste of my own blood, "I did." I didn't even see the backhand coming, but I suffered far worse at the hands of nobles. Mother taught me to be strong, to not show weakness. I staggered but stayed on my feet as the rest of the rogues attacked.

Through the clanging of swords, I heard Celeste's voice in my head, a memory of her saying, "Even the smallest thing can turn the fiercest battle when it is not expected." Then Mother Udele's voice saying almost the same thing. "Even the smallest thing can have a huge effect on the outcome of any event."

I was muttering almost incoherently to myself, "The smallest thing... the smallest thing." As the man loomed over me and raised his sword above his head. I was questing out with all my senses... the smallest thing. I could taste all the metal around me. Weapons, tools, stirrups. I could taste the acrid taste of oxidation of the iron in the blood all around me, the metals in the stones and in the broken Monolith.

I had to blink when his sword went tumbling from his hand, an arrow with the colorful feathers of the Mountain Gypsies in his arm. He started to lunge at me in rage.

Wait, that's it, the smallest thing! Doc Maxwell said that mother's iron levels were low so her cells weren't getting enough oxygen. I looked blearily up at the man as I yanked my hand into a fist in the air, pulling with all of my might, using the last embers of the dying magic inside of me and whispered, "I'm sorry,"

The man's eyes went wide when a red mist sprang from his body and he grasped his throat, his mouth working like a fish out of water. He was gasping for the oxygen his body could no longer provide, as I formed the iron I took from his body into a little metal ball. I let it fall to the ground as he fell to his knees. Life leaving his eyes.

I was swaying and I started to fall, when I heard the heavy pounding of hooves. Time seemed to slow all around me. Like an angel of death, the huge form of Goliath emerged through the smoky battlefield, with a bloodied Celeste riding high in the saddle with a wild look in her eyes. The last thing I saw clearly was her sword sweeping down to take Raneth's head as she passed by like a beautiful and deadly wraith.

My heart stuttered as the world started to fade to black. Celeste was alive! My heart stuttered again, then there was nothing.

CHAPTER 26 – RECOVERY

I woke up in a familiar wagon. I couldn't focus well. I was so tired. The world was alive in a torrent of mists. I was aware of two things. One was that with all this pain, I had to still be alive. And two, the Lupei family was at least four days ride away, how could I be in Sylvia's wagon? I croaked out, "Sylvia?"

Someone grabbed my left hand tightly, it was Celeste. She blurted out with hope tinging her tone, "Laney?!"

The silken mists around me dissipated and I saw an exhausted looking Sylvia standing over Celeste's shoulder where my Lady sat on a chair by the bed. I tried to sit up but winced in pain. Both Celeste and Sylvia put hands on my shoulders to keep me down.

I felt the warmth of bodies around me and tried to focus. I smiled as I saw Ingr curled up on my side with her two tiny goats. Glasses jostled and clinked and the wagon swayed. We were moving. The windows were dark, the only light in the space was the oil lamp on the table. It was still night.

I remembered the Gypsy arrow that had disarmed Raneth in the battle. The Lupei family must have followed us. Sylvia slapped the wall of the wagon soundly twice and we came to a creaking halt. She ran the couple steps to the door and swung it open. She yelled two words in English, "She's awake!" There was cheering and I heard Mother Udele's voice in the distance calling out in the tongue of the people, "Make camp!"

I heard the creaking of wagons as they formed a circle while Celeste just laid her head on my shoulder and wept. I lifted my arm and stroked her hair, pausing when I saw my hand. There was twisted and mangled flesh covering most of it. I held it up to look at my palm and the skin looked much better there, but it had Gypsy symbols raised in the flesh like scars. They glowed faintly.

I looked back at Celeste and continued to comfort her. "Shhhh... It's alright Celeste." She looked up with watery eyes. She looked mad.

I swallowed and she hissed, "Again, I thought I had lost you, Laney! My heart can't take it! Never do this to me again!" I didn't know what to say so I just nodded. The corners of her mouth quirked into a smile.

I cupped her cheek then looked at the window again. "How did the Lupei arrive so quickly? When will Father Sol awaken?"

Sylvia moved into view and exchanged a look with my Lady. Then she said, "The survivors of your caravan arrived at our camp seven days ago Laney, after a five-day trek to us to seek healing for you. We will arrive in Flatlash tomorrow. Then Wexbury three days later, on your Holy Day."

Twelve days? I had been unconscious for that long? I blinked at them then Sylvia continued, "We did not know if you would ever return to us, you had suffered so much injury. I have been healing you as I can. I can still do more, but... your arm leg and face will have scarring. Most of the burns were magic in nature."

I was so tired. I shrugged and closed my eyes and said, "It is no matter, as long as my people are safe now." But then I snapped my eyes open. "Our people?! Is everyone safe?"

Celeste lowered her eyes and then said in a strained voice, "It was a long fought battle, first Lord Linus and Lord Paul fell to Raneth's attacks. They were so varied, I believe he was an Adept. I moved in to take him in single combat as the battle raged."

She exhaled. "Kristof was making short work of the lesser rogues with Bex's gadgets and I don't think they were prepared for Verna and Tennison's rage and physical power." She swallowed. "We fought for almost an hour, dwindling their forces. We had lost Sir Marrin and Randolph before the enemy realized they were no match for the fire of Wexbury. The cowards ran. We chased them knowing they would seek out Poe's support."

Then the corner of her mouth quirked into a crooked smile. "I had not known you had already dispatched Raneth when I rode Goliath in to save you." Then she softened. "As always Laney, you are full of surprises."

The door swung open and Duke Fredrick's form filled the doorway. He was smiling and told Celeste, "And to think, our Squire Laney here dispatched Poe with her toothpick, and that little paring knife. And Raneth with the little spark she holds inside." He shook his head in disbelief and said with a touch of pride that made me warm inside. "Two Adepts."

I croaked out a whine, "Hey, it's a dagger, not a paring knife!"

Everyone chuckled at me, I surrendered and smiled.

A hand rested on the Duke's shoulder. "Fred, leave your Femeie de Sabie to rest. Go make yourself useful setting up camp."

We all chuckled at his lopsided grinning response. "Yes... Mother."

He bowed to Udele as he exited. Then the woman came inside, she smiled fondly at Celeste and laid a hand on her shoulder. "Go now child, get something to eat. Your girl is now awake."

Celeste looked at her as if she were going to challenge her, but then she lowered her eyes. "Yes Mother Udele."

She looked at me with eyes glittering with joy and then she kissed the top of my head. "I'll be right back." I smiled and dropped my hand from her face. Then she left, looking back as she shut the door.

Udele sat in the chair Celeste had been in. She took my hand and gave it a squeeze then looked at the door and said, "That girl. I swear she rarely slept or ate while she sat by your side. I worried more for her than you."

A pang of guilt hit me. She shook her head at me and with a tinge of satisfaction and vindication said, "It seems you were up to the task, and could take far more pain than should have been shouldered by you, my mostenitor." I didn't know that word.

She smiled and asked, "Are you up to trying to stand?" Sylvia made an exasperated sound and Mother just waved her off.

I didn't want to disappoint her so I just nodded then looked down at the three little sleeping heat generators. Sylvia reached over to snag Ingr, the little goats were much distressed about that and hopped off the bed to stand at Sylvia's feet, looking up at their cute little ringleader, asleep in her arms.

I winced as I forced myself to a sitting position. I looked down, I was in some sort of colorful sleeping robe. Udele helped me to my feet, I winced at the pain that shot through me. Sylvia said quickly, "Now that I have repaired the worst of the damage, I can work on those pains. You should be restored as much as I am capable of doing before we reach Wexbury."

I nodded and my hair fell oddly. I reached a hand up and about a quarter of my hair was shaved off on the left side. She gave me an apologetic look. "It was burned and matted, we had to shave it off to see the wounds beneath. It will grow back within a few months." Then she looked down. "I can do nothing more for the burn on your face."

I shrugged and assured her, "I was never going to be pretty anyway. It is no matter." The two virtually glared at me. What had I said? I tried to qualify it, "At least everyone is safe now." Udele closed her eyes and shook her head then kissed the top of mine and Sylvia slid some slippers in front of me and I slid my feet into them as she draped a cloak of dyed rabbit pelts over my shoulders.

Then I furrowed my brow. "In the battle. I thought I saw an arrow of the people."

Sylvia grinned and nodded. "That lazy brother of mine. Dru was

assigned as your garda personala, to watch you, to keep you safe."
Then she said, like it was some sort of common sense explanation
when she saw my confusion, "Your blood bond with Mother Udele
of the Lupei."

I gave an apologetic look for my ignorance and said, "Well,
please thank him for me. He may well have saved my life."

Both of the women waved that off as Sylvia said with humor in
her voice, "By the powers that be Sora Laney, don't tell him that.
His head barely fits in the door as it is." I chuckled. I could see the
pride in her eyes for her brother even though she teased.

Sylvia laid Ingr down gently with her head on the pillow and
pulled the blanket up. The little goats hopped up and settled around
her. Then Sylvia quickly fastened a belt around my waist. It had a
small curved sword hanging in a scabbard on it. She explained,
"The Femeie de Sabie of the Altii mustn't be without a blade. Yours
is being seen to, our weaponsmiths are baffled, it has somehow
changed in nature. They will have it ready soon."

Then the women led me out and down the little fold down stairs.
The camp was full of motion as people were setting things up and
getting a roaring fire going in the center. I saw huge oxen hitched to
the wagons.

The activity seemed to pause, everyone turned to look at us, and
a cheer went up. Udele gave me a reassuring squeeze of the arm and
Celeste rushed up to take me from the women and guide me to a seat
at one of the long plank tables that had been set out. Then everyone

went back into motion.

A huge feast and celebration followed and the children seemed to crowd around me. I was so happy to see that most of our group had survived but saddened at the loss of four more who were swiftly becoming my friends. That is five comrades at arms that paid the ultimate cost of defending what is right.

Duke John was walking around fine, wearing colorful Mountain Gypsy garb, and tugging on his mustache. They must have healed his injuries.

The porters and Dru were busy spinning exaggerated yarns of the battle, to the children and any other who would listen, by the fire. Alexandru's hands were swooping through the air as he said in exaggerated tones, "Then Sora Laney, Femeie de Sabie of the Altii, cried out a challenge as she brandished her enchanted blade, Anadele. With one mighty sweep of her sword, she tore half the Monolith of the Before Times asunder. The ground shook for miles as it crashed to the earth, crushing half the enemy vrajitor." He winked over at me.

I whispered to Celeste, "It didn't happen like that and nobody was crushed."

She was grinning like a fool as she shushed me and listened as our porter, Henry chimed in. "That's how it happened. I saw it with my own eyes."

I started to protest, but Mother was grinning, "Oh shush girl, I want to hear." I slouched in defeat and I caught Fredrick and Lucia

grinning at me. I looked at them in helplessness and Fredrick waved
it off with a smile then turned to listen to the fairytale that Dru was
spinning.

I doubted I could be any more embarrassed as I blushed and ate
some more. I felt as if I hadn't eaten for weeks. I cheered with the
crowd when he got to the fall of Raneth, "Then Sora Celeste,
Femeie de Sabie of the Altii, charged through the fires of hell
consuming the valley. She rode the unstoppable warhorse, Goliath,
with flames shooting from his nostrils as his thundering hooves
pounded the earth as they made haste to Sora Laney's side. With a
single stroke of her vrajitoare blade, she separated the defeated
Raneth's head from his body, ensuring he would not rise again to
perpetrate evil upon the innocents of the land!"

I smiled smugly at the look of consternation on Celeste's face
and stuck out my tongue at her. Then I yelled over the divine
cornbread muffin I was eating, "Alexandru, you forgot the
incredible shot you yourself took to disarm Raneth to save me." I
smugly took a bite of the muffin at the grumpy look he shot me.

Darin Porter lit up at that and said loudly, "Yes! I witnessed that
with my own two eyes. He made the shot from a hundred and
fifty... no from three hundred yards away from where we hid in a
small ravine as Lady Laney fought. He came to protect us and saw
Raneth swinging his huge blade down at Lady Laney and without
hesitation or aiming, he fired off a shot that passed clean through the
enemy's arm. It sent him spinning back to the ground." I grinned at

the exaggeration, I had no doubt it would be six hundred yards after a few retellings.

Henry chimed in to punctuate my thought, "No it had to have been three hundred and fifty yards." The children and some of the adults showered Dru with praise. I was happy to give him a helping of his own medicine.

I chuckled at the look on Dru's face, then asked the Wexbury contingent that was gathered around. "Does anyone believe these fabricated tales?"

Lord John's face went from smiling to serious. Then he said, "Exaggerated or not. The truth dear squire is that you stopped over a hundred men and left the stragglers to me and your brethren as you dispatched two Adepts. One with a little goat charm and a tiny knife, and the other by ripping the very iron from his blood. You are no mere Techromancer now are you Laney?"

I looked at Fredrick, who was about to say something as he shook his head in warning to me, and I thought of Celeste and the battle of York and blurted out loudly for all to hear. "For as long as I shall live, I will swear upon the courage of Lord Samuel in this campaign." I held up my mug of grape juice.

Lucia looked shocked at me, and Frederick grabbed a cup and all of Wexbury present toasted, "Lord Samuel!"

Duke John looked long and hard at me then he smiled and said, "Then I too shall swear upon it when asked, as I do for Celeste at the Battle of York." I gave him silent thanks with my eyes and he nodded once.

He looked over to Fredrick and chuckled, "I hate you Wexbury. Just how many secrets do you keep?"

Fredrick grinned right back. "I hate you too Flatlash." The men laughed together and my Lord raised his mug to John. "Allies for life." Duke John repeated it, "Allies for life."

The festivities wound down with the Three Sisters high in the sky. We retired to Sylvia's wagon just after midnight. Dru and Sylvia said their goodnights and joined their mother on the other side of the partition. I arranged myself around Ingr and her little herd, and was so happy to have Celeste at my back, wrapping her arm tightly around my waist.

Little Eli seemed to materialize from nowhere and slid under the covers in the overcrowded bed. He murmured, "Soras." Then he was asleep before his head hit the pillow with his little sister. Why was everyone calling us Sora? I drifted off with that question in my head.

***

I didn't dream, the nightmare, or seeing, never came, I had already lived it. Over the next couple days, I got stronger and stronger. I was amazed at the story of Celeste routing Raneth, when Verna told me what had happened when Celeste wouldn't. She had stood toe to toe with him and not allowed him to call lightning down on her comrades.

There was a lot of planning between our leaders. A large force

was to be sent south to liberate both Treth and Far Reach, though
they believed any remaining rogues would have dispersed to the
winds after hearing that a contingency of only nine Wexbury
Knights and four Wexbury archers had dispatched over two hundred
and seven of their magic using warriors.

I helped out in the camp wherever I could. I loved reading to the
children, and I was getting much better at making water skins. I
even taught Lady Beth and Celeste how to sew. They thought it
basically the same as stitching up a wound on the battlefield.

We stayed in Flatlash Keep. The Gypsy caravan overnighted on
the Fairy Ring meadow at the base of Castle Flatlash. We feasted
and listened to our Knights and Duke John tell the tales of how Lord
Samuel had made two impossible shots to kill the rogue Adepts and
stave off another Great Mage War. He fell a hero of the realm at the
great battle of the Monolith.

When we awoke to start our three-day journey by oxen pulled
the wagon to Wexbury, there were two stacks of clothing on the
table. Celeste and I were the only ones in the wagon. I looked at
the stacks and blinked twice and smiled then stood in front of my
Lady and put a finger to her lips when she was about to speak.

I poured water from the pitcher into the basin, then turned to her
and reached for her nightdress. She almost backed away with...
fear? In her eyes. I tilted my head and smiled. And reached for it
again and she swallowed and stood still as I undressed her like
Sylvia had done for me in another lifetime, before the battles that

had changed something inside me.

I wiped down my lady with a wet cloth marveling over her perfect form. Then piece by piece dressed her and secured each piece of her new armor on her. Everything, including her undergarments had dozens, no, hundreds of protections, charms, and symbols of luck, adoring them. Everything was buzzing with a warm, soft energy under my fingers. Her breastplate was half the weight of her old one and I could taste a lot of carbon in the steel, strengthening it.

On the breastplate was etched the crest of Wexbury, the crest of a Techno Knight, the crest of the House of Celeste, and then one I recognized burned into every wagon in the caravan, the crest of the Lupei family. I slid her sash on, which had the same crests on it, then a braid of colorful fabric around her neck that hung down beside her sash.

I had to shade my eyes, there were so many charms upon her person now that she shone like an angel. I realized I was breathing hard as I looked at her and licked my lips and calmed down. My eyesight changed, but even with my normal vision, she seemed to almost imperceptibly shimmer.

Then I sat her down and brushed out and braided her hair to one side, and tied it off with strips of emerald and violet fabric. When she turned around, she took my breath away.

Then she stood in front of me, I looked up into her eyes and we stood like that for a few long seconds. I wasn't breathing. Then she reached out and began to undress me. I stood not only naked before her, but naked to the universe as she washed my body down. She paused to trace the scars on my face, my arm, my leg. Then she ran a finger along each and every scar on my back from my flogging.

I had to squint at the clothing and armor she placed on me. If possible, it had more layers of charms than hers did. Then she sat me down and duplicated the side braid I had done for her to my right. Exposing my shaved head and scars on the left of my face more prominently.

I started to reach up to absently touch the scars but she gave me a warning look and I dropped my hand. I stood and grabbed her riding cloak and her sword clattered to the ground. I looked in the cloak and grinned. I went about arming my Lady. Her weapons and their scabbards and sheaths were spelled as well. Then I laid her riding cloak, which was shimmering with power, over her shoulders.

She opened my cloak on the table then smiled. In a gleaming new scabbard was Anadele, with her shining, spell covered hilt wrapped with a new leather grip. She crinkled her nose as she strapped my dagger to my boot and she made a squishing motion as she squinted an eye. I rolled my eyes at her and grinned. Yeah, I got it, a tiny knife.

Then she put my tool pouch over my shoulder and hesitated when she turned back to my riding cloak. She reached out and picked up a single, delicate white glove that looked to be woven in the finest silks. It was glowing brightly and thrumming with power.

I used my sight to walk down through the dozens upon dozens of layers of enchantments and charms on it.

She looked at my right arm and then me expectantly. I held out the withered and scarred thing and she slipped the long glove over it. It went up almost to my shoulder and the aches and pains that Sylvia could not ease, seemed to vanish. I clenched my fist, no pain. I smiled at Celeste, then she draped my new riding cloak over my shoulders.

We put on our leather gauntlets. My right arm looked odd with a gauntlet and then white silk running up to my shoulder. Then I looked up and froze. Celeste was inches from me looking down at me, emerald sparks drizzling from her eyes. I wasn't breathing again as she just seemed to take me in, then she lifted a hand and cupped my right cheek. She whispered in a voice I had never heard from her before, "You are so beautiful Laney."

I blushed and she wouldn't let me look down. I smiled shyly and said, "And so are you. Lady of my heart."

She kept me immobile with those amazing eyes for a few seconds longer. That had been possibly the most intense moment of my life. Then she turned me to the mirror and said, "Shall we go see what mischief our Gypsy friends are up to Lady Laney?" I blinked, my facial scars seemed to be shimmering slightly as a result of the huge amounts of magic of the people on my person.

I turned away from my reflection, looped my arm through her offered arm, and said, "I would be delighted Lady Celeste." I silently exhaled and then we stepped out into a cheering crowd of Gypsies and knights.

After a huge breakfast buffet provided by our hosts, Duke John, and Duchess Camille, Celeste mounted her charger. Then on my third try, to the chuckling delight of all around, I mounted Goliath. I ignored the teasing and looked up regally and before Celeste could, I stole her thunder since I heard her chuckling with the rest. I raised my arm to the sky then let it drop, pointing forward.

The war horns of Flatlash keep sounded their deep rumble and the Gypsy caravan lurched into motion as we followed the Flatlash honor guard out of the keep, for our last leg of the journey home. Celeste had her horse cantering by my side as I ignored her grinning self. I made a point of not looking at her and I patted Goliath's neck. "Ignore them, handsome boy. You're the only horse for me."

This got me a giggle from Celeste, I broke and shot a silly grin at her and she leaned across her saddle to bump shoulders. That was how our next three days went. Mother Udele met with Celeste and me, then Duke Fredrick each night. I grew even closer to the amazing people in the Lupei family.

Then we rode tall in the saddle as we passed through Wexbury Minor. The Knights patrolling the external village took off like arrows at breakneck speeds to inform the Keep of our return. We went up the little rise by the livestock grazing fences and saw Castle Wexbury rising out of Wexbury Keep.

I faltered and Goliath weaved nervously to a stop. Celeste was instantly beside me looking at me in concern as I silently sobbed. "Laney?" I took some rapid breaths trying to calm myself. I reprimanded myself. Control it, don't let it control you. Be strong. Then I was able to take a long, deep breath and centered myself just as I heard all the metal around us starting to raise.

Then I whispered to her and gave an embarrassed smile as a tear rolled down my face, "I'm sorry. This has been the most amazing adventure of my life, something I would never have dreamed of. But I am so very glad to be home."

She nodded and smiled and took in the sight of our keep and voiced her agreement, "Yes... there really is no place like home."

Alexandru rode up beside us and rested his arms across the pommel of his saddle, barely holding his reins. He looked at the keep then back at us and nodded with a smile. Then made an ushering motion with a hand. "After you Soras."

We started moving and the caravan started up behind us again as Celeste asked him, "Just what does Sora mean anyway? All the Lupei are calling Laney and me that."

He chuckled as he turned around to ride away from us and called back with humor filling his voice, "In your tongue, it means Princess. Did you not think of the price of the blood bond of your house to Udele? You are her heirs now, my... Soras!"

His laugh faded behind us as Celeste and I looked at each other, going pale as she said, "Oh shit." I nodded, so succinctly said by my Lady. Then we started chuckling to each other and shaking our heads. We could hear the bells of the church heralding our return in the distance.

What an adventure this has been indeed.

EPILOGUE

I was looking in the mirror, absently running my silken gloved fingers across my shimmering facial scars, at the castle barber. Jace came running in, gasping for breath. My hair had grown in nicely in the past six months, and Giselle, the barber, had just styled my hair brilliantly, I looked more like a girl than a pubescent boy with the feminine style.

I grinned at my little brother as he held a finger up as he panted. Then he blurted out, "He's going to do it, Laney! Now!"

I gave Giselle an apologetic look as I ran for the door, snagging my riding cloak from the hook by the door and tying it around my neck as I ran with my brother. My cloak billowing behind me as I grumbled, "The fool is going to get himself killed!"

We reached the grand staircase and I slowed to allow the first class of children, from the new schoolhouse, past on the tour of the great library of the Techromancy Scrolls. Mother had arranged the visit. It was not long after we had returned to Wexbury that Duke Fredrick succumbed to mother and my pressure about mandating every child in the realm be educated.

The children gasped when they saw me and there was murmuring, "It's Lady Laney!" or "That's Anadele on her hip. It can split lightning." I blushed.

Though the official story of the great battle of the Monolith painted Lord Samuel as the hero of the day we didn't anticipate the

stories that the Gypsies, who carnivaled at the keep for an
unprecedented two months, would spread. Nor the fact that our
porters and coachman, who were commoners like I had been, would
spread the real, if not exaggerated, tales through the famous
Wexbury grapevine.

A small girl, possibly four or five years old, stepped up to me as
Jace and I stood by the railing so the children could pass. Her
brown eyes were so big and wide as she smiled shyly in recognition
of me. "You're the Penny Lady. Mommy and I sawed you in da
Market. I wanna be a Techno Knight like you when I'm growed
up." I blushed, I wasn't a Techno Night yet, not until later that day.
The new Instructor of the Keep, Jacklyn, was stepping up to the girl
to take her hand.

I signaled for her to wait. I asked the girl, "What's your name
little one?"

She smiled hugely and said, "Misty Cobbler."

I reached into a pocket of my tunic and pulled out a small
handful of penny vouchers and placed them in her hands. "Well,
Misty, can you help me out by giving each of the children here a
penny voucher for their families? It is important for an aspiring
Techno Knight to care for those under her protection."

The little girls eyes went wide and she ran to the other children
with Jacklyn in tow. Then I remembered why I needed to make
haste. We burst out into the courtyard and ran toward the livery. I
had to smirk a little that I was actually getting faster than Jace now.

I had never been in better shape or felt stronger in my life with all the training that came after our misadventure to Far Reach.

I saw Bex on my old hay wagon, fiddling with the electric motor and steering linkages he had tinkered together. Brenda was demanding he stop the foolishness. I grinned, like the poor man could ever stop. He'd do anything that woman told him but that.

Dozens of people were standing around, watching with curiosity.

❦Then he pushed a lever and the wagon started moving forward. He had been trying to recreate a motorized conveyance like the Wizards of the Before had used. He was likely to break his fool neck. He almost fell off the wagon as it started moving then he stumbled forward and got into the drivers bench and grabbed the steering levers. The wagon kept gaining speed toward the castle wall.

His eyes went wide and he turned the wagon toward the courtyard gates as it continued to build speed. I yelled, "Bex! Stop that contraption!" Jace ran after him.

He yelled back, "I... don't think I can. I forgot to make a way to control the motor." Brenda and I looked at each other and I sighed and looked around. Goliath was in the courtyard being exercised by a stable boy. I ran at Goliath, shouting, "Move aside!"

The stable boy got out of the way as I dove at Goliath, snagging the pommel of his saddle with my silk gloved hand and slung myself up, mounting smoothly. He was already in motion before I took the reins and shouted, "Hya!" as I kicked his sides gently.

He huffed a hot breath through his nostrils. He loved when I gave him all the rein he wanted. I laid across his neck as he stretched out and we thundered off after the silly tinker. I swear, if he broke his neck on the day we became knights, I was going to kill the man.

We were gaining on the still accelerating wagon down Lord's Way. I could hear Bex screaming for people to make way. Everyone was running to the side of the road, a poor man carrying a basket of baked goods dove to the side, spilling his load.

We were almost to the Roundabout when Goliath stopped gaining. That thing was fast, there were few horses that Goliath could not beat. Bex was screaming like a woman who had a mouse run across her feet as he went barreling around the Roundabout, two wheels of the wagon lifting from the ground.

Some speed had bled off there and I was able to catch up. Goliath came alongside the wagon and we were perilously close to the back wheel as I leaned out of my saddle and reached for the lever at the motor to shut it down. My fingertips brushed it as the wagon kept accelerating away from us. Damn!

As we chased, and rapidly approached the Belt, I swallowed at the congestion on Lord's Way all the way to Market. This was not going to end well. But Bex must have realized this too. As soon as we Passed the strip of multi-story buildings of the Belt, he veered left and the wagon exploded through the rail fence and it skipped down into the Warehouse District.

He skirted between the buildings and Lord's Way, looking back at me with wide eyes as he held up the broken handle from the little friction brake that he thought could stop the wagon. The small grove of trees at the end of the Warehouse District signaled that we were out of room, and out of options, as the wagon hurtled through another fence and went airborne as he passed through the trees. I could hear his girlish wail then a huge splash.

We thundered through the trees and the picnic grasses beneath them and I pulled Goliath up short. There was my wagon, mostly submerged in the lake, with Bex trudging out of the water, laughing maniacally, full of fear, adrenaline, and elation, still grasping the brake handle in one white-knuckled hand. He looked like a wet gangly scarecrow as he shouted, "It worked!" Then added almost comically as Brenda arrived on a borrowed steed, "Just a couple minor bugs to work out."

He grabbed a floating tube as he slogged out of the water and I dismounted. Brenda slapped the back of his head hard then kissed the man. "Idiot." He grinned at her.

Then he looked worriedly at the tube. It recognized it as the tube he kept the parchments with his designs. He popped the top and pulled out a parchment then exhaled in relief. I snatched it from his hands before he could react, and asked as I looked at the drawings, "What scatterbrained scheme are you working on now?"

He took the parchment back as he shrugged. "Just a lighter than air vessel to explore the uninhabitable lands."

I squinted and furrowed my brow. "Like the balloons the Gypsies float in at Carnival?"

He nodded. "Yes, but much larger and with fans to propel it instead of being subject to the whims of the wind."

I shook my head in wonder, trying not to show excitement for the idea, no need to encourage the man. "Only you Bex, only you." I looked around at his mess as we all mounted up, him behind his woman.

I said as we headed up to Lord's Way, "We need to get some men over to pull that out of the lake and repair the fences when we get back to the castle."

He nodded in embarrassment, but then sat tall and asked us, "Did you see? It worked. Travel without horses. I just need to devise a way to control the motor from the seat and a better braking system."

To silence him Brenda and I both yelled out, "Bex!" then we shared a secret look of pride. He really had done it, a motorized conveyance. Was there anything we couldn't accomplish in these modern times?

We all rode high in the saddle as we made our way back to the castle, as people in the market stared at us. We needed to get ready. I scooped up Jace with one hand and deposited him behind me in the saddle as we passed him at the Belt. He was truly fast to have made it all that way so quickly.

Celeste was at the Livery pacing when we returned. She

virtually caught me as I dismounted and she motioned a stable boy toward Goliath as she pulled me along toward our quarters. She said, "You're going to be late for your own ceremony."

I nodded and grinned at her. "Bex did it. His contraption worked. Though he almost broke his own fool neck."

She smiled with a nod. "I had no doubt the brainy guy could do it. Half the scholars and Techromancers have secretly been monitoring his progress." That was news to me. But he has sort of become a sensation, as the weapons smiths have been adapting and refining his powered blade concept to help our Knights stand against rogues.

My Lady helped me gear up and she did my hair up in a braid and paused as she looked at me in the mirror, just holding the braid in both hands.

She had done that a lot lately. After the troops had been sent south, and Treth and Far Reach were liberated, and our part of the spoils of war amounted to tens of thousands of gold coins, she would often slip into thought.

I looked at her in the mirror and she snapped out of it when I quested with my eyes. She shook her head then smiled and said, "Oh, your Techno Knight sash that will replace your squire sash at the ceremony. I hope you don't mind, I designed your crest."

I looked at it and it had five crests, Wexbury, Techno Knight, the House of Celeste, the crest of the Lupei family, and the fifth... I grinned up at her then ran the fingers of my silk gloved right hand over a crest with a platypus with a lightning bolt behind it, in the colors of Wexbury.

She shrugged. "The noble and adaptable platypus. A fierce fighter like our Lady Laney." I hugged her then pulled away when she stiffened up.

I looked up at her and tilted my head in question. She looked... sad. "What is it, Celeste? You've been growing distant."

She shrugged and whispered, "You're going to get your title today Laney." Like it was an explanation. I prompted for more and she closed her eyes and said, "You'll be assigned your own quarters." My heart sank though I knew it was inevitable. Then she opened her eyes and whispered an admission, "I was hoping you would stay... forever."

My heart sped up. Did she mean what I had hoped with all my heart? I felt tears gathering in my eyes as I shook my head and made an admission of my own, my heart felt as if it were breaking, "I... can't my Lady. It would be too painful. I've... fallen in love with you." I closed my eyes tightly and felt tears spill down my cheeks. I didn't understand all the emotions assaulting me. She would hate me now.

I heard a sob and looked at her. She had a hand covering her mouth and her green eyes were overflowing with tears. She was nodding her head and I had a lump in my throat as hard as stone. Her voice cracked as she said, "I'm in love with you too, my impossible herder... the girl who will not run. Stay with me always?"

I nodded dumbly as some new warmth filled me. My body arched and my hands flew back as blinding white, warm misty energy exploded from me. There was a soft whump of implosion then everything in the room was knocked over. I looked at Celeste through new eyes, and she was even more beautiful than before, strands of silky white emanating from her. I realized I had ignited, again, it took Celeste's love to unlock the power. I could feel the world as I never had before, I could feel all the life around me. This is what Mother Udele must have meant when she said that I had to bloom again.

I looked at the Lady of my heart, and she just smiled and leaned down to capture my lips gently with hers. My toes curled and my heart was singing with joy as I realized that I was hers, and she mine.

It felt brand new, as though the adventure of my life was beginning anew, and I wondered what the future had in store for us. All I knew was that we would face it together, hand in hand.

the end

Books in the Techromancy Scrolls series...
Adept
Soras
Masquerade
Westlands (2017)
Avalon (2018)

Books in the Urban Fairytales series...
Red Hood: The Hunt
Snow: The White Crow
Ella: Cinders and Ash
Rose: Briar's Thorn
Let Down Your Hair
Hair of Gold: Just Right
The Hood of Locksley
Beauty In the Beast
No Place Like Home (2017)
Shadow Of The Hook (2018)

Books in the New Sentinels series...
Djinn: Cursed
Raven Maid: Out of the Darkness
Fate: No Strings Attached
Open Seas: Just Add Water (2017)
Ghost-ish: Lazarus (2018)

Books in the Drakon series...
Awakening
Dragonfall

Books in the Valkyrie Chronicles series...
Return of the Asgard
Bloodlines
Folkvangr
Seventy Two Hours
Titans

Books in the Bridge series...
Trolls
Traitor
Unbroken

Books in the Fracture series...
Divergence

Romance Novels by Erik Schubach

Books in the Music of the Soul universe...
(All books are standalone and can be read in any order)
Music of the Soul
A Deafening Whisper
Dating Game
Karaoke Queen
Silent Bob
Five Feet or Less
Broken Song
Syncopated Rhythm
Progeny
Girl Next Door
Lightning Strikes Twice
June
Dead Shot

Music of the Soul Shorts...
(All short stories are standalone and can be read in any order)
Misadventures of Victoria Davenport: Operation Matchmaker
Wallflower
Accidental Date
Holiday Morsels

Books in the London Harmony series...
(All books are standalone and can be read in any order)
Water Gypsy
Feel the Beat
Roctoberfest
Small Fry
Doghouse
Minuette
Squid Hugs
The Pike
Flotilla

Books in the Pike series...
(All books are standalone and can be read in any order)
Ships In The Night
Right To Remain Silent
Evermore

Books in the Flotilla series...
(All books are standalone and can be read in any order)
Making Waves
Keeping Time
The Temp (2017)

Novellas by Erik Schubach

The Hollow

Books in the Paranormals series...
Fleas
This Sucks
Jinx (2017)

Short stories in the Fixit Adventures...
Fixit
Glitch
Vashon (2017)
Descent (2017)

Short Stories by Erik Schubach
(These short stories span many different genres)

A Little Favor
Lost in the Woods
Rift Jumpers: Faster Than Light
Scythe
Snack Run
Something Pretty
MUB (2017)